THE STORM KING

THE LOST GOD BOOK THREE

SHEILA MASTERSON

THE STORM KING

THE LOST GOD BOOK THREE

SHEILA MASTERSON

Ebook: 9781960416087

Paperback: 9781960416094

Hardcover: 9781960416100

Cover Design and Ivy: Andrea Laguer

Hardback Case and Map Design: Mike Sisak

Editing: Erin at EKB Books

Proofreading: Mike Sisak

*To all those who have pulled themselves back from the abyss
by sheer force of will.*

*And to those who have come for us in every darkness and sat with us
until we could walk out on our own.*

A NOTE FROM THE AUTHOR

Dear Reader,

THE STORM KING deals with mental health struggles (including grief, depression, anxiety, and suicide ideation), fertility issues, war, violence, threat of sexual assault, death, profanity, and explicit sex. I've attempted to treat all sensitive topics with the utmost care, but this content might still be challenging for some readers. Please take care of yourself.

Happy Reading,

Sheila

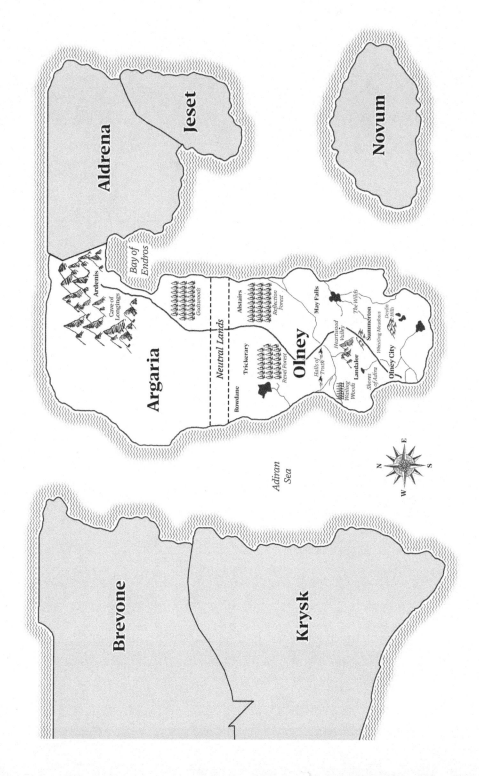

BEFORE

XANDER

The first thing Xander Savero learned in hunter training was how to protect what was vital.

Before anything else, hunters learned to defend what they couldn't live without: the throat, the gut, the lungs, the heart.

He defended them in a fight. He defended them in the woods. He even defended them in sleep, curled into a ball with a blade under his pillow.

That training was only exacerbated by the hypervigilance of spending his formative years behind enemy lines.

It was fitting that forgetting that important lesson was his downfall. He'd simply expected it would be a blade, not a beautiful woman, that broke him.

Xander had forgotten everything he'd learned when he fought Cecilia Reznik in the wild, instantly opening his stance to her. No doubt she'd noticed and assumed it was a move meant to bait her, but he knew it was a mistake. It was involuntary, as if his heart knew to make room for her, as if his magic recognized hers and bent to it, as if his body had understood something numinous that connected them even then.

Even in sleep he couldn't help but let her in. Many nights he woke sprawled wide for her to curl into, so her cheek could rest just above his heart.

Love was a thief, robbing him of something he did not know he possessed. It could only happen that way—like a crime—a thing that happened entirely without his permission but cost him all the same.

He'd faced down many enemies, and nothing scared him as much as that beautiful girl with a bow in her hands who had the unique ability to steal his heart before he even noticed it was gone.

Xander stared at the letter, his name written on the front in Cece's loopy handwriting. He was equal parts terrified and excited to read it. He darted down the hall before Evan could grab him and drag him into yet another exhausting meeting, and paused in the corridor leading to his parents' old rooms.

The air seemed stiller, perhaps even colder, as if marked by the memory of their deaths. Shaking off the chill, he continued down the dim hall past the doors that led to sitting rooms with furniture carefully wrapped to protect from dust, until finally, he reached their bedroom.

The door groaned open, and he stepped inside, pressing his back against the wood as if bracing for ghosts. He didn't know whether to be relieved or disappointed that he found none.

He walked across the room, knelt next to the fireplace, and pulled aside an old bookcase to reveal a small passageway. Crawling inside, he slid the case back into place behind him and scrambled down the short corridor to his secret sanctuary. Dust tickled his sinuses and he fought off a sneeze.

Daylight cut long triangles into the stone wall above his head as he rose to his feet in the small room. Though the castle was full of passageways, this was a simple hollow that led nowhere. He'd found it as a boy when he'd been trying to learn all the passages as well as Davide knew them.

A lump formed in his throat, the memory rising in his mind out of nowhere.

Davide, so much taller than him, all gangly limbs and awkward elbows, trying to fold himself into the space beside Xander. His brother had riffled through the collection of books before smiling at Xander. *"What does it feel like? The storm magic?"*

Xander snapped back into the present, a dull pain pressing behind his eyes. He was still so unpracticed at memory recall, but he was grateful for every glimpse, no matter how it wore on him.

He looked at the stack of magic books still sitting on the short table in the corner. He'd stolen them from the royal archives after his magic saved his life and his father had discouraged his pursuit of it.

"You've already made yourself a myth. What do you think will happen if you go out and start practicing your magic?" Damian had said. *"You'll become just another witch struggling for control. It would be foolish to let everyone see your weakness. Focus on combat instead and become fearsome enough to gain the respect of the army you will someday lead."*

Though his father had a point, it was lonely having so much magic brewing in his body and no idea how to channel it. The king didn't care about his restlessness, so Xander threw himself into combat training and spent his free time reading magic books in secret. Over time, Davide helped add to his collection, encouraging Xander when no one else was looking, which was the only time an heir could be seen defying the king.

Xander laughed to himself as he brushed his fingers over the satchel of dried herbs from when he'd tried his first spell. It had not come nearly as naturally as storm magic, but his mother's mother had slipped him a few simple things to try. This space had been where he hid his practice.

Now he was hiding again, but instead of dodging his father or his guards, he was hiding from his responsibilities.

When Xander was young, Castle Savero felt like a prison. He couldn't walk down the hall without his guards or Evan on his tail. He couldn't turn a corner without people bowing to "Prince Alexander."

He'd hated that enough. But when he had started training and had shown such promise, his joy was dashed when Davide reluctantly admitted that none of the hunters were fighting him with full effort because he was the prince.

Everywhere he went, the world catered to him, while at the same time he wasn't allowed to be his true self. Most of who he was needed to stay a secret. That was why spying suited him so well.

He liked anonymity. For once he could prove his skill without the world catering to him. The challenge of stealing information from sources without them even realizing they'd given it up was thrilling. In Argaria, he was placed on a pedestal and never really given the opportunity to shine. No matter how he saw himself, the kingdom and even his own father saw him as a spare. He asked to go to Olney at fourteen to do the one thing Davide could never do. His parents fought about it for days, his father immediately seeing merit in the idea, his mother adamant that he was too young. In the end, King Damian won, as he always did.

Xander was eager for the freedom of being unknown and no task would better cleave him from his old life while still making him a hero. He could not be a better king than his brother, but he'd always been a better fighter and a more charming liar.

He warred with opponents, he warred with who he was, and he warred with being the expendable son. Fate had a sense of humor in making him a very reluctant king.

He picked up the intricately carved wooden box beside the herbs, opened it, and looked at the stack of Cece's letters inside. He hadn't been brave enough to respond to a single one. Over the past few weeks he'd hidden in the passageway to read them, as if he could hide from the hurt of missing her. He'd only tucked them away to keep Evan out of his business.

The newest one burned in his palm. He wanted the comfort of her words.

The chain beneath his tunic shifted. Xander pressed a hand to his chest, the metal of his wedding ring warm on the jagged scar above his heart. He could not wear it on his hand and deal with the whispers about his state of mind, but at least he could keep some small piece of her close to his heart.

He'd been alone his whole life but now he felt lost without her. Cece broke him open and he was uncertain how to close and heal over such a wound. If he had designed the woman of his dreams, he couldn't have done a better job. Her biting wit, her intelligence, her skill with a blade and bow. She was a perfect combination of deadly beauty and courage. She'd ruined him.

How had he let it happen? Years of training flew out the window the first time he kissed her. He knew then he'd sacrifice anything for her. He might not have been willing to admit it, but he knew.

He hadn't realized that would mean losing her and his mind. He hadn't realized there could be a torture as potent as protecting her love for someone else, because the loss of Rainer would wreck her more than the loss of Xander. It was a brutal thing to know, and yet he'd endured it for her.

Because she was it. She still was.

A stunning goddess had ripped out his still-beating heart, even as she'd literally sewed the wounded organ back together.

She was the first person he'd ever shown his heart to, and she would be the last.

"*This is what love does. It makes you the sharpest weapon to cut those you love. It leaves wounds that can't be healed. Love makes both of you weak,*" Cato had said.

The trickster was right about that. It had wrecked both of them.

It had also saved them. If Xander hadn't loved Cece so much, he never could have protected her weak spot from Cato. If she hadn't loved him so much, she wouldn't have been able to bring him back from his brush with death. She wouldn't have had the faith in him that he could come back from losing his mind. It was little consolation, but it was something.

Xander's deal with the trickster god, Cato, had cost him everything. Even his own mind had been lost to him for a while. Though Cato's influence and corruption vanished the moment he stabbed Xander on the beach, there were times Xander wondered if it was lost still.

Xander had been working with a tutor for months to cultivate his own memory witch abilities. He wanted to recall in precise detail his history with all his loved ones who had died and the short time he shared with his wife.

Ex-wife. He shuddered, his chest suddenly too tight to draw a full breath. The word was violent—carving him hollow with the memory of the shattered look on her face when he'd told her their marriage was over.

At times, the vivid memory magic made the loss so visceral it felt like he was back in each painful moment—his mother offering her blessing on his wedding night, Davide protecting him to the end, watching Cece die—but it hurt him more not to see them. Remembering was hard, but forgetting might as well have been forgetting himself. He had never seen himself as clearly as he did when reflected in their eyes.

For three long, cold months, he'd filled his nights with alcohol and a parade of what-ifs.

If he hadn't been gone so long, he would have noticed the change in Davide sooner. If he'd been there, maybe they could have ruled their kingdom together. If he hadn't made a deal with Cato to keep Cece to himself, she might have chosen him anyway.

It would be easy to blame Cato for all of his problems, but he knew they were mostly of his own creation.

Most nights he kept the dark at bay by drinking himself into oblivion. Others he walked the grounds until he was too exhausted to think anymore. The rest of his time was spent alone in his room as if sitting vigil for the love he lost. Some nights he sat in the guest suite, where he and Cece had spent their first night as a married couple, and stared at her wedding dress. It still faintly smelled like her and he wondered if that scent was magic or a curse.

Evan had tried his best to pull Xander out of it, but there was nothing that drew him from the depths of his pain.

Then the letters started.

Every week, a new letter from Cece arrived. They were tentative at first. Short little notes about things happening back in Olney.

Did he hear that the Olney Huntgames were postponed? New trade routes were being discussed with Novum. Would she finally get to cross the sea and see the moonrise city of Estrellas? Was he okay, and if so, why did he not say goodbye?

Over time they got longer. Sometimes it was like she spilled everything in her heart onto those pages in rambling tales that made him laugh before making him miss her so desperately it felt like his chest would cave in. Other times they were clever, carefully constructed and beautifully written. Her years of reading and telling stories were clear in her craft.

Still, others were haunted and heartbreaking and told of the immense grief and guilt that she felt for surviving when so many others died and when she'd caused so much death. Those were the ones that broke him because they were honest and unguarded, the ink dotted with tears. He imagined her pacing the gardens in Olney in front of the bench where they first spoke.

At first, he'd thought she was just writing for his sake—out of some misguided sense of pity. Over time it became clear that despite choosing to spend her life with Rainer, she still missed Xander's comfort. She still counted on him to see her darker side without judgment. He knew she wanted a reply, but he had no idea what to say. What was between them felt unfinished and tenuous and he wasn't sure what his careless words might do.

Not writing back was the easiest way to shove down the little bit of hope that reared up every time one of her letters arrived. He busied himself with trying to run the kingdom, but it was hard to care about anything.

Xander never wanted to lead, and he constantly felt like he was doing something wrong. He saw the disapproval and disappointment on the faces of his advisors, heard the constant jabs about how he'd spent more of his life in the court of their enemies than their own.

It was all made worse by the murmurs that he wasn't really his father's son, but a bastard child of the queen and her consort who didn't deserve the throne.

His people didn't trust him and he didn't blame them. Xander didn't trust himself anymore.

After spending months under Cato's mind control, he wasn't sure if he'd ever trust himself again. He knew what was true and what

Cato had planted, but all the memories still existed and they filled him with guilt.

He couldn't decide if it was a blessing or a curse that his love for Cece hadn't faded at all.

A knock on the bookcase made him jump.

"Are you going to hide in there all night hoarding your letters?" Evan called.

Xander sighed heavily. Of course Evan knew about this spot. Foolish to think he wouldn't.

Xander looked at the letter again, placing it on top of the others and vowing to come back for it soon.

"I promise not to read them, but honestly, the hoarding them to yourself is as bad as the closet full of her clothes that you refuse to put in storage or at least send to her to wear," Evan called, his voice muffled by the bookcase between them.

Xander sighed heavily, shutting the letter in the box before crawling back through the passageway and pushing the bookcase aside. "What good is being the king if I can't get a moment of peace?"

Evan helped him to his feet, brushing cobwebs from his shoulder. "You have to decide on the trade terms from Aldrena. They've been nervous about Vincent's battalions along their land routes and they want permission to come via sea instead," he said.

Xander walked out of the bedroom and down the hall to his den, slumping into his chair by the fire and pouring himself a glass of whiskey. It was a safe, Cece-less room. One she'd never visited and therefore held no memories of her, though Xander had imagined her spread out for him on his desk many times when he was bent over battle maps and boring paperwork.

"More of this, then?" Evan asked, waving a hand at Xander's drinking.

Xander leaned back in the chair. "What's the downside of letting them come by sea?"

Evan shrugged. "Your father always felt that allowing Aldrena to freely come and go by sea could lead to a surprise attack on both land

and sea. That said, he wasn't dealing with Vincent's men attacking our land trade routes."

"My father—" Xander started but the words fizzled out on his tongue. He took a swig of whiskey. "Which father?"

Evan froze, hesitating a moment before crossing the room, pouring himself a whiskey, and sitting in the chair beside Xander. "Are you going to give credence to these rumors?"

Xander narrowed his eyes at his friend. "Are you going to tell me that there's no truth to them?"

Evan sipped his whiskey, studying his friend over the rim of the glass. "Xan, I honestly don't know. I tried to find out for sure for years with no luck. But as the person whose job it is to protect you, I have to tell you that looking into it won't lead to anything good. Where there is smoke, people will assume there's also fire, and this is not a good time to instill more doubt since your contempt for your new role is obvious to basically everyone."

Xander frowned, studying Evan, looking for a lie, but his heartbeat was as steady as his voice. It was rare there was such an important secret that Evan didn't know.

The two were interrupted by a shift in the air.

Death came in many forms, but tonight he arrived in an elaborately embroidered tunic, cashmere breeches, and a puff of cinnamon- and ash-scented smoke, like a market magician.

Xander narrowed his eyes, looking from the god of death to his friend. "Is this an intervention?"

"Are you going to give me an answer about Aldrena?" Evan asked, arching a brow.

"Whatever you think is best," Xander said.

Evan wanted him to be more assertive, but Xander was no more worthy of running the kingdom than anyone else. He could not wrap his mind around the enormous responsibility.

Evan shook his head, knocking back the rest of his drink. "I cannot run this kingdom alone."

Xander ran a hand over his beard. "And I cannot be responsible for more harm. I don't know what I'm doing."

The last time he forced landowners to raise wages for their workers, they'd responded by firing a portion of their staff, leaving the poorest of the poor even worse off than they already were. Every time he tried to make things better for everyone in Argaria, he only seemed to create some new problem. It felt like he was in a sinking ship, trying to bail out water as more and more holes popped up.

Evan frowned at him and then turned to Grimon. "He's all yours." He rose with a huff and stormed out of the room, slamming the door behind him.

If Teddy were alive, he'd chase Evan down and smooth things over. Then he'd come back and talk through everything with Xander and tell him how to apologize—how to be *better*. Without their late friend, their friendship was more strained than it had ever been, and Xander had no idea how to fix it because he could not fix himself.

Xander turned his gaze back to Grimon. His den didn't feel big enough for the two of them. It felt like the stone walls were closing in, though it felt like that most days now that he was in charge.

"You're not also going to storm out?"

Grimon gave him a brittle smile. "Good to see you too, Your Majesty."

"To what do I owe the honor, Grim?"

The last time Xander had seen the god of death, Grimon was pissed at him. Now he eyed Xander sympathetically and that was all the king could take. Grimon was the last god Xander wanted pity from. His silence was stifling.

"Death makes poor company," Xander said.

"Only one of us looks like death."

Xander chuckled darkly as he gulped down his whiskey. "Why do you care, Grim?"

"Because Cece cares. Your people care. You have a kingdom to protect. Wallowing won't make it disappear. I'm here to warn you that while you wallow, your cousin Vincent gains strength."

"I'm doing my best," Xander said.

"Personally, I simply wish you'd approach your rule with the same enthusiasm you reserved for seducing Cece," Grimon taunted.

The god of death baited him, but he couldn't muster the frustration to be hooked.

"We cannot undo the past. We can only learn from it and move forward."

Xander barked out a laugh. "How?"

"One foot at a time."

"Spoken like someone who's never had to live a mortal life. Also, this is more like one literal battle at a time. My consolation prize was advisors who whisper about my parentage behind my back and in front of my face, a throne I never wanted, and another Savero trying to steal it."

Grimon chuckled. "Disappointed that your considerable privilege doesn't come with an instruction manual?"

Xander knew this tactic well. Years of spying meant he could always tell when he was being worked. Grimon was trying to lure him into a fight, but Xander was completely exhausted. He was already giving his blood, sweat, and every ounce of battle strategy he'd learned to the kingdom. He did not have more to offer and he was aware of how he was falling short. At any given time, it felt like he was equally loved and loathed by the people whose allegiance he desperately needed.

"Are you just here to scold me or do you have another purpose?" Xander asked.

Grimon's eyes flashed with anger. He reached into his cloak and Xander flinched, unsure what to brace for, but when the god of death pulled his hand free, he was holding a blue velvet cloth. A soft hum filled the room. Whatever he'd brought was some sort of magical object.

"I don't think it's my color," Xander said.

Grimon glowered at him. "That's just the wrapping. The prize is inside." He slid away the fabric, revealing a small hand mirror. The hum grew louder.

"I do enjoy looking at myself," Xander said.

Grimon's pale eyes narrowed. "I can take it back with me; I just thought you might want to try it. It's the only one in existence. Forged with Goddess Aelish's truth magic."

"What does it do?"

Grimon handed him the mirror. Xander gripped the cool silver handle, turning it from side to side, trying to sense how it worked.

"It reveals truths."

Suddenly Xander wanted to smash it into pieces small enough that he couldn't glimpse anything. He looked up at the god of death.

"Now why would I need that?"

Grimon's mouth slashed into a wicked grin. "I can't imagine why. The mirror has a will of its own. It wanted to be here."

Xander arched a brow and took another sip of his drink. "And did it tell you that?"

"You joke, but it has its ways. You hear how loud it hums now that I'm here. You are seeking a truth and the mirror can show you." Grimon shook his head. "It is not a limitless gift. It can only show your most desired truth."

Xander eyed it warily. "What does that magic cost?"

"The courage to look."

Xander set it on the table beside him a little too quickly, tossing the cloth over it. "Well, I will certainly have a glance should I think of any truths I wish to know."

He took another long gulp of whiskey, set his glass down, and crossed his arms. Curse Grimon for bringing that godsforsaken mirror—for letting Xander know it existed. There was not a snowflake's chance in an Olney summer he'd look in that thing. He did not want to know the answer to the question that could end his reign and send his kingdom into peril. His longtime desire to know the truth of who he was had died along with his brother.

He did not need another reason to doubt himself, just like he didn't need another reason to fear becoming King Damian.

"Xander, the time for sulking will come. This isn't it. If everyone liked you, you wouldn't be doing your job. Well-liked kings are lazy and you're doing hard work. You could learn a thing or two from Cece, you know. You absolutely wrecked her, but she kept going. Even when it seemed hopeless. Even when she had no idea how to. She did it. You won't know what else could be for you if you can't let go of what was."

Xander scrubbed a hand over his face and looked into the fire. He took a fortifying gulp of whiskey. "I have no interest in seeing what could be when what *was* nearly destroyed me. Why tempt the fates with the prospect of my happiness?"

Grimon stared at him as if expecting him to say more. "Fine. Waste away. Wreck your kingdom. Wreck everything that you all sacrificed for because you're too selfish to fight when your heart is broken. Don't say I didn't try."

Grimon disappeared in a puff of smoke, leaving behind a burnt cinnamon scent.

Xander tilted his head back, squeezing his eyes shut. Grimon could say whatever he wanted. He'd never run a kingdom. He'd never had his heart broken, if he even had a heart.

Everyone was a critic. Grimon and Evan might want Xander to be a leader, but he was terrified of making the wrong choice again.

He had learned his lesson. He would protect what was vital. There would be no more bargaining with gods and he'd never again trust his heart around a beautiful woman with a bow in her hands.

PART I:
THE RETURN

1

CECILIA

C ecilia dreamed she was dead. It happened so frequently, but the darkness closing in around her with no ribbon to lead her out was always terrifying.

She sat up in bed, blinking her eyes open and pressing her hand over her chest. Her heart thundered beneath her clammy palm.

Gull calls punctuated the distant sound of waves crashing on the sand beneath her cliffside cottage. The fire in the hearth still burned, but the kettle wasn't steaming. Rainer had been gone for a while.

Blinking against the midmorning sun shining through the cottage windows, Cecilia rubbed her fingers over the green ribbon tied around the bedpost.

"Brave with my hand. Brave with my heart," she whispered.

She had a spell for courage, but not one for letting go. She needed to create her own.

The blanket slid to her waist as she rolled to the edge of the bed. The cold floorboards under her bare feet sent a shiver up her legs. She grabbed the sweater Rainer had left on his pillow and pulled it on as she stood. She swiped the blank paper from beside the bed, ripped it into smaller scraps, and jotted notes on each.

Once she had them all written out, she crossed the room to the fire and set the kettle over it to make tea, then padded to the kitchen to grab some dried lavender from the bushel hanging from the ceiling.

The floorboards creaked as she walked back to the fire, pairing each sprig of lavender with one of the scraps of paper. One by one she offered them to the fire, murmuring the words to herself like an incantation.

"*I am at peace with my father's death.*

I am at peace with Teddy's death.

I am at peace with the exchange I made for my magic.

I am at peace with all that I have saved and all that I have lost."

One by one she watched them burn to ash, waiting for contentment to hit her, trying not to feel disappointment when she felt no closer to letting go.

When she was young, it had seemed there was no problem that magic couldn't fix. But she could not magic away her grief. She could not heal the bargain she'd made. She could not soothe Rainer's anxiety that he would lose her because she still felt half-lost. Magic could do nothing for them.

"Maybe try again tomorrow," she said, turning to make her way to the sunlit spot in front of the window seat.

Cecilia folded forward over her legs to start her morning stretch routine. The series of breaths and movements made her feel grounded, especially after nights plagued by dreams of leaving her body.

She moved through the familiar series, sweat rising on her skin as her muscles warmed. Her legs burned as she moved slightly faster, as if a bit of vigorous exercise would be enough to chase the ghosts from her haunted heart.

She'd died and come back. Death wasn't something to be feared. She'd already triumphed over it.

And yet...

Cecilia felt as if she was somehow less—like she'd arrested her momentum toward death temporarily but now there was a pressing compulsion to rush toward that void. Grimon had warned her. "*It will be painful both physically, mentally, and emotionally. No one returns without a bit of darkness. Something must die off for you to be reborn, so understand that you will not be the same."*

The dying wasn't the hard part. It was the coming back that was the problem.

No matter how she tried to shape herself into familiar roles, nothing quite fit the places where she'd lost bits of herself. It was like trying to fit into a dress that was cut for someone else.

Cecilia had been made and unmade, and now she had the strange sensation of trying to rebuild herself from nothing.

Too often she found herself playing the character of her old self. Fumbling for her words a beat too late, needing to think about how she should react to the people who stopped her in the village on her walk home from the healer's clinic.

"Thank you, Goddess," they said in reverent tones that made her uncomfortable. As if there was another choice for her.

She rose to her feet, crossing the room. She pressed her palm to the spine of the book that she'd stashed her dagger behind. The sound of metal hitting wood was a relief. Even from afar, the weapon had a magnetism. Though the thick volumes of fairy tales hid it well, she could not stop checking that it was there and not still gripped in Rainer's shaking hand as it slid into her chest. She braced her palm against the leather spine.

She was accustomed to the melancholy that grew inside of her. She simply hoped that it would leave her be. Every time she closed her eyes, the image of the dark maze came to her again.

In every dream, she felt eyes on her. As if someone was watching her struggle with survival. It was as if the more settled her life became, the more she braced herself for something to go horribly wrong.

Why can't you just be happy?

The kettle squealed, shaking her from her thoughts. She poured herself tea and settled onto the window seat, looking out at the sea.

The pleasant ache in her legs reminded her she wasn't a goddess anymore. Her body was mortal and fatigued as such. She still had some additional mind and memory healing abilities, but they were a shadow of what they'd once been, and she tired much faster.

Holding such power had been both thrilling and terrifying—a relief and an enormous burden. What was left of that power felt much more manageable and simultaneously like not enough.

Cecilia ebbed and flowed as the days went by. Some days she felt more herself, but then the tide pulled back and she lost what ground she'd gained. It was like she'd been floating in the ocean, relaxed and happy, when suddenly she was caught in an undertow. The more she fought the darkness and grief, the more it pulled her under.

She thought that she might have been worthy of love once, but lost that worthiness in the fight to save her kingdom. She might never be worthy again. Perhaps the real damage Cato did wasn't to the world around them or the people he killed, but to those who survived.

Cecilia hadn't counted on being so haunted. It seemed simple in the fairy tales, but maybe all those neatly tied-up stories had led her astray.

Maybe happily ever after didn't really exist. Maybe what came after was just a bunch of broken, grieving people trying to survive imperfectly in a world that would never be the same. Maybe their happily ever after was the lot of them trying to figure out who they were now that they had been irrevocably changed.

Is that something to grieve? Am I really just grieving myself? And if so, which version of me? The me who existed before she ever left to finish the Gauntlet? The me who stood in the forest begging her best friend to love her enough to choose her over his duty? The me who fell in love with a hunter and liar who turned out to be a prince? The me who trusted all the people in her life were being honest with her? The me that laid down her life for the man she could not bear to live without?

It had to mean something. Cecilia had to make it all mean something.

This was supposed to be the easy part. Loving Rainer had always been second nature. But it was impossible to untangle herself from all that had happened.

She'd murdered to save those she loved. She'd come back from death. She'd killed the last living god.

She was a hero revered in her kingdom, a woman deeply loved by her fiancé, and a witch reborn—but she truly had no idea who she was.

She tried so hard to be the sunny, hopeful girl she'd been, but even peace felt hollow and far too fragile for all she'd sacrificed.

It should have been enough to survive, but Cecilia didn't just want a life. She wanted to *live*. Instead, she felt trapped inside the horrors, unable to free herself from the frozen fear that kept her suspended in a ghost of a life.

The cottage door creaked open and Rainer stepped inside with a linen towel wrapped around his shoulders.

"I thought I felt you wake up," he said.

She retraced her emotions, hoping she hadn't let too much grief pass through their bond, but he looked happy.

He crossed the room and pulled her into a hug.

She squealed, squirming away from him. "You're cold and wet."

Rainer laughed. "You were right. It's a bit too cold to swim, but I had to try. I miss it."

It was as if her restlessness had seeped into him, too. Rainer struggled to settle back into the steady rhythms of their life, and for someone who'd been so regimented for so long, he was lost.

Still, he gave her a dazzling smile and kissed her, his lips cold and salty against hers. She brushed the towel from his shoulders, running her hands down his chest.

He slid his hands to cup her backside. "Want to warm me up?"

Cecilia laughed. "And have your ice-cold hands all over me? I don't think so. Go take a bath."

Rainer kissed the tip of her nose before making his way to the washroom. The admiration on his face made her squirm because she didn't feel worthy of it. Not when she couldn't give him everything he wanted.

Clastor had assured her that coming back from death and surrendering most of her goddess power did nothing to affect the exchange she'd made. Rainer seemed to have made peace with that, but Cecilia couldn't help but see how his eyes lit with longing whenever they passed families with small children on market day in Olney City.

Rainer's love was bright as the sun, painful to look at directly and impossible to ignore. She didn't deserve it. Not when she felt so defeated by the simple act of being herself. And certainly not when she couldn't give him every single thing he wanted.

Cecilia couldn't stop thinking about her Aunt Clara's favorite teacup. When Cecilia was eleven and Rainer thirteen, they'd been fighting with practice swords in the kitchen and knocked it down. It shattered on the floor and Cecilia's heart broke with it. Her mother, Rosalee, had hand-painted it and it was a one-of-a-kind gift that her aunt used daily.

Rainer, seeing her distress, had hastily and meticulously glued it back together. His hands were like magic, his brow furrowed in concentration, teeth chewing his lower lip as he worked until it was back in one piece. They tested it and it worked perfectly. Aunt Clara even said it was an improvement that gave the cup more character, but Cecilia had cried and cried. She couldn't stop looking at all the cracks, knowing that they'd ruined something beautiful and it would never be perfect again.

She felt the same now. Rainer was looking at her like she was back in one piece when all she could see in herself were fissures where pain still grew. Instead of being smoothed down by the struggle, she felt sharpened.

She needed to get Rainer to stop hovering; to get her mind to stop turning constantly.

She stepped into the washroom, using her magic to warm the bath for Rainer.

She met his eyes over the steaming water. "I spoke with Lyra at the healing clinic yesterday. I was thinking—" She swallowed hard, suddenly nervous he wouldn't like the idea. "I was thinking I would start taking more hours."

He studied her, and she squirmed under his assessing gaze. "You're already working pretty long hours." The words were careful.

She blew out a breath. "It's temporary. Just until we get through this backlog. Think of all the people I could help. I already have to turn people away every day, Rain. It's hard to say no when they need my help."

Though she was a mediocre healer, the months of working in the clinic had helped her learn to use that magic more efficiently, and the remnants of her goddess power were even more valuable to the people of Olney. It was only a glimmer of the magic that had healed Sylvie's grandfather's memory. Where it had once been easy to weave a mind together, now it took her exhaustive concentration to do such intricate work, and instead of one treatment creating a permanent fix, her patients needed to come back regularly when they started to forget again.

Cecilia hadn't expected to miss the power after resenting it so much.

Rainer brought his hands to her shoulders. "I'm worried about you."

Of course he'd notice her weight loss and troubled sleep. Her clothes hung off of her so severely she'd been to see the seamstress the previous week to get everything taken in again.

"Twice last week I had to come get you because you were so tired you could barely make the walk home without my help," Rainer said, a crease forming in his brow.

Reaching up, she brushed her thumb over the wrinkle. "I found a worry, but I'll fix it in a hurry."

He grabbed her wrist and kissed the scarred skin. "I'm serious. I'm worried about you."

Cecilia frowned at him. "Maybe we can compromise and my handsome fiancé can bring me lunch every day?" She ran her hands over his chest, letting her fingers linger on his golden scar.

Rainer shook his head, biting back a smile. "Oh, you think you can flirt your way out of this?"

She shrugged as she unbuttoned his pants, sliding them down his hips. "Usually works."

He pulled her into a kiss. She tried to relax, but he drew away a moment later, clearly sensing the tension in her body. The rhythm between them had always felt so steady and effortless, and now it was as if they were eternally out of step.

He frowned, climbing into the hot bath. "Fine. Take the hours, but I reserve the right to renegotiate if you don't take it easy, and I'm not afraid to call in reinforcements. Sylvie is just a letter away."

Cecilia smiled as she left to make Rainer tea. She missed Sylvie and Cal desperately, but they were busy trying to help Xander keep Argaria on track, acting as the Olney ambassadors to the neighboring kingdom. Their absence left a gap in her social schedule, which she filled with work and occasional dinner with King Marcos and Queen Regent Elena. While Cecilia was happy to see Marcos come into his own as king, court dinners still left her feeling like she was playing the part of a lady and looking around, expecting her father to walk into the room at any moment. Leo Reznik's death still left her breathless at the strangest moments.

But of all the strangeness in her new life, the thing that confused her the most was Xander's absence. It wasn't as if she'd expected him to stay for her. He had a kingdom to run, but he'd fled without a word, leaving her to deal with all the messiness between them as if it was her responsibility alone.

She'd written fifteen letters to Xander and received not a single reply. She wasn't sure what she expected. He was trying to run a kingdom—one he never wanted to rule—on the heels of grieving his entire family, one of his oldest friends, and her. He was busy. But it disturbed her how easily he'd moved on when she still felt so wrong.

In the heavy quiet of night, she was dogged by the guilt, shame, grief, and rage, all of which swirled around in an impossible vortex in her head. So she wrote to Xander. At first, she did it because she was hurt. He'd left without a word. After all they'd been through, she'd expected a goodbye at the very least. She didn't want him to suffer, but she couldn't fathom that something that had meant so much to her meant nothing to him.

Her letters turned into the one place she could pour her heart out. The words were messy and raw and jumbled like her insides, and her tears blurred the ink in spots. She wondered if Xander would notice, but she was comforted by the knowledge that he would never judge her.

She didn't know why she wouldn't let Rainer see it. She knew he could feel it. She knew he woke her up when she was crying in her sleep and kissed away her tears, whispering that it was going to be okay. Rainer could weather it all and just be there for her when she was ready.

"There is no part of you too dark and scary for me to look at. No part of you is less lovely than the whole," Rainer had said months before.

Yet her tongue stayed tied.

Rainer was everything that was good in the world. Through it all, he remained compassionate and loving. She didn't deserve him, but she was terrified to let him see that because then she would be alone.

It was just the two of them now, and she didn't know if she would survive if Rainer saw the bitter, broken parts of her.

2

EVAN

Evan handed the reins of his horse to the stable hand and shivered. His skin was sticky with sweat and dirt and several other people's blood. The pungent scent made his stomach turn. Sometimes his enhanced hunter senses were more burden than help.

He turned to look at Xander. His friend looked as exhausted and beaten down as Evan felt. Normally they relished a good fight, but neither felt particularly good about the flurry of border skirmishes they'd been facing down for months, and Vincent had just taken over yet another city along their borders. For all of their effort to beat him back, he seemed only to be growing stronger.

Evan, Xander, and several battalions of the Argarian Hunter Army had fought five small battles on their northeastern borders in the past three months, all of them victories—until today.

They were fortunate most of the army had made its way back to Argaria after the Battle of Goddess Cecilia, as the people were referring to what happened months before, when she fought Cato outside Olney Castle. She'd given most of the army hope to live, which meant many hunters were reluctant to rejoin the ranks. It helped that

Xander bolstered hunter wages, and most of the men seemed happy to see a hunter on the throne, no matter where he'd been trained.

But Evan was failing at every turn. He couldn't figure out how this opposing army followed Vincent when he was never present at any of the battles. To make matters worse, Evan could not get any useful information out of the prisoners they'd captured.

Xander had even granted him the freedom to have some former slayers root through the prisoners' memories, so long as they didn't suck them dry of memories and leave them husks. But each time, they came up with conflicting descriptions of Vincent or simply hadn't met him.

It was impossible to fight an invisible enemy. The frustration of trying to face down Cato was fresh in Evan's mind. That failure to protect his friends made him desperate to do better. But try as he might, he could glean no details of what Vincent looked like. Even his best spies who had infiltrated Vincent's army had never actually met the usurper.

His failure frustrated him to no end. Since he'd started hunter training twenty years ago, his success and value in Argaria had depended entirely on his ability to peel secrets from the people least willing to part with them. It was the only thing he was good at and it had given him a sense of purpose. There was so little of his life that was in his control. His network of spies and his ability to connect with sources allowed him to secure a place in King Damian's inner circle and to help protect Xander, even from a kingdom away. He liked the work of putting a puzzle together. He was driven by the challenge of outsmarting an opponent.

Cato was the first adversary Evan had come up against that he hadn't been able to best, and the fresh loss stung. Especially when he thought of all the havoc his friends had been through.

He tried to call up Vincent's face in his memory. As children, he and Xander had known Vincent, but it had been fifteen years since they'd seen him. When Xander's uncle had attempted to usurp the throne and was banished to the eastern wastes, Vincent was only sixteen. He'd been gangly and too tall, with dark hair and desperation to prove himself. His only defining feature was eyes so dark they were nearly black, with small flecks of gold. They'd yet to capture anyone who came close to fitting the bill. It was infuriating.

Xander was quiet beside him as they walked from the stables into the castle. Still grieving, he was hard to read these days. It was difficult to tell if the far-off look in his eye was the result of thinking about Cece, the bone-weariness that came with running a kingdom, or a hangover.

It could have also been a result of the ever-present question of his true parentage. That kept Evan awake at night. At least if Evan knew the truth, he could have a contingency plan, but he still didn't have any way of confirming one way or another.

Cal waved to them from the bottom of the stairs by the council meeting room.

"Thank gods! There you are! Lord Spellman called a council meeting. Sylvie is doing her best to stall until you get back, but you know how he is," Cal said breathlessly.

Evan sighed. Lord Edward Spellman was a power-hungry pest who made strategic jabs at Xander's competence daily.

In the months since they'd returned to Argaria, Cal and Sylvie had made themselves invaluable allies at court. It was no secret that the wealthier class of Argaria was wary of their young, untested king. Many considered Xander to lack both the experience and the culture to lead the kingdom. They thought of him as an outsider.

While Xander had done a great job of winning over the common people by fighting alongside his soldiers in the small border towns, the nobility still stuck their noses up at him, and after stories emerged of how he'd fled with his goddess wife and fell under Cato's control, they felt their doubts were justified.

As if they knew anything of what Xander had suffered. As if they knew anything of the man he had the potential to be. Evan had always felt protective of his friend, but now there was a newfound vigilance given the tremendous scrutiny that came with being king.

Xander did little to help the cause—fighting and drinking his way through his grief. It was difficult to keep him focused.

Evan was a strategist, but he was not born to rule a country. He understood battle tactics, but he'd never had a broken heart. He had no idea how to soothe his friend, and he found court politics exhausting.

That's where Sylvie shined. He'd learned to lean on her more and more in these situations not just because she had a mind for it, but because she ruled masterfully over men. Their world was not one that embraced strong, intelligent women, but she was an expert at walking the line between flattery and manipulation. It was mesmerizing to watch. He did not need a distraction, but she was impossible to ignore.

Evan, Xander, and Cal burst into the council room. Evan could read the relief in Sylvie's eyes when she saw them.

"There you are!" she said. "I apologize for delaying this meeting, Your Majesty, but I was so clumsy I spilled the water pitcher all over my parchment and needed to clean it up. I'm here now and ready to take notes."

Half the men in the room were smiling indulgently at Sylvie. Evan aspired not to be one of them, but he could tell by the glimmer of triumph on her face that he'd failed.

Xander nodded at Sylvie and crossed the room, his mouth in a grim line. He was clearly pissed, though it was unclear if his anger was directed at the opportunists on his council, his cousin's violence on their borders, or himself for not immediately mastering being king. He poured himself a large glass of whiskey and noisily began to remove his armor. In the past, Evan had often needed to protect his smart-mouthed friend from saying too much, but now Xander had learned how to effectively use silence as a weapon. Weak men always felt a need to fill the quiet.

Xander unbuckled the last of his armor, letting it clatter to the floor as he walked to the head of the table. Edward Spellman yielded his place to the king. Xander sat down in his chair and wiped a smear of blood from his face.

"I'm sorry for my delay. As you can see, I was out defending our lands from a would-be usurper," Xander said harshly.

Evan was so relieved Xander was finally rising to the occasion and at least attempting to look like a king in the council room.

The quiet was heavy, the air thick with the scent of blood and sweat that dirtied both his and Xander's clothing and armor.

"Your Grace, we sincerely apologize," Felix Bidell sniveled. "We hadn't thought you'd be back so soon or we would have waited. Lord Spellman was only concerned for the primary defenses of the castle."

Evan tried not to roll his eyes. Felix Bidell was a wealthy fishing merchant and was as set in his ways as he was old. Evan occasionally checked to make sure he was still breathing when he nodded off during council sessions. When he was awake, though, he was always eager to back up whatever plan Edward Spellman proposed.

"I'm always thinking of the protection of our great kingdom and its people first," Lord Spellman said. That was a lie. He was always thinking about money first. He was the largest and wealthiest landowner in Argaria and biggest pain in Evan's ass.

Christopher Lamotis leaned back in his chair, trying not to grin. He was an old friend of Teddy's who was elevated to nobility and a council seat when a distant uncle died. Beside him, Teddy's older brother, Reese Reynolds, who had inherited his seat on the council from their late father, winked at Xander. The two were the youngest members of the council and they loved to watch the older men squirm.

Evan would get a full report later from Sylvie, but he was certain that Chris and Reese had been in favor of waiting for the king and his top advisor before starting.

"Was it a successful defense, your grace?" Richard Chavers asked.

Evan was relieved that someone was concerned about the actual safety of their people. Richard Chavers could always be counted on for that at least. He was resistant to the alliance with Olney, which was frustrating, though understandable since he was a retired war hero who'd spent his career fighting off Olney hunters. But he did seem to genuinely care about the security of the kingdom and the fearsome reputation of the Argarian Hunter Army.

"Yes, it was successful, though not without its cost. Lives were lost and homes were burned. We should expect some more people seeking refuge in Ardenis in the coming days," Xander said solemnly.

"If we need more supplies brought to town I can have an additional grain shipment within the week," said Vaughn Salvatore. The wealthy grain merchant had been notably tight with his supply in the past. Perhaps Xander's bad mood was more compelling than Evan expected. "Perhaps Lady Brett could go arrange for it."

Sylvie smiled pleasantly at the suggestion, but Evan ground his teeth. The men of the council were always trying to assign her administrative tasks that would normally be handled by servants. It was condescending.

"Nonsense, Salvatore. We need Lady Brett here at the meeting. She already does so much for us. I'm certain she could run the kingdom if we all wanted to take a week off," William Arvato said.

Sylvie preened at the compliment. "That's a very generous sentiment, but I think we all know I could not do what all of you do."

Xander arched a brow at the exchange and Evan scowled. William Arvato had recently taken over his late father's textile business and his seat on Xander's council. William could be counted on to support Xander's decisions so long as they were aligned with his interests, and Evan was grateful that he was so pragmatic. He was less appreciative of how much William flirted with Sylvie. Unfortunately, Evan admitting that would mean showing the council his weak spot, and it would undermine Sylvie and her hard work. If the council knew she was involved with Evan they would take her even less seriously than they did now.

Corin Archer cleared his throat, eyeing Cal and Sylvie. Like many of the council members, he resented that Xander had added the two ambassadors from Olney to the council and, while he didn't say so publicly like Spellman and Bidell, his discomfort was clear.

"Can we move things along? I have a fleet returning this afternoon and I'd like to be there on time," Corin said.

The man never missed an opportunity to remind the council how busy he was or how much they relied on his shipping fleet and well-established routes for interkingdom trade. Evan couldn't tell if those reminders were driven by pride or a desire to impress the older members of the council, since Corin himself was only a few years older than Xander and Evan.

"By all means, let's proceed," Xander said.

They continued with the tense session as Evan and Xander reported their experience from the front lines.

When the meeting was finally over, the council cleared out, leaving Xander, Sylvie, Cal, and Evan in tense silence. Evan's head ached from exhaustion and dehydration.

"They're getting bolder," Cal said, rubbing the back of his neck. "They balked when I asked if they were going to wait."

"You're forgetting they also suggested you and I could skip this meeting," Sylvie said, grinning at Cal.

Cal shook his head. "They did."

Sylvie's guardian was remarkably even-tempered and, although the council did not like a foreign influence among them, the hunters of the Argarian army had taken him in with excitement. He'd become Evan's eyes and ears among them since Evan had risen too high to effectively blend in. When Evan worked under King Damian, there was enough distance between him and the king to convince the hunters of the army that Evan was one of them. But now, as Xander's proxy and best friend, the power dynamic had shifted such that he could not be seen as anything but a leader, and no one wanted to be honest with their boss.

"It's not enough to save the world," Xander said softly. "You also have to be ready to rule it."

"You planning on doing that anytime soon, Your Grace?" Sylvie asked. Her blue eyes narrowed on Xander.

Cal sucked in a breath, looking to Evan to resolve the tension as he had so many times before. But Evan didn't want to. He wanted to know how Xander would explain himself to the woman who had given up her comfortable life in Olney to prove her worth as something more than a bride to be claimed by the most strategically aligned guardian.

Evan was as dazzled by Sylvie's strategic mind as he was by her beauty, but he'd be damned if he let her know it. If she thought she had him, she'd be bored, and he could not have that. It was less about playing games with her and more about convincing her he was a worthy ally, even when he knew he would never be. She was a lady— a brilliant one, at that—and he was an orphan with no land or status. His only power came from his best friend, who was barely hanging on as king. He could not win her with a distinguished family lineage or massive wealth like all the men who tried to woo her back in Olney. He had to find another way.

Evan waited, expecting Xander to snap at Sylvie, but he just sighed and leaned his head back, looking at the stone ceiling.

"I'm doing my best, Lady Brett." He finished his whiskey and poured another.

Cal took that as a signal to leave, excusing himself politely and hovering at the door to wait for Sylvie. The two were bonded, which meant that they often came as a pair, and although Cal was aware of Evan's relationship with Sylvie, he rarely let her out of his sight unless she was safe with Evan. The three of them had agreed that was how it had to be while tension in the kingdom was still so high and some saw Cal and Sylvie as outsiders trying to destroy Argaria from within the castle walls.

Sylvie stood abruptly to follow Cal but paused at the other end of the table. She slammed her hands down on the mahogany wood and squared her shoulders to face Xander.

Desire pulsed through Evan's blood. He liked to see her fire, especially when it wasn't directed at him.

"It's a good thing I don't tell Cece anything about you, even when she asks," Sylvie huffed. "She'd be so disappointed to see the state you're in. She spent all her magic saving you and you know what it cost her. You dishonor the faith she had in you with your blatant disregard for your responsibility."

Xander flinched at the words. They were cold, efficient, and lethal

—a different kind of weapon—meant to be a harsh dose of reality and one that only Sylvie could deliver thanks to her regular correspondence with Cecilia.

"Get it together, Xander!" Sylvie turned on her heel and stormed out of the room, the swish of her dress fading down the hallway.

"She's just stressed," Evan said.

Xander rubbed his hand over his face. "If anyone understands passion from a spirited witch, it's me. I don't hold it against Sylvie. She's right. I just can't seem to figure out how to move forward."

Evan crossed his arms. "You could try moving Cece's clothes out of your room, maybe even blowing off some steam with one of the lovely women I've sent to you in the evenings."

Xander waved a hand. "I'm not interested in whores. I've never had to pay for it before. Why would I start now?"

"Because you're a sad sack of shit and any woman who spends time with you should be compensated for such poor company," Evan said.

Xander tilted his head back and laughed. "Fair enough. Still, I'm not sure I have an interest in that type of company. As for Cece's things, I just need a little more time."

Evan knew it was a lie, but he let Xander have it for now. It was good enough just to hear him laugh.

"I should—" Evan gestured after Sylvie. Xander nodded in dismissal, and Evan rushed back to his room.

When he pushed through the door to his bedroom, Sylvie was already pacing the floor, having let herself in through the secret passage that connected to her bedroom. It was convenient, though their secret was likely not as well-kept as either of them pretended. Still, Sylvie preferred to hold to the illusion of propriety.

"You need to stop coddling him," Sylvie said, her hair loose and spilling down her back like a golden waterfall. "You're constantly making excuses for him. I know he's lost the most. I get it, I really do, but it's hard for me to muster sympathy for a man who's had wealth, power, and influence his whole life when I've had to fight so hard for my own."

Evan stared at her. She was smart and so cutting. One moment she was managing a room of men, truly making them believe they were smarter than her while pushing them toward exactly what she wanted, and the next she was suggesting better trade routes and more favorable terms with neighboring kingdoms. The woman was born to be a queen. Too bad he wanted her to himself. He couldn't fight off a smile.

"What?" Sylvie gave him a baffled look, which immediately shifted to one of scolding. "No. Don't give me that look."

"What look?" Evan asked, prowling toward her.

"The look that says that you're about to kiss me until I forget how mad I am."

That was exactly what he wanted to do.

"I have no idea what you're talking about."

She braced a hand on his chest. "I need my anger right now and you need to hear it, Evan. I have sympathy for him. Xander is my friend, but he cannot fall apart right now. If I'm impatient with him, imagine how everyone else feels. I'm the one most likely to cut him a break. There are no breaks left. He's on his last limb with the council, and we need an actual plan."

Evan sighed. "I know. I promise I will fix it. I know he needs to do better. I know his best doesn't feel like enough, but that's why we are here, right? We help balance him out. Still, I have a few ideas. I will fix this. There are five eligible princesses in the neighboring kingdoms, several that have already sent correspondence. He needs an alliance and he could certainly do with some company. I just need to find the right moment to spring this idea on him."

Sylvie's shoulders relaxed, appeased by the idea of Xander married off. "Good luck with that. He won't even choose an artist for his royal portrait."

"He'll do it. I can convince him," Evan said.

The skepticism on her face wavered. With gentle fingers Evan tilted her chin so she met his eyes.

"Now can I kiss you until you forget how mad you are? Perhaps also until I forget how frustrated I am? Maybe even until we are both so exhausted we can get a good night's sleep?"

Sylvie grinned in spite of herself and Evan felt triumphant. Each smile was a victory stacked in his favor. When it came to Sylvie Brett, he'd take what he could get.

3

XANDER

Xander was lost in a flood of memories as he stalked through the halls of Castle Savero, fresh off a battle with yet another of Vincent's battalions. He expected to feel more frustrated, but the persistent grief that dogged him had numbed his extremes.

Five months as king and all he had to show for it was a constantly shifting border, a council full of opportunists, and a relentless depression that made even Argaria's warmest month seem as drab as late winter.

He walked down a long corridor. Candlelight flickered, casting shadows that made it feel like the walls were closing in. Portraits of past Savero kings glared down on him. It was silly to feel their judgment. They were just paintings. Still, they were reminders that the Saveros had ruled over Argaria since the kingdom split from Olney. His ancestors had kept the kingdom together, and now he was failing to do the same. He paused in front of the portrait of his father.

The painted rendition of Damian Savero stared down at Xander, a battle-worn scowl on his face. Xander tried to recognize something of his father in himself, but Davide had always been more like him—brutally strategic with sharper features—while Xander favored his mother—warm and kind with more humor in his face. He only risked this kind of staring late at night when there were few servants and courtiers to gossip about why the young king might stare so long at a portrait of his father.

He'd spent just as long looking at Arthur Randal, the famous Argarian hunter and the queen's longtime consort. There were so many questions that he wished he could ask his mother. Despite that desire for the truth, he had not yet summoned the courage to look in the truth mirror Grimon had brought him. It sat tucked away in his bedside table, its magical hum a constant taunt.

An ache formed behind Xander's sternum as he looked at the empty space next to his father's portrait where Davide's nameplate hung with nothing above it. His brother had been king for too short a time to be painted. Xander had hired a memory witch artist to pull the memory of his brother so that eventually Davide would be as perfectly preserved in paint as he was in Xander's mind. He deserved to be remembered along with the rest of the Savero kings.

However flawed he might have been, Davide saved Xander when it mattered, and he'd been under the influence of the same cruel god.

Now an entire family tree had been hacked down to a single branch. Xander was the last Savero—the entirety of his family's legacy. Unless, of course, he counted the rogue branch—Vincent, his only living relative, who wanted him dead.

He looked at the empty space next to Davide's nameplate. Evan had been pestering Xander for months to have his own portrait done, but having his likeness on the wall next to his brother and father would offer the opportunity for his detractors to point out the subtle differences in their features and use it as some kind of proof that the rumors were true.

Xander swallowed around the grief and loneliness and continued down the hall. He pushed open the heavy door of his bedroom and was about to drop his armor when movement caught his eye.

A beautiful, scantily clad blonde woman was poking through the scraps of paper on his desk. She didn't seem to notice his entry, but he could recognize her by the faint rose and jasmine perfume she left on the air.

"Looking for something, Mika?" he asked.

She froze momentarily before tossing her shiny hair over her shoulder and turning to smile at him. "Your Majesty," she said with a curtsey.

Xander rolled his eyes. "I've told you before to just call me Xander when we're alone. I can't stand the ceremony."

Of course Evan would send Mika up after a fight. Evan was still trying to treat him like the old Xander, and the old Xander loved a good fuck after a good fight.

The problem was, this wasn't a good fight—it was a painful, drawn-out war with an invisible enemy who had access to seemingly endless funds—and he wasn't the old Xander. He was a heartsick mess disguised as a king.

Evan might not have had any real magic, but he still tried to summon the old version of his friend—as if appealing to a version of Xander that no longer existed would draw forth the same confidence and attitude.

Mika stared at him, her brow scrunched with faux worry. When no reprimand came, she continued sifting through the papers. A scrap floated off the edge and fluttered to land at Xander's feet.

He looked down at the sketch of eyes. On paper, they were black and white—crude in charcoal—but in his mind, they were the same bright blue as the Adiran Sea on a clear day. He didn't know why he couldn't stop drawing Cece. It didn't help the loneliness, and it only succeeded in littering his desk with pieces of his ex-wife like torturous snowflakes.

Xander washed his hands, hair, and face in a fresh basin of water.

He pulled off his bloodied tunic and turned to meet Mika's dark eyes. Her gaze raked over his bare chest appreciatively.

"There are a lot of half-written missives here," she said, forcing a casualness to her voice.

"Leave it," he said curtly, knowing she wouldn't let it go so easily.

She didn't. She did not fear him. Instead, she licked her lips and began to read. "'*My love, I wish I could take away everything that hurts you. It breaks my heart each time I receive one of these tear-stained letters. You, of all people, don't deserve to hurt any more than you already have. I'm sorry that I dragged you into this mess. There aren't words for—*'"

"Enough," Xander said, snatching the half-written letter from her hands.

"Why are there so many unfinished? Why not send them?" Mika asked.

"Because there aren't words big enough. Because every time, my words feel too trite to contain what Cece was to me—what she is to me. Because each time I start, it reminds me where my heart really is, and that's not with this kingdom...where it should be."

The immensity of his loss could not be summed up in a letter. Even if it could, he would not burden Cece with his pain. If she knew, she'd ride across the two kingdoms and he would have to let her go all over again.

That's why he ended up sketching her—her eyes, her lips, her smile, the curve of her hips while she napped beside him. Now it seemed ridiculous. He should burn it all. Better not to have his pain on display to anyone else.

But when he looked up, Mika's gaze bore curiosity, not judgment.

Xander tossed the unfinished letter into the fire, then pulled on clean clothes. He grabbed a glass and the decanter of whiskey, then sat down in his chair to watch his words burn. Mika perched on the arm of the chair opposite him.

"Do you want me to take off my robe?" she purred.

Xander almost laughed at the question. The robe was lace and completely transparent. It did nothing to block the view of her elaborate lace slip and her smooth, fair skin. She ran her fingers over her collarbone enticingly.

"I've told you before, no matter what Evan has suggested, I have no desire to sleep with you. You're a beautiful woman. Please don't take offense. I am just hopelessly in love with someone else."

She gave him a wolfish smile. "I could make you forget."

He laughed bitterly. "Spoken like someone who has never had the real thing. I have half a mind to let you try."

Her eyes softened the slightest bit. Mika had a good poker face, but what he respected most about her was her honesty and intelligence. When Evan started sending him women, Xander chose Mika for her ability to converse—and for the fact that she looked nothing like the brunette goddess who haunted his dreams.

"Fine, then why do you ask me to come here every night?" Mika asked.

"I don't. Evan does because he thinks it will help. I don't mind your company because I'm lonely and I miss—"

Mika's eyes brightened with recognition. "You miss talking to her."

Xander ran a hand through his hair. "She was...*is* brilliant. Funny and smart and so easy to talk to. I just miss having an ally—someone that I trust—who can give me a perspective that's different from my own."

Mika considered it. "So, no sex?"

He flashed her the smile that had separated so many women from their good sense in the past. "I make no promises, but for the foreseeable future...no sex."

Mika's shoulders relaxed. "It's just as well. Men are fun on occasion. It would be an honor because you're the king and also your skills are well-reviewed. But in general, I prefer different company."

Xander looked at her, puzzled.

"I prefer women," she clarified. She looked as if she was expecting him to react poorly, but he just smiled.

"Me too," he said blandly. "We have more in common than I expected."

Mika laughed. She placed a gentle hand on his shoulder. "In my experience, the ache never really leaves, but you become more accustomed to the feel of it."

Xander studied her, swirling the amber liquid in his glass. There was no falseness in her face, and her heartbeat was steady. He liked Mika for this very reason. She understood how to reveal herself a little bit at a time, how to omit what she wasn't ready to share without overtly lying, and how to tell a good story.

"What happened with—"

"Ivy," Mika said, holding his gaze. "She was hurt by a reckless man. I can never forgive. Never forget. Never stop trying to even the unsettled score between us."

The intensity in her dark eyes and the threat in her words left him breathless.

"I'm sorry," he said.

She blinked and forced a grim smile. "It was a long time ago."

"Then may his memory be shorter than yours so you have the element of surprise," Xander said.

For a moment, her face was unreadable, then she nodded. "Well, I've told you mine. Now tell me about yours. You never speak of her and yet I think you see her in every silence."

Xander had become good at deflecting and steering conversations back to the person who'd asked the question. He could do it again now and Mika would say nothing because he was king. But it had been five months without Cece and he was bursting with thoughts of her.

"I never wanted to fall in love," he said, more to himself than her.

He'd said those exact words to his mother the first time he'd seen Davide in a relationship when Xander was just thirteen. He'd been baffled by something that would make his brother act so idiotically. Davide seemed to have lost himself, following Lady Davis Carrington around like a lost puppy.

His father was always a believer in never showing a real weakness. Rather, King Damian invented false ones. *If you show an enemy an easy wound to tear open, they won't look for a true weakness.* Those words were formative, and they were what helped Xander protect Cece from Cato.

But as his eyes passed over the painting above the fireplace, he knew his weakness would forever be on display to the world. Cece had sent him back to Argaria with her favorite of her mother's works, *Little Storm*, which depicted a four-year-old Cece gazing out over the ocean with a wild swirl of color around her. Xander had recognized Cece in the artwork the first time he saw it, when she welcomed him home to her cabin. In the accompanying note, Cece had written that he'd always seen her exactly as she was. Now he wondered if she just wanted to pay him back for hurting her by giving him a reminder to torture himself with daily.

He swore he could smell the summer scent of her skin each time he looked at the painting, feel the swell of her storm magic when she was upset, hear her laugh when he said something dirty.

He downed the rest of his glass of whiskey.

"Want some?" he asked.

Mika nodded, and he poured her a glass as she sat down in the chair next to his.

She held up her drink in a toast. "To the ones who broke our hearts."

He clinked her glass and downed his drink before pouring another. "It's only fair you know that I broke hers first. More than once, I think."

"Tell me more. I've heard the rumors, but I'd love to hear the real story."

He considered lying. He and Mika typically stuck to light topics and court gossip. He found comfort in their mundane conversations. He considered telling the bare-bones version with none of his own thoughts or emotions, but what would be the point? Evan had been trying to get him to talk it through with someone. Mika had been chosen in part because of her discretion.

So he started at the beginning.

He spoke about going to Olney to prove something to his family. He talked about the first time they met. He explained how the huntmaster asked him to keep an eye on his daughter, how he'd fallen for her from afar without realizing it. He left nothing out, swigging his whiskey as he went until he was drunk enough to tell the hardest parts.

Mika was quiet. She asked questions that made it clear she was genuinely interested. He supposed it was a good story. He wondered what Cece would think of his version.

By the time Xander finished, he was pleasantly numbed by the booze. The end was the hardest part. He should have been living happily with the love of his life. Instead, he was trying to run a kingdom of people who saw him as an outsider, while the only family he had left chipped away at his credibility.

He'd made terrible mistakes. He'd broken Cece's heart. Perhaps this was the punishment he deserved. The fact remained that this was his new reality. He was alone. Cece was miles away. The only things he had were her letters and the painting.

"Let's go for a walk, shall we?" He stood abruptly, ignoring the way the room tilted, and tossed Mika his robe, which would act as a more substantial cover than hers.

He walked into a passageway on the far side of his room with a bottle in hand. Mika's soft footsteps echoed against the stone behind him as she followed. He took the stairs down through a tiny hallway where he had to duck his head, and then back up, pushing through another secret door that dumped him into a bedroom.

"Where are we?" Mika asked.

Xander smiled faintly at the arrow marks in the wood door of the room. "This was her room when she was here. She wasn't allowed to do much, so she shot a bunch of arrows into the door. She drove my friend Teddy crazy, but he was so good with her."

Mika took in the room. It hadn't been touched since Cece left, except for the maid who cleaned it each week. The one exception was that he'd had her clothes moved to his bedroom closet so that her scent lingered. A book of Argarian mythology rested on the nightstand, and one of her shawls hung over the back of a chair by the fireplace.

"Is that why you stay in your old room instead of the king's rooms?" Mika asked.

He shook his head. "My parents died in the king's chambers."

Mika looked stricken. "I'm sorry. I knew that, I just didn't think—"

"It's okay. Everyone thinks the question and doesn't ask."

Xander's words were slurred, but Mika was good enough to pretend not to notice. She took the bottle from his hand and took a long swig.

"Want to see my favorite spot in the whole castle? Davide and I used to sneak up there all the time when we were kids, and it drove Evan crazy."

Mika grinned and nodded, following him out of the room. There were few servants in the halls at such a late hour. It was easy enough to sneak up the winding staircases to the highest wall in the castle. The darkness of the new moon made the stars seem exceptionally bright above them.

Below, in the city of Ardenis, torches and candles flickered on porches and windows like glittering fireflies. Everything had a glowing storybook quality.

It was so stunning that Xander barely noticed the icy chill in the air. Down below, the breeze was minimal, but high on the castle walls, a stiff wind cut into him.

"It's beautiful, but Xander, it's quite cold, and I'm not sure how safe it is to be up here. The winds seem unpredictable," Mika said.

Xander chuckled as he sat down on the lip of the wall, his legs dangling over the edge.

Mika sucked in a sharp breath. "Your Grace—"

"Xander," he corrected.

"Xander. I don't think you should be so close to the ledge. It's not safe."

He sighed and looked down at the ground far below them. "Nothing is safe when you're the king."

"That may be true, but this seems exceptionally reckless. Also, I'm not dressed for it." She placed a gentle hand on his shoulder.

"Are you afraid of heights?" he asked.

"No, I'm afraid of falling."

He laughed. "Aren't those the same?"

"No," she said. "Either way, I don't think that you being that close to the edge when you've had so much to drink is wise."

He groaned. "You sound like Evan."

"Perhaps you could see me back to my room. I'm not really dressed appropriately for this cold," Mika said soothingly.

She was clever, but he wasn't ready to step away from the edge yet.

"Fine. If you insist on staying here, I need to change into warmer clothes, okay? Do you promise you'll still be here when I come back?"

He turned and met her pleading gaze. There was real fear on her face, like she could not decode the sudden shift in his mood.

"Please?" Mika whispered.

Xander sighed heavily and laid back, his knees still bent over the edge of the wall. "I promise to stay right here."

Even he wasn't sure that he meant it, but she looked satisfied, quickly dashing back through the stairwell door.

Xander stared at the night sky for a few minutes, picking out constellations he knew and trying to remember the stories associated with each. He and Cece had done that when they were alone on her final Gauntlet run and he wanted to help her sleep. He'd mixed in real ones with fake ones, trying to make her laugh over the absurd stories he made up.

He'd been bold once—reckless in the way someone who had never been truly humbled could be. Now Xander was all unspent thunder and wasted lightning. Now he was a paper doll of a man who'd never really been worthy of Cece's love in the first place.

Name the fear and it loses its power. Davide had shared those words before he died and from beyond the grave, and though Xander had named terror after terror, they'd become no less compelling.

I'm afraid more people will be hurt by my failures. I'm afraid I will bring my friends down with me when I fail. I'm afraid I am my father's son and also that I'm not. I'm afraid I will never love again—that I will never be truly loved and understood.

The list was never-ending.

Pushing himself up to a sitting position, Xander stared down at the kingdom below. He was failing them. He was letting his people down. Maybe, more importantly, he was letting down the woman he loved—who had made a huge sacrifice for him. He didn't know how to be a good leader. Lowering taxes on the poorest classes had earned him nothing but scorn from his council. He'd raised hunter army wages, but only heard how it should have been done sooner. There was no winning. Every move Xander made was met with criticism, and he was exhausted.

He'd been raised to be a soldier and spare heir, and everyone in his life had always looked at him like he was too much. Too energetic, too extreme, too flirtatious, too playful. He always seemed to be too much of the things no one wanted and not enough of what they did.

Grief was like water, seeping through the cracks of his mind. There was nowhere it could not reach. Xander fixated on Cece because she was still here, still breathing, still miraculously grounded in this realm. The rest of his family hadn't chosen to leave him. They'd been taken. It hurt more that she decided not to be with him.

He was so incredibly low. He did not want to die, but he wasn't sure he could keep living. He felt trapped in a sort of middle place, as if he'd never come back from the brutal chest wound Cece had healed. He brushed his hand over his heart where the topography of his chest would forever be marked by his most vicious scar yet.

She hadn't meant to leave it, but she didn't have the luxury of being neat when he was teetering on the edge of death. It felt appropriate, almost comforting, to see it there every time he looked in the mirror—a focal point for the constant ache of being hollowed out by loss.

The door swung open, and Xander knew without looking that Evan was standing there.

"Xan," he said, taking a tentative step toward him. "What are you doing?"

"Just taking in the view."

Evan was breathless. "Mika came to get me."

"Traitor. I should have known she's one of your little spies," Xander sighed.

"How about you move away from the ledge, Xander?" Evan's voice was tight with fear.

"You don't get the same view from back there."

"I'm not joking."

Xander turned and winked at him. "Neither am I."

"What would Cece think about this?" Evan asked impatiently.

"She'd probably sit right down next to me."

Evan blew out a breath. "You're probably right, but what would she think if something happened to you? She worked quite hard to save you, and now you're acting like a spoiled prince instead of a king."

Evan was infuriatingly well-versed in guilt.

"I know you miss her. I miss her too. She certainly kept things interesting. She was much better at keeping you in line."

Xander laughed as Evan made his way to the edge and sat down next to him. His hand formed a firm grip on Xander's shoulder.

He met Evan's dark eyes.

"What are you doing, Xan?"

Xander swallowed hard. He felt the sharp ache in his chest, as if he hadn't been drinking at all. "I don't know."

"It's time to step back from the edge. It's time to put one foot in front of the other. It's time to be the kind of leader that only you can be."

"An idiotic one?"

Evan sighed. "No. A human one. A flawed one. This kingdom doesn't need another pompous ass like Vincent at the helm. It needs you. You recognize your weak points. You rely on other expertise when you should. You're a better leader than even I have given you credit for, Xan. That's on me."

"You're just saying that," Xander said.

"I'm not. I don't do lip service. You know that. But you know what else you know?"

"What?"

"That if something happened to you, it would break Cece's heart. She would blame herself."

Xander swallowed hard. Even through the haze of drunkenness, he knew Evan was right. He couldn't do that to her.

Worse, he heard the hitch in Evan's voice—Evan, who had put all his faith in Xander, who had followed him to Olney and back. Evan, whose fate and future were tied to Xander's whether he wanted them to be or not.

"Now, Sylvie is making some of your hangover tea. Why don't we go back inside and get you to bed?"

Xander stood and reluctantly took a step back from the edge. He put one foot in front of the other and stepped away from the brink. There had never really been a choice for him but to go on living.

4

EVAN

Xander was falling apart, and Evan could do nothing to hold him together, though it wasn't for lack of trying.

Evan had more than twenty years of intensive study under his belt. He was practiced in Xander Savero. He knew Xander preferred to sit back and let an opponent attack first so he could spot their weakness faster, he knew the way he covered true feelings with humor, and he knew the way Xander tried to fuck his way out of feeling anything at all.

But five months ago, that version of Xander died on a beach in Olney. Evan couldn't help feeling like he could have stopped the momentum of Xander's life if he'd just been there to keep him from kissing Cecilia for the first time or, at the very least, from making a deal with Cato.

He still felt a tinge of fury when he thought of the day Xander had commanded him to stay in Argaria.

"You'll be safer here," he'd said.

The words were ridiculous. Until that point in their lives, Evan's sole purpose had been to protect Xander—sometimes from other people, but usually from himself. Xander had made a point of keeping their friendship as equitable as possible by never once giving Evan a command until that moment.

"You'll help my father and keep me in the know of the things he does and doesn't want me to know," Xander had said, so nonchalant at fourteen, as if he was taking a holiday and not inserting himself in a precarious place behind enemy lines.

They'd planned to go together. Teddy was supposed to stay behind and use his father's access to the king's council to keep them both informed. Xander's last-minute command had been made worse when Evan looked to Teddy for support and his friend had offered a sheepish smile. It was the first time Evan had been blindsided by the two of them. He'd made sure it was also the last.

Xander was impulsive, so Evan made himself vigilant. He'd learned things about everyone important in his kingdom and in Olney. He'd traded favors and bedded women and closed himself off until he was a vault of valuable information.

He'd spent his formative years revolving around Xander, who seemed content to seek out danger like it owed him money. Teddy had once asked Evan if he resented playing babysitter from such a young age. It always bothered Teddy that King Damian treated him and Evan like family when he needed something and ignored them the rest of the time. He'd expected the king to be more paternal, since he'd had a hand in raising and training Evan.

But Evan hadn't needed a father. He'd needed a means to make his own way in the world, and King Damian had given him one.

In time, Evan realized that Xander had placed deep trust in him. He was more valuable as a spy than a protector, but the idea of letting Xander go alone filled Evan with guilt. It left him feeling like there was a debt he couldn't settle. That hadn't been Xander's motivation, but it had been the result all the same, and it made Evan feel a misguided need to make up for it now. No matter how many stupid things Xander did, Evan was always there to defend the king.

But seeing his friend with his legs dangling over the castle wall had gripped Evan with a vise of panic that was still clamped around his chest a full day later.

That was why he sat down at his desk in the late evening, candle wax dripping onto the hardwood surface. Despite his better judgment, he wrote to Cecilia for the first time in months.

———

Cece – Last night, I found Xander standing on the edge of the castle wall staring down like he was ready to jump. I don't know what to do. Can you come?

———

Soft footsteps padded along the floor behind him. A shadow fell over the letter.

"You can't send her that," Sylvie said.

He sighed. "I know. I just don't know what to do."

Sylvie ran her fingers through her hair and tightened the sash on her red silk robe.

Evan liked her ruffled. In daylight she was so curated, so careful to be seen in a specific way, in the best dress, in the best light. But he thrilled in seeing this softer side of her glowing in candlelight. He liked it even more that she couldn't stand to miss what he was up to.

If he got up, she got up too. She wanted to be a partner, and he had desperately needed one in the wake of Teddy's death. She did not fill the void his friend had left, but she was a great listener and a wise strategist. She knew how to wait and he thanked the gods for that.

She tossed the letter into the fire. "Cece cannot give him what he needs, and he has to understand that. If she comes here now, he's going to ignore everything that needs to be done and obsess over her."

Sylvie made a good point. It was impossible to know if Cecilia's presence would make things better or worse. Evan knew if he sent the letter she would come running. He'd watched Xander break her heart, and she still fought for him. He was confident she would keep fighting now, but she deserved to be happy.

It was nearly impossible to be both a good friend to Xander and a good friend to Cecilia. She needed time and space to heal, while what Xander needed was her.

Evan knew she worried because she wrote to Sylvie all the time. He knew Cecilia was struggling. As much joy as she'd found with Rainer, she was grieving. She was managing her own losses, and asking her to come here and continue taking care of his best friend wasn't fair to her.

He flashed back to the conversation he'd had with Xander that morning. The king had blown off his questions like he was worrying over nothing.

"Xan, how bad is it really? I've been trying to let you figure it out, but last night—"

Xander hadn't met his eyes. *"Last night, I was just taking in the view of my kingdom."*

"Neither of us is stupid enough to buy that."

Xander still hadn't looked at him. He stared into the fire.

"I was going to write to Cece—ask her to visit. I thought maybe it would help."

Xander had looked over at him at the mention of her name. *"She's dealing with enough. She doesn't need to worry about me."*

"So she's still writing to you?"

"Yes."

Evan knew she was. He just wanted to know if Xander had written back yet. *"And what does she say?"*

Xander had been quiet for a moment, looking back to the fire. *"She's just trying to keep herself together like the rest of us."*

Evan never considered for a moment that Xander's broken heart would have led him to that castle wall. Xander's hunter training was all about survival, and if there was one thing Evan knew about his friend, it was that Xander Savero was a survivor. While he wasn't a strategist, he was resourceful, fast, and a good improviser. Evan had underestimated how badly love had wrecked his friend.

Evan had been on high alert from the moment Xander returned to Argaria. He hadn't understood how Cecilia had successfully gotten her claws so deep in Xander so fast. Evan was surprised to find an alarmingly honest woman whose expressive face meant she'd make a terrible spy. Cecilia, Goddess of Mind and Memory, had made Evan's life terribly complicated.

He'd still had his doubts, but Teddy won him over.

"Watch him with her. Look at the way his face lights up when he sees her across the room. Look how she makes him laugh. Look how she loves his extremes. You should talk to her more. The two of them are so much alike. She loves him," Teddy had insisted.

Sure enough, when Evan paid closer attention, he saw the way the two echoed and understood each other. He saw the way Cecilia scolded Xander for how over the top he was, all while loving it.

Evan had watched people tell Xander to be less—*don't be magical, don't be affectionate, don't want so much.* For the first time, his friend met someone who liked him exactly how he was. When most people looked at Cecilia and Xander, they probably saw two young people who couldn't keep their hands off each other, but Evan saw the truth. They were two people who'd been told the same things by the world around them but refused to make themselves smaller so others would be comfortable.

He accepted then that Xander had met his match. What he couldn't grapple with now was how to pull his friend back from the brink of that love. Xander gave him many scares over the years with his reckless behavior, but he had an instinct for self-preservation that Evan could count on. Seeing him literally on the edge was unsettling.

Evan was floundering. Even with Cal and Sylvie's help, he struggled to keep a kingdom in line. Vincent's attacks had not only depleted their resources in soldiers and funds, but they'd depleted something much more valuable—the confidence the court had in their new, untested king.

While Xander showing up himself at small border fights bolstered his popularity among the common folk who lived there, it did nothing for the nobility who stuck their noses up at him as if he was a foreigner. They thought training as a commoner and living an ordinary life was a weakness instead of an asset. As if understanding the majority of his people was a bad thing.

The more word of his hands-on fighting and courage spread through town and into the outskirt villages, the more his council challenged him and the more Evan had to find ways to smooth over conflicts among the king's council members.

The complaints were many. *He was wasting resources. Does he not trust his generals to lead his army? He needs to learn to delegate.*

The whispers were ludicrous. The same people would be declaring Xander a coward if he failed to show.

Evan learned years ago there was no pleasing those people. Unfortunately, it was his job to try. Holding the official title of Royal Advisor meant that he needed to watch Xander's back. He was accustomed to doing so, but not with so many knives coming at it at once. He missed Teddy daily, not just because he needed his help, but because Teddy found the good in everything. He and Xander were the optimists, while Evan embraced the pessimism he was born of.

It was of no benefit for the prince's young guard to assume anything but the worst. A prepared guard was an asset, and an idealistic guard was a liability.

He had no idea who to count on.

Sylvie sat in his lap and kissed his cheek. "You worry so much. You carry the weight of the kingdom on your shoulders."

Evan leaned back in his chair and took a long gulp of whiskey. Sylvie's eyes bore into him. She trusted him to find a solution. She'd given up a good life in Olney to build something here—to prove she could be more than the sum of her looks and her ability to pit suitors against each other.

"What if I wrote to Rainer?" Evan said, pressing a kiss to her collarbone.

"You don't know each other very well," she said.

"And yet we understand each other. Rainer is perhaps not the best strategist for court politics, but he might be the strategist for managing Xander."

Sylvie arched an eyebrow. "True enough. He's been managing

that wild woman his whole life. Gods, you should have seen her when she was younger. What a terror. Gods bless Rainer McKay for the things he dealt with. She was always picking fights with much bigger men and insisting on finishing them herself."

Evan laughed. Cecilia was the best archer he'd ever seen, and he had no doubt she'd been mopping the floor with seasoned elites since she was old enough to hold a bow, but fighting hunters was another thing altogether. Especially since she was the huntmaster's daughter. Evan had seen firsthand what Nessa Ducrane—the Argarian huntmaster's daughter—went through just for being a woman and attempting to train with the rest. She put up with more shit than anyone else twice over.

"Ev, why do you take care of him as though he's still a child? The two of you aren't bonded. You're not his guardian. You could choose to do anything else," Sylvie said.

He frowned at her. Xander and Teddy were the closest thing he had to family, and he would do anything for them...would have done anything for them.

He still couldn't come to terms with the loss of Teddy. It left him with a wild desperation to hold on to what he still had. He found himself walking through the castle, expecting to find Teddy around any corner. And every time he went to a council meeting and saw Reese Reynolds, it was like having the air knocked right out of his lungs.

While Reese was several years older, he looked so much like his little brother it was startling. The only apparent difference was the sharpness in Reese's gaze. While Teddy's eyes had always been bright and joyful—almost young at times—Reese was a strategist to the core. He was suited to the council and a valuable ally. Still, he couldn't take the place of the friend they'd lost. Teddy left a chasm that nothing else could fill.

Evan floundered, trying to fill both roles and failing.

"Xander's my oldest friend, and he has no one else. His family gave me everything I have. I would not be here without them, and I would not be here without his friendship. Moreover, he has never once treated me like I am less than him, other than in a fight." Evan grinned. "He's the kind of leader this kingdom needs. I know he isn't there yet, but I know he can get there. I know you don't understand, and you don't believe in him. But can you believe in me?"

Her face softened. "I always believe in you." She kissed him gently. "Let me make you forget your worries for a little while, darling."

So he let Sylvie peel off his clothes and make him forget there was anything else in the kingdom but her.

5

RAINER

As much as Cecilia had been transformed by her rebirth into the world, Rainer had been transformed by the hope it brought him. For so long he'd been a ball of worry, a pessimist always expecting the worst, but beneath the constant buzz of anxiety, a new hopeful feeling had taken root in him.

Unfortunately, that meant he'd agreed to meet with Raymond McKay to give the man a chance after months of silence. Their reunion was not off to a strong start. His father was either running late or making a point about his time being more valuable than Rainer's.

Rainer shifted in his chair, looking out at his mother's garden. It had gone to seed. Cecilia had helped him maintain it for so long, but with travel and preparation for the Gauntlet over the past few years, it had been impossible. It was sad to see it in such a state of disrepair. The least Raymond could do was hire an earth witch to tend to it once a season.

The more time ticked by, the more Rainer's nervousness twisted his stomach in knots—either because he hoped Raymond would be moved by his son's near-death and finally see him as more than a way to increase his social standing, or because Rainer knew that was a fantasy.

For as long as he could remember, he'd wanted his adoptive father's approval. Logically, Rainer knew how wrong it was that he'd been made to feel like he was only worth what social currency he could provide the man who raised him. But even at twenty-seven, Rainer could not rid himself of the impulse to prove that he was a worthwhile investment.

It was irrational, but he'd been conditioned by years of desperate attempts to please his father and by the reality of his true parentage. Deep in his heart, Rainer knew he was falling short of his birthright.

Finally, the floorboards outside the office door creaked, heralding his father's arrival.

Raymond strode into the room and sank into the leather chair behind his desk. His hair was woven through with more gray than the last time Rainer had seen him. His stomach was also rounder, and the lines on his face more severe.

"I wasn't sure you'd show up," Raymond said.

The smallest flicker of hope lit in Rainer's heart. At least he seemed to recognize that Rainer had good reason not to show up at all.

"You always show such contempt for my concern. Why show up now?" Raymond asked, instantly smothering the fantasy that he would ever accept Rainer as he was.

Rainer sat a little straighter in his chair. "I suppose I came because I've been offered a second chance and would like to make the most of it."

Raymond frowned. "Yes, I'd heard about that. My son nearly dies and gets engaged and I have to hear about it from gossip in town."

"Last time I nearly died, you couldn't be bothered to even visit me at the healer's clinic. I didn't see the point of reaching out. You have no idea what it cost me—no idea what I've sacrificed."

The words were steeped in bitterness. Rainer swore he wouldn't let his father get a rise out of him, but he was already failing.

Raymond leaned back in his chair, pressing his hands together.

"You've done exactly as I asked, though I'm not sure being engaged to her will carry the same weight it would have if she'd retained her goddess powers."

Rainer frowned. "I didn't propose to her because you suggested it. I've been in love with her for years."

Raymond scoffed, waving a hand as if to ward off emotion. "The reason doesn't matter. The real question is, what's next for you?"

Rainer sighed. It was the exact question that had plagued him since the Gauntlet ended. He'd spent a misguided month at the healer's clinic trying to help Cecilia and the head healer, Lyra, but he felt more in the way than anything else. His anxious energy did nothing to settle the patients, and he mostly just moved them from one bed to another. After a few weeks, Lyra very nicely but firmly told him that although his heart was in the right place, he was more a hindrance than a help to their work.

It was just as well because, despite his morning swims and occasional workouts with Cecilia, he missed the relentless physical training his body had grown accustomed to over his years as a guardian. So he went back to what he knew—fighting.

He trained young guardians whose families could afford private lessons in swordplay and volunteered time with the hunter army. He competed in recreational tournaments, but none of it filled him with the same sense of accomplishment.

Rainer sat up straighter, forcing the words out in a rush. "I accepted an apprenticeship with a carpenter."

His father's eyes went wide. "A carpenter?" He slammed his fist on his desk. "I paid a fortune to have you whipped into the finest warrior in the kingdom and you're going to waste your unparalleled talent on building crooked tables."

Rainer could have said that since he'd wasted his unparalleled talent trying to please a man who would never be satisfied, carpentry seemed more productive. He could have said that he'd become too accustomed to his training and it ceased to clear his mind in the same way. He could have said that even after months, the memory of Cecilia's death had left him breathless and sweating with anxiety in the middle of the Olney City Market until his teacher stuck a block of wood and knife in his hand and told him to carve. From the first scrape of metal on wood, the rush of thoughts in Rainer's head hushed to whispers.

The carpenter had held up a wooden rose and told him to make one just like it. The carving was delicate, intricate, and Rainer sat hunched over his little block of wood for four hours until the market was closing down for the day and the movement startled him from his trance. His neck was cramped, his hands were sore, and his carving looked like a blob. Rainer had expected the carpenter to laugh at his efforts, but the man patted him on the shoulder and told him to come to his studio the following day and try again.

For two weeks he'd gone back every day, continuing to carve away while he watched the carpenter make short work of much more complicated projects. Yesterday, he'd offered an apprenticeship that Rainer had been thrilled to accept—until now.

Rainer wrung his hands, dragging his thumb over the crescent scar on his outer palm. He was so tired of wishing for more from the man who raised him. Frankly, he was tired of thinking of the man as a father at all.

Raymond McKay would never change, and being around him would always leave Rainer certain of the ways he was falling short.

Rainer stood so suddenly he nearly tipped his chair. "Well, this has been enlightening as always, but I think I've had enough of your conniving for one lifetime. Thanks for the congratulations and for reminding me exactly why I didn't bother to share the good news with you personally."

He crossed the room and wrenched the office door open, striding into the hallway.

"It's easy to make me the villain, but I think you know your birth father would have been just as disappointed in your choices," Raymond called after him.

Rainer wished he'd escaped fast enough to miss those words, but they crawled under his skin and remained burning and burrowed there.

He slammed the front door, hoping he'd never set foot in that house again. He'd already taken the few items of his mother's that were left and tucked them away for safekeeping. He could hardly stand to look at them because they served as a reminder that Maura had always been as kind as Raymond was harsh.

Storming away from the estate, Rainer tried to slow his racing heart. Raymond was right. He was wasting his potential, but he'd always felt like something was missing in him—something vital, the absence of which left him scared and weak when he should have been brave.

He paused and leaned against a tree at the edge of his father's estate, trying to calm the pulsing panic in his chest.

Cecilia had died in his arms. That moment marked a complete loss of identity. Not only had he lost the person he loved most in the world, but he'd failed at his most sacred duty. *From this day to my last day, I promise you my sword and my strength.* He'd been desperately trying to keep to that vow for years, until that day months ago when he'd failed.

He'd thought those words were a promise, but they were only a wish. He knew Cecilia better than anyone in the world—knew how she was always the first to sacrifice herself for someone else. Gods, he'd watched her sacrifice her happiness for him for years when she kept her mouth shut as he paraded women in front of her. And yet he had let her wrap her bloodied hand in his and push that blade into her heart.

For a few short moments, he felt the emptiness of a world without her, and even though she was back, the memory cast a shadow over every part of his life.

Rainer was terrified all the time, and she would not let him in. That morning he'd tried to confront Cecilia after hearing her awake and sobbing in the bathroom in the middle of the night, but she'd smiled and said it was just a bad dream.

Then she'd brushed her thumb to his brow and sung her rhyme and acted as if everything was fine. But it wasn't. She'd never been so remote—so utterly unreachable. He'd always known what she needed and for the first time in his life, he had no idea how to help her.

His chest tightened and his breath grew short. *Not now, please, not now.* He leaned his back against the tree, the bark snagging on his sweater. He pulled a half-carved flower from his pocket, turned it over in his palm, and prayed the sensation of something solid would ground him. But his heart beat harder, his breath grew shallower, and no matter how he tried to concentrate on the wood, his mind filled with flashes of blood and tears and star flowers.

He sank further down the tree and rested his forehead on his knees. *Breathe.*

A surge of warmth in his chest calmed him. *Cece.* She'd kept their bond closed over the past few months, but he must have been stressed enough that she felt compelled to take care of him.

Rainer buried his face in his hands, overwhelmed by a swell of love so in contrast with the leftover shame from Raymond's contempt. Feeling Cecilia there on the other end of that connection, alive and well, made him weak with gratitude.

Their whole lives, they'd loved fairy tales, but now that they were living a happily ever after, it wasn't all it was cracked up to be. They were both wounded in their own ways, but Cecilia carried a weight from which he had no idea how to unburden her. He loved her so much, but he could do nothing but watch her struggle and give her the opening to know he was there when she was ready.

He hadn't missed the way gentle touches made her flinch now, whereas she'd leaned into them before. As if she couldn't stand to feel something so soft in a world that had been so brutal with her. She always seemed guarded—braced for battle—and if he wasn't careful, he'd find himself her adversary instead of her ally.

Since the first time he'd taken her to bed, he'd felt the way the last little bit of space between them had disappeared, but now he saw in small ways each day that she fought hard to construct a new wall. It broke his heart to watch how she hid away.

No matter how he tried to draw her out, she resisted. The more she withdrew, the more anxious he became. The more he fussed over her, the more impatient she grew with his incessant attention.

He couldn't help it. It wasn't so much that he felt he owed her for what she'd done. He simply wanted her to be able to reap the rewards of her sacrifices. Instead, she continued to shrink into herself.

Despite her diminutive size, Cecilia's presence was large. She seemed poised to take up whatever space required, able to spread wide and fill cavernous rooms or just enough to remind a proud hunter to back down. It was easy to take her confidence for granted when he saw that in action, but when she woke from a nightmare and crawled into his lap, she seemed incredibly frail curled against him. He felt truly helpless to do anything for her.

Everyone thought they wanted to carry their loved ones' pain, but it was brutal to feel every hurt Cecilia felt. She had depths that he didn't, and when she fell low, she fell very low. It was so hard to know someone's pain like that and not be able to do anything but be there.

All he had to offer was himself, which felt woefully inadequate. It always had.

"*I'm just for you, Cece,*" he'd whispered in the moonlight as he held her trembling body.

"*Just for you,*" she'd repeated.

Then her lips would find his. Gentle, then passionate, then desperately seeking. Whatever clothing they wore was tossed aside. He couldn't hold her close enough, couldn't touch enough of her, couldn't kiss her long enough.

Much as he enjoyed it, he knew this tactic for what it was: an attempt to replace true intimacy with physical intimacy. It was only a treatment for the symptoms of her pain. It was not a cure, and once she'd fallen asleep peacefully beside him, he'd lay awake, watching her, praying to any god who would listen to take away the fear that still lived in her dreams.

He pressed his hand to his heart, sending a shock of love back through their bond. He turned the block of wood over in his hands, pulled out the blade the carpenter had given him, and started back in on the carving.

His heartbeat slowed and his breathing settled. He sat there for the better part of an hour until a pile of wood flakes lay in the dirt beneath him. He flexed his fingers, taking in his handiwork. It looked nothing like the star flower the master carpenter had assigned him. Every day of the last two weeks, he'd been assigned the same star flowers—Goddess Cecilia's star flowers, which had become a symbol of hope and renewal in Olney. Every day, Rainer tried to replicate them in pine and every day he failed to make anything as delicate and detailed. But he was getting closer.

He stood, tucked his tools away, and walked the rest of the way home to the cottage. By the time he pushed through the front door, he was calm.

Cecilia was poised on the window seat, backlit by the sunset, the late afternoon sun shining on the red and gold highlights in her hair. It was loosely pinned up, waiting for her to take it down. She played with the sash of her robe. It was barely knotted, revealing a glimpse of her thigh-high socks and the lilac ribbon stays that held them in place.

Gods, he loved those little ribbons and the swath of her thighs above them. He swore she only wore them because they made him mindless.

He ran a hand through his hair, trying to master his expression.

"How was your day?" she asked with a sexy grin.

He eyed her skeptically. *This again.* "It was okay."

Her lips tugged into a knowing smile. "Perhaps we could make it better?"

All at once, he knew she was avoiding talking yet again. She dropped her robe, standing naked before him in nothing but those thigh-high socks. All the blood in his body rushed south.

"I hate when you do that," Rainer said.

His eye was drawn to the golden scar on her chest. The sight of it never ceased to leave him breathless with love for her.

"You don't look like you hate it. You look like you like it quite a lot." She stared at his tented pants.

"I hate it because it empties my head of every thought," Rainer sighed.

"Sometimes it's good to forget your cares for a while." She grinned.

"And sometimes it's a strategic way for my lovely, naked fiancée to avoid conversations we need to have."

"Nonsense. Where would I have learned such a technique?" She realized immediately it was the wrong thing to say.

Rainer gritted his teeth. The spell was broken. Xander was where she learned it. He'd taught her how to avoid her hurts with sex.

She arched a brow. "That still makes you jealous?"

Rainer nodded. Jealous was an understatement.

"Perhaps you could dispel some jealousy by trying to wipe the memory from my head with something better."

She knew exactly how to send him over the edge. Rainer swept her into his arms. He kissed her as he sat down on the edge of the bed with her in his lap. His hand slid between her thighs, brushing lightly against her. She gasped. He pulled back to meet her eyes as he slid a finger inside her. He wanted that same intensity they'd had before—the gentleness, the eye contact that made it impossible to look away. But she squeezed her eyes shut and dropped her forehead to his shoulder.

"Cece," he murmured, but she wouldn't look at him.

She whimpered as he slid his finger in and out. Her hands gripped his shoulders and she moaned loudly.

"Cece," he repeated.

Still, she wouldn't meet his gaze. Instead, her hand slid inside his pants, wrapping around him with a gentle stroke.

"Stop," he said.

She froze, jerking back, eyes wide. "What's wrong?"

He leaned away from her and took her hands in his. Gods, it was torture to stop her when he wanted her so badly all the time. Their connection buzzed to life every time she was in his arms, but he had to get through to her.

"I can't do this anymore," he whispered.

Her bright blue eyes clouded with panic, her hands tightening on his. "What?"

"Oh gods, no, not like that. Sorry, I just...this...sex. I can't."

She laughed nervously. "What? Why?" She tried to look casual, but a whole host of emotions buzzed through their connection— anger, embarrassment, confusion.

Of course she didn't understand. She'd only been with one other person, and it was clear that Xander had never turned her down.

"It's not that I don't want to. You're so incredibly tempting," he said.

"Then what's the problem?" She slid her hands over his chest.

Trepidation dimmed the light in her eyes. She had no clue how to navigate this kind of rejection. Rainer needed to tread carefully.

He cupped her face in his hands. "Cece, I want you every day, all the time. It's maddening and distracting how much I want you. What I can't do without is our connection, and right now, you refuse to do that. I don't want to just be with you. I want to connect with you."

She frowned, her anger simmering in their bond. "You never seemed to mind before."

"It did bother me. I should have said something sooner. Don't get me wrong. You are unbelievably sexy, and I love being with you. The problem is that you refuse to let me in. You leave our connection closed most of the time, you won't talk to me about anything you're feeling. A quick, passionate tumble is great. But it's been weeks since you've really looked at me."

She pulled away from him, and anxiety clenched in his chest.

"And why shouldn't I, when you've been so selective about what parts of me you could love in the past?" she asked.

He recoiled. It was a fair accusation.

The Cece I know, my best friend, would never get joy out of hurting someone. But I saw you enjoy hurting Davide. Even if he deserved it. Even if you were just paying him back. I hate to see this war change you.

He'd said those idiotic words after Cecilia broke Davide's hand months before, and he wished every day since that he could take them back.

When she was afraid, she always went back to that. She started hiding so Rainer wouldn't see anything unpleasant about her. He wished he could take back the words he'd said in a moment of weakness that made her feel that way.

"I'm sorry that I ever made you feel like there was a part of you I couldn't love. That was wrong," he said. "I love and want to see all of you. Even if it's hard. Even if it's not what I want to hear. Even if it's dark and scary and you think it's too much for me. I love you. Not part of you. Not just your beautiful face. I love all of you. And now that I've had it all, I can't settle for less."

"So if you can't have all of me, you're just done?" she asked, standing and turning her back to him.

"No, sweetheart, of course not." He closed the distance between them and wrapped his arms around her. "I just can't do intimacy without the actual intimacy."

She cringed—actually cringed in his arms. She pulled away. Furious, stormy blue eyes stared into his. Her rage was ready to boil over. He braced himself for the impact.

"Can I fuck other people, then?" she asked.

Rainer's anger flared. He wasn't expecting that, even if he should have. She loved to push him. She wanted a reaction.

"You're not my property."

Her eyes narrowed to angry slits. She took a shaky breath. Rainer waited for her to yell, but instead, her posture relaxed. A wicked grin tugged at her lips. She laid back on the bed.

"What are you—"

He didn't even get the words out before her hand slid down between her legs and she whimpered softly.

Rainer stopped breathing. He was so utterly outmatched by Cecilia, all he could do was watch. She blinked her eyes open and grinned at him.

"I guess I'll just have to take care of myself," she whispered. Her head fell back as she moaned.

He stared at her hand, unable to speak. She knew how much he loved to watch her. She fully intended to torture him until he gave in. Gods, he loved her, even when she drove him crazy.

"You have permission to take over anytime you want," she said in a sultry voice.

"Cece—"

She moaned.

His self-control wavered at the sound. He needed to get out of the cottage immediately.

"Enjoying yourself?" he rasped.

"Immensely. You know how much I like when you watch. Want to know what I'm thinking about?"

She said the filthiest things when she got like this. It was a game to see how hard she could make him before he fully lost his mind and pounced on her. She knew exactly what he liked.

Walk away, Rainer, he screamed at his body, but his feet were glued to the floor. His eyes were focused on the movement of her hand.

She panted, her cheeks flushed. "I'm thinking about—"

Rainer didn't wait to hear. He forced himself to turn and leave the cottage. He walked straight down the cliff trail to the beach. He tossed his shirt into the sand and plunged into the icy sea, hoping it would be enough to settle him down.

He swam for an hour, but he couldn't stop picturing her splayed out on the bed just for him.

He forced himself to swim until his skin was chilled and he could think of something other than Cecilia. He needed a plan if he was going to survive this brand of warfare.

———

After two weeks of the same madness, Rainer was teetering on the edge of sanity and self-control. He busied himself with organizing the bookshelves. Cleaning and organizing had always helped him think through problems.

He shifted several of their old volumes of fairy tales, but one book would not push flush to the back of the shelf. Something was blocking it. He pulled out the book and behind it found Cecilia's Godkiller dagger.

He hadn't considered it until then, but she no longer carried the blade, as though she couldn't stand the weight of it. Just seeing it made his blood turn to ice with the memory of the last time he'd held it.

When he ran down to the beach that day, months ago, he had no idea what was in store for him. He only knew Cecilia's fear, sharp and bright and cutting, and he ran to her.

All he could think of was getting to her, until Cato was slicing into his chest, and Rainer looked helplessly into Cecilia's wide eyes as she screamed. It was a loud, inhuman scream, as if the knife was in her chest instead. It may as well have been.

Rainer underestimated her bravery, even after he'd seen it so many times over the years.

Cecilia knew the moment she put her dagger in his hand. She knew she would die, and she knew it would hurt, but she convinced him anyway. Her face betrayed nothing as she kissed him and said goodbye in her own secret way.

"*Brave with my hand,*" she'd said to him.

"*Brave with my heart,*" he'd answered.

But she'd been the one who lived those words at that moment.

He had no idea what it was to possess that kind of courage. It wasn't fair the way she still carried the burden of it all.

Turning the blade over and over in his hand, Rainer tried to see a way to remind her of that courage. Finally, he tucked the dagger into one of his bags in the back of the closet before returning to the bookshelf. A book on guardian training tipped onto the floor, unfurling to a page on the final guardian exam and, all at once, an idea formed in Rainer's mind.

As much as he wanted to solve this problem for her, he'd learned from making that mistake before. Cecilia needed to know that she could do it herself.

She was so stubborn, but he had one last idea to make her face whatever was making her hide away. He knew she would be furious, but he also knew if he did nothing, she would continue to withdraw into herself.

He set out at once to find someone who could help him make it happen.

———

Rainer added a log to the crackling campfire and took one last glance over their surroundings. It was too dark to see much other than the horses stirring on the other side of the tent where his friend, Anders Everett, had gone to rest.

When Rainer shared his plan, Anders patted him on the back and wished him luck with Cecilia's wrath. Still, he offered to help with the horses.

Doubt crept into Rainer's mind, but he had to go with his gut, and his gut said that Cecilia needed to be pushed.

Rainer sat down on a log by their fire.

Cecilia slumped down beside him with their wine canteen in her hand. "I thought the point of finishing the Gauntlet was not having to camp out in the woods anymore."

Rainer smirked. "I thought it would be a nice change of pace from being at home."

"But it's cold." She snuggled into his side and took a long drink from the canteen, then held it up to him.

Rainer shook his head. She'd already had quite a bit with dinner and he wanted to keep a clear head.

"I still don't understand why Anders is here."

"He's not really here," Rainer said.

Cecilia tilted her head up to glare at him. "Then why is his tent right over there?"

"He's going to stay with the horses while we take a short walk tomorrow."

The lie came disturbingly easily to Rainer. Fortunately she didn't press, and he didn't have to make up a more elaborate lie to cover for the fact that Anders would be leading her horse back to town. Rainer was so grateful that it was already growing dark when they arrived. He'd timed it intentionally so that Cecilia wouldn't recognize where they were. He was so nervous she'd notice that he kept offering her wine, and now she was clearly a bit tipsy.

"Why don't I tell you a story?" Rainer said.

She glanced around. "But we're out in the open."

"I thought we could sleep under the stars."

Her face lit up in a way that made him doubt his whole plan.

"Fine," she said. "Tell me a story."

Rainer was barely five minutes into his story when Cecilia drifted off to sleep. He kept her there, sleeping soundly against his chest, until the first hint of dawn dragged up the horizon. Then he tucked her against her supply bag and kissed her goodbye.

He'd been approaching things all wrong. The shape of her sadness was too large for him to inhabit. He could not deliver her from it, could not fill every secret hollow of hurt with love, much as he wanted to. She needed to be her own hero.

Rainer hesitated, looking back at her sleeping form in the distance. It was too late to back out now, so he turned and left her alone in the wild.

He knew her the best. If she was lost, he would help her find herself. Rainer would remember her even when she couldn't. Cecilia Reznik was unforgettable.

6

CECILIA

Cecilia woke to sunlight warming her face. Birds squawked in the trees above her. She had a vague memory of Rainer carrying her, of waking with her cheek against his firm chest, of smelling his skin as he kissed her forehead and placed her on the ground. She didn't remember him settling in to hold her.

She shot upright and blinked her eyes open, her hands reaching blindly before her gaze adjusted to the light. Rainer was not beside her.

The way the light slanted through the canopy above her suggested it was at least midmorning. She was at the edge of a clearing just outside the woods, a blanket pooled in her lap and a pack tucked beside her. Anders's camp was broken down and the horses were nowhere to be found.

She stood and turned in a slow circle, trying to assess where she was.

"Rain?"

There was no answer. She tried again, louder, but there was no sign of him. She dug through the leather pack, pulling out a canteen, food, and a slip of paper with Rainer's neat handwriting.

———

Cece – I love you too much to let you continue to flounder in your grief. I know I can't save you, much as I wish I could. You'll have to save yourself. I know you remember the way home. – Rain

———

She read the message four more times before she understood. After all her antics the past few weeks, he wasn't messing around. He'd really left her out here in the wilderness in the middle of the night.

Cecilia cursed, shoving the note back into the bag and climbing to her feet.

She shaded her eyes with a hand and looked further past the edge of the clearing. Pink and yellow wildflowers trembled in the morning breeze and as they shifted, she caught a glimpse of a white marble marker.

She ran toward it. Moss had settled into the etched words in the marble, but it was easy enough to read: *To Guard Wisdom, Memory, and Magic, you must first master your mind.*

Her magic swelled, searching through the web in her mind until it snagged on something.

———

Cecilia was seventeen years old and Rainer nineteen. They stood in the same spot in the clearing she was now.

"Are you sure you want to do this? You know you don't have to," Rainer said, his brow creased with worry.

"I know," Cecilia said.

"You don't have to prove anything to everyone. Anders has always been an asshole to you, but he's not right."

"I hate to admit it but he is actually right. Winning the Huntgames only proves that I'm the best hunter. I want to prove that I can hang with the guardians."

"It won't make him nice to you," Rainer said. "Passing the Guardian Final Exam is not necessary for you. No one seriously doubts your skill, not even Anders. I don't like the idea of you spending three days in the wild like this. You have no idea what you'll run into, and once you start, you know that you're on your own. You won't be able to use your magic because of the wards along the course that block it."

"I know. I can do it. But you have done it and I want to do it too. Don't go where I can't go, Rain."

He smiled faintly.

"I can do it," she said.

"I really would like to just throw you back on Zeke and carry you home right now. This goes against every instinct," Rainer said.

She brushed her thumb over his brow. "I found a worry, but I'll fix it in a hurry."

Rainer smiled indulgently.

"I'm more than prepared. You drilled the route into me. I will see you back at the cottage in three days."

Rainer studied her face with the same resigned anxiety he always exhibited when she wanted to do something he hated. He'd had the same look on his face while he trained her for the Olney Huntgames and every time she'd done something stupid or reckless since.

"No unnecessary risks," Rainer insisted.

She grinned at him, taking his hand in hers. "Who can say what's necessary other than adventure, Rain?"

He rolled his eyes but pulled her into a tight hug. "I'm serious, Cece. No detours. Come straight home. I won't be able to help, and I won't be able to feel if you need help, and I hate that." He mumbled the words into her hair, but she understood.

"Would you prefer to feel me in peril and know you can't help?" she asked, grinning as she pulled away.

She faked confidence for his sake. Now that she was facing down three days separated from him, she felt less bold than she had to start.

He kissed the top of her head and turned to leave her alone as he rode away.

Taking her first steps into the clearing, she felt her connection to her magic sever. She was truly on her own.

———

Cecilia blinked her eyes open.

"Asshole!" she shouted.

There was no point in screaming about it. Rainer wouldn't hear her, wherever he was. She hoped he would at least feel her anger.

"This is supposed to make me feel better? Abandoning me for a three-day hike?"

It was a waste of energy and a waste of time. She was three days from civilization at the start of the course that determined if guardians were ready for fieldwork. She wouldn't be able to use any magic. Three days in nature with nothing but the thoughts in her head was a nightmare.

At seventeen, she'd done this hike to prove to her longtime bully, Anders Everett, that she was just as strong and capable as him. Now she would do it again to prove to Rainer that she was fine. The only way out of the trail was through, so she started the hike.

A golden Olney guardian crest gleamed at the trailhead. As she stepped over the threshold, she felt the connection to her magic sever. Turning back, she spotted several markings at the corners of the stone. She knew little about magical wards, but they were part of what kept guardians from following their witches into the Gauntlet caves. Wards were old magic, rarely used anymore, and absent from her collection of memories—likely because the witches who created the Gauntlet didn't want anyone learning how to take down their protections.

As Cecilia walked through the stifling quiet, beginning her climb up a steep hill, her mind wandered to all the things she'd been avoiding for months.

She was always divided. Part of her longed to let Rainer in; wanted to curl up in his arms and never leave—to be seen, heard, and loved. It wasn't like she wanted to keep him out, but the moment she'd come out of the dark and drawn air into her lungs, she'd felt a door slam closed in her heart.

Her heart was beating. Her lungs were breathing. She was alive. But it felt like death had placed a veil between her and the outside world. Life had lost some of its color, or perhaps she had lost her connection to its usual brightness. She did not have a name for the isolation, but even when she was surrounded by people, even when she felt Rainer's love bright and fluttering and wrapped around her heart, she somehow felt alone.

And Rainer kept looking at her like all was well. So she'd tried to settle in to their second chance. But the moment her life slowed down and she finally held still, all the grief and guilt that she'd postponed while they saved the kingdom crashed down on her at once.

She could not expect Rainer to accept the ugliness when she couldn't accept it herself.

It was impossible to keep a distance between them. No matter how she tried to keep him out of their bond, he still sneaked through.

War broke people in quiet ways even far away from battlefields. It had broken her mind to the point she still felt the ripples of it, a cold sweat that broke out on her skin when a wave of panic hit out of nowhere. The war was over but her vigilance remained.

No matter how much she reminded herself she was safe, she could not shake the feeling that at any moment a split might open in the air and Cato would step through, and the nightmare would begin again.

"He's dead," she said aloud, startling a wren from the raspberry bush beside her. "Cato is dead."

But she'd been dead, too. And now she was here on this rocky, godsforsaken trail, her heart pumping as if it had never stopped at all.

She brought her hand to her chest, pressing her fingers in until her linen shirt tugged over the golden scar. The sensation sent a shiver through her. It was always sensitive, but touching it reminded her that she was safe and calm and alive.

"Scars are just reminders that you are stronger than the thing that tried

to break you," Rainer had once said when they were children. But she wasn't sure that was true.

That scar reminded her that she had been broken by death; that she'd needed to be saved by Rainer—and while that was romantic, it also came with a strange pressure to be well. She had always dreamed about the kind of love that was strong enough to conquer death, but she'd meant it metaphorically. She felt as if she'd crossed back over the veil and left worthiness behind.

"I am at peace," she said to herself.

The heavy foliage around her swallowed up the words that sounded more question than incantation in her ears.

She sighed and kicked a rock in frustration. Rainer was so impatient. She did not understand why he couldn't just let her sort through things in her own time. The past few months, it was as if the more he struggled with his identity, the more eager he was for her to settle down with him. He had not pressed her to set a date for their wedding, but she felt the unspoken question in every silence.

It made her feel like a crutch, not a partner. They'd always struggled to have their own identities when they were so closely entwined in each other's lives, but she resented that he used tending to her as an excuse to not tend to himself.

Relying on each other too much before had been a mistake that cost her dearly. When Rainer revealed he'd known who she was for four years and hadn't told her, the entire foundation of her life had been knocked out and she'd lost her entire sense of self because it was so connected to him. Now she could see the ways the Gauntlet ending had done the same for him. He did not know how to exist without her safety as the center of his world, and she felt burdened by the weight of his attention. She did not want to build a life where they only existed in relation to each other. She wanted a relationship where they grew and supported each other's dreams. Finding that balance was a challenge.

For most of her life, their bond had been a comfort—Rainer constantly reminding her that she wasn't alone. But now it was smothering, as if she couldn't get a moment of peace even inside her own heart.

Rainer's love had saved her. And still, she didn't trust him to love her enough to step into the dark with her. She didn't trust him enough to see her grief and despair without trying to fix everything for her. And here he was, proving that he could not help but try to do just that.

Her thoughts were a restless tempest that threatened to steal too much of her focus, so she paid attention to her feet. One foot in front of the other, one step at a time, she would get back to Olney. Every step of the way, she planned how she would kick Rainer's ass once she got home.

It took her hours to get to her stopping point for the day. When Cecilia hiked up the steepest part of Clastor's Summit at dusk, she cursed Rainer's name. Her feet were blistered and screaming in her boots, and the muscles in her legs were on the brink of failure with the effort.

Grief had made her weak, and that would not do. She slipped, banging her knee against the rough rocks and tearing her leggings and skin.

She was so close to the top, but every muscle in her body was screaming for her to stop. She couldn't. Even if she wanted to, it was much too steep to rest, and the loose rock was too unstable. She kept climbing.

When she finally reached the top, she collapsed into a heap. Sweat soaked her clothes, and the chilly night air made her shiver. She crawled to a nearby tree, leaned against its base, and miserably ate some cheese and bread from her pack. She looked out on the valley below. In the distance, she saw faint lantern lights in Olney City and the rise of Olney Castle. She shivered against the autumn air as she pulled her blanket around her.

"I hope you're happy, Rainer McKay," she muttered as she leaned her head back against the tree. She wondered if she would even be able to sleep out there alone. The questions didn't remain long. The exhaustion of the day ensured she fell asleep quickly.

———

The next morning, she woke stiff and not at all well-rested. She'd always envied Rainer's ability to fall asleep anywhere. It had become a joke, the way he could lie down and seemingly find sleep in seconds. He liked to say it was a sign of a clear conscience.

I wonder how clear his conscience is this morning. She hoped he was worried sick. It served him right, leaving her out here alone when she was so out of shape and distraught.

She quickly ate breakfast and packed her things, heading down for day two of her travels.

Despite her rage, she'd had some time to sort her feelings. There was grief for the people she'd lost, guilt for the lives she'd taken, fear that Rainer would stop loving her, and devastation that she couldn't give Rainer everything he wanted.

Cecilia could not shake the nervousness from her body.

She hiked into the valley and struggled across a low point in the river, water roaring in her ears as she fought the current. She pulled herself onto the opposite bank and collapsed onto her back in the shade of a lemon tree. Her mind wandered to Teddy. He would have found this whole ordeal hilarious. He'd find a way to make things light, even when she was furious.

By the end of day two, she'd run out of fury and was left with nothing but grief and guilt. Guilt felt safer, so she thought of all the people who had sacrificed for her and all the lives she'd taken without a second thought. She tossed and turned all night, unsure how to release the weight of it.

In the morning, she was exhausted and left with nothing but grief and devastation. Her body was leaden as she forced her blistered feet to march the last few miles to her cottage. Tears streamed down her face as she blindly made her way through the wilderness.

Cecilia wasn't ungrateful to be back from the dead, but she felt she'd been broken and reformed. There was a sense that she'd brought something back with her, but rather than an entity, it was just her own grief and fear. As if the pause between life and death held her in such suspension that everything she'd been holding off collapsed on her at once.

Her return had been joyful, and she was able to hold back the tide for a while, but then it grew larger in every silence.

There was no part of her that regretted her choice, but the aftermath was devastating.

Rainer had asked her once what it had been like. It took a few months for him to work up the courage to ask, but she just stared at him, unblinking, torn between telling him the truth and saving him from the nightmare. The point had been to save Rainer—not drag him down to drown alongside her in her grief and pain. Explaining to him what she'd been through would only make him feel guilty. The closer Rainer became, the more afraid she was he'd see it.

She didn't know how to unwind the grief that seemed to weave its way through her entire being. She'd had her heart broken, metaphorically and literally. One left her feeling like she could not trust herself. The other buried a phantom pain in her chest so that every time she rolled her shoulders back, she felt a twinge where the dagger had entered.

That was not something she could easily explain, nor did she want to share it.

She was so lost in thought she didn't realize how much ground she'd covered until she walked by the white marble pillar at the end of the trail and felt her magic swell in her chest again.

Cecilia drew up short, the scent of the sea hitting as she descended the trail. In the distance, she saw her cottage, gilded sunlight making the salt-withered paint appear vibrant.

Familiar fury washed over her as she approached, and she was happy to have reconnected with that anger in time to confront Rainer, but when she threw the front door open, he was nowhere to be found. Instead, she peeled off her boots, grumbling as she pumped in cold water for her bath. She didn't bother to use her magic to heat it before climbing in and scrubbing three days of dirt and sweat from her body.

When she emerged from the washroom in clean clothes, Rainer

stood in the doorway, freshly shaved and bathed, eating a lemon cake. He held one out to her, regarding her casually as if it was just a normal day, though she read his underlying wariness through their bond.

"How could you leave me out there alone in the state I'm in? You knew I was out of shape. You knew I couldn't handle it," she said. It was a costly admission.

"You look no worse for the wear," he said plainly.

"How could you leave me on my own?" She wanted so badly to just feel angry, but her eyes were already burning with tears. Her anger was being eclipsed by hurt. She bit her lip to keep from crying.

"You were already on your own," Rainer sighed. "You pushed me out. I just forced you to see it in a more literal way."

His gaze was so intense, as if he could see right through her. He took a step toward her, as if sensing her wavering control.

Cecilia tried to hold it back. She didn't want to give Rainer the satisfaction of knowing his plan worked. She was too angry to keep him from everything she'd been tucking away.

"You left me alone. What if I didn't remember?"

"I knew you would." His tone was placating, and it just made her more furious. "You needed to see now, just like you needed to years ago."

She crossed her arms. "To see what?"

"That you could save yourself. You needed to know that you could still do it—that you still had the will to." The crease in his brow disappeared and his voice grew softer. "I couldn't do it for you."

Cecilia blinked away furious tears. Her chest tightened and her breath grew shallow. She hated this feeling. The intense feeling of panic had come on in a rush a few times over the past few months, leaving her hazy and curled in a ball on the floor at the most random times. It felt like dying—like the whole world narrowed to just sucking in the next breath, like her body was rejecting life.

"You left me out there alone." She choked out the words between gasps, ignoring the pinched look of concern on Rainer's face.

Why was this happening now? She was mortified and frustrated with her hands for shaking so badly, with her heart for thundering so loudly she couldn't think, with her body for being so fragile when it used to be so strong.

"I didn't," he whispered.

"You did."

"I was right behind you the whole time," Rainer insisted.

"Spare me the emotional platitudes," she said with a dismissive wave of her hand.

"It's not a platitude. I was literally right behind you the whole time."

She froze, staring at him in disbelief. "I would have felt you."

"I thought you did three different times. You turned and looked right at me, but you didn't see me in the trees," he said. "I needed to know you'd be okay."

"You were there the whole time?"

He reached a tentative hand to cup her cheek. "Every step of the way. I knew that you could do it alone, but I wanted to be there anyway, just in case."

"Just in case," she repeated.

"I know I've spent most of our lives doing it wrong," Rainer said. "I should have let you stand beside me more instead of making you stand behind me. I just know that when you hurt other people, it hurts you. Instead, I made you feel like I thought you were helpless. I made you feel restricted. Maybe it was for my own benefit...so I could feel like you needed me. Either way, I know that I needed to let you prove to yourself that you still can."

She was speechless.

"Cecilia Reznik, I knew you the first moment I saw you. I knew you again when we were bonded. I will always know you. I want you to choose to be mine. Because that's the only way someone could ever have you—if you choose them. It felt like you chose me before, but it has not felt that way since—"

He blew out a breath. He refused to say it—like the words alone would haunt him.

"Since I died."

He flinched but didn't pull away. "Tell me how to help you. Talk to me. I know you're up crying at night. I see you write Xander letters. If that's what you need to do, I want you to do it. But I want to know how you're feeling. I can't imagine what you're going through, but I hate that you're going through it alone—that you won't let me see or comfort you."

Her lip quivered. "You were right behind me the whole time?"

He nodded.

"I came back for you. I should be okay. So many people didn't get to come back—"

"You have a right to feel whatever you do." He pulled her onto the couch next to him.

She looked at him skeptically. "Really? You're not going to freak out? You're not going to run? I don't think you'll like what you find."

"There's nothing about you that I don't want to see. I crescent promise. I want to know all of you. Will you let me?" Rainer asked.

"I still see the light go out of Teddy's eyes. I still see my father falling to the ground. I still see you and Xander bleeding out. I still see the faces of all those hunters that I killed without a second thought. I wanted to do it." Tears streamed down her cheeks as she spoke.

"You were scared and beaten down and overwhelmed. You need to give yourself a break. You went on and saved even more hunters from both kingdoms after that. You figured out how to not have the same thing happen again," he soothed.

She shook her head. "They were someone's children, someone's husbands, someone's fathers, and I killed them. And I got to come back. Sometimes I—" Her voice broke, and she stopped. "Sometimes I wish I never came back."

Rainer's devastation hit her through the bond.

Most days it felt that way—like she'd never feel peace again. Rainer could not understand because he was good. He had only ever killed because he had to—to protect her. She kept waiting for him to realize that he shouldn't love her, all while she selfishly prayed that he would.

"Is that what you wanted to hear? You might wake me up every night to make sure I'm still alive, but I wake up every morning feeling like I don't deserve to be," she said, furiously wiping away tears.

The hurt had no beginning, middle, or end. She rode it around and around in an unending spiral, spinning out forever, leaving her dizzy and sick and breathless. Every time she thought it might be over, it circled again and all she could do was wait for the dizziness to pass.

He was quiet for a moment. "You have to stop punishing yourself. It's enough. You've been through so much. I know I don't even know it all. You've saved all of us countless times. You saved me more than once, and it cost you a lot to do it. I hate that you had to carry the burden for all of us, but those hunters would have been killed either way. Either by me, you, Evan, Olney hunters, or Xander. They were there to kill us—to invade. You acted out of self-defense. You have to forgive yourself."

"I don't deserve it," she whispered.

"Yes, you do."

She leaned her head back and sighed. "I don't. I'm not like you."

"What if I had slaughtered them all?" Rainer challenged.

"You didn't."

"What if I was the Lost God, and the moment I came into my power, I didn't know how to control it? What if it was my father that I loved so much who was killed in front of me? What if it was you with a knife to your throat? I would have killed them all. Make no mistake, Cece. I would have done the same thing, and I wouldn't even feel guilty now because I would kill every man in the warring kingdoms if they tried to hurt you. I would have enjoyed watching everyone who wanted to harm you die a horrible death."

She didn't say anything.

"We've been through a war that no one ever prepared you for— maybe not one in an open field, but a mentally grueling one," Rainer said. "You've had your heart broken over and over, and I watched you pick yourself up no matter how you felt. You fought for everyone else, but now you won't fight for yourself. You made me stab you in the heart to save me. You have given everything, every part of yourself, to me and both kingdoms. And you did that even after we all lied to you, even when we didn't deserve it. You have a right to feel what you feel, but I won't listen to you say for one moment that you don't deserve to be here."

She looked at him, tears clouding her eyes. She shook her head. She stood and paced the floor. He stood in her path and stopped her. He brought a hand to her cheek, and she leaned into it.

"Rain, I'm so broken. I am afraid I'll never again be the girl you fell in love with. I don't know how to fix it. I wanted to be strong for you and for everyone else," Cecilia rasped.

"I know you're strong. I've seen you be strong in the face of things that would have broken me. You don't have anything to prove to me. You don't need to do this yourself. Will you let me help?"

Cecilia hesitated. She wanted to let him. She truly did, but she was so scared.

He tilted her chin up so she'd meet his eyes. "Don't keep yourself from me, Cecilia. My soul is sworn to yours just like my heart is—just like it will always be. I spent years letting you walk into the dark alone, but the Gauntlet is over, and I will do it no more. I will come for you in every darkness, and I will carry you out, or I will sit with you there until you can walk out on your own."

She placed her quivering hands against his chest. He'd followed her through miles of wilderness to make sure she could do it. "You were right behind me the whole time?"

"I was, and I always will be," he said softly.

A storm tore through her. She threw her arms around Rainer's waist, buried her face in his chest, and sobbed. All the fear and grief and longing in her roared to the surface.

Cecilia cried for the girl she'd been when she left Olney to finish the Gauntlet, who had her hope crushed and her heart broken. She cried for Teddy, who had so much life left to live. She cried for her father, who hadn't lived to see her happy with Rainer. She cried for Xander's parents, who were murdered in their sleep. She cried for Xander and the beautiful, charming, carefree prince and hunter he'd

86

been—for the joy that had been destroyed when Cato ruined his mind and their relationship. She cried for the hunters she killed on the beach. She cried for the children she would never bear, and she cried for all the times over the past year and a half that she'd been scared out of her mind but kept on going.

She sobbed until her legs gave out, and Rainer pulled her into his lap on the floor and held her until there was nothing left in her eyes and her body was a desert.

The place where she'd been most hurt—where all her love and grief poured out like blood from a wound—was the same place where the love entered. Rainer could not fix it, but he could hold his hand to where it hurt. Sometimes that's all there was to do: simply witness someone's pain and hold them through it.

Rainer carried her to the bed, tucked her in, and wrapped himself around her like he could insulate her from the pain. For the first time since she'd come back to life, she let him lie in the dark and hold her pain along with her until she could walk out on her own.

7

EVAN

Evan stared down at the letter from King Marcos Teripin. It was as much a warning as a relief.

Our alliance is new, but I am happy to offer assistance if needed.

Marcos meant well, but if he was miles away and that aware of Argaria's struggles with Vincent Savero, that meant other kingdoms would be too.

Worse, being the weaker side in an alliance would leave them forever at Olney's mercy, and while Evan had come to trust Marcos during his short time in Olney, a king could only garner support for an alliance if the people and his advisors saw value in it. If Argaria became a burden, Marcos would be forced to cut them loose whether he wanted to or not. His duty would always be to his own kingdom first. Much like Evan's duty was to Argaria above all else.

That was why he'd left Sylvie alone and naked in his bed to read through a pile of correspondence. Xander should have been the one doing it, but he was useless and broody once the sun set. So all the responsibility fell to Evan.

The letter from Marcos arrived along with two inquiries, one from the Kingdom of Aldrena and one from the Queendom of Novum, both about opening diplomatic relations now that the war with Olney had ended. Evan saw the requests for what they were—an interest in establishing a more personal alliance. Both kingdoms had unmarried princesses.

The idea had occurred to him, but after months of trying he'd still not found the right moment to bring it up without risking Xander immediately shooting it down. Evan needed to be precise in his timing, but it was becoming increasingly obvious that the moment needed to be sooner rather than later.

Talking about marriage at all was a precarious thing. While he knew Sylvie had come to Argaria to prove her value as more than just some wealthy guardian's wife, Evan wasn't foolish. She likely had unspoken expectations of him after spending every night for the past year in his bed. If he brought up marriage now, even in the context of a political marriage, it would become a cloud hanging over their otherwise effortless relationship.

Evan poured himself a glass of whiskey and took a burning gulp. Then he picked up the next, more worrying message. Breaking the wax seal, he opened it and held his breath as he read. When he finished, he leaned back in the chair, rubbing the bridge of his nose, listening to the soft patter of feet on the floor behind him.

"Is it from Cece?" Sylvie asked.

He shook his head. "News from the front."

Sylvie crossed the room quickly, but Evan folded the letter before she could read the gory details. While Cecilia was a storm that wanted to tear through the world and leave no prisoners, Sylvie's vengeance was surgical and precise. She had her own plans for Argaria—her own scales of justice that needed balancing—and he didn't want to be an obstruction to that.

Sylvie leaned her hip against the table and looked down at the letter. "It's him again, isn't it? He's still doing it."

Ever since Sylvie learned about the trail of violence Vincent left in his wake, she'd refused to speak his name. Each time the reports came in of haunted women left behind as Vincent's army ravaged villages, Sylvie's anger grew and she spent longer hours volunteering at the Temple of Aurelia. The priestesses of Aurelia ran a shelter, and Sylvie spent her scant free time ensuring they had all the resources they needed and survivors were taken care of.

She always returned to the castle stoic and quiet, with a faraway look in her eye that frightened Evan. He admired her hard work but worried about the toll it was taking on her.

Evan cleared his throat. "Yes, it's more of the same."

"I should go see if they need me—"

"Syl, it's the middle of the night. Any survivors won't even arrive until the morning. You should rest."

She looked into the fire, a stubborn tilt to her chin, her hands clenched into fists at her sides. "We have to beat him, Evan. I know you are trying—I know Xander is trying, but it's not enough. He's been better, but people need to see him as a leader."

"I know. I swear we are really close. Please don't doubt me now. I need you."

Her face softened.

He counted on Sylvie to help him hold the reins of a struggling kingdom. In many ways, she was the perfect operative. People expected Evan to be strategic, but Sylvie was unique. Her beauty and charm were like a finely sharpened blade to extract information without anyone noticing. More than that, she was a comfort to him personally and a bright light in a stressful time. He needed her to be patient a little longer.

"I have to bring this to Xander. I'm sorry. I'll be back as soon as I can, but feel free to go back to bed without me," he said.

Leaving the room before she could argue, he darted down the hall and hurried toward Xander's sitting room.

Some small, delusional part of him hoped to find the king involved with the woman Evan had sent earlier in the evening. He'd searched high and low for someone who slightly resembled the former princess. Finally, after months of searching, he'd found Elle, a brunette with long, wavy brown hair and bright blue eyes so much like Cecilia's that even Evan had done a double-take. It took weeks of vetting to prove she was who she claimed she was—a woman from a poor village in rural Argaria who worked at a brothel in Ardenis to send money home to her parents. Evan knew Xander could take care of himself, but he was still the king, and vigilance was necessary for anyone coming close to him.

As Evan cut down the hallway, thunder rattled the windows. Thunderstorms were uncommon in the fall, unless Xander was burning off some magic.

Evan caught the eye of the guard outside Xander's rooms. "Is he alone?"

The guard shook his head. Evan let himself into the empty sitting room and paused outside the bedroom. He strained to hear anything through the thick wood door, but the rain battering the windows muffled anything else.

"Xander?" he called.

No response, but then there was a sound like a gasping breath.

Evan shoved the door open so hard it slammed into the stone wall.

On the far side of the room, the balcony door had blown open and rain pelted the stone floor as the curtains billowed against the wind. Evan's gaze landed on Xander. He was sprawled on the bed, pinned beneath Elle, but she was still fully dressed.

Lightning flashed and Evan realized that Xander wasn't straining because he was lost in passion. His eyes were bulging, his face almost purple. Elle was killing him.

Before Evan could move, a bolt of lightning shot through the window and struck Elle, launching her across the room. She crumpled to the floor, unconscious. The guard from outside the chamber burst into the room, his sword drawn.

Xander coughed and sputtered, trying to sit up. Evan ran to his side.

"What the fuck?" Xander choked. "It's like she sucked all the air from my lungs. She must be—"

"A fire witch." Evan had sent his friend a fucking fire witch who looked like his ex-wife, and the woman had nearly killed him. "Are you all right?"

Xander nodded. "I'm more embarrassed that she got me down so quickly."

"You should have just stabbed her," Evan said, his tone sharper than he intended.

"I'm fine. I thought you'd want to question her and didn't want to kill her if she had information. I just needed a moment to get the storm going."

Evan could not get his body to move, his limbs still frozen in fear. "You could have died."

Like Teddy. He hadn't meant to give voice to that particular thought, but the adrenaline coursing through him shattered his self-control. Evan knew well that it only took a moment of misjudgment to lose a friend.

Xander said nothing, his gaze fixed on the woman. "I told her to get out the moment she arrived."

"She was vetted. I thought she would help you blow off some steam."

Xander placed a hand over his heart. "I don't need to blow off steam with a poor imitation of my Cece."

He crossed the room to the mantel and tipped a jar into his hand. Then he knelt next to Elle and pressed a hand to the back of her neck, whispering quiet words.

It wasn't until Evan recognized the scent of burnt chamomile that he knew it was a soothing spell. He'd only seen Xander use it a few times before.

"She'll sleep until I wake her. Now get her out of my sight."

The guard who'd been poised in the doorway, unsure what to do, quickly scooped the woman from the floor and disappeared from the room.

Evan's whole body felt made of stone, his heart still pounding as he tried to find words to express his relief, concern, or the sudden, twisting grief in his chest. In that moment, he desperately missed Teddy. Most of the time, he could overlook the void his friend left in his life. Cal and Sylvie had become invaluable allies, and they had different skills. But standing in Xander's room as the storm calmed outside, all Evan could see was how ill-equipped he was to deal with this situation.

Competence had defined him for so long, but the reality was clearly laid out in front of him. He needed more help. He could not protect their kingdom, run a network of spies, *and* figure out how, exactly, a well-vetted assassin had slipped through his defenses. Worst of all, he could not be both advisor and friend to Xander.

Xander closed the balcony doors and crossed the room to his whiskey. The crystal decanter clinked against the glass as the king poured with shaking hands. He tipped back the glass and drank it down in one gulp before pouring another.

He poured one for Evan and handed it to him. "Why are you here? Are you checking that your present was well-received? Honestly, I do love a dangerous woman, but perhaps not one who is actually trying to murder me."

It was too soon to joke, but that was how Xander coped.

Evan stared at the amber liquid in his glass for a beat before knocking it back. "Duly noted," he said. He tried to comb through his memory to figure out how he'd messed up.

So few people knew he was having Elle vetted. Only Reese was involved in the vetting process and Evan trusted Teddy's brother to validate her background. Reese had always been loyal and extremely valuable since he was both handsome and cunning in a disarming way that got both men and women to open up. Evan didn't want to doubt him, but he couldn't rule out the possibility.

It was much more likely that a servant had somehow overheard what he was looking for, or simply assumed that a woman who looked like the former princess would be a compelling option. But that meant that there were adversaries within the castle who wanted Xander dead.

Dread settled in Evan's stomach. He was out of his depth and he needed help, but he had no idea who he could trust beyond their core group of friends.

He was good at reading people, as was Sylvie, but neither of them could read a person's emotions and tell if they were being genuine like Cecilia could.

Xander rubbed a hand over his face. "So why are you here in the dead of night?"

"Vincent's men are moving about our borders. They took Varain before our men could get there and beat them back. They appear to be readying an attack."

Xander's face wore a weariness reserved for someone much older. "I am so tired of this constant jockeying for position."

"We could stop it." Evan hadn't meant to blurt it out. It was a long shot and probably the entirely wrong time to try, but he was desperate.

"How?" Xander asked.

"An alliance. You could marry someone—a strategic ally."

Finally, the king turned to look at him. His eyes bore into Evan. "I did marry someone. Someone beautiful and powerful."

"And then you ended that marriage by breaking her heart."

Xander flinched and looked back at the fire.

Evan wasn't trying to hurt his friend, just bring him back to reality. He knew it was wrong to read Cecilia's letters to Xander, but he read all the king's correspondence, and he needed to understand what was going on in Xander's head.

He tapped each finger on his left hand to his thumb to settle his growing apprehension. He rushed through the words. "You chose to let her go with a clear mind. The reality is that now a very precarious peace relies on you. Marcos is doing the same in Olney. I've heard rumors he expects to marry within the year. Olney is a good ally, but we are weak, and if we become a drain on their resources, Marcos will have no choice but to cut us off. It's bad enough that he's offered to send men. Things would be less precarious if you chose a wife who provides you with an ally to keeping the peace—not to mention an heir."

"How can I give a heart that I no longer own?"

Evan sighed. "You know as well as I do that your heart has nothing to do with this type of alliance."

This was a familiar brand of brooding for Xander, though it had never been so severe. They might not have been bonded like witches and guardians in Olney, but Evan knew Xander almost as well as if they were.

"We need to find you a new wife as soon as possible. I've given you the time to grieve and hide, but we are beyond that."

Xander said nothing, still staring into the fire.

"She went through a lot to keep you alive," Evan said.

"To keep him alive," Xander corrected.

"She saved you first and even if she didn't know what it would cost, she did not hesitate. Do not let that be in vain."

Xander crossed his arms. "I don't need to be reminded that I have a duty to honor her sacrifice. I know exactly what she sacrificed. I was there. I watched her die," he said. "I have no interest in another marriage."

"And yet it's necessary. There's no need for another love match. Just an alliance that secures peace. I want to hold an event—for prospective queens—"

"No," Xander said firmly.

"It would be short and sweet. An easy way to find an ally and secure this delicate peace."

"No."

Evan rubbed the back of his neck, searching for a way around the inevitability of the only motivator he had left and the only two people he trusted enough to help. "Given what happened tonight, I can admit that I am out of my depth with the protection of both you and this kingdom. I am going to reach out to Rainer and Cece to see if they will come and help. Cece in particular has an uncanny ability to read people that would be very valuable if we are bringing a bunch of strangers to court."

Xander turned slowly to look at Evan. "She won't come here again. She hates me."

"If she hated you, she wouldn't write so much."

Xander shook his head. "Rainer wouldn't let her."

Evan cocked his head. "You think any man can stop Cecilia Reznik from doing whatever she wants?"

Xander laughed. "Fair enough, but I haven't written to her in a year. Her letters stopped weeks ago. She won't come when she thinks I've ignored her all of this time. I think you underestimate her stubbornness."

"And I think you misunderstand it. She's proud. She will be eager for an explanation."

Evan was not one to pray, but he whispered a sort of silent prayer in his head that Xander would go along with it.

Xander pursed his lips as he scrutinized the fire, considering. "You sincerely think she will come?"

"I doubt she could resist."

"And what of Rainer?"

Evan shrugged. "He's pragmatic. Any chance to get you married off and away from his fiancée is a win for him. Even if he hates the idea of you having access to her, he would sacrifice it for peace and to have her free of you."

"How do you know?" Xander asked.

"Because we've occasionally been writing." Evan shifted uncomfortably. He hadn't strictly intended it to be a secret, but it hadn't come up.

Xander sighed. "It would be good to see her."

Evan arched a brow.

"As a friend, of course," Xander said.

Evan tried not to roll his eyes. Xander didn't know how to be Cecilia's friend. He only knew how to love her intensely.

Evan had been fooling himself, thinking that Xander's obsession was all Cato's influence. He remembered well when Xander was twelve and wanted to learn to be the best swordsman in the kingdom. He had trained himself to exhaustion for months. He refused to rest no matter how Davide, Evan, or Juliana begged. He was so single-minded he'd collapsed in shock during training one day, and the healers had to put him on bed rest for a week.

Xander turned to face him. "Fine."

Evan tried to hide his surprise. "Seriously?"

He knew he should have been worried that the presence of Cecilia Reznik was still so compelling to his friend. He'd expected Xander to fight harder against his idea of finding a queen. It was a big gamble. Things could go very well, or descend into more wild chaos. Either her presence would inspire Xander to show up, be his old charming self, and win over an allied princess to make her jealous, or he would relentlessly pursue his ex-wife and blow up all of their lives.

Both options seemed just as likely. But the fact remained that Evan needed people he could trust to help protect the king while they secured an alliance.

"Do you want me to second guess?" Xander asked.

"No," Evan said, more forcefully than he meant. "I'll send out invitations tomorrow. Any requests?"

"No one who looks like Cece. They all need to look drastically different. I cannot bear the sight of someone that resembles her in these halls."

Evan nodded. "Done."

"And I reserve the right to choose no one if they're not a good fit."

Evan squeezed his eyes shut, praying silently to any god who would listen that such an outcome wouldn't be the case. "Absolutely. You're the king, after all."

Xander was quiet for a long while as they both drank. "Do you really think Cece will come?"

Evan sighed. "Yes, I know she will. The question is...will you be able to choose someone else if you're looking at her?"

Xander took a large swallow of whiskey. His eyes lit with mischief. "You said it yourself. She's almost as jealous as I am, and I'll be looking everywhere else."

Evan sighed. This was either his best or worst idea so far. Only time would tell.

———

"I'm shocked," Sylvie said as she slumped into a chair by the fire in disbelief. "He actually went for it."

"You doubted me?" Evan teased.

"You, never. Xander, constantly," she said. She took a sip of wine. "Do you think he meant it, or is he just going to be himself?"

"What does that mean?" Evan asked.

Sylvie cocked an eyebrow as if to say he knew exactly what that meant.

Evan shrugged. "I share your skepticism, but I also think that it couldn't hurt to have some faith in him. I've known Xander my whole life, and people constantly underestimate him. He's used to low expectations, but he's risen above them every time. Why are you here doing what you're doing if you have no faith in him?"

Evan was surprised by the sharp words, but he was tired of defending Xander to the rest of the world. He didn't want to also have to defend him to the one person who was supposed to be on Evan's side.

Sylvie rolled her eyes. "He's not a child. He needs to start taking things seriously."

"In my entire life, Xander only ever played games he knew he could win. He bedded every woman he could." Evan laughed to himself remembering the litany of letters he'd received from Xander's bodyguard in Olney over the years, all of them detailing Xander's "leisure activities" and the "considerable security risks" of a prince who couldn't keep it in his pants.

He'd been no better when he returned to Argaria twice a year during hunter army leave. He spent his time drinking with Evan and Teddy and chasing women in every spare moment.

Evan took Sylvie's hand. "He has always chased women and thrilled in the challenge of winning someone over, but he never wanted to keep anyone until Cece. I'd never seen him so open. She is the only thing he ever wanted not for the sake of besting someone or proving someone wrong, but because he simply loved it. I may not get it. You might not either, but I can recognize that he's lost something. He's heartbroken, and he needs some grace."

"I've done nothing but give him grace and ask others to," Sylvie said. "I've manipulated the council into giving him chance after chance, but Evan, at some point, he needs to get it together."

"And why must it be on your timeline?" Evan asked.

He didn't mean to be so blunt but he hated having to convince her to give Xander grace. Sylvie yanked her hand from his and swallowed hard.

"Why can't you respect that I want to protect Xander in the same way you want to protect Cece?" he asked.

Sylvie shook her head. "She died, Ev. She was gone. She lost her ability to have children, her father, her whole sense of self. She's still fragile."

"And Xander didn't lose? He had a malicious god in his head for months, driving him out of his mind, ripping away the only thing I've ever seen him truly want. He is flawed in inconvenient ways—I'll be the first to admit that. But every time you treat him like he's unworthy, you reinforce what he's been told his whole life—that he isn't good enough, that he doesn't matter, that he's superfluous to the order of rule. Give him a godsdamned minute to get back on his feet, Sylvie. It may not be up to your schedule, but at least he's trying."

"It's not about my damn schedule! It's about the kingdom's. War waits for no man, Evan. You know this. Don't let your soft spot for Xander blind you to the fact that our hold on this court, this kingdom, and this truce with Olney is precarious."

"And don't let your love of your friend blind you to the immense responsibility you have to be smart and diplomatic, Lady Brett."

She scowled at him. It was maddening that she looked so beautiful when she was angry.

Sylvie stormed out of the room. She slammed the passageway door behind her, leaving Evan feeling as torn as he'd felt all year.

8

CECILIA

Rainer stepped out of the surf. Sunlight glistened on the water trickling down the lines of his chest and stomach. He ran his hands over his face and hair, sloughing off extra seawater. He walked toward Cecilia, flashing her a brilliant smile.

Cecilia didn't bother to hide her gawking from where she rested on a blanket in the shade of the cliffside. *Gods bless these morning swims. I wouldn't mind staring at him shirtless and soaking wet every morning for the rest of my life.*

Rainer was so effortlessly sexy. She didn't understand how she'd ever resisted pouncing on him with their constant proximity.

Over the past few months, her grief had lifted quite a bit, allowing them a tentative sort of intimacy. Rainer was romantic and thoughtful, often stopping to see her at work and bring her lunch or a carved wooden star flower to add to the bouquet he'd been working on. But she could never fully relax and enjoy it because she couldn't tell if he did it out of desire or because he didn't trust her to reach out for support.

Coming out of the worst of her grief felt like a fog had been lifted from her life. It wasn't perfect, but it was good. When she had bad days, she tried her best to lean on Rainer. Sometimes she succeeded.

Sometimes she bit his head off for being so kind when she was so angry and raw. Sometimes her feelings were so confusing she sat with her palm over his heart, passing some nameless hurt through their bond, and it was enough to know someone else felt it too.

They fell into a rhythm, and she tried to stop punishing herself for her failures. She worked normal hours at the healer's clinic, although she still insisted on working for free, and when Lyra protested, she proposed that any clients who had means could donate to shelters and families in need in Olney City.

Every mind she healed felt like paying a sort of penance for all she'd done. It helped to ease the guilt and grief she felt. Slowly but surely, she found herself able to breathe again. The grief and loss weren't gone, but they became less oppressive.

Neither she nor Rainer talked about setting a wedding date or having children. Those were the two topics that still seemed too precarious to tackle, but they had plenty of time to get to them. Cecilia told herself she'd bring them up when she felt stronger. She hated that she could not seem to take this last step forward. Their future together was being held hostage by the past. She wanted a clear head and a light heart when she finally married him.

Steady days slid into steady weeks and then steady months. Now it was the one-year anniversary of her new life—an event she was unsure if she should celebrate or completely ignore. It felt strange not to mark it, but what more could she say than "I'm still here"?

She looked down the beach at the white stone obelisk that marked the best and worst day of her life. People thought it was a pillar of courage and joy, but to Cecilia it looked like a tombstone. It marked the end of her old life and the beginning of the new.

It reminded her that she'd killed Cato. It also made her wary. If she could return from death, what if he could, too? He didn't have a soul bond, but he was the trickster god. A year had passed and still the vigilance would not leave her.

King Marcos had insisted on holding a Festival of Hope in remembrance of the battle she'd won. The king told the people it was a way to honor those who lost their lives, but that didn't stop people from piling flowers on her death marker. She knew Marcos was trying to walk the line between being a good friend to her and a good king to his people. She hated the attention, but she'd made herself a symbol of hope. Whether she liked it or not, the people of Olney were grateful that the war was finally over, even while they were lost without the constant anxiety of it hanging over them. This festival gave them a place to channel that restlessness.

Cecilia forced her attention back to her handsome fiancé as he strode across the sand.

Rainer raised an eyebrow. "See something you like, Cece?"

She hopped to her feet, closing the distance between them. "As a matter of fact, I only see things I like."

Rainer grinned, pulling her close.

"You're getting me all wet," she squealed.

"Am I?"

His teeth grazed her earlobe, and her body went liquid. He caught her, sweeping her into a kiss. She wrapped her legs around his waist and he marched blindly back to the blanket, carefully lowering to his knees before guiding her down and settling over her.

He covered her in salty kisses, melting away her swirling thoughts about the day. She never wanted him to stop. It didn't matter that they'd done the same thing every morning all week. It made it no less intense.

She placed her hand against the scar on his chest and gently dragged her thumb over it. His whole body stiffened at the sensation. Their golden scars were extremely sensitive and seemed to have magic in them. When he touched hers, she felt a shiver of desire and a burst of love ricocheting through her body.

His hands bunched the hem of her bathing gown up over her thighs. He pulled back, kneeling between her legs. Rainer kissed the freckle on her left little toe and the one inside her left knee.

She knew if they were back in the cottage and she was naked, he would kiss the rest of his favorite freckles. The one inside her right hip bone, the one under her right breast, and the three that dotted up the left side of her neck. Seven freckled stars that made up the constellation of Cecilia.

"My favorite constellation," he would whisper as he traced it with his lips.

By the time he got to the last one, she'd be a boneless mess. He did it so often, yet it never lost its potency. Perhaps that was what it was to share true trust and intimacy with someone.

His stubble scraped the sensitive skin of her inner thighs, grounding her back in the present moment.

"Rainer," she breathed.

"If you say my name like that again, you're going to relieve me of my last shred of self-control."

"If you keep kissing my thighs like that, you're going to relieve me of mine." She groaned as he did it again.

He'd taken to keeping stubble all the time because he knew how much she loved the look of it, but at that moment, she was more mesmerized by the feel of it.

"How do you do this to me, Cece? Will it ever stop?" he whispered against her skin.

No. It wouldn't. It hadn't. It didn't matter how frustrated, lonely, or depressed she felt—she always wanted him. The bond around her heart seemed to swell in an intoxicating way when Rainer was close.

"Please," she begged.

He grinned at her and pressed another kiss to her thigh. "How do you feel?"

She hated that question so much. She hated that she had the same knee-jerk reaction every time, but he asked it so often. "I feel annoyed that you just stopped kissing my thighs to ask how I'm feeling."

Rainer sat back on his heels, his gaze coming to rest on the flower-covered memorial. "I thought you'd want to talk about it today."

She scowled at him, trying to roll the sudden tension from her shoulders. How could they be so in sync one moment and so off the next?

"How do *you* feel?" she asked.

"Thank you so much for asking, Cece," he said, his tone full of sarcasm. "I feel—" All the tension bled out of his face at once and his green eyes met hers. "I feel breathless every time I think of what you did. I feel angry at myself that I didn't see through your trick. I feel so incredibly grateful that you are here with me still." He kissed the inside of her knee again. "Grateful that I can kiss these beautiful legs anytime I want. I feel blessed and damned by the memory of that day, and I feel a crushing rush of love for you every time it comes up."

His love swelled in her chest, chasing away her anger and replacing it with warmth. Cecilia pulled him into a kiss.

She still didn't always love herself, but Rainer reminded her how to be better at it on the days she struggled.

"Take me home," she whispered. "I don't want to talk about my death. I want to celebrate my life."

Rainer lifted her to her feet. They quickly gathered their blanket and rushed up the trail to the house. They burst through the cottage door breathless and flushed, kissing frantically. Cecilia pulled off her dress and slipped off her underwear as they stumbled toward the bed.

Rainer shoved her up against the bookcase, one rough hand cupping a breast, the other slipping between her legs. She moaned into his mouth as his fingers brushed over her.

He dropped to his knees, hooked her thigh over his shoulder, sliding his tongue over her. He drew back and met her gaze. "Does this make you feel alive, Cece?"

He slid a finger inside her as he worked her with his tongue.

"Gods, yes," she groaned.

She was torn between leaning her head back to enjoy being worshipped and tipping her chin down to watch the intensity on his face.

He added another finger, and she was completely lost in the pleasure sparking through her body. His hand moved faster, his tongue insistent and rhythmic against her. She gripped his hair with one hand. Her other hand slid along the bookshelf, struggling for purchase. Every nerve in her body vibrated with need. She was so close her legs shook violently.

The orgasm hit her all at once, spiraling warmth spreading through her whole body. Her standing leg gave out and she flailed, knocking several books off the shelf before Rainer could catch her and pin her in place.

He held her gaze as he slid his fingers out of her and sucked them into his mouth. "Makes me feel alive, too."

Her legs finally seemed sturdy enough that she unhooked her thigh from his shoulder. She bent to climb on top of him right there on the floor, but her gaze caught on the book she'd knocked from the shelf. A letter with a scarlet seal—the Savero royal seal—stuck out.

She frowned. "Is that—" The air rushed out of her lungs. Was it a letter from Xander? Had he written back to her and Rainer had hid it?

Rainer followed her gaze. "It's not what you think." He picked up the book. Several more letters tumbled onto the floor.

Cecilia froze, staring at them. There were at least ten, all with the same scarlet seal. The betrayal chased the remnants of pleasure from her body.

Was Xander finally writing back after a year? Did she care? She was disappointed to realize she did. *Pathetic.*

"It looks like you've been hiding correspondence," she said.

Rainer gathered up the letters and held them to his chest, apprehension sliding through their bond. "Perhaps it is what it looks like."

"From Xander?" Cecilia asked.

Rainer shook his head. "They're from Evan."

A startled laugh tore out of her. "You expect me to believe that Evan, true wordsmith that he is, has written you—what is that—ten letters?"

Rainer shook his head and held out the top one from the stack. It was addressed to Rainer, and it was not Xander's neat handwriting, which meant it was either addressed by a servant or Rainer was telling the truth.

She opened it, but it wasn't a letter. It was an invitation.

———

His Highness, Alexander Maxwell Savero, King of Argaria, cordially invites you to a three-week courting festival.

———

Xander was looking for a wife. Cecilia had no right to be jealous. She'd let him go. And yet, she felt a twinge of irritation that he not only found her easy to ignore, but also easy to move on from.

A year after he'd dissolved their marriage, she still felt unprepared to enter into a new union, despite her immense love for Rainer. But Xander was ready to tie his life to someone else's as if she'd been nothing but a minor detour in an otherwise exciting life.

Perhaps Cato's manipulation had been more compelling than she realized and, without it, Xander no longer felt anything for her.

At the bottom of the invitation was a handwritten note, but it was all in some sort of code. Rainer guiltily reached into the book and handed her a cipher paper. She placed it over the letter and began to read.

———

Rainer,

I know this is awful timing with the anniversary so soon, but I'm afraid I can't put off the request any longer. Things have gone from bad to worse here. The rumors of Xander have run rampant, Vincent's army is chipping away at our eastern border, and last night Xander fended off another attempt on his life. By some miracle, Xander has agreed to a political marriage to help strengthen his claim to the throne and hopefully dissuade Vincent from his attacks. With so many strangers at court, I need people I can trust. I know that Cece's safety is paramount, but I am asking as a friend and a person who saw firsthand what you all went through to secure the safety of our two kingdoms. If Vincent succeeds in his bid, the peace we have all fought so hard for will be gone.

The festival begins the full moon before solstice. Please say you will help.

E

———

Cecilia stopped reading. All her breath was trapped in her chest. Xander was facing danger from all sides, and Rainer hadn't told her.

Finally she looked up at him, her hand trembling with rage as she blew out a breath. "Were you going to tell me?"

"Yes, of course I was going to tell you everything tomorrow. Today is an important day."

"And the other letters?" she asked. "Why did you hide those?"

Rainer ran a hand through his hair. "You were doing well, and I didn't want you to backslide."

"I have been worried about Xander since he left without saying goodbye, and now you are telling me you've had honest news about him—not just Sylvie's placating messages about him training with the hunters in his army—and you didn't think you should share it?" She shook her head, storming away. "I suppose you'll tell me now how it's too dangerous, and I have done enough for these kingdoms and they can figure it out themselves."

He frowned, crossing the room and righting his sword, which they'd knocked over in their rush. He slid it from the sheath, running a finger over the crescent moon engraved on the hilt and the words on the blade. *Brave with my hand.*

She'd replaced her old dagger with the one that matched his sword. It hung from its holster on the headboard, beside the green ribbon favor.

She hated seeing him with a sword in his hands. It wasn't as if he'd given up training these last few months. If anything, it seemed he was out there more, even as he'd started his carpentry apprenticeship.

Buy a man a sword. Pray he never has to use it. What a foolish thing to do. Cecilia had bought the weapon because she thought it would make him feel accomplished, at peace with the end of their quest. It was a trophy he could hold in his hand instead of the one carved into his chest.

But it had only seemed to convince him that he needed to use it, and she didn't like the hint of longing in his eyes when he looked at it.

He'd won three swordsmanship tournaments in Olney in the past year. Cecilia watched from her place of honor beside King Marcos, a mixture of fear and lust burning through her body. Even she could admit that it seemed a waste for a man so talented to lay down his weapons.

But thinking of Rainer in real battle again rattled her. They'd fought beside each other for years, but she wanted to insulate him from danger the same way he did for her.

A tense silence grew between them. She couldn't help but feel betrayed—couldn't shake the feeling that where there was one omission, there would be more. She tried hard not to carry the wounds of her past relationship into this one, but it was difficult not to when she'd been cut so deeply.

"I don't need another relationship where I'm kept in the dark about something important," she said. "I thought we were doing well."

"And I thought you'd stopped searching for any reason to push me away because you're scared to be happy," Rainer countered.

"I'm not scared to be happy," she snapped. "I'm scared to trust myself. I'm scared of being blindsided like I was twice before. I'm scared of the rug being pulled out from under me and falling so hard I won't be able to get back up."

It wasn't as if she had really succeeded in keeping him at a distance. She was so hopelessly in love with him, the idea that she could save herself from hurt was pure make-believe.

"I'm really angry that you didn't tell me. Of course, I know that you're trying to take care of me, but you can't coddle me into being ready. You owe me honesty."

"And do you owe it to me as well?" Rainer challenged.

It was a trap. If she agreed, he'd have freedom to ask anything he wanted and she'd have to answer truthfully. "Yes."

He tucked his sword into its spot next to the bookcase and turned to face her. His expression twisted from anger to fear to love. "I swear I was going to tell you everything tomorrow. I just wanted one last good day before we had a new problem to solve. One year ago, I lived when you died and it feels like no time has passed—like I'm still holding your empty body and wanting to lie down beside you—" His voice broke and he swallowed hard. "I know that you are well now and I know that you still have bad days where you're more distant, and it has nothing to do with me. But I love you so much and I can't help wanting to share all of your burdens."

He rubbed the back of his neck and sighed. "And yes, I would like to feel as useful and capable as I do when I have a sword in my hand. I'd like the purpose of a mission. I've felt aimless and incompetent in this apprenticeship, and while I know that's the point, a trip north, even to see Xander, would be a welcome reprieve."

Cecilia stared at him, searching for a hint of what he wasn't saying on his face. Rainer had started to push out of his comfort zone, but now he seemed eager to go back to the business of saving the kingdom and their friends. Or maybe he simply wanted Xander settled with someone else because it would neutralize the threat of him coming back for her. While Cecilia knew that there was nothing her ex could say that would win her back, she understood Rainer's desire to see proof of that. After all, they'd only seen Xander in his right mind for a moment. There was no telling what he was like now.

"What do you think, Cece?"

I think I want to know why he hasn't written back to me. I think I'm scared out of my mind of being pulled into another fight that's not really mine, and losing. I think I want to decline the invitation only marginally less than I want to accept it.

She wanted closure—to know why he found her letters so easy to ignore. For a year Xander had felt to her like a dangling thread on a sweater that she couldn't stop tugging at. She wanted to feel like the loose end of him was tied up—like she'd meant something to him, if only temporarily. Cecilia wanted to face Xander and feel certain that her broken heart had mended enough that she could marry Rainer with a clear head and a full heart.

She put her hands on her hips. "I think I made a promise to Queen Juliana before she died. I think I owe her enough to protect Xander, even if he's not my husband anymore. I think you're going to need to buy me some really pretty new dresses."

Rainer pulled her into a hug and kissed the top of her head. "I've always really liked you in red."

He wasn't the only one.

9

XANDER

Xander cut through the busy streets at the south end of Ardenis, wondering how long he had before Evan or one of his guards noticed he was gone. In daylight, Castle Savero looked like a fairy tale setting with its tall towers, but standing in its shadow Xander felt nothing but haunted by a legacy he was failing to leave. He pulled his hood lower down his forehead to block everything out.

One month had passed since he'd agreed to do the very thing he was born to do—marry a wealthy, politically advantageous princess. And still, he felt no closer to accepting his fate.

He cut through stalls in the winter market, enjoying the hustle of being out in the streets. The opportunity to sneak away on his own had only presented itself a few times since returning to Argaria. Each time, he'd met a heavy scolding from Evan for being so reckless. He'd heard the same thing since he was a boy, and he had no interest in changing now.

Being king was even more of a prison than he'd imagined. Xander couldn't even walk the streets alone anymore. He had almost no privacy whatsoever, and when he did have it, it was almost exclusively spent worrying about what he was messing up for the kingdom.

While the common folk—like those in the winter market—sang his praises, the aristocracy was not happy with his choice to cut taxes on lower- and middle-class citizens of the kingdom so that they could try to rebuild after years of war. The rich who'd lived off of the backs and hard work of those people for centuries saw any ground they gained as a personal threat to their old way of life.

It was frustrating that people hated change so much that they fought against things that would help them live more sustainably and provide for the poorest in their communities. No matter what Xander did, he couldn't satisfy everyone.

Xander had every intention of creating equality. He didn't understand why he should be elevated above anyone else, especially after living most of his life as a common hunter. When he'd held that job, his primary focus was simply keeping himself alive and spying. Now his primary job was keeping a whole kingdom of people alive—and spying. It was an impossible task, but he was running on spite. The more his advisors suggested he couldn't do something, the more Xander wanted to prove them wrong.

Part of Xander relished the opportunity to be strategic and make decisions for the kingdom that were in his people's best interest rather than in service of his own power. Xander loved King Damian, but many of his decisions had been driven by ego and not the good of their people. Xander was glad for the opportunity to change things, as difficult as it was.

Now, with the possibility of Cece showing up, he wanted to impress her. Still, as he became more involved, he felt a greater need to have something to show for the second chance he'd been given.

Each misstep was an opportunity to learn more about strategy. It had never been his strength, but he was learning in a true trial by fire. Xander found the challenge exhilarating, even as it was draining.

It still somehow managed to be less draining than the excitement over the prospect of a new queen. He was exhausted from the incessant chatter about the princesses who would attend and the endless questions the staff asked.

"Does His Highness prefer brunettes? Blondes? Redheads? Does he

prefer a wife who has a mind for politics or simply one who is pretty and pliant?"

What idiotic questions. They all knew exactly what Xander preferred. He preferred a fierce witch with expressive blue eyes—the unspoken name in every conversation. He preferred Cece.

He couldn't say that because Evan would have punished him with hours of paperwork if he had. His friend never let him out of his sight, as if lack of supervision would lead to disaster. As if he hadn't protected himself behind enemy lines for half his life. As if he was choosing to still be in love with Cece.

He'd considered for just a few desolate moments while he was under Cato's influence that perhaps his love for her had been manipulated. But after a year of trying to convince himself otherwise, his heart remained stubbornly in love with her.

Ultimately, he would choose whichever woman made the most logical sense. The princess from Aldrena would be an obvious choice given their shared border. With Argaria's southern border firm with Olney, securing their northeastern border with Aldrena made the most sense.

Walking deeper into the winter market, Xander was greeted by colorful tents and banners and the smell of pastries, candied nuts, and roasted chicken. Each small booth was a blur of noise, scent, and sound. It was nice to be lost in it, although he worried about how safe it was to have so many people packed so close together with so many open flames. They could easily lose their livelihoods if someone knocked into some hot coals.

He was thinking like a king. The old Xander would have simply enjoyed the sights and sounds, the pretty girls and the people-watching. This Xander had nothing to do but brood over the fact that he had agreed to a three-week-long event, by the end of which he'd need to choose a new wife.

He paid for an ale at one of the stands and drank a long gulp.

"Bad day?" the brewer asked.

"Bad year," Xander replied.

"Ah, to be young. Is it about a girl?" the man asked.

Xander laughed. "It's about *the* girl."

The man whistled out a breath. "You wouldn't be the first one seeking solace at my booth for such a thing. What is she like?"

"She's like the first warm day in springtime and also like the furious spring mountain storms that pop up out of nowhere and tear through everything in an instant," Xander sighed. "She's undeniable."

As Xander took another sip, his hood slid back slightly, and the combination of the view of his face and the story of lost love must have given up his identity. The old man's eyes went wide in recognition.

Thanks to the fanfare about Rainer and Cece's miraculous soul bond and her killing Cato, the whole kingdom knew that Xander had been tortured by the god of manipulation and influence. He'd been relegated to a subplot in their sweeping love story, a mistake that needed righting, a barrier between Cece and the true love of her life. The stories might not have bothered him if they weren't so true. If it didn't make people look at him with pity in their eyes, as if they could comprehend what he'd suffered.

Cece could like storytelling all she wanted, but as far as Xander was concerned, storytelling ruined everything.

The old man started to bow. "Your Majes—"

Xander held a finger to his lips. "I'd prefer to have a quiet afternoon and blend in with my people today. Easier to see how things really are when people aren't making them appear perfect for your royal eyes."

The old man nodded, his gaze both reverent and understanding. "It's an honor." He handed Xander another ale. "On the house."

Xander handed him a handful of coins. "I'm quite certain that it's my responsibility to help stimulate our struggling economy."

The man hesitated, as if too proud to take it.

"I'll tell you what. You go give an ale to that stern-looking fellow over my left shoulder twenty paces back, and we'll call it even," Xander whispered.

The man nodded conspiratorially, disappearing behind him. He returned a moment later, and Evan stepped up to Xander's left shoulder.

"When did you make me?" Evan asked.

Xander arched a brow at his friend. "I knew you were there the whole time. You may make a point to not use a scent, but you smell like jasmine and vanilla from Lady Brett."

Evan grimaced at him and opened his mouth to chide the king.

"I know you're concerned about the attempt on my life, but let me enjoy my ale in peace, and for once, just fucking relax and enjoy yours," Xander said. "This might be the last time we're out here as normal people for months. Consider it a command."

Evan sighed heavily, but he stood there and drank beside his friend like they had since they were teenagers, when they would sneak out to get into trouble and chase girls. Back then, Evan had been slightly more adventurous.

Xander tried to remember when his friend had become so cautious. When they were younger, Evan disapproved of Xander's reckless nature, but he had a cocky self-assurance that implied the two of them were skilled enough to get out of any jam. Evan's fun side was another casualty of Xander's ascent to the throne.

When they finished their ales, the man at the booth offered them another round, but they thanked him and continued on.

"We should go back," Evan said. "It's not safe so far from the castle grounds."

"These are my people, and I'm a warrior. I'm safer here than the rest of them," Xander sighed. He pressed on through the market until they came to the open square.

A clear voice cut through the midday noise, and people had gathered around to listen.

"Who is that?" Xander asked.

"Just a town crier," Evan said. "I'm sure we needn't bother ourselves with whatever nonsense is going to come out of his mouth."

The crier's voice sliced through the boisterous market. "Listen, one and all! King Alexander Savero is an imposter to the throne! In the east, a new king rises. Vincent Savero, the true heir to the throne.

He has proof that Alexander Savero was born of love between the queen and her consort."

Xander's breath left him in a rush. He watched the crowd carefully. Did they share his doubts? Xander had always thought he'd looked enough like King Damian not to raise any questions. The only features Xander had inherited from his mother were his hazel eyes and warm smile. The rest belonged to someone else, though Xander wasn't certain whether it was King Damian or his mother's consort.

A rumble of disapproving boos came from Xander's supporters in the crowd, but just as many people stopped and listened attentively.

"We should go," Evan whispered.

Xander shook his head, riveted to the scene. "Does this happen a lot?"

Evan stayed silent, but the tic in his jaw made it clear it did.

"Why didn't you tell me?"

"Would you have cared?" Evan challenged.

Xander wanted to argue, but it probably wouldn't have seemed real to him if he hadn't seen it with his own eyes. His mind flew to the mirror that Grimon had given him. He'd had it for months. For all his courage in a fight or even in the council meeting rooms, he had none when it came to facing his true identity. It was complicated. If he was truly Damian's son, that meant he could inherit the man's cruelty and selfishness. If he was Arthur's son, he had no right to the throne that someone much crueler was trying to steal.

There was no good answer to the question. Until he knew how he would respond to both options, he couldn't bear to ask.

He watched Evan out of the corner of his eye, wondering what his friend would do if he knew Xander had critical answers so close at hand.

The crier's voice tore through the hum of the crowd again. "The imposter king sits upon the throne, and he's the very reason why we struggle so. The gods are angry. Aurelia withholds her bounty in the harvest because an usurper sits on the throne."

Hushed murmurs cut through the crowd.

"Oh, for gods' sake, what a bunch of sniveling nonsense. These people can't possibly—" Xander stopped when he realized even more people had come to listen.

Several tapped their fingers on their foreheads, lips, and hearts in silent prayers to the gods. Their scant harvest had everything to do with the unexpected early frost—one that he'd long suspected was a gift from storm witches who followed Vincent. Xander and several other storm witches had gone out and tried to prevent the worst of it, but the farmlands were vast, and it was hard to cover enough area, especially when it felt like the storm was fighting back.

The onlookers were eating it up. The very people he was working so hard to help believed this random town crier over Xander.

"Vincent is burning their villages and I'm fighting him back. Why do they care more for a scandal than the truth they've seen with their own eyes?" Xander asked.

"The drama?"

"Who would sponsor this?" Xander asked.

Evan shrugged. "I have my guesses, but no proof. Spellman has hired criers to rail against your tax breaks to the poor or middle class in the past, and he is your number one dissenter on the council. He's been known to stir up trouble before, though it's unlike him to directly challenge your throne. It also doesn't make sense for him to do so with his daughter, Eloise, having a chance of becoming queen. I imagine he'd want to keep you in power, not toss you out."

Xander sighed heavily. "Would marrying Lady Eloise Spellman resolve that issue, do you think?"

Perhaps Xander could give Lady Eloise Spellman more consideration. She was a beautiful woman with black hair and light green eyes. She had nice manners and a beautiful smile. She oozed the kind of subtle sensuality that left many of the men at court drooling. Still, her overreliance on court traditions and fancy manners was a little over the top for him. The old Xander would have loved her, but the post-Cece Xander enjoyed more subtlety.

The crier took a deep breath, winding up to speak again. "Alexander Savero grew up in Olney and belongs more to them than to us. He married an Olney goddess and then dissolved that marriage. He's fickle and unreliable." Several gasps went through the crowd. "Now his whore ex-wife lives in Olney, hoarding our secrets for their new king."

Xander almost lost it, but Evan's hand clamped down on his forearm, freezing him in place and bringing him back to his senses. Even more folks had gathered. The poorest of the poor in their rough tweed and burlap clothing. They were the most superstitious of his people. They relied on faith when their bellies were empty. It hurt to see them manipulated by lies that preyed on that devotion.

"Worse, he's locked us into a useless alliance with Olney, a weak kingdom with yet another unproven king. Olney has been our enemy for centuries, and now he's letting them move freely about our lands. It's not safe! When the time comes, take up your arms and fight for the true king of Argaria, Vincent Savero. Together, we can take back our kingdom!"

A good deal of the crowd murmured in agreement, but the rest pelted the man with rotten produce and insults. Xander watched in satisfaction as they chased the man from his crate, and he slunk away down the street.

"We should follow him," Xander said.

"I will follow him. You should go back to the castle. You have a big weekend. You should try to get some rest before then. Maybe detox a bit," Evan said, eyeing him critically.

Xander was sure he looked a mess. He'd come directly to the market after his morning training. He was sure he still had dirt on his face, and he hadn't shaved in days. The beginnings of a beard dusted his jaw—one born of neglect rather than an intentional choice.

"Fine," Xander said.

Evan slunk away, and Xander made his way back toward the castle walls, feeling a crawling irritation toward the man who stoked tensions out of peace and the people who were so easily swayed.

Xander made his way up the hill toward Castle Savero, the wide iron gates looming. A reminder that as much as he'd settled a bit in his role as king, it still felt just as much a privilege as a prison.

10

CECILIA

Cecilia tucked Rainer's book of fairy tales into her saddlebag and struggled to fasten the leather straps. They were leaving for Argaria in the morning and while Rainer was in town fetching the last of the supplies they'd need for the ride, she adopted his nervous habit of checking that they'd packed anything they could need.

It was a relief that they wouldn't have to sleep in the forests and keep from the main trails. For the first time in their lives, they were traveling outside their kingdom for fun. For years they'd needed to hide, and she'd only been able to observe small village life from afar. If she had her way, she was going to eat her way from Olney City to Ardenis and have a drink in as many bars and pubs as possible.

The door creaked open. "Thank gods you're back, I cannot get this bag closed," Cecilia said, turning toward the noise. It wasn't Rainer.

Grimon stood in the doorway, looking unsure if he should stay or go.

"Grim—" Her voice was raspy, anxiety flaring in her blood, her memory magic instantly hooking into the memory of him in the death maze, offering her a way out. It happened the same every time she saw him.

A tight fist of fear gripped her heart until Grimon took a tentative step into the kitchen and the movement broke her trance.

"Are you well?" he asked.

Cecilia forced a tight smile. "Of course. I just don't like surprises. What are you doing here?"

He brushed his jet-black hair back from his forehead and closed the distance between them. He bent and fastened the straps on the bag she'd been struggling with.

"Taking a vacation?" he asked.

"Actually, we're headed to Argaria to help Xander choose a new wife."

"Is that the type of things ex-wives do? Planning to enter yourself into the running?" Grimon asked, a glimmer of mischief in his eye.

"Been there. Done that."

"Many times, if memory serves," Grimon teased.

Cecilia shrugged. "The man hasn't returned a letter from me in a year, so I'm planning to give him a piece of my mind, but he's not the one who invited us. We've been summoned by Evan because of all the unrest with Vincent Savero."

"Of course. The voice of reason in the north," Grimon said.

The god of death looked around the cottage, smiling faintly at the penciled notches on the cottage doorframe that marked her and Rainer's heights at different ages. He'd never been inside the cottage. He'd only ever met her on the beach or in the garden.

"Why are you here, Grim? Did you just want a chance to poke around our home?"

"Didn't your father leave you his estate?" he asked.

Cecilia tried not to flinch. She'd grown up in the estate, but it still felt more her father's home than hers. The cottage had always been her haven, and the thought of moving back into her father's space filled her with grief. She could barely even step into the house to see Aunt Clara without feeling his absence in every silence.

"We like it better here," she said.

"It's—" Grimon looked around the space as if trying to find an inoffensive adjective. "Quaint."

She rolled her eyes. "I'd love to see your underworld mansion."

"You'd love it. Lots of dangerous things to see there." Grimon looked out the windows. "Where is your husband?"

"Not officially my husband yet," she said, an edge of irritation in her voice.

"Of course," Grimon said, his gaze burning into her. "Do you have plans to make it official?"

Cecilia crossed her arms. "Did he put you up to this?"

The god of death had a laugh like pleasant doom and it sent a shiver down her spine. "Rainer is terrified of me."

"He is," Cecilia said, unable to fight off a grin. "Yes, I have plans to make it official. I'm just waiting until—"

Until things feel settled in the two kingdoms? Until I feel settled in myself? Until some mystical thing falls into place, and it somehow feels like the right time?

The truth was that she was unsure what exactly was holding her back. She was certain she wanted to marry Rainer. Certain she'd love him the rest of her life. Certain that she couldn't imagine a life without him beside her. Still, she'd hoped to feel more at peace before she settled down.

"I'm waiting until the right time," she finished. "But I'm glad you're here. I was going to summon you before we left. Will you give King Marcos and Xander your favor so it's easier to pass correspondence back and forth while we're gone? In case of trouble."

"I thought you said you were going to stop making me a messenger."

Cecilia stuck her lip out in an exaggerated pout. "Please? It would help a lot."

Grimon waved a hand. "Fine. I'll go give your king a healthy fright."

She laughed. "It won't be his first time. Now, you don't normally show up without a purpose. What brings you here?"

He pulled a small item from his pocket and handed it to her. "I have something for you."

She took the green velvet pouch, loosened the ties, and dumped the contents into her palm. Three golden rings tumbled into her hand, along with a scrap of parchment.

———

Dear Cecilia, Here are the warded rings you requested. I went to a great deal of trouble to find them for you, so put them to good use. You're welcome. – Devlin

———

She'd hoped desperately that he'd find them back when Xander was under Cato's control. They could have prevented Cato from influencing him. Cecilia had almost forgotten about them, assuming that if Devlin had been searching for years, it was likely a hopeless cause.

"Why would I need warded rings that protect against godly powers?"

A hint of doubt flickered in Grimon's icy blue eyes, there and gone so fast she would have missed it if she wasn't watching.

Cecilia took a step toward him. "I am the only one in this realm who has even a hint of godly magic, pitiful though it might be. Right?"

She stared at him, her body wound tighter than a bowstring. She was desperate for assurance to settle the relentless vigilance in her body.

Grimon cleared his throat. "I think it's less a matter of need. Devlin has always been quite literal. You ask him for something, he does it if he can. He hates a challenge he can't rise to, and he loves a puzzle. He's been hunting for those rings in earnest since last year, so I suspect he just wanted to cross the task off his list."

She eyed Grimon warily, certain he was hiding something, but uncertain what. "Have you—" Just starting the question left her breathless, but she needed to ask. She needed to put her anxiety to rest once and for all. Cato was dead, and she just needed Grimon to confirm it. She cleared her throat and took a deep breath, waiting for her heartbeat to slow. "Have you seen Cato in the Otherworld?"

Grimon frowned, and the edges of him began to blur. "I'm afraid I have quite a busy day and I'm struggling to keep form—"

Cecilia stalked toward him. "Don't you dare run off without—"

Before she could reach him, he faded into a wisp of smoke that smelled like burnt cinnamon.

She tucked the rings back into the pouch and added one last task to her list.

———

Winter had chased the blooms from the roses in the queen's garden, but Cecilia still chose her favorite bench as her meeting spot for Marcos.

She followed the well-worn trail to the bench and felt the strange, disorienting sensation of glimpsing the specters of other versions of herself in the garden. The angry brooding she'd done before her last Gauntlet run, a giddy future self disappearing around a garden hedge, stealing kisses in the shadow of the willow tree on the far garden wall. She saw herself bringing her own daughter to sit and talk about her week, just as Cecilia had done with her mother years ago.

The afterimage of that future was burned into her heart. Logically, she knew there were many ways to be a mother. Her Aunt Clara had been like a mother to her, and so had Maura McKay. Their love felt no different to her than Rosalee's. But the grief was not logical. It was ravenous.

Cecilia could not reckon with the part of her that felt cheated by the choice that wasn't really a choice—the exchange that wasn't something she could opt out of. She'd only been twenty-two when she walked into the Cave of Longings. She thought she had all the time in the world—until she didn't. Even if she'd decided that at some point she didn't want to have children, she wanted to have the option. She felt frustrated with her body, with her magic, with the way she could do nothing about the choice she'd made at her weakest.

That was the true barrier that had slowly formed between her and Rainer. Brick by brick she'd built herself a wall and hoarded her private hurt behind it. She didn't know how to share without hurting him, too. He wanted so badly to belong—to be loved and accepted as part of a family. She knew they would make it work and they would be so happy if they were lucky enough to adopt, but the grief remained that she could not give the man who had given her a second chance at life the thing he wanted the most. Even if he was okay with the idea of it now, he might not feel the same way in the future.

Cecilia smoothed her green cloak as if to shed the unwelcome feeling. She self-consciously patted at her hair, which was slowly falling out of its pins and not at all appropriate for an audience with the king—even if that king was her childhood friend.

She needed to make sure King Marcos was taken care of before she left for what was sure to be a lengthy journey. With winter setting in, it would take almost two weeks to reach Ardenis, three weeks for the festival and wedding, and another two weeks home. They expected to be gone for nearly two months and she still felt unsettled, as if something was energetically off-kilter in her world.

Cecilia pulled two rings out of her pocket, leaving the third tucked away. To the untrained eye, they looked like simple gold bands, but Cecilia felt a subtle power pulsing around them.

Soft footsteps echoed on the path and Marcos rounded the corner with his guardian, Anders, on his heels.

"Your Majesty," she said, dipping into a curtsey.

He waved his hand, dismissing the gesture as unnecessary. It was strange to bow to someone who'd been her first friend.

In her opinion, Marcos made a much better king than his father. He had an eye for diplomacy and understood how to manage the egos of his court and advisors. Most of all, he was kind and preferred very little circumstance. While his father would have enjoyed making Cecilia bow to him, it clearly made Marcos uncomfortable.

"What can we do for you, Cece? We need to be back soon, or someone will notice the king is missing," Anders said.

Cecilia fidgeted, trying to shake off the pang of guilt. She knew what she was about to say would probably only add to the king's already full plate. "I'll just get to it. I suspect something is amiss."

"Something?" Anders asked skeptically.

Cecilia frowned and thrust her open palm toward them. "I know it sounds strange, but I just have a persistent, uneasy feeling. Rainer and I will be gone for a couple months and it would put my mind at ease if you both wore these rings."

Anders and Marcos each took one of the rings from her palm.

Marcos held the ring up to the light as if trying to spot its magic. "It's enchanted?"

She nodded.

"Is this why the god of death showed up to randomly offer me his blessing and resentful messenger service?" Marcos asked.

Cecilia laughed. "Yes. I'm probably overreacting, but I—"

Marcos placed a hand on her shoulder. "I understand. The fear never leaves."

She nodded solemnly. Of course he understood. Cato had taken over his mind and made him behead his own father. He was probably trapped in the same nightmarish cycle she was.

"Do not take the rings off, ever, unless I specifically ask you to, and even then ask for the password. The password will be 'Rosalee.'"

"Your mother's name," Marcos said solemnly.

Cecilia nodded. "If I show up and I don't say that word, do not take the ring off. If anyone asks, it's a new tradition you started with your king's guard to show their loyalty and commitment to their king."

"What do they do?" Anders asked.

Cecilia clasped her hands and rubbed her thumb on her inner wrist. "They protect you from godly influence."

Both men's eyes went wide.

Anders looked baffled. "Do we need protection from you?"

She shook her head. "It's just a precaution. It doesn't hurt for you both to wear one at all times." Cecilia licked her lips, her mouth suddenly dry. "You can go, Anders, but will you stay for a moment, Marc?"

Marcos nodded as he slid the ring on his finger, and Anders turned and disappeared down the trail.

"I intentionally gave you both the password while he was here, but I'm giving you a separate one," Cecilia said, glancing down the path to make sure the guardian was far enough away not to hear them. "If he knows yours, he could give it away, and I want no points of failure in this. So if I show up and ask you to take the ring off, I will also say 'Wisteria.' Now repeat it back to me. You should only take the ring off if I tell you to and say—"

"Wisteria."

Cecilia paused, waiting for the dread in her body to evaporate. It didn't. "That's all I needed. Thank you for taking the time to sneak out here. Summon Grimon anytime you need to send a message, and he'll get it to me right away."

Marcos turned away but didn't leave. "Cece, I have nightmares about what happened almost every night. Do they—do you think they stop at some point?" He turned to face her again. "He wasn't a very good father, but I still loved him. I dream almost every night that I'm still trapped in my mind, watching my hands kill him."

Marcos cleared his throat and shook his head like he was trying to rid himself of the memory. Cecilia felt the same sense of foreboding she'd been experiencing for days. After so much time, something about the frequency of his nightmares set her on edge.

"I'm sorry, Marc. I didn't get to you in time," she said, her gaze dropping to the grass.

He touched her shoulder tentatively. "No, that's not why I was saying it. It's just, Rainer mentioned once in passing that you suffered from nightmares, and I thought maybe you would understand."

"I do," she whispered. "The ring might help. Do me a favor and send me a message through Grimon if the nightmares stop after you start wearing it."

"You think it's a remnant of Cato's influence on me?" Marcos asked.

She shivered at the thought. Was Xander having the same experience?

"Maybe. We've all been through a lot." She knew it wasn't comforting, but she wasn't sure how to ease his mind when her own was spinning so much.

"I'll let you know."

The king turned to leave and then stopped at the edge of the trail. "Actually, you reminded me—I wanted to ask your forgiveness and settle this...awkwardness between us about what happened years ago."

Cecilia's memory magic swelled, immediately calling up the memory that she instinctually knew he was referring to.

She struggled to keep a straight face. "I don't know what you're talking about."

Marcos smiled. "I'm talking about the time I tried to kiss you when we were younger, and you punched me in the face before having a ghost scare the literal piss out of me."

Cecilia burst into laughter. It was the first time they'd ever spoken about what happened between them so many years before—the very reason Marcos had always been so wary around her.

"I'm sorry, it's not funny. Marc, I've genuinely always wanted to apologize. It was an overreaction. I panicked."

"No, it was presumptuous of me to try. Everyone liked to flirt with a prince, but no one would be so bold as to kiss me. By the time I figured that out, I was afraid I was getting too old. I didn't want to be bad at it. I knew so few girls, and you were the one I knew best. I thought it made sense."

"I'd never been kissed," Cecilia said. "I was waiting for—"

"Rainer," Marcos finished.

She nodded.

"I figured it out after the fact. You were always prone to extremes but never such violent ones," Marcos said.

Cecilia placed a hand on his shoulder. "I was too embarrassed for you to know I hadn't been kissed and didn't want you to try again. I'm sorry. It wasn't personal."

"I know." Marcos laughed, running a hand through his dark hair. "I was young and dumb, but I'm trying to be better—" He cleared his throat and tugged on his tunic. "I'm trying to be a better man for this kingdom. I loved my father, but he wasn't a good listener and never admitted when he was wrong. I want to learn from his mistakes and that means clearing the air with powerful allies."

"Consider it clear," she said, pulling him into a hug.

It was a wonder to see how far Marcos had come from his timid youth. He'd grown so much in the last year.

As he escorted her out of the garden, a flicker of hope burst to life in her heart. If Marcos could rise to the occasion and thrive in the role of king, perhaps Xander could, too.

In two short weeks, she could clear the air between them. Perhaps she and Xander would be able to put the past to rest, start over as friends, and Cecilia would finally feel ready to settle down for good with Rainer.

11

RAINER

The journey to Argaria started peacefully enough. Rainer and Cecilia encountered other travelers and, for the first time, they stayed in small villages at boarding houses instead of in the wild. Cecilia delighted in walking through small towns, sampling their delicacies, looking through shops, and learning new folk dances in pubs.

She enjoyed anonymity after being the center of attention for so long. Even now, in Olney, people approached her with reverence and gratitude. Rainer knew she appreciated the recognition of her hard work and sacrifice, but it was yet another thing that made her feel othered from everyone else. In the small towns along their route, she was just a lady who could blend in, enjoy herself, and not worry about being thanked for dying.

Rainer drank in her joy and relished the opportunity to try new foods from other parts of the kingdom. Cecilia teased him as he named different spices he tasted in each meal, while she just rated everything as delicious, gross, or tolerable.

Her anger had cooled over his lie of omission and the hidden letters. But her quick forgiveness only made Rainer feel more guilty. After all the lies she'd been fed under the guise of protection, he should have known better than to repeat an old mistake. But she was so empathetic and he was afraid of Xander's struggles bleeding into her right as she was healing. He was going to tell her once she was a little more steady.

She'd said nothing else about it. She watched him work on his carvings, complimented his slight improvements over their journey, and asked questions about how the apprenticeship worked. Her pride in him was obvious and that meant more than he could express.

Even with carpentry to ground him and the excitement he felt about starting the next level of his apprenticeship when they returned to Olney, he still felt aimless. The truth was, he was excited to have a mission.

Since completing the Gauntlet he'd felt rudderless, towed along in Cecilia's fight with no purpose of his own but to keep her safe. He thought after what had happened, he'd had more than enough violence. But after a year of normal life, Rainer felt no closer to moving on from his warrior past. Evan's request for help gave him one last assignment, and perhaps knowing it was the last one would allow him to finally settle down and enjoy their hard-earned peace.

He thought he'd laid his ambition to rest. The relentless desire to be a hero had nearly cost him the most important person in his life. But, once again, he was ready to march right back into danger just so he could have a way to prove his worth. Raymond McKay's reprimands were still fresh in Rainer's mind.

Cecilia was in good spirits, joking and telling stories as they traveled through familiar terrain, but the closer they got to Ardenis, the more unsettled she seemed.

Rainer made love to her every night. At first, he convinced himself it was to ease her anxiety, but when they were just a day out from Castle Savero, and he took her up against a tree like a desperate teenager, he finally admitted to himself that it might be to ease his own.

She was more than happy to oblige, teasing him about his insatiable appetite. He knew she loved to feel desired, to feel his desperation, to wield control over him in those moments. Truly, she held his heart in her hands every time, and he knew it would never occur to her to do anything but care for it.

Cecilia wrecked him every day with her begging. *Please, Rainer.* She got frenzied so quickly.

He loved that she was as impatient and bossy in bed as she was everywhere else. He loved when she told him what to do almost as much as when she told him to do whatever he wanted.

The first time she'd said those words to him, he'd embarrassed himself. He couldn't form words, and she'd collapsed in a fit of giggles at the look on his face. He'd been thinking about taking her to bed for so long, all the options flooded his brain at once. Now he'd become accustomed to reading her moods and determining which way she would go. He loved to rile her up and see how she would unravel. He honestly had no idea what she would do from day to day, and it added to the thrill of being with someone he loved so much.

Although Rainer was more experienced, Cecilia was a first in so many ways. The first woman he'd been with who he'd loved. The first woman who wasn't just a lady. The ladies of the court were proper and self-conscious, sometimes shy. Cecilia was self-assured, confident, so fucking sexy it drove him half out of his mind. Not to mention that her training meant she had flexibility and stamina that blew him away.

Still, Rainer couldn't shake his anxiety as they cut through Ardenis and found themselves in front of Castle Savero's gates.

Cecilia handed their invitation to the guard and told him their names. The man's eyes went wide. He pressed his fingers to his lips and his heart and bowed his head reverently.

"Goddess, welcome back."

Cecilia smiled tightly as the guard waved men over to take their bags inside. Cecilia walked onto the castle grounds without another word. A servant greeted them in the main hall, led them up to Cecilia's old rooms, and disappeared to fetch bath water for them.

Cecilia looked around the room, her arms tucked to her sides as if afraid to touch anything.

"Are you nervous about seeing him?" Rainer asked.

He knew it was unreasonable to envy the remnants of affection she held for Xander. She'd chosen him, not Xander. But he wasn't foolish enough to believe that she was over the man when she'd written to him nearly every week for a year.

"I'm nervous about whatever has kept him from replying. I'm afraid I'll go looking for him and find him unrecognizable. I'm worried that he'll say something that hurts worse than his silence," she said.

The air rushed out of Rainer's lungs. It was, perhaps, the most honest she'd been in months. He was so relieved.

"I'm sure he will be happy to see you and, even if he's not, he'll be grateful for your help," Rainer assured her.

Cecilia seemed just as on edge even once they were settled in their room. He wondered if it helped or hurt that she'd been put in her former bedroom. He watched her take stock of the room he'd never laid eyes on. Her robe still hung by the door, a book of poetry on the nightstand. Tracing her fingers over arrow divots in the wood of the sitting room door, she smiled.

As Rainer looked around the room, he noticed similar marks on the wood around the windows, on the mantel, in the armoire, and even on the side tables and nightstand.

"I know what you're thinking," she said. "I'm why we can't have nice things."

Rainer laughed and took in the rest of the room. His room was technically next door, for the sake of appearances. Cecilia immediately searched for the passageway to his bedroom. Although they lived together at home, Rainer still kept his apartment for propriety's sake. The only reason they were able to cohabitate was that the cottage was on the very edge of town and relatively secluded. It was frustrating to go from their private space where they could touch and kiss each other whenever they wanted to being back in the spotlight in court. Since they weren't yet married, they were expected to show restraint publicly.

Court custom meant that Rainer could only kiss Cecilia's hand at public events. It was archaic and ridiculous, but it would have been a scandal for him to kiss her in front of anyone else. Since Xander's hold on his kingdom was precarious enough, Rainer would have to show some restraint. They didn't want to give the council any more complaints to use against Xander, and even if it would be a minor scandal, it was one they didn't need.

Cecilia looked in the closet but found it empty of anything except the new clothes that her former maid, Sena, had already brought in and hung nicely, along with a bow and quiver of arrows. Rainer assumed it was the same contraband with which Teddy had provided her. She touched the bow lightly before turning away and making her way across the room to look out the window. When she thought Rainer wasn't looking, she went through the motions of shooting her bow. He'd caught her doing the same thing multiple times over the past few months, though she always denied it or pretended she was just stretching.

She still refused to shoot her bow. Rainer didn't understand it, but he'd learned when to push and when to let go. He didn't blame her if she chose to lay down her weapons. She'd fought hard.

They settled in, bathing and eating a small feast Sena brought them before she wove Cecilia's curls into an absurdly intricate updo. When she finished, Cecilia looked beautiful but so unlike how she did at home.

The dress was more scandalous than anything Rainer had seen her wear in Olney. Although Olney's dress for women was more revealing than most other cultures because of its warm climate and proximity to the sea, Cecilia always kept her necklines higher and her hems lower. He wondered if she would have preferred wearing skimpier dresses and only now had the opportunity to do so without fear of scrutiny.

Rainer was sure she'd still be scrutinized, though it was different to be in a foreign court without the expectations of being a lady and the huntmaster's daughter. She was the former princess, a goddess, the subject of a new fairy-tale romance after coming back from death for him, and she'd likely be the center of attention as much as Xander at the event.

She spun in a circle, and the scarlet silk fanned out around her. When she came to a stop, she grinned, and he took in the slit up her right leg. The neckline plunged, the edge of her scar peeking out from the lace-trimmed silk covering the swells of her breasts.

Still, he felt like she was continually becoming more herself. Every day she grew into a more mature, joyful, graceful version of Cecilia. The melancholy came and went, but she found her way through it, and when she couldn't, she asked for his help. He felt as though he was getting to know her all over again, and it was a beautiful thing to fall in love with new sides of her each day.

Rainer wondered if he could ever truly know her. If they found each other lifetime after lifetime, if he had an eternity of time with her, could he know all of her? He didn't think so. Cecilia was her own universe, and he never stopped learning her, never stopped finding new things to love, never stopped wanting to explore her. It was an intimidating and comforting realization.

Cecilia was more than the sum of her history, more than heroics, more than the emotions that tore through her like a storm. She was a beautiful mess of wild, unbridled love and joy and flaws and longing, and she was his.

In the back of his mind, Rainer worried the choice of a more daring dress was simply to catch Xander's attention, as if she'd need help to do so.

She met Rainer's gaze in the mirror and smirked. He swore she could read his mind, despite her insistence to the contrary.

"I'm just for you, Rain," she said, trailing her fingers down the lace neckline of her scarlet silk dress to the golden scar over her heart.

She liked to whisper the phrase in private moments that were sacred to them both. When her eyes met his in the dark. *I'm just for you, Rain.* While he moved inside her, breathless, vulnerable, and unafraid. *Just for you.* As she curled into his lap, sobbing from a nightmare. *I'm just for you.* Trying to convince both of them what was real.

He might not have known all of her, but deep down, he knew her heart. He knew the light in her eyes because it was the same light that guided him through his own rage and grief.

He grinned at her, his fingers gliding along her shoulders.

"Rainer McKay, don't you dare touch my dress or hair," she scolded.

"But you look so very tempting. How could I possibly keep my hands to myself?"

His fingers glanced down the neckline to her scar. She shivered against his caress. He pulled her into a kiss. Before she could protest, his hands were in her hair, unpinning the masterpiece Sena had created, scattering hairpins along the stone floor. He simply kissed her for a long time until he struggled not to do more, his hands trailing up the slit in her dress. Finally, she pulled away.

"You are a menace," she complained.

Rainer swallowed her words in another scorching kiss. He kissed her until he felt no more anxiety buzzing through their bond, and instead, it heated with desire.

Finally, he pulled away, grinning at her. "You're so flushed. You almost match your dress."

Her eyes narrowed in accusation. "You did this on purpose."

He couldn't contain his satisfaction. "Maybe. I suspect when the king sees you, he will know exactly what you were up to. Plus, he'll smell me all over your skin."

She shook her head. "You are so—"

"Clever? Dashing? Prepared?" Rainer offered.

"Possessive."

Rainer shrugged. "I underestimated him once and nearly lost the love of my life. I won't make the same mistake twice. Now, do you want to be mad, or do you want to kiss me?"

He taunted her with her own words. She kissed him begrudgingly.

He tried to play down his fear over her seeing Xander again. Since they left Olney, he'd been plagued with thoughts of Xander winning her over yet again. He couldn't shake the persistent sense of foreboding about leading her into this mess. Maybe he'd been selfish when he guilted her into showing up for this. He wanted Xander settled so that she would feel more settled. So that maybe she'd finally set a date for their wedding. He selfishly hoped that Xander getting remarried would give her a sense of finality. Maybe then she'd finally feel ready.

His mind looped and coiled. Maybe it was too soon for all of this. Maybe being where they'd both been prisoners before would set her in a spiral again. Maybe the grief and loss would come roaring back, and it would only ruin their progress.

"Why must my hair always be caught in the crossfire?" she asked, interrupting his rushing thoughts as she slumped in front of the mirror and did her best to sweep her curls back and hold them in place with a jeweled comb.

Rainer's guilty smile reflected back to her in the mirror. "It's the version of you that only I get to see. I like taking your hair down because it's when you look the most like yourself," he said as he kissed her shoulder. "Just for me."

She smiled at him despite her frustration.

He took her hair down every night. He loved doing it. It was a ritual that was more intimate than he'd imagined it could be. She melted for him each time as he gently worked, kissing her as he slowly untangled each pin, loosening her curls with his fingers. She loved it, though he sensed she loved it far less when he did it right as she was getting ready to leave for an event.

"You look incredible," he said, catching her gaze in the mirror. "Are you certain we need to attend? I'd love to have you to myself in that dress."

"Don't be nervous."

He shrugged. Nervous was his natural state of being, and this situation was far from natural. He hadn't even been fully transparent with her about the state of Xander, though he assumed she'd find out soon enough.

"I'm going to try to find Xander before I head to the ballroom. I'd rather get the reunion out of the way in private rather than in front of the entire kingdom."

Rainer raised an eyebrow. He sensed her determination. She wanted something from Xander and Rainer was afraid to know exactly what it was.

"I'm certain Xander will be on his best behavior," she assured him.

"That's what I'm afraid of. He's always been aggressively affectionate."

She laughed. "That's one way to put it, though I doubt it's a concern given his lack of correspondence. He's moved on."

She sounded certain, but Rainer was not so sure.

She grinned at him but said nothing. Perhaps coming to Argaria was the right choice. As much as Cecilia brought out Xander's best and worst behavior, he also brought out a certain stubborn defiance in her. It could be good for her to reconnect with that.

"I will be down in the ballroom when you're ready," he said.

She nodded, and he wished she looked more confident.

"I suppose I've put off this reunion long enough," she said, taking one last look in the mirror.

She stood on her toes and kissed Rainer quickly before ducking out of the room.

Rainer whispered a silent prayer to the gods that traveling all this way to help their friends was the right choice.

PART II:

A FACELESS VILLAIN

12

XANDER

Xander leaned his forehead against the cool, stone stable wall. He wasn't exactly hiding from the princesses and attendants that had swarmed his court overnight, but he also wasn't exactly *not* hiding. The stable seemed to harbor the only quiet to be found on the massive castle grounds.

Soft footsteps cut through the silence. Evan did that when he wanted Xander to know he was coming, rather than popping up out of nowhere and risking a blade to the throat.

"Can I not have five minutes, Evan?" he asked. "Am I not king of this godsforsaken kingdom?"

The scent on the air made him freeze. Lavender and lemons—Olney in midsummer.

Surely he must be dreaming. Xander smelled it all the time: in his dreams, on the wind, everywhere. He missed her so much. Still, it was never quite so strong.

Evan had tried to temper his expectations over the past few weeks, saying there was only a small chance she'd be there. Xander was afraid to turn and find out he'd imagined everything, but she was standing there.

Cecilia Reznik, the love of his godsdamned life, stood in the

Argarian Royal Stables as if no time had passed. The shock of seeing her ran through him like a bolt of lightning. She was the storm always waiting to sweep him away, and he was eager to let her.

Every time he laid eyes on her was like welcoming his undoing.

He pinched himself.

She smiled, and it was as though he'd just watched Rainer carry her bloody body from the beach. As if she'd just broken his heart into a million pieces and he'd fled back to Argaria to try to reassemble himself with nothing but memories and her favorite of her mother's paintings.

He'd had months to prepare himself to be okay, but one look at Cece and all the progress he'd made immediately unraveled.

She took a few steps into the stable, the lantern light illuminating her in a glow. She was breathtaking, so much so that Xander sometimes wondered if something extra animated her, since she still retained remnants of her goddess powers. Beyond that, Cece was lovely simply because she was so remarkably alive, vivid, boisterous. She never seemed to fully still, some part of her always in motion, as if her body was trying to keep up with her quick mind.

"My love." His voice was a hoarse whisper.

Another smile tugged at her lips. "Xander."

Gods! The way she said his name. How could something so simple wind him up so thoroughly? Grief had crushed him for months, but the sight of her pulverized anything that was left. How was it possible that she was more beautiful than he remembered? His memories were perfect and yet somehow she seemed more vital in the flesh.

His hand itched to reach for her, his lips to kiss her.

Not yours, he reminded himself, but his heart remained unmoved.

She would slap him and tell him not to do it again if he tried. Still, it might be worth it to see if she kissed him back. Easier to beg forgiveness than to ask permission.

But wasn't that mentality your whole problem to begin with?

He let out his breath, and the burning in his chest eased. She looked resplendent in her sexy scarlet gown. Delicate, scalloped red lace peeked out over the swell of her breasts from the edges of the plunging neckline, and a long slit up the side of the skirt revealed a glimpse of her leg. It was a surprisingly daring choice. She'd always dressed more modestly back in Olney. Now she seemed content to leave as little as possible to the imagination, and he couldn't help but wonder if she chose this dress to attract his full attention.

If so, it worked. Xander was certain there had never been anyone as merciless as she was compassionate.

Cece's hair fell in a tumble of loose curls around her shoulders, with just the front swept back from her face with a sapphire and pearl comb. He recognized it right away. It was the comb his mother had gifted her on their wedding day.

He swallowed around the lump in his throat. "New dress?"

She waved a hand at the fabric. "This old thing?"

"Cece, you know that I think you look best in nothing at all. Whatever you wear is simply icing on an already exceptionally lovely cake."

He was comforted by the familiarity of her pinked cheeks.

"I still love doing that." He grinned.

"You are a hopeless flirt."

"And you are the love of my life."

Her face shuttered. She did not like that at all. Well, too bad. It didn't make it untrue.

In the moment she was thrown off, he noticed a faint sadness in her eyes he'd missed before. She forced a smile back into place, but she couldn't hide from Xander. Rainer might have been connected directly to her heart, but Xander had studied her for a year before speaking to her, and for six months as her husband. He knew every secret thing written in her eyes.

Cece took a tentative step toward him. He knew she was trying to read his emotions, like she did whenever she was unsure. She would only find the swirl of confusion, love, frustration, and grief that he'd felt ever since she'd chosen Rainer.

Xander moved toward her—a moth drawn to flame, happy to embrace his doom. He knew he was staring, but he couldn't drag his eyes away. He'd destroyed himself once for her before, and he'd do it a thousand times more. When it came to Cece, he simply could not help himself.

"Love, you know it's treason to kill a king, right?" He paused for effect. "Because that dress might just be enough to send me to an early grave."

She laughed. All he could do was stare at her and try to breathe through the swell of love that rose in his chest at the sound. Everything about her was a rebellion against what was expected of a lady in the court of either kingdom: the scandalous dress, the unbound hair, the look in her eyes. She was a temptation the gods had designed just for him.

"Are you trying to say I look nice?" she asked.

"I'm trying to say that you look stunning—exquisite. There really aren't words for how lovely you look. Someone should create a new language for it. Are you trying to torture me?"

"Of course not." She rolled her eyes, but he caught the hint of satisfaction in her smile.

He leaned closer. "You know what seeing you in red does to me. Is that why you wore this color?"

"Not everything is about you, *Your Grace*. Has royalty really gone to your head so quickly? My fiancé also likes me in this color."

"How could he not? But I also notice how you wore your hair down." As he said the words, he brushed her hair over one shoulder, sliding a finger up her neck. She maintained eye contact, her face placid, though he could feel her heart race at the touch.

It shocked him how easily they fell back into their old games. His relentless flirting came so naturally. Her defiant resistance made him just as spellbound as it always had.

"I'm not very good at doing my own hair for these things. It's easiest to just leave it down." She kept her voice calm as he circled her, but her heartbeat kicked up.

"And your comb? Was that also just out of necessity?" He breathed the words right next to her ear, and she shivered against him.

He loved this game they played. He loved it more when they were together, but after so long without being near her, he couldn't stop himself. Consequences be damned.

"No, that I wore for you." She smiled as he walked back in front of her.

The admission caught him off-kilter.

"Why?" he asked honestly.

"Because I thought you might want it for your new wife and because what we had still means something to me. If you'd read any of my letters, you would know that."

He'd read every single word she'd written at least a hundred times, probably more. The creases in them were nearly worn through from all the folding and unfolding. They were what kept him going, though he wondered if Cece knew.

He looked at her lips, imagining the words of each letter coming out of them. *Gods, those lips.* He would do anything to kiss her again— to hear the breathy little sounds she made when he kissed her neck. He hadn't so much as looked at another woman that way. Cece had ruined him for any other woman.

She stepped forward and the lantern lit her eyes the same shade as the Adiran Sea. He'd been stunned to silence when he arrived in Olney and saw the summer sea for the first time. He'd been stunned the same the first time he looked into her eyes up close.

Xander's life had been forever cleaved in half the moment he held her in his arms by the river and kissed her. All the chaos in his life could likely be traced back to that moment. He was as grateful for it as he was tortured by it, but he wouldn't have it any other way.

"I've read all your letters, Cece."

Her brow wrinkled in indignation. "Then why didn't you reply?"

"Things have been busy."

It was a shitty excuse, and he knew she probably saw through it. Her mask of composure wavered. If he didn't know her so well, he might have missed it, but he saw the slightest hint of more than just her calm external shell.

"It's been a year, Xander. I needed—" She stopped herself and took a breath, steadying her voice. "It would have meant a lot to hear from you." It was so like her to not admit to needing anything.

"Well, you might have missed it, but I'm king now. There's a never-ending to-do list and trying to appease a whole kingdom and stabilize it after an attempted coup has been complicated."

Her eyes dimmed with hurt. "I've written a lot of them. It wouldn't have taken much to just write a line or two back to let me know you're well."

He wanted to tell her how every time he went to put his thoughts to paper, they spun around his head like a vortex of grief and loss and longing. Instead of saying that, he continued to act like an ass. It was safer.

"And what does Rainer think of your letters?"

"I don't have anything to hide from him."

Xander leaned closer, twirling one of her curls around his finger. "I want to kiss you very badly right now."

Fisting his tunic, she leaned closer, the thin silk over her breasts pressed into the heavy velvet of his shirt. Her lips brushed the shell of his ear as she said two words that nearly brought him to his knees.

"I know."

Only she would be so fearless before a king.

She backed away and gave him a triumphant smile. For a moment all Xander could do was stare at her. He had always been—and was once again—out of his depth with her.

Xander laughed, running a hand through his hair. "Gods! Does Rainer have any idea how lucky he is?"

She bit her lower lip. "I try to remind him a few times a day."

"I bet you do. Where is your shadow, anyway?" He looked past her, expecting to see Rainer lurking in some nearby shade. "I didn't think he'd let us have so much unsupervised time."

"He's not my keeper. He wanted to give you some space."

"Maybe his overconfidence is to my benefit. What do you think, Cece? Quick and dirty? I know how much you like it up against the wall."

She laughed it off but couldn't hide the flush climbing up her neck. "As much as you'd enjoy that, I'm not sure that Rain would appreciate it."

"I seem to remember that he was pretty lenient when it came to your desires. Does that not still hold true?"

She crossed her arms. "Don't start."

Evan brought her here to help root out the spies in their midst, though perhaps he also did it to get Xander to be the kind of man he should be: a leader, a hero, a king. Seeing Cece now made him want to do just that. The problem was that he didn't want to do so to impress a bunch of foreign princesses—he wanted to impress her.

Before seeing Cece in that beautiful dress, he probably could have come close to convincing himself that someone else would do, at least on a surface level. Seeing her now, he knew no one ever would. He would love her madly until the day he died. There was no one else who could compare. It went deeper than lust, deeper than her beauty, deeper than her saving his life when he hadn't deserved it. It was all of her—the untamed wildness she held onto through all of her suffering and the beautiful hope she inspired in other people. It was the way she'd seen him and pulled him out of his shell. She was the brightest star in his sky, and even without godly meddling or influence, Xander was just as in love with her as he had always been.

Xander did not realize how much he'd been counting on her to drag him up out of the dark. It was only her hands he'd recognize by touch alone, delicate and soft but for the calluses from her bow. It was only her scent he'd follow blindly through the labyrinth of grief. It was only her light that illuminated the way out of the dark forest of hurt.

But now that he was looking at her, he saw how treacherous this gamble was. One misstep and he'd never reclaim himself. How easily he could plunge back into dark water. How quickly he could be swept away from shore to a place not even she could reach.

The danger should have been sobering, but he'd learned nothing and was still just as thrilled by it.

She rubbed her thumb over her inner wrist, her eyes darting

toward a noise down the stable corridor. "I'm just here to help," she said.

Xander wanted to challenge her—to say, "*I thought you were here to lead me out of the underworld, to breathe into me so I can stop living a half-life and finally become whole.*" But he could tell immediately that something was different. She carried a new edginess, her eyes darting over her shoulder like she'd been running for a year and these two weeks of slowness would allow her ghosts to catch up. He'd expected her to do the haunting, but she'd arrived haunted.

"I was hoping we could talk about some things. Perhaps tomorrow when the excitement of the party has faded," she said.

Xander frowned. He knew what this was. She was going to try to pry the secrets from his heart. She wanted answers, and he had no interest in giving them up. Frankly, he had no interest in examining them at all.

He ran a finger down her arm. "Of course, just meet me in my chambers and we'll have a very *private* audience."

"Xander," Cece chided, swatting his hand away. She brushed her hair back over her shoulder. The neckline of her dress shifted and the very edge of the golden scar on her chest peeked out from the scalloped lace.

There'd been talk about that scar and about her great love story with Rainer McKay. The woman who'd come back from death and given up her immortal life with the gods to be with her one true love. Funny that the two of them had loved their fairy tales so much, and had themselves ended up one of the greatest love stories in the land.

"Can I see it?" Xander asked, meeting her eyes again.

She tentatively brought her hand to her chest. Her hesitation wasn't about modesty—he'd seen her naked plenty. It was the intimacy of what the scar meant. It was that he'd been there to witness it, that he'd seen her come back.

He'd watched her die. He'd felt his heart break as the light left her eyes. And then he'd watched her come back to life. He'd let her go because of what that scar meant. Her letters captured the way coming

The Storm King

back had marked her life, but he'd not seen how it had marked her body.

She pulled the lace to the side, revealing the full scar. It was roughly two inches wide, and even in the dim stable lighting, it seemed to shine.

"Grim's Gates," he whispered. Without thinking, he reached out to run his fingers over it. She shivered at his touch, but she didn't pull away. "Does it hurt?"

"No, it's just very sensitive," she whispered.

His eyebrows shot up, and then, because he was a reckless idiot, he ran his thumb over the scar again, harder.

She shuddered and cursed, swatting his hand.

Xander chuckled. "Have I ever told you that you have the filthiest mouth I have ever heard?"

Cece crossed her arms. "As I recall, you've always been a fan of my filthy mouth."

Suddenly all he could think about was her mouth wrapped around him, and just like that, she was back to having the upper hand.

He shrugged. "You're not wrong."

"Good to know that you still have the same boundary issues you always have." She rolled her eyes, but he could tell she was ruffled.

"What can I say? Kings take what they want."

He expected her to have a quick comeback, but her heated gaze locked on his. Something chimed out a warning in the back of his mind. He should step away. Put space between him and the thing that could brutalize him. He should protect his heart from the woman who had pulverized it. But he was snared by her eyes.

Finally, she looked away. "Your court is waiting, Your Majesty, and I can feel my love getting impatient." She brushed her fingers over the scar as she started toward the doorway.

Xander watched her retreat with a sinking sensation in his stomach.

He had not just loved Cecilia Reznik. He had survived her, and he was not sure he could do it again.

13

CECILIA

Cecilia took a deep breath outside the ballroom doors. The crisp northern air felt good.

She didn't know how Xander always managed to ruffle her. She'd hoped she would see him and feel nothing. Instead, the wounds she thought long-healed were still startlingly delicate, waiting for the slightest encouragement to split and start bleeding again. The love that was once so grand and sweeping had dulled to an ache behind the scar in her chest. In seeing him, she'd realized she was missing a part of herself that she could never fully recover, or maybe that she didn't want back. He'd seemed eager to return it to her by ignoring her letters, but now he flirted with her as if they'd skipped over all the pain between them and looped back to where they started.

Xander was so unaffected while she was so raw. She didn't want him to hurt, but his easy flirtation made her feel alone—not just in her grief, but in her entire memory of their relationship.

It felt as if no time had passed, and his seduction confused her more after a year of silence.

"Like it's just a game to him," she whispered.

She lifted her hair away from her neck and fanned herself with her hand.

"Did he already get to you?" a voice asked.

Cecilia jumped, her hand flying to the dagger on her thigh.

Evan walked toward her, seemingly straight out of the darkness.

Hunters and their silent lurking.

She met his eyes. "I don't know what you're talking about."

He smirked. "I do. I've seen that face many times after Xander planted one on you in public after he charmed the pants off you when we were on the run."

"I get it," Cecilia sighed. "Do I look that undone?"

Evan shrugged. "I would try to pull it together before you see Rainer. I did convince him that this was a good idea."

"I know. I was the one that didn't want to come." She took a breath. "Xander seems the same. I know he's not. I believe what your letters said, but he was the same to me as he's always been. Worse, maybe."

Evan pinched the bridge of his nose. "Oh, gods. What did he do?"

"Just the usual. Offered to fuck me against the wall," Cecilia said.

Evan shook his head. "Well, I'm glad he's still in there. He's not been himself in a long time."

Grief and guilt swelled in the air around Evan. He was usually better at locking his emotions down. Of all of their friends, he had always been the hardest for her to read, but it seemed the year had taken a toll on him as well.

"I know I'm here to help keep him safe, but I'm a bit worried my presence isn't going to help him find a queen," Cecilia said.

"You bring out the best and worst in him." Evan rubbed the back of his neck. "Gods know he needs to get married and have an heir sooner rather than later. The peace in this kingdom relies on it." He studied her, his gaze passing over her dress suspiciously. "You are going to help with that, right?"

She leaned back against the white stone wall. "I can certainly try, but I consider myself to be lucky with one miracle in my lifetime. I'm not sure I should push my luck in hoping for two."

He crossed his arms and leaned a shoulder against the wall. "Cece, I'm going to ask you something, and please don't be mad at me for asking."

She nodded.

"Why haven't you and Rainer set a wedding date?"

She winced and looked away. "It's complicated. I wasn't myself for a while. It's hard to move on thinking of everyone we've lost—"

"Survivor's remorse. It's normal, Cece. Teddy would want you to be happy. He was loyal to Xander, but he was also kind of obsessed with you and Rainer's bond. I think he would have been at peace with how this all turned out."

Cecilia stiffened at the casual way he talked about a young life exchanged for hers. It still broke her weary heart.

"Is that all?" Evan asked.

She narrowed her eyes at him. "What else would there be?"

Evan gave her a knowing look. "Well, you wore that very stunning dress. I thought maybe you were still in love with the king."

"Maybe I knew I was seeing the man who ripped my heart out, and I wanted to remind him what he was missing," she said pointedly.

"Fair enough. He's still in love with you."

Cecilia sighed, wrapping a curl around her finger. "I'll always love him. If it wasn't for Rain—" She let the words trail off because it was too painful to think about possibilities. Now that she was back in Argaria, she could see a hundred fractured versions of her future— shards that reflected a life that would have been so different but so happy. It might have been easier if Xander had been angry or cold; if she hadn't felt the raw energy in the air between them; if she could blame her past on a naive lack of judgment instead of a true under- standing of a heart that was so much like her own. She wanted seeing him to free her from caring. But it had only made her more desperate to understand him.

"I couldn't give him what he needs anyway, Evan," she said quietly. If she were queen, there would be no heirs. "What we had, we can't get back. It was another casualty of war. I can't—" Cecilia's throat grew tight with emotion. "I can't give him what he needs and what he deserves, and I don't know how to get back the trust we lost."

"I assumed as much. I thought maybe you could find a new trust."

She furiously blinked away tears. "It was always going to be Rainer for me."

Evan looked like he wanted to say more, but he pressed his lips into a thin line and nodded.

"Do you know why he hasn't written me back?" she asked.

Evan's face pulled into a pitying smile. "I don't. You'd have to ask him."

She nodded, looking up at the starry night sky. She smoothed her dress and tried to steel herself for a room full of Argarian lords and ladies. "How do I look now?"

His lips twitched in the barest hint of a genuine smile. "Like you're ready for battle."

Evan opened the door, and Cecilia entered the ballroom.

She felt Rainer's eyes on her immediately. As she walked toward him, he smiled and she couldn't help but return it. He took her hand and kissed the crescent moon scar on the outside of her palm, leaning down to level his mouth against her ear.

"I wish we weren't in front of all these people so that I could give you a greeting appropriate for how incredible you look in that dress," he whispered.

Cecilia's cheeks heated as she leaned into him, ignoring the gawking stare of the crowd around them. She reached up and brushed his hair back from his forehead. She didn't blame people for staring. He was so handsome, she couldn't stop staring either.

"You look pretty good yourself, Guardian McKay."

"Perhaps we should skip the party and just go upstairs," he whispered.

Cecilia considered the idea. He laughed and kissed her inner wrist.

"Gods, could you two be more disgustingly happy?"

Cecilia turned and grinned at Cal Bennington.

"Cal! I didn't know you were going to be here for this part!" Cecilia said, pulling him into a hug.

Several onlookers raised their eyebrows. While it wasn't appropriate for Cecilia to hug a man who wasn't family or a husband in public, she hadn't seen Cal in a year and she didn't care.

"I go where Sylvie goes, and Sylvie goes where Evan goes, so here is where you'll find me, Rez. Sorry we couldn't be there to receive you two. Sylvie had me acting as escort to one of the princesses. As if I don't have enough to do helping her and Evan and wrangling your lovesick ex-husband. Speaking of His Majesty, does he know you're here?" Cal's gaze cut across the ballroom in search of the king.

"Yes, I've already been appropriately harassed," she drawled.

Cal laughed. "I bet you have in that dress."

Cecilia was happy to see him so at home. The mountains clearly agreed with Cal. He looked handsome and happy and easily ignored the scrutinizing gazes around them. Of course, he was always happy-go-lucky and seemed to rally in even the worst circumstances, so maybe it wasn't the court as much as his nature.

"How is the king?" Rainer asked.

Cal arched a brow and leaned closer. "You want the courtly answer or the honest one?"

"Is he that bad?" Rainer asked.

"He does nothing other than spar, shoot, and drink. Evan seems to have him looking better today, but he's a mess. He rarely sleeps, and he's constantly haunting the halls of the castle at night."

"Are you sure he's not just chasing around the ladies of the court?" Rainer asked dryly.

"No, according to Evan, he hasn't so much as looked at a lady since—" Cal caught himself before finishing the sentence.

Cecilia tried to keep her face placid. She knew without looking that Rainer was waiting for a reaction.

Cal shrugged. "But this ball is a good sign. I wouldn't worry too much, Rez."

"Do I look worried?" Her voice was too high-pitched.

"You look flustered. You have since you came in from seeing him," Rainer said.

Heat rose to her cheeks. "I do not."

"You do." Rainer shook his head. "I felt a burst of surprise and then a rush of heat through our connection. That's like the Xander Savero special. Are you going to pretend he didn't try to kiss you?"

Cecilia raised an eyebrow.

"Gods! Did he already try to kiss you?" Rainer rubbed a hand over his face.

"No," she mumbled. "But he did offer to give me a quick roll in the hay in the stables."

Cal choked on his whiskey.

Rainer's anger and jealousy whipped through their bond. "I'm going to kill him."

"You can't say things like that, Rain, and for the love of the gods, please don't give him the satisfaction of seeing you bothered by it, or he will never stop," Cecilia whispered.

"He'll never stop anyway, Cece, and you know it. He can't help himself with you," Rainer insisted.

She placed a placating hand on his arm. "That's why we are here."

"I still don't understand why Evan thought this was a good idea," Cal said quietly as arriving members of the court were introduced.

"Because Evan knew something like this would draw Xander out. He trusts you," Rainer said plainly.

Evan was a master tactician, and he must have known that Cecilia would come and her presence would bring out the competitive edge in Xander, but she and Rainer had been on their own for so long. She'd forgotten what it was like to be at the center of Xander's attention.

Cecilia turned back toward the stairs, where Xander was expected to enter before a parade of potential queens. She bit back a giggle. The entire spectacle was something Xander would hate—the formal music, the extravagant flowers covering every surface, the judgmental lords and ladies analyzing his every move.

A horn blared, the guard introduced Xander, and the room

hushed as everyone bowed to their king. He looked every bit his old self, full of cocky swagger as he walked down the stairs and into the ballroom. He came to a stop next to Evan and several nobles. The entourage looked up the steps expectantly, but Xander's eyes were fixed on Cecilia.

"Must he look at you like that?" Rainer grumbled.

"Isn't that how he always looks at her?" Cal teased.

Cecilia chewed her lower lip as she realized many of the eyes in the room were picking up on the king's gaze, and most of those eyes knew their history. She felt the disapproval and distrust wafting off of the crowd the same way as when she was first introduced as Xander's fiancée. It seemed they still thought she'd bewitched their king. She couldn't hear their whispers, but she could see the judgment in their eyes. It didn't matter that she had saved both kingdoms and ended the war. They still didn't trust her.

"Easy there, Rez. Don't let them see you sweat. You saved him. You saved all of us. You have nothing to prove," Cal whispered.

She squeezed his arm. "Thank you, Cal."

When she looked back at Xander, his gaze finally slid to the top of the stairs. A parade of young women in bright dresses descended the great staircase one at a time. Each one seemed more lovely than the last. Xander was charming as ever, greeting each of them and kissing their hands.

Cecilia watched each of their faces as they realized their prospect was indeed a handsome young king and not an old gray one. Cecilia tried to shove down the strange pang of jealousy that ached in her chest.

She had no right to feel that way when she'd been moving on for a year. She tried to reason with the feeling. *I am happy with Rainer. I made the right choice. I don't regret it.* It was all true, but a stubborn possessiveness remained. Xander had so many of her firsts and moving on had broken her heart. No matter what her friends claimed about his mindset, Xander made it look like forgetting her was easy.

"What do you think based on first impressions?" Rainer asked.

Cecilia watched Xander's gaze travel over the six potential princesses.

"I think perhaps the princess of Novum. She looks less prim and proper than the rest, and I bet she can hunt," Cecilia whispered.

"You're probably right. Many women in Novum learn how to use a bow, and it's expected as part of their way of life," Cal said. "I actually heard that she was supposed to be the leader of the Novumi army, but when word went out that Xander was available, her mother sent her here."

Cecilia frowned. Novum was technically a queendom, though the rest of their world still regularly called it a kingdom. For centuries the rule of Novum had passed from queen to queen. Cecilia was surprised that a woman would be so eager to trade her daughter for an alliance, especially one who already had such an important role.

The musicians started to play, and the crowd swelled as noblemen asked the princesses to dance.

Cecilia elbowed Cal in the ribs and nodded to the opportunistic nobles. "Perhaps you can bag yourself a princess, Cal."

He blushed, sipping his whiskey. "I'm not looking at the moment."

"Do tell!" She was delighted at the prospect of Cal finally finding love.

His eyes shot across the room to a pretty blonde woman laughing with one of her friends. Cecilia recognized her from her time in Argaria. It was Lady Tanya McGraph, whom Teddy had been smitten with. He'd told Cecilia that Tanya was a good woman—beautiful, intelligent, and kind. The exact type of person who would be perfect for Cal.

When Cal said nothing, Cecilia squeezed his arm. "Good for you, Cal."

Rainer clapped him on the shoulder, but Cal just waved a hand. "It's early. I'm trying not to get ahead of myself. We're all just focused on this right now. Who do you think he'll pick?"

Rainer placed a hand on Cecilia's lower back. "I'll make you a wager right now, Cece."

"Oh, really?" she said. "Let's make it interesting, McKay. I'll bet you two weeks of breakfast in bed that he picks Princess what's-her-name from Novum."

"I'll take that action, but I'm going to bet something slightly different. I'm going to bet that he's going to pick that demure little princess of Aldrena," Rainer said.

Cecilia laughed in disbelief. "The willowy blonde with the perfect curtsey? Are you mad? There's no way in Grimon's Underworld he will pick that bimbo."

"Oh yes, there is. This is all performance art, Cecilia. Xander will pick her just to drive you out of your mind. If he picks her, mark my words, he has no intention of marrying any of them, and he's just doing this to get a rise out of you."

Rainer had convinced her this was a good idea, but he seemed uneasy now. She wasn't sure what had set him off.

"That is—" she began, but Xander asked Princess Perfect Curtsey of Aldrena to dance. "Oh, for Clastor's sake!"

Cal clapped a hand on Rainer's shoulder. "You're good, Rain."

"You can't take it back now. Looks like you're going to have some very early mornings ahead of you," Rainer teased, wrapping one of Cecilia's curls around his finger.

"As I recall, I was never supposed to be made to get up before ten in the morning for the rest of my days."

"Oh, gods! She sacrifices her life for mine, and now I'll never hear the end of it," Rainer said. He tried to make it sound light, but she could tell by the sudden dread in their bond that she shouldn't have said it. "Cece, would you like to dance?"

"I would love to," she said, placing her hand in his.

Rainer led her toward the dance floor, but they were intercepted by Evan before they could start to dance.

As much as Cecilia wanted to know what they were up to, she also desperately needed a drink. Making her way across the room, she grabbed a glass of bubble wine, which she drank much too quickly. She pushed her magic out, trying to take the emotional temperature of the crowd.

"Lady Reznik?"

She turned to find the princess of Novum standing behind her. Cecilia's breath caught. From afar, she was radiant, but up close, she was one of the most stunning women Cecilia had ever seen. Cecilia felt another stab of jealousy.

As if the princess's beauty wasn't enough, she also wore a dress that was unlike anything Cecilia had seen. The neckline plummeted. The silk was finely embroidered with silver thread and sparkling crystals on the bodice. The lavender shade of the silk complimented her warm brown skin, and the diamond-encrusted circlet braided into her hair made her eyes sparkle. The princess was tall, regal, and elegant, but her strength was evident in the tone of her shoulders and arms.

"Your Grace," Cecilia said, dipping into a curtsey. "To what do I owe the honor?"

"I know your story and I was hoping you would be willing to chat with me about the king," the princess said, handing her a glass of bubble wine.

She was certainly forward.

"Of course," Cecilia said. "Forgive me, but I didn't hear your name when you were introduced."

"Princess Jessamin Orum of Novum."

Cecilia restrained herself from asking a hundred questions about Novum, which lay just across the Adiran Sea from Olney. She and Rainer had read numerous books about Novumi mythology and an entirely different set of deities that Cecilia was eager to learn more about. She wanted to ask about the city of Estrellas, where the residents watched the moon rise low on the horizon and had festivals every full moon. Visiting the city was one of Cecilia's dreams.

She shoved down her questions. "Lovely to meet you."

"Charmed." The princess smiled politely. "I understand you were once briefly married to His Majesty."

Princess Jessamin was all business.

"Yes, I was. It was a marriage of necessity."

Jessamin looked at her skeptically. "I was given the impression it was perhaps more than that."

"Xander was a kind and charming husband. He's a good man, if that's what you're wondering. I hold him in very high regard."

"That's good to hear," Jessamin said as they strolled toward the doors that opened to the courtyard. "I'm curious, though, why you would be here for this occasion."

"A fair question, Your Grace. Xander and I remain the best of friends, and he asked me to attend."

"To help him choose a wife?"

"Yes." Suspicion flared in Cecilia's stomach, but Jessamin's emotions were calm—more curious than threatening. Cecilia really tried not to read people normally, but wasn't that the whole reason Evan invited her—so she could assess threats?

Cecilia didn't like someone questioning her presence. She was certain Evan wouldn't want her to share the true reason she was there. Cecilia's greatest asset in this operation was that people didn't know she could read them. Better to be a jealous ex-wife than a magical spy.

"I'm a trained hunter, Lady Reznik, much like yourself and the king. Novum is a queendom, and as such, the queen's daughters are trained to lead the military."

"I've heard as much."

"Then you must know that I would notice things that others might miss."

"I'm not sure I know what you mean," Cecilia said, baffled. They'd moved closer to the door to the courtyard so it was easier to hear each other speak over the music. A cool breeze ruffled Cecilia's dress, and she felt suddenly nervous.

"The king has not torn his gaze from you all night. Since I started talking to you, he's been watching," Jessamin said.

"How do you know that he isn't watching you, Princess? You are very lovely and your dress is one of a kind."

Jessamin frowned at her.

"I meant that as a compliment. I don't think I've ever seen prettier, more unique beadwork. Everyone else looks the same," Cecilia said.

Jessamin's eyes softened slightly, then narrowed again. "And yet it's not me that the king looks at. Not any of the princesses. Only *his* princess. The Lost Goddess. The woman who saved his life and broke his heart. Do you really think he's in the right mind to choose a wife?"

Cecilia choked on a sip of wine. "You know my story?"

Jessamin rolled her eyes. "Everyone in Novum knows your story."

Cecilia waved a hand. "Royals don't get to choose marriages based on love. This is a marriage of necessity. Xander will always do what he has to in order to help his people. He's sacrificed a lot."

"I'm the middle daughter, Lady Reznik. It is a blessing and a curse. I did not get the same attention and scrutiny from my mother, but I was raised to lead our army, like King Alexander. I am here out of duty and for no other reason."

"But why marry you off when you've been leading an army?" Cecilia asked.

Jessamin smiled tightly. "The world changed. Argaria and Olney being allied means that my mother found herself in the middle of the sea with no true allies. Since His Grace prefers women, I was sent here instead of my little brother."

The story reminded Cecilia of how she felt when she was leaving on her last Gauntlet run—powerful in the field but powerless at home. "That's horseshit."

A surprised laugh burst from Jessamin, breaking the tension between them.

Cecilia's cheeks heated. "Apologies, Your Grace. I—"

Jessamin held up a hand and grinned. "No need to apologize. Your honesty is refreshing, and rare."

"Meaning no offense," Cecilia mumbled. "I am sure you'd make a wonderful queen, and I actually think you would be a great match for Xander. It's just unfortunate you have to sacrifice your hard work for someone else's desires."

Jessamin pursed her lips. "We all must pay a price eventually." Sadness sparked in the air around the princess. "That's quite a dress you're wearing if you're not trying to impress the king."

"My fiancé picked my dress," Cecilia said, trying for demureness and likely failing miserably.

"Of course. You and your guardian share a soul bond so strong that he tethered you to the living world when you died. It's a very romantic story," Jessamin said. "Although I have to assume it's been embellished." She waved a hand. "Meaning no offense. In Novum we say all good stories need a little sparkle."

Cecilia brought her finger to the neckline of her dress and drew the lace to the side, giving Jessamin a glimpse of her scar.

"Gods," Jessamin breathed. "It's true."

"What would be the purpose of lying about that? I died. It was heartbreaking and painful and horrible, and then I came back, and that was also painful but really wonderful and horrible. And to address your accusation, Rainer chose this dress because he loves this scar and what it means, and he thinks that I should show it off."

Jessamin looked chastened. "Apologies, Lady Reznik. I shouldn't have been so callous."

Cecilia gave her a tight smile. "You're a foreign woman in a strange court. I won't fault you for being on your guard. I've been in your shoes."

Jessamin smiled, her eyes scanning the room before she turned back to Cecilia. "I must ask. If the king was so incredibly smitten with you as the gossip suggests, why is it that the people seem so wary of you?"

"Because I'm a witch, and they all assume I bewitched him to fall in love with me."

Jessamin shook her head, meeting the eyes of a lady glaring at Cecilia and cocking her head to the side. "*Look away*," she mouthed.

The woman's face went red and she turned around.

Cecilia couldn't contain her giggle of surprise. She'd never seen a royal do such a thing in public.

"What?" Jessamin asked, giving Cecilia a conspiratorial grin.

Cecilia smiled around the discomfort of actually liking a beautiful woman who could very well become Xander's wife. It was clear if they met in any other circumstances, they would be friends. She clenched her fists at her sides. *She could be working you, Cece. She might be trying to win you over.*

She forced herself to keep the conversation going. "They aren't bad people. They just didn't know me, and then overnight, I was engaged to their charming young prince. It would have seemed a strange match for anyone who didn't know I was the Lost Goddess. I don't blame them for their contempt. Plus, most of them think I broke the prince's heart."

"Always easier to make the woman the villain," Jessamin said. "And the men get an excuse to forever be guarded."

Cecilia appraised Jessamin with new respect. She was not at all what she imagined a princess to be.

"Truer words have never been spoken, Your Grace," Cecilia sighed. "For what it's worth, just based on first impressions, I would bet on you. Xander isn't interested in delicate women. He'd much prefer someone who can hunt and ride. I think you would make a great match. Xander likes a challenge, so don't make it too easy on him, or he'll get bored. He's a pompous ass, but he's also impossibly charming, and when it comes down to it, he's kind and thoughtful."

Jessamin nodded. "He certainly is handsome."

"And he knows it," Cecilia said, and they both laughed.

Jessamin's gaze darted over Cecilia's shoulder, and she stood up straighter. "He's coming this way."

Cecilia forced a smile to her face and fought not to let it drop when she came face to face with Xander and the beautiful blonde princess on his arm.

14

XANDER

It was almost too easy. Cece's eyes lit with challenge as they passed over Princess Clare. Xander loved to get a rise out of her. Clare was the obvious front-runner given Aldrena's borders with Argaria, but she was also the antithesis of Cece, with her elegant movements punctuated by perfectly practiced small talk.

"Princess Jessamin, Lady Reznik, I'd love for you to meet Princess Clare Pyke of Aldrena," Xander said.

Jessamin and Cece curtseyed. Xander felt Evan's eyes burning into him from across the room. He could practically hear his friend's exasperated words: *Leave Cece alone, Xan. You're making a first impression tonight.*

How on earth could Evan expect that of him? She'd thrown down a challenge with that dress that kept drawing his eye to the swell of her breasts and the golden scar over her heart. How could he possibly behave himself when she'd clearly forgone undergarments? After a year of being ignored, she had dressed to ensure he could do so no longer. Her tactics were remarkably effective.

"Now, what are you two conspiring about?" Xander asked, looking from Jessamin to Cece.

Jessamin looked mildly bored as she glanced from Clare to

Xander. Cece pressed her lips together like she did when trying not to laugh.

"Princess Jessamin and I were just chatting about her latest hunt. We both enjoy working with a bow so much. Do you shoot, Princess Clare?" Cece asked pointedly.

Xander kept his face placid, but excitement bubbled through him at seeing Cece jealous enough to take a shot at her perceived competition. It didn't matter how much time passed; he hadn't learned his lesson, and he got no less enjoyment out of winding her up.

"I'm afraid I've never been taught to shoot. In Aldrena, women aren't usually allowed to try such things," Clare said sweetly.

"What do you do for fun?" Cece asked.

"I love needlepoint and hosting afternoon tea with the ladies of the court."

Cece's smile was flawless, but Xander read the lack of sincerity in her eyes. "That sounds lovely. We should have tea while you're here."

"That would be so lovely. And perhaps you could come as well, Princess Jessamin," Clare continued.

Jessamin looked like she would rather gouge her eyes out with a dull blade, but she forced a smile and said she would love to. It was easy to see why she and Cece had gravitated toward each other. Jessamin was a second daughter, raised to lead their army, similar to what Xander's upbringing would have been had he remained in Argaria instead of going to Olney to spy. She was probably as thrilled to be here as he was.

Clare took a step toward Cece. "I would just love to hear about your adventures of saving His Majesty and about your beautiful love story with your guardian."

Xander fought to keep from rolling his eyes when Rainer appeared and stepped behind Cece, placing his hand on the small of her back.

"Rain, we were just talking about you." Cece leaned into him and placed her hand on his chest, her fingers dragging over his tunic.

Rainer grinned at her indulgently.

"Is it true that you both have matching golden scars over your hearts from when you saved each other?" Clare asked earnestly.

This was not going at all how Xander had planned. The last thing he wanted was to relive that day or be reminded whose love saved her and whose love had nearly cost her her life.

"It is," Cece said. "You can see the edge of mine right here."

Xander looked from the scar to her eyes, taking a sip of whiskey to try to rid himself of memories. Her cheeks warmed and her heartbeat kicked up.

"Gods! That is remarkable," Clare cooed. "I hope to love someone that much someday." She looked at Xander and sighed.

His chosen princess for the evening was laying it on a bit thick. Still, her fawning had its desired effect.

"I hope you all won't mind if I sweep my beautiful fiancée away for a dance," Rainer said.

"Oh my gods! I didn't know you were engaged. Let me see the ring," Clare said as she reached for Cece's hand, holding it up so the emerald flashed in the candlelight. "It's beautiful."

"Thank you. It was my mother's," Cece said.

Clare tilted her hand in different directions to get a better look. "How lovely to have a family heirloom."

"It is," Rainer said. "Her father gave it to me and told me he'd always hoped we would end up together. He knew it would mean so much for Cece to have that blessing from him, and he knew how much the ring meant to her."

The words were like a physical blow. Xander had always looked up to Leo Reznik, and it stung that he'd only approved of Xander because of Cece's endorsement, while whole-heartedly offering Rainer his approval.

Rainer met Xander's eye. Although the princesses were enthralled by the story, the message to Xander was clear. *I won. Back off.*

"Cecilia's father was a good man and a good judge of character," Xander said quietly. The words cost him, but he knew his place. Rainer was the nice guy, and he was the playboy king. "Well, I promised Princess Clare a drink, so I suppose we should do that, but I'd love to dance with you later, Princess Jessamin."

Jessamin smiled politely as he bowed. Xander led Clare toward the bar as Cece and Rainer wandered onto the dance floor.

Sipping a glass of bubble wine, Xander listened to Clare talk about her winter holiday celebrations in Aldrena. He tried to ignore his ex-wife, but he kept catching glimpses of her scarlet dress out of the corner of his eye. Some foolish part of him had hoped to feel less of a pull toward her, but that was too much to ask for.

He'd underestimated her anger. She'd made it clear that she chose Rainer, and deep down, Xander had always known she would. He didn't think she'd be so affected by his lack of correspondence. Though her letters had grown more frustrated over the months of silence, she'd also seemed to be more at peace.

"Princess?" He interrupted Clare's extensive discussion of winter florals.

She looked up at him with wide eyes, her cheeks growing rosy. "I'm talking too much, aren't I, Your Grace? I'm sorry. I'm so nervous."

"Why are you so nervous? It's just a ball."

Clare's shoulders relaxed from their ramrod posture. She laughed and shook her head. She gulped down the rest of her wine and placed the empty glass on a passing tray. "Forgive my frankness, Your Grace, but you are the only eligible king in years who hasn't been old enough to be my father. I don't mean to seem overeager, but I'd always hoped for a husband I'd have at least a little bit in common with. It's just a ball to you, but it's an opportunity for me to have a hint of the future I truly wanted for myself."

Xander held her gaze. Her sincerity was refreshing, and she was a beautiful woman. The old Xander probably would have absconded to some dark corner with her. But he had no idea what to do with her now. He was saved from having to decide when a redheaded princess glided up next to them.

The redhead leaned forward, her breasts nearly spilling out the top of her emerald dress as she curtseyed and batted her eyes at

Xander. She was young, a smattering of freckles dusting her nose, but she certainly wasn't shy.

"Princess—"

"Larissa," she said, holding out her hand and waiting for him to kiss it.

He took it and brushed a kiss to her knuckles. He'd barely skimmed the stack of details Evan passed along about the princesses, but he was fairly certain the only redhead in the group was the princess of Brevone.

"Your Grace," Larissa said. "It seems Princess Clare is content to keep you to herself, but some of the ladies of your court were mentioning what a spectacular dancer you were, and I just had to see for myself."

Xander had to hand it to Larissa. She was as bold in personality as she was in dress.

"Of course," Xander said. He turned to Clare. "Thank you for the lovely chat, Clare. I look forward to speaking more through the next few weeks of festivities."

Turning back to Larissa, he took her hand and led her to the dance floor, hoping to find Cece there. Instead, he spotted her giggling as she ducked out the door with Rainer.

Xander forced himself to smile as he spun Larissa around the floor, but his heart was no longer in it. It fled with Cece as it always did.

———

Sunlight blazed in the dining room windows, making Xander's head ache. He'd had far too much to drink at the ball and it made for a poor night's sleep.

"I had hoped you would have been more focused on your prospects than your past," Evan said, eyeing Xander over the rim of his mug.

Xander shrugged. "Then perhaps you should not have placed her in front of me. I have never been able to be in a room with her and keep my eyes off of her."

Evan frowned at his eggs, pushing them around his plate. "You seemed to hit it off with Larissa."

"Larissa was as expected. Very—" he waved a hand, "nice."

He knew Evan was beyond frustrated with him, but how could he explain that seeing Cece felt like the first moment in months he'd been able to take a deep breath? Her words in each letter had been an anchor, but the sight of her made him feel like he was actually alive.

Xander sipped his coffee. "My gods, that dress! It's like Cece wanted me to stare at her all night. She knows how much I love her in red."

Evan crossed his arms. "All men like a woman in red. I doubt she wore that dress for you."

"Of course she did. I've never seen her wear anything so daring. She looks spectacular."

Evan shook his head. "She didn't seem different to you?"

Xander froze. "Different how?"

"She never let Rainer out of her sight. I'm not sure exactly—"

"Don't hedge. Out with it."

Evan shrugged. "She seems more nervous than she was, even when she was here before. Sometimes when people have been through things like she has—"

"I don't need you to educate me on living through horrors, Evan. I've lived through plenty of my own," Xander snapped.

Xander's mind wandered to the night Evan found him up on the castle wall. He had waited for months for Evan to bring it up, but he remained watchful and stoic, never uttering another word about it.

Xander could not remember a time before knowing Evan. They'd grown up together, spent every day together, and yet it was always clear how they'd needed different strategies to thrive. Evan's success relied on temperance and careful calculation. Xander's was achieved exclusively through taking risks. He could not look at danger without first seeing possibility.

Evan stared at him, looking uncomfortable. He always paused for a moment like he was waiting for Teddy to say something insightful, then frowned when he remembered their friend was gone. Teddy's death had left a lull in all their conversations and a void in the easy rhythm the three of them always shared. He'd almost forgotten the way he and Evan had fought before Teddy had started tagging along like the annoying little brother in their friendship, inserting himself into every argument and seamlessly finding a way to bridge their communication gaps. Now they were too old, too busy, and too repressed to fix it.

"I know you know loss, but Cece is your blind spot," Evan said finally.

"Cece was herself when we spoke. She's never liked to be the center of attention. When they introduced us back at our engagement ball, I thought she was going to vomit in the middle of the dance floor. I wouldn't read into it."

Cece's presence was larger than life to Xander. Perhaps he had been blinded. Her letters had been happier in recent months, though it was clear she'd struggled early on. But it seemed impossible that Evan would see a change in her that Xander had missed.

Evan leaned forward in his seat. "What did you think of the princesses? You seemed to take to Princess Clare."

Xander laughed. "Is she the little blonde one? She's a bit much. No one is that nice."

"I thought you liked her."

Xander gave him a guilty smile.

"Oh, for fuck's sake, Xan. You promised you would actually try."

"I am."

"You're not. You just did it to make Cece jealous." Evan slammed his empty coffee cup down on the table. "Fuck, Xander. This is serious. I have been covering for you with everyone. I convinced Cal and Sylvie that you're taking this seriously. You can't be distracted by Cece. I told her it would help for her to be here, but if it won't, I'll ask her to leave, or you'll just scare her off by being, you know—" he flapped a hand at his friend, "you."

Xander laughed. "But that's who she fell in love with."

"Only because Rainer wasn't an option."

The words left Xander breathless from shock that Evan had spoken them.

"Did you forget that she's engaged? That she quite literally came back from death for someone else? Did you notice that they didn't leave each other's side all night? Did you see them dancing together? They're still disgustingly in love. Even Sylvie complains about it. Cecilia Reznik is lost to you, Xan."

"She's not married yet."

Evan shoved away from the table and closed the distance between them. "Well, I heard them fucking in the sitting room down the hall as soon as they left the ball. They couldn't even make it up a flight of stairs before being all over each other. You said you would let her go, and she's clearly let you go. It's time to face reality."

Xander met his icy stare but said nothing.

Evan stalked out of the room, slamming the door behind him, but Xander stayed in his seat, frozen in place by the cold reality.

15

EVAN

Evan cut down the side hall to the training room, where he wrapped his knuckles and punched the hanging grain bag until he was sweaty and exhausted. He leaned against the canvas sack as sweat dripped from his body, pooling in the cracks of the stone floor.

"Bad morning?"

He didn't need to turn to know Sylvie was there. He'd smelled her jasmine scent the moment she stepped into the doorway. She'd been watching for a while, but he was too mad to stop.

"What makes you say that?" he asked, turning to take her in.

Evan never thought he'd fall for someone who didn't differentiate between day and evening wear, but over time he'd seen how a dress could be a weapon, and Sylvie chose to always be prepared for a fight.

She looked stunning in a dark green gown that left one arm bare and the other covered in sheer lace. It flared out just below the waist, showing off her figure.

"This is a brand-new dress," she said. "Don't even think about doing anything other than admiring it from afar when you're that sweaty."

He closed the distance between them, imagining the dress in shreds on his office floor.

"And who will stop me?" He grasped her arm.

He was trying to get her to practice a deflection he'd been teaching her. She'd let her training slip, focusing instead on court intrigue, and while Evan appreciated the help, he also wanted her to be able to defend herself with so many strangers at court.

Instead of doing as he'd hoped, she bent her arm, drawing him into a kiss. He should have stopped her, but he pulled her flush against him and kissed her back.

Sylvie pulled away. "Are you all right?"

He nodded. No need to give her anger toward Xander more fuel. Defending his friend was a reflex born out of a lifetime of needing to, but at this point, he was tired of repeating excuses that even he didn't believe. There was no strategic advantage to reinforcing something she likely already suspected, and if he voiced Xander's desire to make Cecilia jealous, he'd just be offering Sylvie an opening to start up an old fight.

Most people seemed to be of the opinion that the previous evening had gone well, and it was true that Xander had been charming with the princesses. It was best to pretend Evan was satisfied with the night.

"I was just concerned with how Hank fared at such an event," he teased.

Hank the Houseplant was their inside joke. Because Sylvie liked to keep a clear head at parties, she only drank one glass of wine per event. The rest she'd carry and pretend to sip but instead would dump in Hank's pot when no one was looking. Evan had noticed it because of the pattern she took moving through the ballroom and finally caught her red-handed months earlier.

As if reading his thoughts, Sylvie slid her hand into his and shared the memory of the first time they talked about Hank. He wondered if she understood what trust he placed in her and the surrender it took to feel the gentle press of her magic on his mind and let her in. One of his memories came to life.

———

"Lady Brett, you're killing that poor plant."

She paused mid-pour and smiled at Evan. "Hank can take it," she replied.

"Hank?" Evan said, trying not to laugh.

"Yes, he's an ally and confidant. I give him my drinks so he doesn't get bored at the party."

Evan stared at her, trying to puzzle out if she was joking. He didn't know as much about magic as he should, and it was possible that earth witches truly spoke to plants.

"Gods, your face," she laughed. "I'm joking. Honestly, how are you in charge of so much but know so little about magic?"

"I don't know. I assume you have some way of communicating with them."

Her face softened in surprise. Evan loved watching her expressions. He was learning Sylvie like a new language, and he enjoyed the moments when he got past her perfect armor.

"It's not my strongest magic, so I don't think I feel them the way a natural earth witch would. But I suppose they do have a language. It's kind of like a pulse around them. Some are strong and loud. Others are soft and faint."

Evan eyed the wilted plant. "Hank looks to be a little weak today."

She giggled. "Don't worry. I come back and fix him in the mornings. I try not to do magic in public. I find it's best not to remind the council I'm more than I seem."

Evan met her gaze, and understanding passed between them. He was constantly underestimating her head for strategy. He supposed that was the point. She was beautiful, and if she could get men to pay attention to her astonishing beauty, they wouldn't be paying attention to how she worked them. He'd seen it enough that he should have been immune, but he was ruined for her.

"So, what type of plant is he?" Evan asked.

She shrugged.

"Aren't you supposed to know every plant as someone with earth witch powers?" he questioned.

"Do you know every swordplay move ever invented as a hunter?" she countered.

He grinned. "I suppose not."

"I make it a point to know the poisonous ones."

"So you can kill them?" he asked.

She grinned wickedly. "No, so I can use them to imprison and torture my enemies."

Evan laughed along with her. "Now, that is something I'd truly like to see."

———

Evan blinked his eyes open and met Sylvie's icy blue gaze. "And how is Hank this morning?"

"He is no worse for the wear," she sighed. "You, on the other hand, look like you've gone a few too many rounds with that grain bag." She gestured to his bloody, bandaged knuckles.

He sighed and unwrapped them, allowing her to clean and heal them.

"Is the king not behaving himself?" she asked, keeping her focus on the split skin of his knuckles.

"He's fine."

"I'm not sure Cece helped with her scandalous dress. Good for her for stepping it up style-wise and showing off what the gods gave her, but she chose a particularly interesting moment to do so."

"Do you think she was trying to make a statement?" Evan asked, trying to keep from sounding too interested.

"I think I've never seen Cece show off so much skin. Can't say for sure whose benefit it was for, but the timing is curious. Now, of course, I haven't seen her in close to a year, so it's possible she was running around like that at home as well. But—"

"But?"

"But I saw the way she captured Xander's full attention," Sylvie said pointedly.

"I'm working on it. He liked Princess Clare and Princess Jessamin."

"I think I have a crush on Princess Jessamin," Sylvie said seriously. "That dress! I don't think I've ever seen a woman walk into a foreign court like she owned the place."

Evan cocked an eyebrow. "I have."

"Don't flirt," she scolded, but she couldn't hide a satisfied smile.

That was how Sylvie worked. If he fell all over himself, like he very easily could have, she would have been bored. He needed to be honest but not effusive, and sweet to her in specific moments that didn't put too much weight on her beauty but also didn't ignore it. She was a complicated puzzle that he thrilled at solving. Most importantly, he trusted her. He'd never let a memory witch into his mind for good reason. He was the kingdom spymaster and even though he'd set up contingencies to compartmentalize the most important knowledge, it was a huge risk to let her into his inner circle and his mind. But she never pushed further than he allowed, much as he could tell she wanted to.

"I saw the library signal on my way here," she said.

It was a code they'd set up with the internal castle spy network. A flower petal was placed on the mantel of the fireplace at the front of the library. Its position showed the time the message would be delivered. The library meant it would be in a specific book on a shelf by the secret passage in the back row. Easier for the messenger to get in and out unseen.

"It's set for ten this morning. Do you want to handle it, or should I?" she asked.

He cupped her cheek. "You look far too lovely to get cobwebs on that pretty dress."

She frowned. "I know you want to keep me out of danger. Just make sure you're not also keeping me in the dark."

She kissed his cheek and left.

As he wandered back toward his room, he worried what news the message would bring.

———

Evan knew something was wrong as soon as he entered the passageway behind the library. He rarely met with his spies face to face, choosing instead to leave coded messages in specified locations. When he followed the instructions from the note stored in volume two of the library's *A Brief History of Olney*, he found Reese Reynolds waiting for him in the dark passage.

He paused, Reese's break in protocol setting him on edge. He wasn't truly suspicious of Reese, but he couldn't fight the fissure of doubt that had formed in his mind after the fire witch he'd vetted had made an attempt on Xander's life months ago.

Reese had reason to be angry with Evan and Xander. They'd failed his little brother. People had switched allegiances for less.

Still, Evan could not imagine Reese thinking that Vincent was a better possibility—not when he knew the havoc the usurper was creating.

"What are you doing here?" Evan asked.

"This couldn't wait," Reese said. "I just got back from meeting with one of our messengers."

Messengers were what they called spies in the field.

"It's confirmed. Two of Olney's ancient witches who created the Gauntlet are missing—Ash Rivers and Petra Ryan Light."

"So whoever it was doesn't have the Olney seer?" Evan asked.

Reese nodded. "Correct, but that's only half of the problem. Lumen Ing, is missing as well."

"The slayer program has been disbanded. Who would have use of a slayer as gifted as Lumen?"

It was a stupid question. He knew exactly who would have use of one: Vincent Savero.

A slayer was a talented memory witch who could extract memories with a touch and leave a person a drooling husk. They were experts at torture and information extraction. But the training and development of memory witches in Argaria had changed post-Gauntlet and they no longer used their magic in such a vicious way.

"I still haven't figured out why, but it's extremely unsettling," Reese said. "Those witches hold the most potent magic in the two kingdoms. If they fell under the wrong influence—"

Though most witches were fully mortal, several of the oldest witches in Olney were sustained by their magic over the centuries. Most of them did favors for the gods in exchange for longer lives. They weren't immortal, but they aged slower, and they had the wisdom and magical knowledge to show for it. They were invaluable resources to both Olney and Argaria.

"There were signs of struggle. It does not appear that they left willingly," Reese said.

Evan leaned his head back against the stone wall in the narrow passageway. "Fuck. What could do that?"

"I suppose other ancient witches or—"

"Or what?" Evan asked, meeting Reese's gaze in the dim light.

"Or a god," Reese finished.

"But all the living gods are dead. What use would an ascended god have for witches?"

Evan didn't like thinking of the possibilities. After all, witches had created the Gauntlet, which was a way to store godly powers.

"And to what end? The ascended gods are too weak to do much damage in our realm," Evan said.

Reese shrugged. "Perhaps they don't want power in our realm."

Evan's eyebrows shot up at the thought. A war among the gods in the Otherworld wouldn't be good for anyone. Still, the timing of it didn't make sense.

"But why *now*? Why take a slayer too? I assume there were similar signs of struggle in Lumen's home? Lumen is a fierce fighter."

Reese nodded. "That's what leads me to suspect that it must be Vincent."

Evan wanted to scream or break something. How was Vincent moving through their kingdom so easily undetected? How was he always a step ahead of them? Did he want to steal godly magic for himself?

"Is that all?" Evan asked.

Reese frowned, and Evan was struck for a moment at how much he looked like Teddy. Grief rose unexpectedly each time he spoke to Reese. Teddy would have loved this kind of intrigue, and he would have been great at it. He was a friendly, smiling face that no one would have suspected. Although they looked alike, Reese's eyes were too clever, and while he played the part of a playboy aristocrat, anyone trained would notice that he was more intelligent than he let on.

"That's not all," Reese said. "Spellman has brought his daughter to court, but he's also sought permission to keep more men here due to her presence. I don't like it."

Evan didn't like it either. The man was conniving, but Evan had to grant the request. Lady Eloise Spellman was a great beauty and would carry an exceptionally high dowry. Although court was likely the safest place for her, it wouldn't be out of the question for someone to try to snatch her for ransom.

"As much as I dislike the idea of giving him more power here, I can't stand the thought of something happening to Eloise and having to explain why a lady wasn't safe in Xander's court," Evan said. "All hell will break loose. With all these border spats, the last thing we need is for things to seem unstable within castle walls. The court is already frustrated enough with Xander's rule, and we don't need to give them another thing to be angry about."

Reese nodded. "I wouldn't put it above Spellman to have his own daughter kidnapped just to prove a point."

The words sent a fresh wave of worry through Evan. If that thought had occurred to Reese after spending months on the court council with him, it no doubt had occurred to Lord Spellman as well.

Evan sighed. "I just need to get through this festival."

"Well, that's the other thing. The timing of this is all very convenient," Reese said.

"You think that some supporters of Vincent managed to sneak in with one of the visiting princesses? They've all been thoroughly vetted."

But so was Elle. Evan didn't like the paranoia settling into his body. It was maddening to work so hard and still not know who to trust.

Reese ran a hand through his hair and leaned an elbow against the wall. "Yes, but it's much the same as Vincent. How can we vet someone if we have no clue what they're supposed to look like? Princess Jessamin is a warrior. I watched her train this morning. She's remarkable. She is set to lead the Novumi army if she doesn't make a match with Xander. Does she even want to get married? Seems she has more power without getting married. Why give it up to tie herself to a man?"

Evan considered it. The timing made sense, but he doubted Vincent would hide an asset somewhere so obvious.

"Also, one of my spies reports that Vincent has a personal bone to pick with Xander. Although people rarely gossip about it now the way they did in the past, most people know there was a falling-out between Damian and William, Xander's uncle, after he tried to take the throne," Reese said.

Evan nodded. "Yes, years ago. If you ask me, Damian was a bit cruel. Rather than have him put to death, Damian banished him and Vincent to the eastern wastes near the border—which is basically a death sentence without having to dirty your hands."

Reese frowned. "Do you have any idea why William tried to take over to begin with?"

Evan shrugged. "Damian didn't offer much of an explanation, but why would he have? Xander and I were still young. He wasn't going to explain his thinking to children."

"Apparently there's a story going around Vincent's army," Reese started. "That William was concerned that Damian was ignoring his people's well-being and continuing the war with Olney for the sake of his ego. They claim just before William was banished, King Hector of Olney had offered a truce that Damian wouldn't take. William begged him to take it for the well-being of the kingdom. He pressed hard for it, even asking the general and Huntmaster

Ducrane to throw their considerable weight behind a truce. That was all it took. Damian thought William was coming for his throne and banished him without any ceremony. William allegedly died a few years later, leaving Vincent to fend for himself with a small contingent, and his army has grown along with his resentment. It seems this is personal and he's trying to make himself a man of the people."

Evan felt torn. Damian had been like a father to him, but even as a child he could see the king's shortcomings. He had a tendency to ignore his advisors and make decisions purely for the sake of ego rather than for the good of his people. Evan never questioned it, but now that he was helping Xander run the kingdom, he could see Damian's flaws in sharper focus. Reese's story made sense to him.

"We need to be very careful about the festival events," Reese said.

"We just need to get through the few weeks and—if the gods have mercy on us—the wedding, and then I will feel like we can handle whatever is thrown at us."

Evan knew as a strategist that the time for an enemy to strike was now, not once Xander solidified his strength in the role of king. He knew it was wisest to strike while things were as chaotic as possible.

"I'll inform the rest of the group. We'll need all the help we can get."

"I'd like to meet her," Reese said.

"Cece?" Evan asked.

"Yes. My brother only spoke about her briefly just before he died, but I could tell he was fond of her, and from what you've said, she eased his crossing."

Evan swallowed hard, trying to put the vision of Teddy's death out of his mind—as if his failure wasn't burned into his brain. "She did. Better than any of us could have. I'll let her know. I'm sure she'd be happy to speak with you."

"Well, that's everything I have right now, and I need to be getting back for luncheon with the lords of the court. As if lunch is an excuse to get shit-faced on whiskey in the middle of the day," Reese sighed, pushing off the wall.

Evan shook his hand. "Thank you, Reese. I don't know what we would do without you."

"No thanks necessary. It's what Teddy sacrificed for. Just promise you will all make his sacrifice worth it."

"We're trying," Evan sighed.

He wanted to honor Teddy's memory just as much, but they'd been fighting a losing battle for a year with no real reprieve. If this didn't work out, he had no idea how he could secure a victory for Xander.

16

CECILIA

After their reunion in the stable the night before, Cecilia was unsurprised to find a summons from Xander to meet him after lunch the following day. Her anxiety buzzed as she paced around the room, getting ready.

She could have ignored it, but she needed to give him the last warded ring Devlin had given her. After much debate, she decided that since she was with Rainer all the time, she could protect him, but Xander was much more at risk. He'd been punished enough by godly influence, and two kingdoms relied on him to keep his mind clear.

Cecilia's anxiety was made worse by the reply from Marcos that morning. It was waiting on her nightstand when she woke up, and she grabbed it before Rainer could notice.

Cece – Haven't had any more nightmares. Thank you. – M

Short and sweet and enough to send her anxious mind spinning. She was half-tempted to try the ring herself and see if it kept her night-mares at bay.

Still, it solidified her decision to give the other ring to Xander.

Just in case, she told herself, even as dread crept into the back of her mind.

A knock sounded on the door. Sena stepped inside, holding note and a box wrapped in a bright red ribbon.

"Oh gods, what is it?" Rainer asked, looking up from his tea.

Cecilia untied the ribbon and opened the box to find a blue glass bottle. She popped the stopper, and the scent of vanilla filled the air.

"It's my favorite bath oil," she said with a smile.

Rainer looked affronted that he didn't know something about her.

Underneath the bottle was a beautiful and clearly expensive bit of lacy pale green lingerie that left almost nothing to the imagination.

Xander's behavior grew more puzzling. She needed to air every-thing out with him once and for all so she could focus on the task at hand and get through his wedding.

A nervous giggle burst from her lips as she read the enclosed card.

My beautiful Cece – So you can smell as delicious as you'll look in these bits of lace. A gift for you that's as much a gift for me since I won't be able to stop thinking about what you're wearing underneath your next daring dress. Feel free to model it for me anytime. – X

Rainer read it over her shoulder. "I'm going to punch him in his smug face."

"Don't give him the satisfaction. I warned you that you would just make it worse if you let him see your jealousy. He just wants a reac-tion," Cecilia sighed.

She sniffed the bottle again. It was a test. If she used the oil, Xander would assume she did it for him. He'd also assume she wore the lingerie. If she didn't use it, he'd assume that he'd ruffled her.

"Are you going to use it?" Rainer asked.

She laughed. "Of course. Xander will read into it either way, so I may as well enjoy it."

"And will you wear this?" Rainer asked, lifting the skimpy green lace slip.

She grinned. "Now that depends on you and if you'll be on your best behavior today."

He let out a breath and his shoulders relaxed. "That's motivating."

Cecilia ducked into the bathing chamber and enjoyed soaking in the hot vanilla-scented water. When she came out in the green slip, Rainer pulled her into his arms.

"You do smell delicious. Are you sure you need to go meet him? I'd love to have you to myself," he said as his hands roamed over the green lace.

"Rain," she chided, swatting at his hands and stepping into her dress. "You've already had me this morning."

"And yet, I still want you again," he said.

"You'll get to enjoy this later. We came here for a reason. Let's get this figured out so we can escape this terrible, cold place."

He helped her button a gown over the delicate lace, kissing up her spine as he fastened each button. By the time he got to the top button, she was ready to tell him to undo all his hard work and take the dress off. He brushed her hair over her shoulder and kissed her neck.

She stared at the reflection of the two of them in the looking glass: Rainer in his dark blue velvet tunic and she in her dove-gray dress. It was different than what she typically wore, but the seamstress insisted it was all the rage. The bodice was made of lace embroidered with sparkling pearls that went down the sleeves with a cascading, ruffled tulle skirt. She tended to wear more form-fitting silhouettes because of her smaller stature, but she liked how the tulle moved with her.

"It's a little much. Might slow me down," Cecilia said, twisting from side to side as the dress swished.

Rainer arched a brow. "Is this all I had to do when you were younger? Put you in a big dress so you couldn't run off too far, too fast?"

She laughed. "Maybe."

She pinned the front of her hair back and escaped the room before Rainer could make a mess of it.

Cecilia walked down the hall to Xander's sitting room. She smoothed her dress, taking a grounding breath before stepping inside.

Xander looked up from the pile of papers and bowl of strawberries on his desk. His eyes lit up.

"My love. You're a bit early." He crossed the room and bent to kiss her hand. "You look and smell incredible."

"I know."

He laughed. "Are you wearing everything I sent?" His gaze dipped, and she held perfectly still like a doe caught in the gaze of a wolf.

For all they had been through, when Cecilia saw Xander, her heart didn't put him into the box reserved for people who broke her. Her traitorous heart still raced as if it forgot their history, forgot his lies, forgot the way he ruined her. Her heart only remembered that Xander protected her when it counted and that he'd let her go so she could be happy. No matter how hard she tried to convince herself he was in the box labeled "friends," her heart refused to move so easily.

He took a bite of a strawberry and licked away the juice. Cecilia couldn't help but stare at his lips and think about the way he kissed like he wanted to consume her.

Guilt swelled in her chest. *It's just nostalgia. It's just body memory. It will fade.*

As if reading her mind, Xander grinned. He stepped closer as his gaze dropped to her mouth. He smiled wider, and she cursed, realizing that he heard the way her pulse kicked up in his presence.

You used to love him, you stupid heart.

Xander twirled one of her curls around his fingers. "So soft."

Used to? her heart seemed to ask. She knew as he stepped closer that "used to" was a lie she told herself to keep her life less complicated. She was in love and engaged to someone else. Someone who made her world stop. Someone she'd quite literally come back from death to be with. She knew in her heart that Rainer was the love of her life, beyond a shadow of a doubt.

Yet when Cecilia looked into Xander's eyes, she wondered how she could be certain of anything other than the fact that he was the most infuriating, potent temptation she'd ever laid eyes on. She'd missed him terribly.

"I need to talk to you about something," she said.

"I know what you're thinking about, love," Xander whispered, lips grazing her ear. "I know that expression like the back of my hand. I have seen it many times before."

"Bullshit."

He drew back and cocked an eyebrow as he leaned against the table. "Oh really? Because you only make that innocent little face when you want to inspire your favorite talent of mine."

"How can I pick a favorite when you have so many worthy talents?" she asked.

He laughed, his eyes brightening with mischief. "You're thinking about me laying you down on that desk, hiking up that ridiculously frilly dress, and peeling your little lace undergarments off with my mouth. You're thinking about my lips tracing over your hip bone and my teeth nipping up your inner thighs and my tongue sliding inside you. I'd be happy to oblige, love. You know how I love to make you scream my name. It never sounds as sweet as it does when you shout it in the throes."

A violent flush lit her whole body. "That will not be necessary, and that is not what I'm thinking about."

Although it is now. The memory of the way his lips could spark everything sleeping in her body to life did not feel quite as distant as she'd expected.

"Want to know what I'm thinking about?" he asked.

A challenge, and one Cecilia could not win.

"No," she said flatly.

Xander just laughed. "Too bad, I'm king. I'm thinking about letting you ruin me—wishing I could ruin you back." He sighed. "I'm thinking about you keeping your eyes locked on mine as you drop to your knees and take me between those perfect lips. I'm thinking about how turned on you get from seeing me so helpless in your hot little mouth. I'm thinking about how you can't help but touch yourself while you taste me. I'm thinking about you moaning around my cock while you play with yourself, and it's making me want you very, very badly right now."

How did Xander Savero make her simultaneously so frustrated and so hot? The heat of her flush emanated off her body in waves, and Xander simply ran his fingers over her cheek.

"Gods, I missed that," Xander sighed. "I love all the things that make your skin pink. Making you blush, seeing you flushed from exertion after I make you come, seeing my handprint on your bottom after I spank you for being a wicked little thing."

She cursed herself for ending up alone with him. He had a way of making her feel so incredibly dirty. It was disorienting, and her body seemed unsure whether to be angry, turned on, or both.

"There it is, that anger in those eyes. That's what I've been waiting for," Xander whispered. "You might love the dirty talk, Cece, but I love that hint of defiance in your eyes because it ends the same way—"

"With you in your bed alone, wishing you'd been sweet instead of an ass?" she asked.

He laughed. "No, with you clenching around me like a vise while I bury myself so deep inside you that you don't know where you end and I begin—or with your hand between your legs alone in your bed, wishing you'd let me do just that."

Cecilia stumbled toward the door. She had forgotten the way it felt like her body was an instrument Xander was born to play. A light touch here, a whisper there—he could read the melody running through her and bring it to a crescendo with a brush of his fingers. It was a terribly inconvenient talent.

"Love?"

She realized she'd stopped moving. Her gaze connected with Xander's. It suddenly felt impossible to ask the question she'd traveled across two kingdoms to ask—*Why did you ignore me for a year?*

Maybe she was afraid to know the answer, but now she just needed to get away from him.

"I was just leaving. This was a mistake. I—"

She pushed through the door and ran down the hall. She made a few turns before looking back momentarily to see if Xander followed, only to crash into a firm chest.

Rainer. She knew before she drew away and met his eyes.

"I was looking for you," he said. He rubbed his sternum. "You were sad, I think—"

Sad and confused, and too afraid of the answers to the questions I want to ask, she wanted to tell him, but it all felt clotted in her chest and she was afraid that tearing it loose would do more harm than good.

So she pulled Rainer into a kiss, drawing away when she was breathless. "Take me to bed. I don't want to do anything else today. I just want to be with you."

Rainer frowned. "Is this about Xander?"

"No," she assured him. "Being back here brings up a lot. I don't quite know how I feel, but I want to feel good. I just want to be close to you, and I don't want to see anyone else."

Rainer's face clouded with concern. "Is it the grief?"

"No. Yes? I'm not sure. It's a little of everything. Nostalgia, grief, joy, relief. I just want more of that. I want to be close to you because when I feel overwhelmed, that is all I want."

He nodded, a glint of lust in his eyes. "You, in that dress. It's almost as good as you out of that dress, which is what I want as soon as we get back to our room."

He led her back to their room and she gave him exactly what he wanted.

17

XANDER

Courting was not for the faint of heart. Xander rubbed his jaw, sore from forcing a smile through a two-hour brunch with the princesses. Why anyone needed to sit and eat for that long was beyond him, but his manners were clearly lacking. There had been a few raised eyebrows and Sylvie had spent most of the meal glaring at him from the other end of the table.

It was difficult when he was distracted. He was happy to be back in the privacy of his rooms where he could frown all he wanted and Mika wouldn't say anything.

His friend sat poised on the bed, toying with the edge of her lace robe.

Xander knew he'd come on too strong the day before, but he couldn't slow down when it came to Cece. He had so little time before the courting began in earnest and he wanted to use it to clear the air with his ex-wife. He'd summoned her to his room for a surprise.

He paced, impatiently waiting. Would Cece ignore his request? She'd be the only one so bold as to ignore a king. She might be angry. She might ignore him the rest of her time there. The thought made him feel sick to his stomach.

She burst into the room unannounced and spared him further worry.

She drew up short upon seeing him shirtless. Her lips parted, and she drew in a breath, looking away. She blushed, tugging the hem of her pink sweater down over her dark leggings.

"You can look your fill, love. Nothing you haven't seen before many times," he teased as he tugged on a shirt. "I'm glad you felt familiar enough to enter without knocking."

"She's just making herself at home," Mika purred from the bed.

Cece's eyes darted to Mika. A flurry of emotions crossed her face —confusion, shock, and then anger.

Mika played the part perfectly. Xander was relieved that his moment of weakness on the castle wall months ago hadn't scared her off. She climbed onto her knees at the edge of the bed, allowing her robe to slip and show the swell of her lace-covered breasts.

"It's nice to meet you, Lady Reznik. The king sings your praises. He spoke of your beauty, but he certainly did not do it justice," Mika said, trailing her fingers over her collarbone.

Cece's blush bloomed brighter, her neck and chest turning bright red as she met Xander's eye. "Is this what I've been summoned for? To watch you with some other woman? I came to help you, not play your games, *Your Majesty.*"

"Just call me Xander, love."

She pursed her lips. "That wouldn't be appropriate, *Your Grace.* I'm no longer your wife."

"Doesn't being the king mean you have to listen to me for once?" Xander asked.

"You're not my king."

Xander frowned. "What if I'd like to be?"

The question hung between them heavily.

She licked her lips and frowned at him. "What did you need, Your Majesty? Or did you just want me to bear witness to this performance art?"

"Are you jealous?" Xander didn't bother to hide his delight.

"Why would I be jealous?"

He wasn't deterred. "Mika is simply a dear friend, and we have great conversations. Isn't that right, Mika?"

"It is, Xan." Mika grinned.

Cece's eyes went wide at the nickname, and he saw real jealousy on her face for the first time. "So you just talk? About what?"

"Life. Love. Loss," Xander said.

Cece looked from Mika to him with pure betrayal in her eyes.

He was disappointed that she was more upset with him for sharing stories and intimate details of his life with someone else than sleeping with them. He should have realized that would bother her more.

"Well, I suppose it's easy to make great conversation with you when she's getting paid for her hard labor," Cece huffed.

Xander barked out a laugh. "You know your jealousy only serves to turn me on, Cece."

She rolled her eyes. "Everything turns you on."

"Everything you do does."

"Except writing you letters, apparently."

He truly hadn't meant to hurt her so badly by not replying, though now it seemed obvious to him what a mistake it was. She saw it as rejection. He was shocked that his beautiful Cece could ever think he didn't want her.

"I have something for you, but we need to be alone," she said quietly.

Xander's eyebrows shot up, but he waved Mika off. Mika smiled as she pulled her robe closed and left the room.

Cece reached into her pocket and pulled out a ring, holding it out to him in her palm.

"Is this a proposal, love? Because if so, it's a bad one," he whispered.

The joke broke the tension between them. She'd used those same words on him when he moronically proposed to her years before in a cabin in the mountains. Xander was swept up in her as he always was—as he remained—and the words flew out of his mouth before he could stop them. He'd meant them. His mouth was always ahead of his brain, which was always a step behind his heart.

She'd put him in his place for his poor planning, and rightfully so. If he could do it all over again, he'd do something bold and clever. It wasn't the extravagance that she valued, but thoughtfulness.

"It's a gift. Take it how you will," Cece said, interrupting his thoughts as she slid the golden band onto his right ring finger.

"The answer would be yes, you know."

She tossed her hair and grinned. "Of course it would. I'm spectacular."

He wanted to tease her for her arrogance, but a strange surge of power around the ring stopped him in his tracks.

"It's magic," he murmured. "What does it do?"

"It's warded against the powers of a god."

Xander's eyes went wide. His mind spun too fast for him to process. Rainer didn't have one. He'd checked Rainer's hands as soon as they arrived to make sure he and Cece hadn't eloped.

"Why me?" he asked, dumbfounded.

"Because you lead a kingdom, and I need your beautiful, twisted mind to be clear. You've been through enough godly influence."

Xander eyed her skeptically. "All the living gods are gone. Why do I need protection?"

"It's just a precaution, and the bonus is that it keeps me out of your head."

"As if I could ever keep you out. What if I want you in my head?"

She worried her lower lip between her teeth. Dread sank its claws into him.

"Cece, what aren't you saying?" he asked.

"Nothing. I wanted to ensure you and Marcos were extra careful. You have one, and so do Marcos and Anders. If I'd had more, I'd give them to all of you, but I wanted to make sure the kingdoms were protected during this chaotic time. If anyone asks, it was a gift from me when we were together. Never take it off unless I tell you to, and when I do, you'll ask for the password."

"What's the password?" he asked.

"Reldan."

He sucked in a breath. That first dance they'd shared was as imprinted on his body as it was on his memory.

"Easy to remember," she whispered.

"More like impossible to forget," he rasped.

The desire to kiss her was an ache in his bones. He brushed his fingers over her cheek, but she slunk away. He'd need to do more to bring her out of her shell and stoke her competitive spirit.

He should have been more serious. She'd just given him a tremendous gift that meant more to him than words could express. He could communicate in other ways if she'd let him, but he wasn't about to push his luck when she seemed so skittish.

Words had always failed him with Cece. She was something more felt than spoken. Xander truly did not know how to tell her how much it meant to him without the language of touch, kiss, and skin on skin. With his lips on her skin, he could tell her so many things. Long ago, he'd made a map of her body, a place for *I love you*, a place for *I'm sorry*, a place for regrets and longing and loss and grief and joy and hope. He knew how to move with her, hold her, and touch her to make her feel loved, but without access to such intimate means of communication, he was at a loss.

It was part of the reason he'd failed to write back to her for so long. It wasn't for lack of wanting to. It was for lack of having the language to describe magic.

So he did the foolish thing and dragged her into another one of his games. He couldn't help it. If he stopped playing, Cece would stop playing with him. He had three weeks to pick a new wife, and all he could do was pine hopelessly over the one he'd lost.

"Follow me. I need your help with something," Xander said, making his way out of the room and down the hall. He hated himself for doing it, but he did it all the same.

They walked for a while until they made it outside near what looked like hunter training grounds. Xander smirked as he walked over to a group of hunters practicing knots.

"I was hoping that you could help me with my knotwork. I remember you had a particular talent for it," he said.

Cece eyed him suspiciously, but she wouldn't back down from a game of chicken.

"I'd be happy to help if you're feeling rusty, Your Majesty. You must be so busy with ruling that you've forgotten your basic training. What a shame," she quipped.

She held out her arms, and Xander smiled at her. He firmly wrapped the rope around her wrists. Cece struggled to keep her heart rate even.

"What do I do next?" he asked.

"Tuck the ends through the center knot," she said.

Xander continued to play dumb as she told him how to create the knot. He looked down at her bound hands and then back up at her eyes when he was done.

"Is it too tight? I wouldn't want it to chafe your wrists," he said, running a finger up her forearm. Goosebumps rose on her skin in the wake of his touch.

"No, it's perfect," she said. She refused to look away from Xander's eyes. She licked her lips, and he swallowed hard.

"How does it feel to be helpless?"

"I've never been helpless in my life," she said, feigning confidence.

He leaned in close, her breath dancing over his cheek as she held perfectly still.

"Cece, thank you for this ring. I wish I could express the peace it brings to know that what happened before cannot happen again," he whispered, his lips brushing her ear.

She shuddered and pulled back. He got too close, too fast, and the magic was gone.

"How would you get out of a binding like this?" Xander asked.

"You could just untie me."

"Where's the fun in that?" He grinned.

Then he pulled out his sword and swung at her. Cece spun to the side, grabbed his dagger from his waist, and tossed it aside. He swung out again with his sword, and she jumped back. He sliced down, and Cece caught the flat side of the blade with her foot, then brought her elbow to his chin. His head snapped back, and she swiped her binding along the blade, cutting her hands free before diving for the dagger. She rolled to the side and then threw the blade at him.

He dropped his sword and caught the dagger just in time. The entire group of hunters had stopped their training and stood staring at them.

Xander laughed. "You are still magnificent."

"And you are still a reckless idiot," she huffed, climbing to her feet.

Xander's guards had no idea what to make of the exchange. He waved them off.

Cece stared at him, breathing hard. He thought he'd enjoy riling her up, but the heat in her eyes made it nearly impossible not to pounce on her.

They stood frozen in place, locked in a staring contest neither seemed intent on breaking. She looked away first and it left Xander feeling empty instead of victorious.

———

Sylvie's blonde hair bobbed as she scribbled something in her leather-bound notebook. She was always writing in that thing. Xander was dying to read it, but he'd not yet figured out where she hid it when she wasn't using it. It was below him to antagonize her, but it was her fault for making it so fun.

Xander leaned back in the chair and closed his eyes. This was the one moment of reprieve he'd have the whole day. As soon as he left the quiet of the sitting room, he would need to be on his best behavior.

Sylvie closed the notebook and tucked it under her arm. She leaned her hip against the card table and met Xander's eye. "You will take Eloise Spellman for a pleasant horseback ride of an appropriate length—"

"I'm known for my long and strenuous rides, and my length is entirely inappropriate. I'm a lot to take, or so I've been told," Xander said.

"Of course you have, *Your Majesty*," Sylvie said, not missing a beat.

Xander loved to verbally spar with her. "Are you implying that my lovers would lie to me?"

"Are you foolish enough to think they wouldn't?"

"Perhaps we need another opinion. We could get Evan in here to explain to me how he keeps you satisfied with the appropriate length of his rides—" Xander said, looking toward the sitting room door.

"If you let Evan hear you talking to me about your length or his rides, he'll have you on your ass before you can finish the sentence. Now, tell me you understand." She gave him an exasperated smile. "Xander, I know you to be a compelling and charming man when you want to be. Please, just for the next couple weeks, use that power for good."

Xander grinned. As much as he liked to wind Sylvie up for sport, he liked it better that she treated him no differently than she would anyone else at court. Even Evan showed a bit more deference now, even when they were alone, and Xander hated that.

"If you do anything this first week, please give Eloise your attention, even if for a moment. Her father is an absolute nightmare to deal with and if you at least give her one date, I can make a case that you've done your due diligence," Sylvie said. "When you've returned from your ride, I have arranged a lovely winter garden wine tasting for you and Princess Larissa of Brevone. Not only does she love the winter roses, but her parents import sweet wines from us because she enjoys them so much. I figured she'd like to taste the latest vintages."

"Can't wait," Xander said sarcastically. "You know how I live for sweet wines."

"Oh yes. Please regale me with a tale of how you are a long-suffering rich man who could bathe in that wine if he wished to—"

"Is that an option?" Xander asked. "It might help bolster my temperament."

"If the last year is any indication, alcohol does nothing good for your temperament. It makes you sulky and boring."

Xander laughed. Evan was wise to send Sylvie to see him off on this full day of dates. She was not as easily deterred as the rest of them. He enjoyed the challenge.

"And what lovely evening date will I have tonight?"

"You'll just have to wait and see. Now come here and let me fix your ridiculous hair."

Xander feigned offense. "My hair is perfect."

"Fine, go enjoy your date."

Xander grinned and crossed the room to stand in front of her. Sylvie was perhaps the only woman who had ever been wholly unaffected by his nearness. For every other woman, he'd been a handsome prince or a rogue hunter, but to Sylvie he was a project, and she was nothing if not meticulous about her projects.

She ran her fingers through his short waves, taming them into something he'd not be able to replicate himself. The wildness of his hair had worked for him as a hunter, but as a king he'd noticed that ladies in the court were less impressed.

Sylvie stepped back and admired her handiwork. "Perfect."

Xander winked. "It's about time you admitted it."

She turned him toward the door and gave him a light shove. "Go now or you'll be late."

Xander tried to mentally prepare himself for a date as he walked out to the stables. The truth was that he'd never actually been on one. Seduction came naturally when he was a hunter, but it seemed it was a more complicated game as a king.

Xander stepped out into a brisk breeze. He'd hated winter for most of his life, but he had to admit that it felt like home. He loved the way the winter sunsets were more colorful, and the smell before snow always brought him back to his childhood. But mostly he loved that it felt like a part of him had never left and was ready to reemerge as the weather in the mountains turned.

He silently thanked the gods when he got to the stables and

found Eloise Spellman in riding breeches and not a dress. He could not handle a slow sidesaddle stroll.

She dipped into a curtsey and smiled at him. "Good afternoon, Your Grace."

"You ride, Eloise?" he asked, bending to kiss her hand.

"I love to ride." She cleared her throat and glanced toward her father's guards, who were stationed by the stable entrance. "I haven't actually been able to get out much since coming to live at court because my father thinks it's not becoming of a lady."

Xander grinned. Clearly, Sylvie had thoughts on that opinion and that was why she'd assigned Eloise this date. He'd been expecting to have to help her, but Eloise wasn't interested in playing damsel and he was grateful for that. This date was already going better than expected since it served the dual purpose of actually being an activity Xander enjoyed while also antagonizing his most annoying council adversary.

"And who is this?" he asked, gesturing to her black stallion. It was a beautiful beast and certainly not a beginner rider's kind of horse.

"His name is Midnights," Eloise said as the horse nudged her shoulder with his nose. "He is sweeter than he looks. And who will you be riding?"

Xander took the reins from the stable master. "This is Biscuit."

Eloise barely stifled a laugh. "Biscuit? Meaning no offense, Your Grace, but I'd expected the king would have a horse with a fiercer name."

"Yes, a friend thought it was quite amusing to name a royal horse as such, but he's reliable and I'm afraid that for all the gruff war horses I have access to, I like this softie the best."

On cue, Biscuit nudged Eloise, and she grinned.

"He's also an excellent judge of character, so you can take his approval to heart," Xander said. "Shall we?"

He was prepared for Eloise to ask for a boost, but she mounted with practiced expertise. Xander hopped onto Biscuit, and they took off onto the trail at a gentle pace.

Xander had only ever seen Eloise at court, where she was

pleasant but perhaps a bit uncomfortable. She stayed out of the most gossipy circles and, though her father's wealth meant she was invited to all courtly events, she only showed up for some of them. Xander had long suspected she preferred country living to Ardenis.

"Do you get to return to your family home often?" he asked.

Eloise shook her head. "I'm a lady of marriageable age, which means I have to remain at court should my father need to show me off like prized cattle."

Xander laughed, and she offered a genuine smile. "But you'd prefer the country?"

"Already trying to get rid of me, are you? That's hardly a healthy way to start a marriage," she teased. "I like the pace of city life, but I miss the ease of my time in the country. I can be more myself there than I ever can here, though I suppose I don't have to tell you that."

Xander nodded. It would be nice to have a wife who understood the stress of managing a public persona while not losing the private one.

"I hope you won't take offense, Your Grace, but I haven't ridden in weeks and, as lovely as the conversation is, I understand you're an excellent rider." She looked at the trail in front of them. "The trail is a loop. Do you care to race first and talk on the second time around?"

Excitement sparked in Xander's stomach. Riding instead of small talk and all the while Sylvie thought he was courting. Maybe this wouldn't be so terrible.

"I would love to—"

He'd barely gotten the words out when Eloise and Midnights took off. Xander kicked Biscuit into a gallop, chasing her down.

They rounded the first bend. Eloise had gained even more ground. She was clearly familiar with the trail, and that was working to her advantage. Xander urged Biscuit to go faster. After the next turn in the trail, he caught and passed Eloise.

He was about to dart out of the woods and back toward the beginning of the loop when a blur of red popped out of the brush beside them.

Biscuit reared up, and Xander held on for dear life. It would be truly humiliating if multiple assassins had failed to take him down but a fall from a horse succeeded. He would never live down the shame.

Biscuit finally settled and Eloise came to a stop behind him. Xander peered down at the wide eyes of Princess Larissa of Brevone.

"I'm so sorry, Your Grace," she said from where she was sprawled on her backside. "I did not mean to startle your horse. I twisted my ankle so far from the castle and I was desperate for help."

"Of course you did," Eloise mumbled under her breath.

Xander sighed. It was too soon for these women to already be at each other's throats. He couldn't stand tense silences and judgmental looks for the rest of the festival. He'd expected a certain level of healthy competition between the women, but he should have at least been able to make it through one date without incident.

Xander hopped down and went to Larissa's side. "I'm afraid I would not be a good host if I left a guest in a lurch."

She stumbled into him, brushing her borderline obscene cleavage against his chest and making it unclear which ankle she'd injured, if any at all. He was truly impressed by the seamstress who had created her dress, or perhaps it was the maid who got her into it. Xander wasn't sure who was responsible, only that they had a supernatural ability to show the absolute maximum amount of cleavage.

Xander turned to look at Eloise. Her hair had come loose from its updo and wisps of it hung around her face, her skin flushed from the joy of riding.

"I'm sorry to cut our date short, Lady Spellman. I thoroughly enjoyed the ride. Would you mind terribly riding ahead to let Magdalena know that I'll be bringing Princess Larissa in with her injury?"

"Of course, Your Grace. I am happy to be of assistance to visitors in *our* kingdom," Eloise said.

Larissa's eyes narrowed at the word choice, but Eloise ignored her and turned Midnights toward the castle and rode away.

Xander lifted Larissa onto Biscuit, careful not to shift her dress, then mounted behind her. She stayed sidesaddle, clinging to him like a storybook damsel as they started to ride back toward the stables.

"I can't believe she wore menswear on a date, though I suppose she is only a lady and perhaps she did not know," Larissa said.

Xander frowned. "Are breeches not appropriate riding attire?"

"My mother would disown me if I wore breeches in front of a man who was courting me."

"In my experience, mothers are not always the authority on what attire will have the greatest impact when courting a man," Xander said.

Larissa blushed and tipped her head, her shiny auburn curls bouncing as she shifted. The skin across her nose was faintly pink and dotted with freckles, which made him wonder how long she'd been waiting for her chance to interrupt his date.

"I must admit that while I don't mind a woman in breeches, your dress is very lovely and—" He cleared his throat and she shifted against him. "Sturdy."

"Oh, thank you. I am so embarrassed by my clumsiness. I just wanted some fresh air. It's so stuffy in that castle, and I was hoping to see some snow. I hope the healer can tend to me in time for our wine tasting," Larissa said.

Xander forced a smile. "Our palace healer is very talented. I'm sure she'll have you back on your feet in no time."

"I hope you won't mind me saying that you're very handsome."

"I'd mind it more if you didn't."

Larissa grinned the wide, open smile of someone too young for him. He praised the gods for the reminder. The princess was barely twenty-one according to Xander's paperwork, and while plenty of men liked young wives, Larissa was definitely the type to have an overly romanticized idea of marriage. He could tell by the look in her eyes, and a romantic relationship was more than he could promise.

The stables came into view and he breathed a sigh of relief. He could not wait to drop Larissa off with the healers and retire to his room for a quiet drink. Xander climbed down and helped Larissa off the horse. She feigned a swoon, and he caught her, sweeping her into his arms.

She curled close, leaning her head against his shoulder. Her breath was warm on his neck and her skin smelled like citrus. It wasn't unpleasant, but she clung to him so tightly the scent would be all over him if he didn't bathe between dates.

He charged through the courtyard, into the castle, and down the hallway into the healing clinic.

Magdalena looked up from her herbs. "Your Majesty, who have you brought me?"

Xander set Larissa on a cot and bent to kiss her hand. "Princess Larissa seems to have twisted her ankle. Please give her the best care possible."

Larissa caught his hand before he could turn to leave and for a moment he feared she'd ask him to stay and force him to continue to pretend he cared about her supposed injury.

"Your Grace—" she began. "Xander, thank you for being so gallant and taking such excellent care of me. It's a relief to know that my possible future husband is both caring and gentle."

Xander pulled his hand away and winked. "Of course, Princess."

He darted from the healer's clinic before Larissa could ask him to stay, hoping to escape to his rooms to have a moment of peace. Instead, he nearly tackled Princess Mayella.

She braced herself with her hands gripping his shoulders. "Oh, Your Grace, what a lovely surprise."

Was this how it was to be? Not a single date to be completed, each woman interrupting the last, too impatient to wait her turn. Xander could not possibly handle three weeks of these antics.

"I do so hope she makes a swift recovery," Mayella said. The skip in her heartbeat suggested otherwise.

So it begins. These women will rip each other to shreds the first chance they get. A dull ache formed behind Xander's eyes. Suddenly a wine tasting didn't sound so bad. Maybe he could turn it into a drinking game and get so drunk he'd forget the entire afternoon.

Mayella bobbed her head and dipped into a curtsey. "Your Grace,

I was so looking forward to our date later this evening, but with Princess Larissa injured and Lady Spellman busy cleaning herself up from your ride, I am happy to make myself available to you now."

She looked up at him coyly as if to emphasize her obvious innuendo.

"Do you like wine?" Xander asked.

Mayella pressed a hand to her breast. "I *love* wine," she practically groaned.

Xander restrained himself from rolling his eyes and offered her his arm.

This is how it would be. Six women fighting over him while he fought to keep his attention off the one woman who wasn't the least bit interested.

18

CECILIA

Cecilia was not particularly in the mood to have tea with all of Xander's potential wives, but she'd told Evan and Sylvie that she would help get a read on each of them. Her ability to read people's emotions was a big part of the reason Evan had asked for her and Rainer to help in the first place. Hopefully, a little truth tea would make it even easier by loosening lips and encouraging the princesses to share their secrets.

It was also easier for Cecilia to read emotions on people who were more receptive and open.

She watched as Sylvie poured the hot water over the tea and a mixture of herbs. Sylvie gathered dried lemon rind for bringing truth to light, thyme for cleansing and purifying, and rosemary for clarity. Gathering a bit of each into her palm, Sylvie closed her eyes and laid her other hand on one pot of tea. Her lips moved in a silent incantation and the air filled with the scent of burned herbs.

It was an old spell, one they'd learned in the early years of magic classes, and though Cecilia had never had much use for it, it made her grateful that she and Sylvie had memory magic so that they didn't have to go dig a book out of the royal archives.

Sylvie blinked her eyes open and turned her palm over, releasing the ash of her exchanged herbs and gathering fresh ones for the next pot. She repeated the steps and, once she was satisfied, dusted off her hands and nodded.

"Now we just let them steep for five minutes."

Cecilia nodded, studying the delicate, intricately painted teapots. They reminded her of her mother's hand-painted dishes and teacups at home.

"How are you really?" Sylvie asked. "Couldn't help but notice that you seem unsettled."

Cecilia arched a brow. "What do I have to be unsettled about? My ex-husband searching for a new wife? My fiancé quietly willing me to set a wedding date?"

Sylvie's face softened. "I'm not judging. I can't imagine what you've been through, mostly because you won't talk about it."

Guilt swelled in Cecilia's chest. It's not that she didn't want to talk about it, but it was hard to put into words what it was like to die and then come back.

"But I do think if you don't find a way to start letting some of it out, that dark cloud will drag you down to a place where none of us can reach you. I'd hate to see that sabotage something you fought so hard for."

Cecilia swallowed the lump in her throat and looked away. Was that what she was doing when she let Xander flirt with her? Being in Argaria was like being fractured between the past and the present and still not knowing who she was in either place. The more she tried to hold herself together in all those broken places, the more she felt drawn to shatter them further. She could not seem to shake the reckless desire for oblivion that had followed her back from death.

Still, if carrying that weight and dragging herself back from the edge every now and then was the price she had to pay to be alive again, she would take it.

Sylvie traced a circle in the leftover herbs on the table. "Do you miss your goddess magic?"

Cecilia startled at the question. No one had dared ask her, but she supposed no one understood what it was like to be momentarily powerful in a world where you were not the rest of the time.

"I do. It's still there but it's so limited and, as horrible as it could be and as difficult as it was to control, I liked feeling strong that way. I could certainly help more people at the clinic if I still had the full magic."

"You are worth more than what you can do for other people," Sylvie said.

"You sound like Rainer." Cecilia sighed. "I know that. It's just when you have all this power and then you have only a glimmer of it, it's hard to accept the new limitations. Why? Do you miss the Gauntlet?"

Sylvie shook her head. "The only things I liked about the Gauntlet were the magic and the freedom. I have both here, though I do miss the thrill of learning new magic."

Cecilia hummed her agreement. At the healing clinic, everything was so routine that it robbed magic of some of its wonder. Sometimes it was nice to talk to another witch about the numinous thrill of taming something wild—of bending the world to your will for a moment.

Cecilia glanced around the busy kitchen. They were tucked away in a corner, but the rest of the room was alive with activity, the air filled with the scent of fresh bread and roasted vegetables. The staff buzzed around them like a swarm of bees, agitated to have two ladies in their space, but not enough to say so.

"You seem to have made yourself at home here," Cecilia said.

Sylvie leaned against her stool, a satisfied smile on her lips. "Yes, I suppose I'm more adaptable than even I realized." She glanced out the kitchen window. "Can't say I've adjusted to the cold. It really limits what I can wear."

She gestured to her elegant, icy blue dress. The neckline ran along her collarbone and exposed her shoulders with long lace sleeves. "I hate that I have to sacrifice warmth for fashion and, gods, I do get homesick. Do you know my niece Luna is walking and talking now?"

Cecilia smiled. "I do. We saw them a few weeks before we left. I can show you the memory. She looks just like you and Maeve. She's going to break some hearts."

Sylvie passed her fingers over her forehead, lips, and heart in mock reverence. "From your lips to Desiree's ears. May she always be the heartbreaker and not the heartbroken."

"I'll toast to that," Cecilia said.

"Perhaps not with truth tea, though," Sylvie said. She turned and disappeared into a pantry before emerging a moment later with a bottle of bubble wine and two glasses.

"You really have made yourself at home," Cecilia teased.

Sylvie poured them each a glass.

"To women saving the realm," Cecilia started.

"To men remembering to thank them," Sylvie finished.

They clinked glasses and sipped their wine.

There was an uneasy set to Sylvie's shoulders.

"What's bothering you? Other than worrying that Vincent will strike at any time?" Cecilia asked.

Sylvie offered a tight smile. "I came here to make a real change and I feel like all I've really done is put out small fires before they can spread." She took a sip of her wine and pursed her lips. "I need to do more."

"Syl, did you not just tell me that I'm worth more than just what I can do for people? You're doing plenty—"

"He's hurting women," she said so softly Cecilia barely heard her.

"Vincent?"

Sylvie nodded. "There's a shelter at the Temple of Aurelia. The priestesses take them in and I volunteer there." Her voice grew tight. "I'm not only failing women in Argaria in general by not getting them out from under the control of the men in their lives, but I'm failing the women along our borders who are—" Her voice broke and she looked away.

Cecilia felt sick. The horrors of war always seemed to fall the hardest on women and children. She couldn't imagine what those women were going through, nor what Sylvie suffered seeing that damage day after day.

"That's not on you any more than the men who died during that battle outside Olney Castle are on me. We cannot take responsibility for men and their wars. All we can do is try to end them for good and that is what we are doing here. I get it. I want to do something, too." Cecilia sighed and sipped her wine. "I'm glad you told me. But you're doing an amazing job here. People respect you. I'm so proud."

Sylvie sighed. "I know you're right but it still hurts my heart."

"Then let's turn that hurt into motivation. What did you once tell me? Use that anger?"

Sylvie looked delighted. "Gods, I'm so wise."

"And so modest."

"Why be modest when I can be honest? I am fabulous and everyone should know it." Sylvie preened, finally returning to her confident, calm self. "Now if only Evan would know it, too."

"Still nothing?"

Sylvie shook her head. "I'm beginning to wonder if I made a mistake. Not in coming here or doing what I'm doing. I would never have had this opportunity in Olney. But I wonder if the mistake was in expecting him to be anything but what he is—a spy who keeps all his secrets."

Cecilia wanted to argue with her friend. It was clear to her that Evan cared about Sylvie, and he certainly trusted her, but she could understand that it wasn't enough.

"What will you do?"

Sylvie shrugged, nodding to the tea. "Today I will pour some magic tea and pry some secrets from some princesses. Everything else is tomorrow's problem."

Cecilia followed Sylvie into the sitting room, her finest forced smile on her face.

The princesses were already perched in a circle in the sitting room, all sitting perfectly straight, their faces in pleasant smiles even while their eyes narrowed on the competition.

Sylvie took her time pouring tea, asking a few basic questions to get the conversations started. At first, the flow of the chatter was stilted and tight, but as the servants brought out sweets and the tea flowed more frequently, everyone opened up.

Cecilia started her appraisal with Princess Clare Pyke of Aldrena with her shiny blonde hair, pale skin, and light green eyes. She was petite, like Cecilia, but had an elegance that made her appear taller. She'd received most of Xander's focus at the opening ball, and Cecilia didn't want to think about why that made her feel jealous. On top of Xander's interest in her looks, Clare made the most logical ally since Aldrena shared its western border with Argaria.

Cecilia turned her focus to Brytta Nyvyn of Krysk, the mountainous region across the Adiran Sea. Brytta possessed a cold beauty: a tan, angular face, bouncing brown curls, and sharp eyes so dark they looked nearly black. She took in the competition with obvious contempt, but she seemed to have formed a tentative alliance with two of the other princesses.

Brytta stood by the tea station, chatting with the young redheaded Larissa Varisada of Brevone, which neighbored Krysk to the north. Larissa looked exceptionally young, with a smattering of freckles across her pale cheeks and her red hair coiled into an updo. Her youthful joy was in such sharp contrast to Brytta, making Cecilia wonder what they could possibly have in common, though it seemed most of the conversation was held up by Princess Mayella Sing of Jeset.

Mayella chatted between sips of tea, glancing smugly over the rim of her teacup at her competition. Her stark black hair was thick and shiny and braided into an intricate coronet woven through with flowers. She wore a magenta dress that looked gorgeous against her olive skin.

Then there was Jessamin Orum, Princess of Novum, with her dark skin and light brown eyes. She had a calm, steady presence as she conversed with her guards in their lilac garb. They were world-renowned for their valiant fighting ability and seemed to hover closer than the rest of the princesses' guards. They could have also been world-renowned for their stunning good looks, because all the guards were lovely. Though one wore a scarf that covered most of her face, she had beautiful eyes the same light brown shade as Jessamin's. Cecilia made a mental note to ask Jessamin if she could watch her and her guards train.

Finally, Cecilia turned her attention to Lady Eloise Spellman, who happened to be staring at her. Cecilia crossed the room and sat down beside her.

"Lady Eloise, it's lovely to meet you. I've heard so much about you," Cecilia said. It was a lie, but it seemed polite to offer a boost to the only non-princess in the room.

Eloise smiled. "Lady Reznik, you're kind to say so, though I'm not sure who'd find me worth mentioning."

"Nonsense," Cecilia said, noticing Brytta's sudden interest in their conversation. "Xander told me how beautiful you were at the opening ball, and I think he may have sold you short."

Cecilia worried she was selling her compliments too hard, but Eloise was a beautiful woman. Her dark curls were woven into a loose braid and threaded with ribbon. Her red dress brought out the green in her eyes and a light flush to her pale skin.

"Thank you," Eloise said. "I hadn't realized the king took much notice. They say he only has eyes for you and that you only have eyes for your handsome guardian. Rainer is a bit of a legend in the kingdom, having stolen you from the king and all, though I can understand the appeal."

Cecilia kept her face placid. It was a simple comment. It wasn't as if she didn't notice the way ladies of Argaria's court stole gazes at her fiancé. Eloise's comment gave her the distinct impression that she was more interested in Rainer than Xander. She doubted Xander would want to find himself in second place to Rainer once again, but it wasn't as if she could start something now by asking Eloise what exactly she meant.

Eloise seemed to sense her discomfort. "I meant nothing by it. Only that such a romantic story makes all of us a little flustered."

Cecilia bit her tongue to keep from saying something cutting.

"Lady Reznik, you must tell us all about the king. I understand you know him very well," Brytta said.

Cecilia nodded. "Xander is an open book. I'm not sure what I could tell you that isn't already apparent. He's kind, and he truly cares about his people and his kingdom. He's an excellent fighter. And of course, he's very charming—and he knows it."

They all laughed.

"There are rumors that you had a secret wedding. That sounds very romantic." Clare smiled.

"We did," Cecilia said, forcing a tight smile. "Xander knew I was uncomfortable with the Argarian traditions, so he arranged for us to have a private ceremony with my own customs the night before our public wedding. Of course, we never got to have our big wedding because of the assassination of the king and queen. But the ceremony we did have meant a lot to me."

"He went to all that trouble. That's very sweet," Mayella said, though her pinched face suggested she thought it was bullshit.

"He has a good heart, even though he tries to hide it," Cecilia said. "Tell me, Princess Larissa. What inspired you to be here today?"

"Well, if I'm being honest, I had hoped to have a bit more time before I was traded off to be married," she laughed.

Cecilia found her honesty refreshing and genuine. She wasn't sure how much of it was the tea and how much of it was the girl.

Larissa took a sip before continuing, her eyes darting to the other women as if desperate for approval. "My mother gave me good advice. She'd heard that Xander was kind and young and handsome, and she told me that he was basically as ideal a match as I could hope for. I'm not sure I made the best first impression, but he was so gallant when I hurt my ankle yesterday."

Cecilia tried to read Larissa's energy but only picked up warmth and excitement, which matched the hopeful look on her face.

Sylvie placed a hand on the redhead's. "You were lovely at the opening night ball."

"The king hardly looked at me," Larissa lamented.

"That's because he was so taken with Princess Clare," Jessamin said, her hand coming to her lips as if shocked by her own admission.

Sylvie raised her eyebrows and met Cecilia's gaze at the clear sign that the tea was doing its work.

"Oh gods, I don't know if that's the case. He danced with all of us," Clare said, looking at the other women for faux reassurance.

"No, she's right. The king danced with you the most, although his mood seemed to sour when Lady Reznik left the ball early," Mayella quipped.

"They are such dear friends," Sylvie said, trying to break the tension.

Mayella glared at Cecilia with clear resentment. "Where did you run off to so early?"

"My fiancé and I needed to discuss some details for our upcoming wedding," Cecilia lied.

Sylvie smirked at her, knowing that there was absolutely no conversation at all that went on between Rainer and Cecilia when they went to bed that early.

"When are you getting married?" Larissa asked. She wrapped one of her red curls around her index finger as she spoke.

"We haven't set a date yet, but I'm hoping in May, right after Rainer's birthday. It's so pretty in Olney that time of year."

Sylvie's eyebrows shot up. She glanced at Cecilia's cup as if to check that she'd had the correct tea.

"You have such a sweet love story. I thought you would have been married right away," Mayella said.

Cecilia sat a little straighter. "We've both been through a tremendous amount of loss. Not all of our story is for public consumption. We both wanted some time to heal and help our kingdom heal before settling down. We're still young. We have time."

"But I assume you'll want to have children soon," Mayella continued.

A cold gust of grief blew through Cecilia. She'd had so much time to get used to it, but no matter how much it came up, she still felt wrecked.

"Of course, but we also want to spend some time just the two of us," Cecilia said tightly.

Sylvie was good enough to take over the conversation and allow Cecilia a break to read each of the princesses. She wasn't sure what she was looking for, but she figured today would give her a baseline on each of them. After a few moments, Cecilia settled into a seat.

Xander strode into the room with a wide smile on his face. "What an honor to have so many beautiful women all here for me."

He looked over all of them, but his eyes came to rest on Cecilia. He stared at her for a moment. She pretended not to notice.

"Princess Clare was just telling us about her family's summer vacations on the western coast. It sounds so lovely there. Have you ever been, Your Grace?" Cecilia asked.

"I haven't, but I've heard it's lovely."

"Why don't you have a seat, Your Majesty? I'll pour you some tea," Cecilia said, gesturing to her chair and hopping up to pour him tea from the pot marked as safe by Sylvie.

"That's a lovely dress, Lady Reznik," Xander said. He took the teacup she offered and slid into her seat.

"Thank you for noticing," Cecilia said as she squeezed in beside him. The princesses seemed annoyed at how close they were sitting, but no one else had made room for her.

Sylvie looked from Cecilia to Xander warily, sensing the tension brewing under the surface.

Cecilia was playing a dangerous game, and she didn't even understand why. Did she want to prove something to Xander? To herself? Did she want him to pine for her? Was she really that selfish?

Xander sensed the awkward silence and started chatting with the princesses, leaving Cecilia free to notice their interactions and tune in to their feelings.

It was clear from the start that Jessamin and Eloise were the outcasts of the group. Brytta and Mayella cut them off before they could say much. The other princesses were threatened by Jessamin's nonchalance and the fact that she came from a kingdom that was run by women. On the other hand, Eloise was exiled from the group for not being royal. It seemed the women didn't want to be friendly with anyone they saw as having too much or too little power.

Cecilia tuned her senses into Mayella. Sharp envy and cold jealousy surrounded her, though it only intensified when she looked at Cecilia and dissipated when she was speaking to Xander.

"Truly, I'm just confused about what all the fuss is about. Lady Reznik is a beautiful woman, but nothing extraordinary. When people say she was a goddess, I just expected—" Mayella waved a hand at Cecilia. "I don't know...more."

Mayella's eyes went wide at the admission, as if she hadn't meant to say it, but that was how truth tea worked. It made people more forthcoming and honest.

Xander leaned in close to Cecilia and whispered, "Perhaps she just needs to see you naked, love. That would make anyone a believer."

Cecilia flushed fiercely as she stirred her tea. Sylvie narrowed her eyes at them, and Cecilia leaned away from the king.

"Jessamin, that's such a beautiful gown. All your dresses have such incredible beadwork. I've heard that's a specialty in Novum," Cecilia said, trying to pull her into the conversation.

"It is a lovely dress, though one wonders if you might be a bit cold in such a climate," Brytta said curtly.

Cecilia had heard several of the women whispering about the revealing nature of Jessamin's dresses, but she thought they were all tasteful and exuded confidence she wished she possessed.

Jessamin smiled. "Thank you, Lady Reznik. It is one of our proudest industries. I'm sure most of the women in this room own a dress with Novum beadwork." She turned to Brytta. "It is so kind of you to show concern for my well-being, but our climate is prone to extremes thanks to northern tempests. I assure you I'm quite comfortable, if not from my dress, then from the warm welcome I've received here."

Cecilia nearly sprayed her tea, and even Xander regarded Jessamin with surprised humor.

"I like her," Cecilia whispered to Xander.

"She's your pick?" he asked.

Cecilia shrugged noncommittally. She hated the idea of him with another woman. It was selfish, but true. She couldn't quite wrap her mind around what was happening. She wanted to know why Xander had shunned her for months and wanted to prove to herself that she still had a pull on him, if for no other reason than to remind herself that what they had mattered.

But there was a part of her that felt afraid to be truly happy, as if the second she let her guard down, some villain would spring forth, ready to sweep the happiness away. Her body felt poised for a death blow ever since she'd returned from Grimon's doorstep, and she couldn't seem to stop herself from self-sabotaging to end the suspense.

"Your Majesty, what do you like to do for fun?" Larissa asked, leaning forward to show off breasts that were already barely contained by her bodice.

"I love to fight and train. I play cards. I enjoy chess with the right opponent. I enjoy riding and going on hunts, but I also like things like music and theater. You'll find I'm very open-minded," Xander said.

"I think I'd like anything if I was doing it with you," Larissa purred.

Cecilia bit back a laugh. She wasn't sure if it was the truth tea or if the princess simply pulled no punches. Her approach was a bit over the top, but Xander had preferred that type of overtly sexy woman before he and Cecilia met.

She felt into the energy around Larissa, sensing prickly desire and warm lust. Yet another princess who seemed harmless.

Clare was harder to read. She seemed anxious, sipping her tea quickly like her mouth was too dry. While dry mouth was a side effect of the tea, it could also indicate nervousness. Her eyes kept flicking from Xander to Cecilia to the rest of the girls as if the conversation was moving too fast for her to keep up. Cecilia had suspected she was a bit dull, but this solidified it. She'd been plied with truth tea, but she was so simple she still had nothing to say. Cecilia looked at her with pity.

She moved on to Brytta, who was a bit more animated with a jagged feeling that Cecilia couldn't quite place. It felt like something between anger and longing.

Next, she took in Eloise Spellman, the only non-royal in the mix. Anxiety buzzed around her, mixed with a tightness that felt like frustration.

Finally, Cecilia settled her attention on Jessamin. A slight pulsing nervousness flowed through her, but she otherwise seemed calm and happy. Her gaze occasionally shot to the doorway, where a redheaded member of her guard smiled at her. Each time that happened, Jessamin's shoulders relaxed. Cecilia got the impression that Jessamin was simply biding her time and would have preferred to be out in a training ring with any opponent than in this room full of venomous princesses. Cecilia didn't blame her.

"Ladies, I do apologize, but I must take my leave. Even a king must make time to train and stay in shape for any troubles that might arise," Xander said, excusing himself.

He didn't go far. Xander made his way out to the gardens, in full view from the sitting room where the ladies were enjoying their tea.

Cecilia watched him through the large glass windows. Evan had set up a makeshift training area—clearly for the purpose of Xander showing off since the king had access to private training rooms in another wing of the castle. Xander stripped off his fine tunic so that he was just in his white undershirt, and Evan tossed him a sword. The two went back and forth.

Cecilia watched them spar. Xander was truly a beautiful fighter. Rainer might have been a better swordsman, but Xander was a performer, and he could make anything look good. He was graceful and quick and she could tell from the way he and Evan went at one another that each of them had practiced understanding of the way the other fought. It reminded her of sparring with Rainer.

Before long, the princesses had all gathered at the windows to watch.

"Gods, he's incredible," Clare mumbled.

Xander finished a parry and turned and winked at the ladies.

Cecilia rolled her eyes, but she couldn't tear her gaze away from Xander and the way his shirt had become transparent with perspiration. It clung to his chest and stomach, showing off his incredible physique. He took a sip of water and caught her looking. He smirked at her as if to say, *"See something you like?"*

She shook her head and looked at Sylvie, who seemed just as mesmerized by Evan. Cecilia supposed watching two incredibly good-looking men fight wasn't the worst entertainment. So she stood alongside the gawking women and enjoyed the show.

19

EVAN

The festivities had barely begun, and Evan was already exhausted. He'd finally fallen asleep the previous night after hours of pacing and worrying, only to be woken in the middle of the night by a knock on his door. His men had discovered a scantily clad Princess Larissa wandering the royal wing.

Princesses were already throwing themselves at Xander. What concerned Evan more was that Larissa had either ducked her own guards or they had let her go. Both were problems considering so many visitors at their court; there were too many variables for him to control. He made a mental note to go over Larissa's background check again to ensure they hadn't missed something. Her late-night exploration was probably a desperate move by a princess who was under a lot of pressure, but he needed to be sure.

He'd also posted extra guards in the royal wing to keep himself and his friends safe. They all stayed in Xander's wing since Evan didn't trust anyone else to room so close to the king.

He walked down the hall in search of Sylvie. She was gone by the time he woke up, but she'd left a note about having breakfast with Cecilia.

When he finally found her, she was in the hallway by the council meeting room, nodding as Lord Spellman talked her ear off about making sure his daughter had a fair shake among the princesses. Evan paused at the end of the hall, pretending to read correspondence a ways away so he could listen. He caught snippets of the conversation.

"My lord, Eloise is a beautiful woman. I saw the king took her riding yesterday," Sylvie said. "I agree. They'd make a beautiful couple. Many beautiful children— Why yes, I did know that Eloise is one of five children. How lovely to be so...fruitful."

Evan cringed. Sylvie hated when men used fertility as a selling point for their daughters. She proclaimed their kingdoms held the ideal vision of women as—in her own words—"walking wombs." The first time she'd said it, he laughed out loud, but she hadn't. She'd gone on to explain the hypocrisy of how women were expected to appear humble and poised, all while pleasing their husbands behind closed doors, lest the men stray. It was always the wife blamed for men's dalliances. People whispered that it was just men being men when they cheated, saying they weren't getting something they needed at home, but really it was just greed. That's what ran the kingdom, despite Evan and Xander's interventions.

She told him that even though Cecilia had practically single-handedly won a war, saving thousands of lives, most people would still consider her a poor marriage prospect simply because she couldn't bear children. It was preposterous, but he knew that change happened slowly—much more slowly than Sylvie was willing to stand for.

He brought his attention back to Sylvie. She rested a hand on Lord Spellman's forearm. Evan immediately went rigid. The man smiled at her widely.

"The king is so young and untested. A marriage into such an old, established Argarian family would, I'm sure, wipe away any doubts about those silly rumors," he said.

Lord Spellman would have never dared to say that in front of Evan, but he clearly had no issue casually questioning Xander's parentage to Sylvie.

Evan scrubbed a hand down his face. He thought they had put those rumors to rest, but if Edward Spellman thought it would be advantageous to run his mouth in front of the foreign princesses in the hopes of scaring them away, Evan had no way to disprove the allegations. It didn't matter that there was also no evidence to prove them; spicy gossip traveled faster than bland history.

"Yes, my lord," Sylvie said, a hint of hesitation in her voice. "I'll tell you what. I'll make sure that Eloise gets more one-on-one time with the king. It's no problem at all. You know how much we all value your support, and your daughter is so poised. She'd make an exceptional queen."

Evan was about to save her from the tedious conversation when Lord William Arvato walked around the corner and joined their conversation.

"Lady Brett, what a pleasant surprise. You look radiant today, as always," William said, taking her hand and placing a kiss on it that lasted too long for Evan's liking.

Evan cringed. *Radiant? Is that what she wants to hear?* He supposed the adjective fit, but it seemed a bit much.

Sylvie ate it up, a faint blush on her cheeks. "Lord Arvato, aren't you a terrible flirt this morning?"

Evan frowned. Sylvie looked genuinely charmed, and he did not like that one bit.

"Not a flirt, just simply speaking truths, my lady." He turned toward the man beside her. "Lord Spellman, I heard there was an issue with your men down at the winter market again today. I didn't want to intrude, but it seems there may need to be some debts smoothed over at one of the pleasure houses. Please excuse me, Lady Brett, for speaking of such a topic in your presence."

Lord Spellman disappeared in a huff, and Sylvie smiled at William with genuine relief.

"Thank you, Will," she said.

Evan winced. He did not know they were so casually acquainted. Evan had been so busy looking for threats to Xander he'd missed a threat to his relationship right in front of his face. He studied

William's black tunic with elaborate gold embroidery. It was a bit showy, though standing side by side, he seemed well-suited to Sylvie in her stylish dress.

Evan had seen Sylvie chatting with William after several council meetings, but thought nothing of it. It was what she did. She chatted up the lords of the council in hopes they'd clumsily let something slip. The problem was that he'd somehow missed what appeared to be a blooming, genuine flirtation. Foolish of him, since William was young, unmarried, fabulously wealthy, and, according to many of the ladies at court, very handsome.

Worse, William Arvato did the very thing that Evan regularly failed to do. He lavished Sylvie with compliments and his rapt attention publicly.

In some ways, it was an intentional choice to withhold his affections. If Evan showed his feelings for Sylvie, she could quickly become a pawn in someone else's moves against him. It was also unintentional. Evan had not had a single serious relationship and spent most of his life around hunters. He didn't know how much women enjoyed such affirmation and attention, and he didn't want to be another man fawning over Sylvie just because she was beautiful. He wanted to compliment her mind as much as the rest of her, which he did by giving her genuinely important assignments. Clearly, that wasn't enough, and he needed to figure out how to do more.

Vulnerability had never been his strong suit. Of all of life's mysteries, it baffled him most how someone who had been trained to fight his whole life could learn to willingly give another person the means with which to ruin him. Even if he could suppress the years of training, he'd had no instruction whatsoever on how to explain what he felt. It was a strange mixture of respect, lust, and possessiveness.

Evan couldn't take another moment of flirtatious small talk. He stalked down the hall.

"Lady Brett, Lord Arvato, nice to see you both this morning. I'm sorry to interrupt, but I have a matter to discuss with Lady Brett," he said, not taking his eyes off Sylvie's sly smile.

"Of course. I'll leave you to it." William took Sylvie's hand. "Lady

Brett, you make every day brighter with your very presence. Enjoy the rest of your morning." He kissed her hand again and disappeared around the corner.

Evan sneered after him. "I don't like him."

Sylvie rolled her eyes. "You liked him just fine before. What do you want?"

He hesitated.

"Nothing then? Perfect. So I just let you make me look weak in front of a council member for no reason." She crossed her arms.

Evan frowned. "I was hoping to save you from Arvato's nonsense, not make you feel weak."

"I am done being someone who needs rescuing," Sylvie said.

Evan arched an eyebrow. "Is that so?"

"It is. And I hardly think I need to be saved from a handsome, wealthy man who wants to tell me how lovely I am. I'd prefer you worry about yourself, Evan. If you're not careful, one of them might steal me away."

She was teasing, but it was what he feared, and he couldn't muster a smile.

"I'm kidding, gods, lighten up," she said. "You should worry about yourself, though. Who will save *you* from all these foolish men?"

He grinned at her, holding out his arm. She took it, and his shoulders instantly relaxed. He'd never met anyone who had such a calming influence on him.

"You work too hard," she sighed.

"I could say the same to you," he countered. "How was tea?"

She sighed heavily. "Xander was not on his best behavior, I'm afraid. There was quite a bit of flirting with Cece. What's worse than the flirting, though, is the way he can't take his eyes off of her. There's no way these women don't notice, and that's not exactly the kind of thing that a lady wants to see when she's considering a suitor."

Evan feared that might happen. He was beginning to doubt the strategy of inviting Rainer and Cecilia. While he trusted them implicitly, he did not trust Xander around them. He relished every opportunity to infuriate Rainer and flirt with Cecilia. Cato's influence was gone from Xander's mind, but his obsession with his ex-wife remained.

"Cece could have done a better job of deflecting his affection. She can be reckless. I think she likes pulling his attention," Sylvie said.

Evan cursed. "I was counting on it from him, but not her."

"I know."

"Did anything interesting come out of the truth tea at least?"

Sylvie shook her head. "Honestly? Nothing more than a few sharper words than normal. It seems the princesses are used to being painfully honest with each other. Court cruelty is a second language for a princess."

They walked down the hall and into Evan's chamber sitting room. Sylvie poured them tea from the waiting kettle. Evan felt restless in her presence. He'd always been a caretaker, and he was unaccustomed to someone taking care of him, but he liked it.

"You have to stop juggling like this, Evan. It's impossible to keep every ball in the air. One is bound to drop, and you're killing yourself for a king who seems to resent the very position you work so hard to secure for him."

"That's not fair. You have no idea what it's been like. He is all I've had...my whole life. Xander and Teddy. They were it. We all had roles to play. Teddy was the joy and humor. Xander was the reckless instigator. And I was the one who kept everything together. I kept us safe."

She placed a hand on his arm. "Even you cannot hold the world together with sheer force of will."

They were normally on the same page. It was frustrating that she couldn't see what he was trying to do.

"I have so far. Gods! I'm doing this *for us*! So that we can build a life here. I'm doing this for him, yes—so he can finally stop looking over his shoulder. He's like a brother to me, as ridiculous and frustrating as he may be. But most of all, I'm doing this for you. So that you can live in a kingdom that values women and gives them more autonomy."

She sighed, leaning back in her chair. "I know. I'm sorry. I'm just frustrated and on edge." She took a long sip of tea. "Sometimes I feel like you'll forever be telling me to just wait for the next big emergency to settle. There's always some crisis postponing when I can be a priority. I know you're trying, and I'm not saying this to hurt you, but I'm tired of feeling like I'm in second place to the king."

Guilt settled in Evan's stomach. He knew he'd been doing exactly that, but he hated that he hadn't had a chance to address it before she noticed. His entire survival in the Argarian court had relied on his ability to anticipate issues before they arose.

"I swear I'm trying."

She shook her head. "Every Wednesday I have tea with the royal gardener, who hears more secrets than the high priestesses at the Temple of Aurelia. I attend needlepoint and breakfast with the ladies of the court two days a week, have lunch in the kitchens on Thursdays, and play cards in the secret hunter gambling games in the stables on Friday nights. I am in every council meeting and running circles around your other spies, but any time you need me, I am there. And yet I cannot say the same for you."

Evan reached for her hand. He guided her onto his lap. He cupped her face and pulled her into a long, slow kiss. He loved the way she melted into him. She sighed as he pulled away.

"I know. I am sorry and I will do better," Evan said. "You do look radiant this morning, you know?"

She tipped her head back and laughed. "That really got under your skin, didn't it? Duly noted. All I have to do to get you to show affection is flirt with an eligible lord and have you hear how lovely he thinks I look in my dress."

"I think we both know what you look best in is nothing at all," he said, grinning at her. He slid a hand up the hem of her dress, and she didn't stop him.

"I have to be at a meeting in a half-hour," she whispered.

"I like a challenge," he said.

———

When they were finished, Sylvie quickly pulled her dress back into place and sat down in front of the mirror to fix her hair before kissing Evan goodbye.

She met his gaze, her pale blue eyes filled with hope. He knew what was coming. Every time, she looked so incredibly hopeful, and it killed him to let her down.

"I love you," she said.

The words both thrilled and terrified Evan every time she said them.

She paused, waiting for a response, but he could tell from the look in her eyes she didn't expect one. Maybe that was her strategy— get him into such a deficit that he'd need to climb back out of eventually, like a complicated equation—and if she said it enough times, it would trigger him to say it once.

It wasn't that he didn't feel it. Gods knew he did. It was that it scared him like nothing else in life.

His mother died in childbirth with him, and his father died in battle when Evan was still an infant. His whole life, the only people he'd ever known that he loved were Xander and Teddy, and neither of them ever said it. It was understood between them, unspoken, but just as real as if they'd said the words.

He showed Sylvie. Of that, he was sure. He'd gifted her with dresses from the finest seamstress in Ardenis, surprised her with romantic dates when he could, and showed her with his body every time they made love. He worshipped her.

She was the most brilliant, beautiful woman he'd ever laid eyes on.

It baffled him why he couldn't just say so.

Her disappointment was crushing. She kissed him again and left him alone in his room.

Evan sat down at his desk and unlocked his drawer, popping out the secret compartment and removing a small box. He opened it and held it up to the firelight. His mother's large diamond engagement ring glittered. Sylvie would love it. It was beautiful and ostentatious, but most of all, it was one of the two most important possessions he owned.

When Evan's father died, King Damian put his father's sword and dagger set and his mother's ring in the Savero family vault for safe-keeping. Damian gave him the sword on his sixteenth birthday when he was finally big enough to wield it and the ring two years after, when he turned eighteen.

When Damian had handed the ring to him, he smiled faintly. *"Your father made me promise that I would share this advice with you when I gave you this ring. He said, 'Marry someone smart, or you'll spend your life making dull conversation and worrying. If you marry someone smart, you'll always have another mind to tackle life's problems, and you'll never worry that she can't handle herself. If all else fails, find someone kind. We warriors are rough and aren't good at taking care of ourselves, and it's not such a bad thing to have someone who can teach you how to be kind to yourself.'"*

Evan had taken the advice to heart. Sylvie was both things. She was brilliant—too bright for her own good much of the time. She was also kind in a way few ladies raised at court were. Courtly life inspired competition and pettiness between women, but he'd seen Sylvie befriend every social outcast and scorned woman since arriving in Argaria. She did not care at all what anyone thought.

When he asked her about it, she'd credited Cecilia, saying that Cecilia had never suffered a bully, even if that bully was the entire court. She'd walk right up to the outcast and start talking as if the whole room wasn't staring at them. Sylvie got used to it. Then, she saw the power it gave her to hold her own counsel. Rather than risking her reputation, it let people know she'd do as she pleased and didn't need permission.

Evan was very much in love with and in awe of her. He did not know why he couldn't simply say the three words that would let her know.

He was going to do it. He'd been through brutal battles. He'd fought gods and warriors and princes. He'd faced down plenty of scary things.

Still, telling Sylvie how he really felt—how important she was to him—how he wanted to spend his life with her—that was something he desperately wanted to do.

He just needed to get through the festival. He needed Xander settled, an alliance solidified, and, if the gods would lend them any luck, a bit of peace. Once Xander was taken care of, Evan would fix things with Sylvie. Though, he supposed that was kind of her whole point.

Perhaps he'd been looking at things all wrong. Maybe he was happy to have a life with her, but she wasn't satisfied to be something that always came after Xander.

He frowned as he snapped the box closed and carefully placed it back in its hiding place.

Evan needed a deadline. As soon as Xander was safely married, he would tell Sylvie how he felt. He'd plan something grand, and he'd ask her to marry him. He just needed enough time for the festival to end and Xander to be settled.

They were young, and they both had their parts to play over the next few days. After that, Evan would shift his priorities. It couldn't happen all at once, but he could start to pass some things off to Reese and Chris. There were reliable council members who could handle these things.

Sylvie was right. He didn't need to do everything himself.

He only hoped that he wouldn't be too late and that what he offered would be enough for her.

20

RAINER

Being back in Argaria stoked Rainer's anxiety to a fever pitch. It wasn't that he'd expected Xander not to flirt with Cecilia, but he had hoped she wouldn't enjoy it so much. And all of that as he walked through the very halls where he'd been a prisoner —where he'd first lost Cecilia.

The heat of the fire licked at the back of his neck as he watched Cecilia begin her morning warm-up.

His mind had never been good at resting; even when it had a threat to address, it would always be searching for more. Even when all was well back in Olney, he'd taken Cecilia's disinterest in setting a wedding date as a sign that something was wrong, and now that he was in Argaria with the threat of Xander looming large, all Rainer wanted was to know for sure that she only wanted him.

Much as he wanted a big celebration so that he could finally tell her in front of everyone exactly how he felt after years of holding it back, he would have married her immediately, with no one around to witness it, if only she said she was ready.

He turned the star flower carving over in his hand, gouging the wood to get more detail on the petals. The sound was soothing, matching the rhythm of Cecilia's calm breathing as she moved through her morning stretch routine on the floor beside the bed.

When he had to look and not touch, it had been pure torture to watch her bend over and contort her body into a number of very suggestive positions. Now that they were together, Rainer found it difficult not to interrupt her when she insisted on doing it in just her undergarments.

She pressed onto all fours and arched her back.

"Fuck," he muttered, looking at the curve of her ass in black silk and lace.

"See something you like?" she taunted, pressing her chest toward the floor.

"You have the finest backside in the two kingdoms."

She preened at the attention. "Nonsense. You haven't seen every ass in both kingdoms."

"It's so spectacular I don't need to."

She paused, grinning at him over her shoulder, clearly waiting for him to pounce, but he stayed where he was.

She rolled over to sit on the floor. "What's wrong?"

Rainer shook his head. It wasn't the right time to bring it up. They would get married eventually. "Nothing."

She hopped up and sat on his lap, running her fingers through his hair. "Tell me. I can feel your anxiety. What can I do?"

He sighed. "I have felt restless back here. The two of you are—" He cleared his throat to delay, to think of the right words. "Much as you ever were, and it makes me uneasy."

Her face softened. "I'm just for you, Rain."

He saw the sincerity in her eyes, felt it in their bond, and still it wasn't enough. "I know. I think I would feel better if—"

Her whole body went rigid as the understanding settled in. "If we set a wedding date."

He swallowed hard. "Yes. Several people have asked me. While I don't mind deflecting, I don't like that I don't really know the answer."

"I'm not ready." She looked down at her lap as if embarrassed by the words.

"Why? Do you even want to marry me anymore?" He sounded so sullen and childish, but he couldn't hide the frustration building within him.

She looked wounded by the words. "Yes! Of course I do. How can you even say that? I came back for you, Rainer. Only you. I love you. I want to be with you. But I don't want this dark cloud hanging over me on what is supposed to be the happiest day of my life, and I haven't figured out how to dispel it yet."

He should have accepted the response, but nothing she said would rid him of his anxiety. It probably wouldn't have even satisfied him if she'd agreed. He wanted her to *want* to set a date. He wanted her to be enthusiastic, to push things along as most brides seemed to. He wanted to feel her joy and excitement instead of feeling like he was dragging her toward something she was afraid of. Rainer wanted her to make him feel worthy, but her sacrifice had tipped the scales so far that he wasn't certain he'd ever feel worthy of her again.

"What if you can't dispel it?" Rainer asked. It was an inside thought, the kind of desperation that was meant to live in the darkest corner of his subconscious, never to be spoken aloud, but it crept out anyway.

She stood in a huff and crossed the room. "I'm sorry I'm not able to resolve my considerable grief on the timeline you've deemed appropriate."

"Cece!" he called after her, but she grabbed a dress from the closet and slammed the washroom door behind her. The sound of the lock clicking into place took the fight out of him.

It was official. Rainer was an ass.

He tried to wait her out, but she stayed locked on the wrong side of the door, waiting for him to leave.

Finally, he gave up and headed down to meet Cal by the stables, where some of the princesses' guards were gathered. He found Cal looking in on a poker game at the back of the royal stables.

The makeshift setup featured a round wooden table surrounded by a smattering of hunters and a few princess guards perched on wood crates. They were all in various states of disarray but seemed unbothered by the chill or the stench of horses. Some looked as if they'd been playing for hours, while others appeared fresh and bright-eyed. Whiskey glasses and coins covered the table. It was a bit early for drinking, but they were probably on the night shift and just finishing their work for the day.

"Some of the hunters like to play when they're off duty," Cal explained.

"Does Xander know?" Rainer asked.

Cal laughed. "What do you think? We've caught him in here playing more than once."

"Is he any good?" Rainer asked.

One of the hunters spoke up. "The king is an exceptional poker player."

Several hunters leaned against the wall. Others stood outside the stable door flirting with some of the kitchen servants who were on break.

Everything seemed so normal. If Evan hadn't told them how precarious things were, Rainer would have no idea.

He and Cal watched the game for a few more minutes, several of the hunters stopping to gossip with Cal about the events of the week ahead. Cal talked animatedly.

Rainer was surprised to see his friend fall into the role of spy so easily. Cal had a way of putting people at ease. He told jokes and gossiped about the different ladies at court and who they were involved with.

Several men asked Cal about Lady Tanya, whom he was courting, but he dodged the questions. Rainer had noticed Cal dancing with a pretty blonde at the opening ball, but he was tight-lipped on the subject. Rainer would make a point to ask more questions when they were out of earshot of a bunch of nosy hunters and their exceptional hearing.

Cal and Rainer wandered the stables and then the training grounds, talking to several of Cal's friends and other hunters he didn't know as well who meandered in and out of conversations. Then they made their way to the garden where some of the Novumi princess guards were training.

They watched Princess Jessamin's guards spar, each of them a blur of lilac fabric, leather armor, and fists. The Novumi royal guard was as exceptional as Rainer had been led to believe from the stories. They were fast and strong and cunning.

"Excellent work, Nicholette," their captain said, patting a dark-haired guard on her shoulder. She turned her attention to the scowling redheaded woman who lay panting on the ground. "Maren, that was very sloppy. You're too defensive—not taking your moments to go after her, and you're missing opportunities to take Nicholette down. I know that look on your face. Don't let that temper rule you. Either the rage feeds you, or it feeds on you. Don't be a meal."

It took Rainer a moment to realize that Princess Jessamin was the one calling out the sharp orders. He and Cal bowed, but she waved them off. Her gaze was riveted to the fight.

She called out commands to both fighters. "Don't get cocky, Nicholette. Stay focused. If I can see that tension in your jaw right before you strike, she can, too. I know your ribs are still bruised from your fall on the boat on the way over."

Nicholette stepped away from the fight. She turned to face the princess, crossing her arms, her face full of contempt.

"That was not my fault. It's a hazard to leave a trap door open like that," Nicholette said.

The other guards broke out into laughter but Jessamin hushed them.

"Situational awareness is part of your job. Now get back in the ring and don't be sloppy," she said.

Cal leaned closer to whisper in Rainer's ear. "She leads the Novumi army. I've been watching them train since they arrived. They're even better than the stories say. Their style is so different. I've never seen fighters who move so quickly—not even our finest hunters. I wouldn't want to meet them in the field."

"Why is Princess Jessamin here if she's supposed to lead Novum's army?" Rainer whispered.

"Rumor has it that her mother has been concerned about their lack of active allies and difference in ruler—it makes them a target and a threat to other kingdoms. Evan thinks that she chose now to offer Jessamin's hand because Argaria could use the military knowledge, and she could use having both Argaria and Olney as allies." Cal turned to look at him, apprehension on his face. "Listen, Evan wanted me to talk to you. Given all that's going on, he wants to—" He cleared his throat, shifting his stance, and rubbed the back of his neck.

"Gods, out with it," Rainer said.

Cal shook his head. "Xander insists on being at every border skirmish to show how important all his people are—not just the wealthy ones. But Evan doesn't want him out and about this week without him or me or—"

Rainer sighed. "Or me with him."

"We know you and Xander have a complicated history, but we trust you. Especially when it comes to protecting a valuable target."

Rainer laughed in disbelief—protect the man who was actively trying to steal his fiancée. It was a bold request, which was likely why Evan was having Cal make it. A strategist would know the request would be better received from a close friend.

Rainer groaned. "I know I'm used to protecting someone so reckless, but that's a lot to ask."

Cal shrugged. "Kind of like convincing your fiancée to come back to relive her past so that you can be certain she's done with her ex-husband?"

Rainer blew out a breath. "That's not what I did."

Cal cocked his head to the side. "My mistake. Dragging your fiancée across two kingdoms so you can have a mission to throw yourself into instead of having to build a new life of your own."

Rainer crossed his arms. "Tell me how you really feel, Cal."

A sheepish smile stole over Cal's face. "Just trying to fit a year's worth of friendship into a couple weeks. I have to call it like I see it."

Rainer didn't like that he was so knowable by so many people. What did it say that all his friends could predict how he'd react?

The truth of what Cal said stung, as did the casual nature of the accusations.

He ran a hand through his hair. "I swear I'm trying to rebuild."

Cal patted his shoulder. "I get it. I felt a little aimless post-Gauntlet myself. Getting out of Olney really forced me to think about what I wanted for the first time ever after years of just being Sylvie's guardian. It was difficult at first, but I have more of a life here than I ever have at home because I took the risk." He shook his head and waved a hand toward the stables. "Gods know it's not easy. I took my fair share of scrutiny when we first got here and I had no idea how to even begin with diplomacy. That's Sylvie's thing. I'm just trying to keep up with her. Like always. But at least here I've been able to make my own way without the burden of a history."

Rainer was happy for him, but Cal made what was so difficult for him sound so remarkably simple. It was a little humiliating to see everyone moving on when Rainer was still so stuck.

"It's okay to work at figuring it out as hard as you've worked on everything else. Just don't expect to start with all of the answers. Give yourself the grace your father never has and allow yourself to be imperfect for once," Cal teased. "You'll survive it. The rest of us have been doing it forever."

"I've been doing carpentry and I'm truly terrible at it," Rainer said. He pulled out the half-carved star flower from his pocket.

Cal eyed it skeptically. "Is that bad?"

Rainer laughed. "You know when we used to watch the new guardians at the beginning of training and they'd be all wide-eyed and stunned every day because they thought they knew it all and were only just then learning that they didn't?"

Cal nodded.

"This is like that. Every success is met with learning just how much I still don't know."

"Sounds like a good place to me. A whole world out in front of you with new things to learn."

They fell into a silence, watching the princess guards fight for a while.

A commotion broke out back at the stables and Rainer and Cal rushed to see what was wrong. As they entered the dank space, Rainer's heart started pounding. The jovial laughter of drinking hunters was replaced by a rushing sense of urgency and frantic voices.

The group was gathered around a man that they'd laid across the table.

"Slayer's work," whispered one of the hunters, touching his fingertips to his forehead, his lips, and then his heart in a silent prayer to the gods.

Rainer had only seen someone in such a state once before, when a witch had brought her guardian back to Olney a bloody mess, saying that a slayer had gotten ahold of them. She'd hidden, but her guardian wasn't so lucky. The man was a drooling puddle, wiped clean of every memory that made him who he was. He could barely walk. His eyes were vacant and unfocused, and he couldn't speak.

It was truly horrifying. So much so that Rainer had nearly pissed himself the first time he and Cecilia had fought a slayer in the wild.

"Fetch Magdalena," Cal told one of the guards nearby. He turned back to Rainer. "Should we get Cece?"

"I don't think so. Their healer is likely much more skilled," Rainer said.

Cecilia was skilled with memory but she had never worked on the victim of a slayer. The palace healer was more likely to have that experience, and Rainer wanted to protect Cecilia a little longer if he could.

The healer, Magdalena, appeared a few moments later on the heels of a hunter. She looked to be in her fifties, with smile lines around her eyes and mostly gray hair swept back in a bun at the nape of her neck. She looked over the man before ordering several of the hunters to bring him to her healing suite so she could continue to try to work on him. She didn't look optimistic.

"I'm not sure much can be done," she said, meeting Cal's eye. "Are all our former slayers accounted for?"

Cal sighed. "All but one."

Magdalena turned and followed her patient inside, leaving Rainer and Cal alone.

"There's something else," Cal whispered. He nodded his head to the side, and Rainer followed him farther away from the stables. "The man they brought in. That's Jude Harek. He's Evan's most trusted captain in the Argarian army."

Rainer's mouth went dry. "What do you think they wanted?"

Cal shrugged. "Evan intentionally compartmentalizes knowledge. It's unlikely that Jude would know anything too damaging, but choosing him sends a certain message."

Uneasiness settled in Rainer's stomach as he walked back into the castle and parted ways with Cal.

It was a shitty start to the day, which was why he found his feet seemingly involuntarily carrying him toward Cecilia. He tugged at the connection between them, following the impulse. He found her in one of the sitting rooms having yet another tea with the princesses, Sylvie, and Xander.

She was wearing a new dress. Even from across the room, he could see the way the blue fabric brought out her eyes, as if the seamstress had dyed it to match.

She looked gorgeous. He thought of how beautiful she looked in that dress and sent that love across their bond.

Her eyes closed, and her hand came to her heart, her face the picture of joyful serenity. Rainer loved to watch her in those quiet moments. It was their own private communication in a room full of people. There was something intimate about sharing how much he loved her without words.

Her eyes blinked open and locked on him right away. Without thinking, Rainer did the exact thing he had an impulse to do.

Maybe it was years of shoving down what he wanted, shattering his self-control, or perhaps he just didn't have a single care left to surrender. He crossed the room, and instead of kissing her hand as he was supposed to until they were married, he cupped her face in his hands and pressed his lips to hers in a long, slow kiss.

She tensed at first from the sheer surprise of it, but then she leaned in, her hands on his waist, moving idly against the fabric of his tunic. He wove his fingers through her soft hair, wishing he could stand there kissing her for the rest of the day. They were both a little lost in each other.

Finally, he pulled back, aware of the gasps of the princesses. His cheeks warmed with embarrassment at his lack of restraint.

He cleared his throat and bowed, kissing Cecilia's hand. "Lady Reznik, you look absolutely stunning today."

"Is this your new way of apologizing?" she whispered, stifling a giggle.

"I'm sorry for being an ass." He turned to the rest of the group, heat rushing to his face. "Sorry for the intrusion, ladies."

Rainer walked out of the room as if he'd just done the most normal thing in the world. Following Cal's advice meant doing what he wanted, and Rainer genuinely didn't care what the people of the court thought. He'd kiss his beautiful fiancée whenever he wanted. Rules be damned.

21

XANDER

There was a princess asleep in Xander's bed. It was not one of the visiting princesses trying to win his heart. It was *his* princess, and if she wanted him to stop pursuing her, falling asleep in his bed seemed a strange choice.

He was shocked to see her there. When he'd walked into the room he'd reached for his dagger. The attempts on his life and all the new faces at court had put him on edge. But the only threat that Cece posed was breaking his heart.

She lay sprawled sideways across the mattress, one knee tucked up and an arm under her head, the position highlighting the graceful curve of her waist. Her face was tucked into one arm, but he could see the soft pout of her lips. Her sweater hung low, offering a glimpse of her shoulder. Her nightdress was hiked up slightly, offering a view of her pale legs.

She used to nap like that all the time. He'd find her sprawled out, taking up the whole bed. He had no idea why she was there, but he wasn't ready to wake her.

She whimpered softly, and it sent a surge of heat through his whole body. She had made the same sounds in her sleep when they were together, and they wrecked him.

In the past, every night he'd go to bed with her with the best intentions of letting her sleep through the night by trying to fully satisfy both of them before passing out. And every night, inevitably, she'd fall asleep naked, make those soft little whimpers, and push her ass against him. Instead of going back to sleep, he'd kiss her neck, encouraging more of those sounds until she was fully awake and asking for more, and he'd slip inside her.

It would start soft and slow and lazy, but inevitably it would always end with him flipping her onto her belly so he could get deeper, so desperate to have all of her the same way she wouldn't be satisfied until she had all of him.

It was more than just the sex he missed. It was seeing Cece open up, and in a more metaphorical way. There was a moment right before she climaxed where this look came over her, and she was so beautiful and raw and full of love. It was always gone just as quickly as it appeared, but he lived for trying to extend it.

She sighed in her sleep, and he had to fight the urge to climb into bed and hold her again, to feel the way her body curved against his as she slept. He wondered if she would let him or if she would try to punch him. He took a sip of whiskey, trying to chase away the impulse as he looked into the fire.

"Xander?"

He whipped his head back around. Cece's eyes fluttered, heavy with sleep.

"My love, did you miss being in my bed so badly you needed to sneak in while I was out? I'm glad you remembered that you have a standing invitation anytime you want. If you want to snuggle, you only need to ask. I must admit, I missed seeing you here." His voice sounded more hoarse and strained than he intended.

She propped her head on her hand and smiled sleepily. Funny that he'd spent his whole life not connecting to the women he slept with and, for the most part, sleeping alone after any encounters, only to find himself desperately missing sleeping beside her. It shocked him how quickly it became a habit. How much more at peace he felt with her tucked against him.

"I was waiting for you." The sultry sleepiness in her voice sent a shock through him. "I thought you'd be back sooner. I wanted to talk, but I haven't been sleeping well, and it was so nice and warm with the fire. I must have just passed out."

"Or maybe you just found the place where you belong, and it felt so comfortable you fell asleep there."

She pursed her lips, trying not to smile.

For a moment, he could pretend that the past year hadn't happened and that he was just busy doing some kingly business, returning to find his beautiful queen waiting for him. It was the way his life should have turned out—and likely would have—if he had just been honest with her.

"Rainer keeping you up too much with his lukewarm lovemaking?" Xander teased.

She frowned. It was a petty comment. Xander knew from the supreme lack of tension in her body that there was no way she was feeling unsatisfied. Still, he was curious about what made her feel bold enough to come to his room alone at night.

"Jealousy looks bad on you, Your Majesty. One wonders why it's a look you wear so often," Cece said, flopping back on the bed to stretch. She arched her back and reached her arms over her head, jutting her chest out before pressing herself up to a sitting position. "I wanted to know how it's going. What do you think of the princesses so far? It's such a short period of time to get to know them."

"Ahh, you're looking for secrets. Worried someone is going to take your place after today?"

"I'm curious to see if I'm going to have to get up early and learn to cook. I really don't want to lose the bet I made with Rainer," she said.

She shook out her hair and again arched her back in a way that instantly made him think of how she looked riding him. He had to shift in his seat to avoid becoming more aroused.

He really needed to bed someone. A year of self-imposed celibacy, combined with Cece's presence, was killing him. When he met her eyes, she smirked like she could read his mind. She was definitely doing it on purpose. She watched him drink her in, holding perfectly still under his gaze.

"And who did he bet on?" Xander asked.

"I can't tell you that or I'll affect the outcome, but if I lose, it means I have to make him breakfast in bed for two weeks. You know how much I love getting up early and cooking," Cece said.

She walked over to him, stealing his glass and taking a long sip of his whiskey before sitting down in the chair next to him. The familiarity of it was both comforting and jarring.

"I have to admit, I'm a little disappointed that you're not here as some magnanimous early birthday present to me. What a gift it would be to hear you come undone for me after so much time."

Cece stared him down, trying to keep her face tranquil, while a flush spread up her neck to her cheeks. "Perhaps you should just listen at my bedroom door at night, and you'll hear what you're missing."

"Is that an offer? I wouldn't mind listening to you two...or watching, for that matter," he said, only half-joking.

She cocked an eyebrow. "I suspect you wouldn't like what you see."

"What would I see?" he asked.

"There aren't words for it. You have to see it, but it would break your sweet little royal heart," she said, taking another sip of Xander's drink.

"I'd risk it to see you naked again." He smiled.

She threw her head back and laughed with her whole body in a way that melted his heart. "I did miss this."

"I know, love. Me too."

She tilted her head to the side. "Then why have I not heard from you in a year?"

Xander couldn't explain it now—not when he was exhausted and overwhelmed at the prospect of marrying someone else in a few weeks' time. Some part of him had hoped he'd see her again, and she'd hold no sway over him—that the magnetic draw to her had been purely Cato's influence, or perhaps that time and nostalgia had made her grander than she was. But that was not the case. In fact, it felt worse. The more she deflected his flirtation, the more determined he felt to try to hook her in. It was completely pathetic. *He* was completely pathetic.

"Nothing to say? Fine." She brushed his hair away from his forehead. "Are you actually trying to like one of these women?"

"As much as I can."

It was complicated with Cece around, yet it would have been impossible without her there. Evan took a calculated risk inviting her, and Xander had to respect how well his friend knew him. If she hadn't come, he would have just dismissed the whole thing.

Cece's arrival raised the stakes. He wanted her to see him at his best. He wanted her opinion on the women as much as he wanted her jealousy.

Seeing her here was strange because, in many ways, she was exactly as she had always been. And still, Xander could see the way grief had chipped away pieces of her. He could see fear in her where there had been none before. It only came in glimpses, but he was desperate to see it, to truly know it like everything else about her. She was a mystery he couldn't stop himself from wanting to untangle. The more she opened, the more he wanted to see. The fact that she wasn't his to unfold anymore was entirely his fault, and it still stung even after a year.

She closed her eyes and brought her hand to her heart. Her face displayed her tranquility, and she sighed. He knew that face. It was the face she made whenever Rainer sent something through their bond. She once described it to him as a rush of love to the heart, almost like the sensation of a rush of blood to the head. When they were together, it had driven him insane that her guardian had this secret, powerful way of communicating with her. It still made him crazy with jealousy.

"Everything okay?" Xander asked.

"Yes, I just wouldn't be surprised if Rain was here in a few minutes. He's looking for me."

"No doubt he will be disturbed to find you here."

"Doubtful. Rainer trusts me. It was his idea to come back to Argaria in the first place, and he had to convince me."

"You didn't want to come?" Xander tried to keep the hurt out of his voice, but he was sure she saw it.

She swallowed. "It's been—really hard. I didn't want to get sucked back into another mess. It seems there's always one more thing we need to do before we can just settle down and heal and enjoy our lives. I wanted to see you but I died last time we were all together. A part of me did die, if I'm being honest. I wasn't looking to take more punishment." She finished the whiskey, and he poured her more.

He studied her beautiful, worried face. "I shouldn't have made it about me."

"It is about you, Xan. You lost everything, and you deserve to be happy now. I want that for you. I want to help you, and if it was as simple as that, I would have come here without question. It's everything else that scares me. You never do."

Her words were brutal in their kindness.

"Part of me wishes I did. I wish you were worried about losing your heart again. I hate that your heart is safe around me when mine is always in peril around you."

She blew out a breath. "You know how I feel about Rain. He's it."

"It was always going to be him," Xander said.

Cece frowned. "Maybe. I'm not saying this to hurt you, but we'll never know for sure what would have happened if you'd just been honest from the beginning. I hope you'll learn from that for this next relationship."

They were quiet for a moment. Xander felt momentarily crushed by the weight of his mistakes.

"It's fair to say I would have never stopped loving Rainer, and I would have never stopped wanting him. He was always in my heart."

"And you're happy now?"

"I'm getting there. Some days, it feels like I'll never fully be there. But with Rain, yeah, I'm happy. He's the sweetest person I've ever known. There aren't words for what I feel. You've always been sexy and very flirtatious, but Rain just has the biggest heart, and he's so kind."

He grinned at her. "Go back to the part where you said I'm sexy."

She rolled her eyes. "You know you're sexy. You have six princesses swooning over you. You don't need me to tell you, and you don't need my attention."

"But what if I want it, love?"

Cece frowned. "If you want it, you're going to have to tell me what that sound is."

Xander froze. He'd become so numb to the incessant sound of the truth mirror Grimon had given him, he'd not considered that she or any other witch who wandered into his room would hear it. The mirror had grown more persistent, louder over the past few months. Occasionally, he'd walk into his room after a long day and find it inexplicably sitting on the bed or his bedside table. The more resistant he was to looking at it, the more aggressive it became.

"What sound?"

Cece pursed her lips. "You're usually such a good liar."

There was a light tap on the door. Saved by the clingy guardian.

"Come in," Xander called.

Rainer walked in, looking from Xander to Cece.

"Hi, Rain," Cece said, grinning at him.

"When you said you were ducking out for a bit, I thought you meant a bit, not the rest of the night." His voice was calm, but there was a tic in his jaw.

Cece must have sensed it. She crossed the room, resting a hand on his chest and standing on her tiptoes to kiss him. When she pulled back, Rainer's shoulders relaxed slightly.

"Everything good?" he asked, looking over at Xander.

"Yes, I just came up to talk to Xander and fell asleep while I was waiting. Just a little girl talk."

"I was looking forward to Cece's expert counsel," Xander said, stealing back his whiskey from where Cece had set it on the table and finishing the glass before pouring another.

Rainer gave her a suspicious look. "Lady Reznik, I certainly hope you're not using your considerable influence over the king to try to win our bet."

She feigned offense. "I wouldn't dream of it, and as you well know, no one can control the king—not even the king himself."

"I never have been able to control myself when it comes to you, love," Xander said with a wink.

Cece frowned at him, stealing a glance up at Rainer. He wrapped his arms around her from behind and tucked a kiss into her neck. She scolded him half-heartedly, but it was impossible to miss the joy on her face.

"So, who's the front runner?" Rainer asked.

"Princess Clare is very sweet."

Cece's outrage was swift. "I don't like that woman. No one is that nice."

"Just because you are not that sweet doesn't mean no one is," Rainer said.

"I am plenty sweet," she said, craning her neck to look up at him.

"You seem a little more sour now," Rainer teased.

"You're perfect as you are. Sour and sweet, like a lemon cake," Xander said with a smile.

Cece grinned, triumphant, and Rainer rolled his eyes.

Xander knew he should behave, but he enjoyed pushing Rainer. What else would he do with his time? Actually court a princess? He turned his gaze on Cece. "Though I must admit, every time my lips or tongue brushed your skin, all I ever tasted was sugar."

Rainer bristled. "I'm not afraid to punch a king."

Xander should have stopped, but he didn't want to. Riling up Rainer was an old pastime and the habit was hard to break.

"Oh, love, I forgot to mention that some of your old dresses are in the closet there still, if you need anything," Xander said. "There are also some of those lacy underthings I used to peel off with my teeth."

A beautiful blush lit Cece's face.

"You're probably surprised there's any left, considering how many I shredded because I was desperate to be inside you," Xander said. "You know, I've never properly thanked you for saving my life, love."

She gave him a warning glare. "Yes, you have."

"No, I haven't. There are so many ways I'd like to thank you."

She tensed as if reading precisely what was on his mind.

"I'd like to thank you with my lips and my tongue and my hands. I'd like to thank you bent over the desk in my study and splayed out on my bed and up against the wall. I'd like to thank you until you're screaming my name loud enough for the whole castle to hear you. I'd like to thank you until you're too sore or exhausted to move."

Cece tried to look annoyed, but she only succeeded in looking turned on.

Rainer's hands fisted. Xander met his eyes, cocking an eyebrow in challenge, curious what the guardian would do.

Did Xander have a death wish? Maybe. But what good was having their whole group of friends back together if he couldn't at least get a rise out of Rainer?

Rainer's eyes closed and a serene look passed over his face. All the tension left his body. When he blinked his eyes open, he kissed the top of Cece's head.

"Fun trick," Xander muttered. He hated that bond.

"Xander, stand up," Cece said.

He stared at Cece as she crossed the room to meet him.

"Stand up," she repeated.

He put down his drink and stood.

"I should have done this when I first got here instead of playing your silly games."

She wrapped her arms around his waist in a tight hug, leaning her head against his chest. The sweetness of it almost knocked him over. "Xander, I missed you, and I care about you, and I'm glad you're all right."

"No one has done this since—" he started.

She met his eyes, her face a mask of devastation. "No one has *hugged you* since me?"

Xander hugged her back, burying his face in her hair and holding her tight to his body. He didn't realize how badly he needed it until that moment. All of his emotions had felt bound up for months, but now they threatened to unravel him all at once. The urge to cry was so foreign he hardly recognized it. He immediately pulled back on his emotions.

"Relax, Xan. I'll stay right here as long as you need," she whispered.

A rush of warmth lit in his chest, spreading through his limbs. It had been so long since he'd felt her goddess powers. He didn't know she could even still use them. Squeezing her tighter, he was vaguely aware of her waving Rainer away. To Xander's surprise, the guardian nodded and left the room.

"Why were you waiting here for me tonight?" He sounded so pathetic, but the question was nagging at him.

She drew away, and frowned. "It can wait. It's not important right now."

"Why haven't you set a date?"

She rolled her eyes and blew out an exasperated breath. "Not you too."

"It's just that you came back for him and all. I assumed you'd do it in short order."

She chewed her lip and said nothing, but frustration was painted all over her face—in the stubborn tilt of her chin and the wrinkle in her brow. He wished he could read her mind.

"I missed you so much it physically hurt. I don't think I ever realized how lonely I was until I had you to talk to. I still love you too much," Xander whispered.

"I know," she said, squeezing his hand. "Why don't you lay down, and I'll sit with you for a while?"

He frowned.

"It's not a trick. It's meant to be a comfort. Evan is strategic, but he's not exactly warm. Why don't you let me take care of you tonight? I'll remind you what it's like to have someone there for you. Maybe inspire you to pick a new queen," she said hopefully.

He didn't say anything, just turned and moved toward the bed. He took off his boots and shirt and climbed under the blankets. Cece laid down next to him, on top of the quilt.

"You're just here because you feel sorry for me," he sighed.

"I feel no such thing," she scoffed. "You're an incredibly handsome, wealthy man who rules a kingdom. I feel no pity for you. I simply care about you. We all need someone sometimes. It's okay to admit that you need comfort, Xan. I won't tell anyone."

She ran her fingers through his hair, and he almost moaned. He loved when she did that. She grinned knowingly as she continued to move her fingers in soft, languid circles. They lay in silence for a long time.

"You taught me how to love. I'm sorry that I taught you how to stop."

She frowned. "I never stopped."

He wanted to challenge it so she'd convince him. He wanted to kiss her—to feel that love. That would be a terrible idea, though, because if she let him kiss her, he'd never want to stop. Months of pent-up longing reared up inside him. She could kill him with desire, and he'd let her.

"Don't leave yet," he whispered. It was pitiful, but having Cece close made falling asleep alone feel unbearable.

"I won't. I'll stay until you fall asleep," she said.

In the fading firelight, Xander wondered if anyone would ever be as good at loving him as Cecilia Reznik and if he would let them if they tried.

22

CECILIA

After a day of watching Xander stroll and flirt with all the princesses, Cecilia's face was sore from forcing a smile. Rainer was still off with Cal trying to hunt down answers among hunters and guards. He had sent word that he wouldn't be back until late. He and Cal hoped the combination of alcohol and gambling would encourage looser lips among the hunters.

Alone in her room after dinner, Cecilia paced restlessly. Finally, when she could no longer stand the silence or facing the court vultures, she decided to search out Xander and get the answers for which she'd traveled across two kingdoms. Last night he'd seemed upset and clearly missed her but she didn't understand how he so easily ignored her all of this time.

The suspense was making her crazy, but her desire to know the answer to her question had finally overpowered her fear about what that answer would be.

She ducked down the hallway, stopping short when she spotted Princess Clare Pyke of Aldrena in the corridor.

"Are you lost, Your Grace?" Cecilia asked, dipping into the slightest curtsey she could manage.

Clare jumped, noticing Cecilia for the first time. "Lady Reznik,

I'm afraid I may have made a wrong turn, yes." Anxiety buzzed like a cloud around her.

"Interesting that you ended up here," Cecilia said. "The guest suites are in another wing entirely."

Clare shrugged and blushed. "I was looking for the king."

The enormous, intricately carved wooden doors of the Savero royal archive towered behind the princess. Cecilia's eyes narrowed.

"And you thought you'd find him in the royal archives?"

Clare turned and looked at the doors. "Oh, is that what this room is? It was locked, but from the scene on the door, I thought perhaps it was a war room or council room of some sort, and I heard the king has council meetings in the evenings." The princess shifted nervously.

"Probably best that you leave the king to his work. If you don't understand that a king is a busy man, I'm not sure you'll make a great queen," Cecilia said pointedly.

The princess raised her eyebrows and frowned. "It appears you're the only one who knows what he needs, Lady Reznik. Perhaps you could give one of us a chance to learn." Clare's blush burned brighter as she spoke. "I really like him, you know."

"You don't even know him," Cecilia snapped.

"I know that he has an ex-wife who seems to still want all of his attention and who is protective enough to stand in my way. That at least suggests he's a man of quality. Three weeks is a short time to stand out with so many women competing for his attention. I just wanted a moment alone with him, of which you seem to get plenty."

Clare turned and disappeared down the hall before Cecilia could say more.

Cecilia continued down the hall and knocked on Xander's bedroom door. Xander beckoned her inside without asking who it was.

"Honestly, you need better security. Aren't you supposed to be the king or something?" she said as she walked into the room.

Xander grinned. "My love, what a pleasant surprise! Did you rethink my offer to properly thank you?" He gestured to the bed.

She laughed. "No." She looked at the pile of correspondence on the table next to Xander. "Oh, you're busy. It's not important. I can come back."

He held up a hand. "Nonsense. What's on your mind?"

She hesitated, and he motioned to the seat next to him. "Well, first of all, I just think you should know that Princess Clare was prowling about the halls near the royal archive, spouting some nonsense about wanting alone time with you and that she thought the royal archive was your meeting room. I don't trust that woman."

Xander arched an eyebrow. "As you've said before, love."

"She has quite an anxious energy. I think she's hiding something."

"And is that something that she wants me, and it makes you jealous?" he taunted.

"No." Cecilia crossed her arms. She hated that he might be right. She was not objective about these women. How could she be? There was no one who seemed good enough for Xander—not after all he'd been through. Not after the way he'd protected her at his own peril. He deserved someone who was unselfish and thoughtful—someone who would protect him.

Xander chuckled. "Very well. I'll mention it to Evan."

Appeased, Cecilia relaxed into her seat slightly.

"And did you come here just to talk about Princess Clare?" Xander inquired.

He poured her tea as she sat next to him, fixed it with lemon and sugar, just how she liked it, and waited for her to speak.

"Will you please answer the question I've been asking you since I got here?" she asked.

Xander stared into his glass as if the answer was hidden there. "Which question is that?"

"Why did you not write me back? Why did you leave without at least letting me know? What you went through—" She let out a shuddering breath. "What I went through—" Her voice broke and she placed her hand over her heart, trying to soothe her racing pulse. She squeezed her eyes shut, trying to block out the memory. The pale imitation was burned on her eyelids so that even when she wasn't calling up the memory, it was always waiting there. The fear was as wild and fresh as it had been when she was lost in the dark maze of death.

"It was selfish of me to come here for my own answers, but I want peace so badly. I trusted you so deeply and you broke that trust. That was one thing. But then you walked away and never looked back. Like it was *easy*. And now I feel like I cannot trust myself with Rainer. I cannot believe that he couldn't do the same if I can't give him what he wants."

Guilt swelled in the air around Xander.

"I am not telling you to make you feel bad," she pressed on, her words flowing together in a rush of breath. "I know you have your own pain and I know you owe me nothing, but I had an idea of what we had together and I've spent a year wondering if it was just a fantasy I invented in my mind. What if Rainer just feels like he owes me for what I did for him? What if he is still in love with a version of me that doesn't exist anymore?"

Xander frowned and rubbed his temples. "I can't believe I'm saying this, but I'm doing it just for you, Cece. Rainer will want you no matter what. Are you blind or just foolish? Or simply afraid to let him love you?"

She startled at the words. She was afraid of Rainer's love and afraid of the way love had hurt her so brutally in the past.

"I'm afraid he will think I'm enough now, but that eventually I won't be," she said.

She had never said the words out loud, and they wrecked her. It felt as though they'd been cut right out of her heart.

"There are so few things that I know for certain," Xander offered. "I have watched Rainer go from being a staunch rule-follower to a rebel breaking apart the very system he lived within for so long and kissing his beautiful fiancée in front of a room full of royalty. I'm certain he will love every version of you. But rest assured that if for some reason he can't, and he decides to be the world's biggest fool once again, I will be waiting to swoop in and steal you away for myself."

"I don't deserve it," she whispered.

"You do."

"I've done horrible things," she said, wiping away tears.

"We all have. We are flawed, but your flaws make you beautiful, Cece. One of a kind and even more compassionate than you already were. You are a good person deep down."

She sniffled silently, and he rubbed comforting circles on her back. "It's not fair of me to rely on you."

"Well, I say it is, and I'm king, so—"

She giggled as she pulled back and looked at him. She brought her hand to his cheek, meeting his luminous hazel eyes. "I want you to be happy."

Xander sighed in frustration. "My love, what makes you think I am unhappy?"

"Just your face, your emotions, and the way you still chase me."

"I will always chase you, Cece. It's a reflex to pull you close."

She sighed, unable to stuff down the guilt. "But you deserve happiness."

"Well, perhaps your definition of happily ever after and mine are different."

She stared at him. She'd been trying to force him into her version of happily ever after. She hadn't stopped to consider his definition of the concept might be different.

Xander laughed. "Speechless. That's a first."

"I'm sorry."

Maybe Xander wouldn't be happy married. Perhaps he'd feel as trapped by it as she'd felt before her first Gauntlet run. Didn't she resent the system that neatly coupled people up like it was their duty to live happily ever after? Hadn't she felt like the walls were closing in even when she was in love with him, and she was staring down a marriage?

"I know," Xander sighed. "I can't help feeling like maybe you think it will assuage your guilt for being happy if I'm settled."

"It's not that." She played with the sleeve of her dress. "Well, maybe that's part of it. I want you to have what I have. I want to see that spark back in you, but not for me."

Xander tugged at one of her curls, watching it coil back into place. "You're such a beautiful liar. You always want me to pine for you, and don't offend me by pretending you don't. Rainer may be steady and passionate in his own way, but you enjoy my sense of drama."

Even after months apart, he saw her. It was all true. She wanted him to move on as much as she wanted to know that she'd solidified a place in his heart. It didn't come from cruelty as much as the desire to know that what she felt was real, no matter how short-lived it might have been. His lack of correspondence irked her.

She'd hoped to look at Xander and feel some old pang in her heart, not a relentless desire to prove how much she mattered to him. Sylvie used to talk of closure as a way to find peace when a relationship ended, but Cecilia and Xander had vowed to spend their lives together, and Xander's deal with Cato tore that apart and left her doubting any part of his love had been real. After months of being ignored, she wanted to be assured that she meant something.

"I want you to feel settled," she said. "To feel seen. You are too good of a person, and too wonderful of a husband, and much too good in bed to be so lonely and morose all the time."

Xander winked. "I never expected more than this. My life is not exactly how I imagined it to be, but it's the same result. I will marry a beautiful, powerful princess. In time, I'm certain I will love her in my own way, but I have no desire to cheapen what we had by replacing you."

"I'm irreplaceable," she teased.

"You are that." The longing in his eyes was unmistakable.

"I'm kidding, Xan."

"I'm not."

She stared at him, eyes narrowing. "Oh, my gods! You're *scared*." She leaned back in her chair and shook her head. "I never thought I'd see something frighten you after all we've been through."

His eyes went wide, and his fingers tapped his thumb furiously. It was rare to see his anger directed at her, but now Cecilia felt it coming off of him like waves of heat off summer sand.

"I'm not scared," he gritted out.

She snatched his glass and sipped his whiskey. "I don't blame you. I hurt you. Why risk opening yourself up to that again? I remember well what Davide told me when I was on the other side. Give your fear a name and it loses its power. What would you name this one?"

Xander spun her chair toward him, caging her in with his arms so his face was inches from hers. "I'm not scared."

"You are more of a coward not to admit it. Name the fear, Xander."

The air grew tense between them, the storm brewing, past and present colliding. This was not why she'd traveled across two kingdoms, but she could not stop her gaze from dropping to his mouth. She was so tired of being careful, so tired of the pressure of being grateful and kind to people who thanked her for dying, so tired of the pressure to be happily ever after.

"If I'm a coward, then you are too," he said. "You're afraid if you let me in, you won't be able to throw me back out again. You still love me, too."

Cecilia frowned. "Of course I do. It was never a question of loving you. I've never stopped. But I could not be with you when I didn't trust you. And I couldn't live without Rainer. I made the only choice I could live with, and it almost killed me."

Relief broke over his face. "Well, you have another choice to make now," he said, his gaze dropping to her lips.

She swallowed hard, barely breathing. "What choice?"

"Whether you would like me to make love to you all night until you're too exhausted to move. Or if you want to run scared back to your fiancé, who had no problem seducing you away from me. I promise you, love, if you let me, I will have you coming so hard they'll hear you screaming back in Olney. I haven't properly fucked anyone in months, and I've dreamt of being inside you every night since the last time I was. I will worship you like I always have. I'll make you feel filthy, just the way you like. I'll even let you blame it all on me afterward. You can pretend you didn't enjoy it. You can pretend you won't be dreaming of my mouth on your pussy for weeks. You can pretend you won't touch yourself, thinking of the way I fuck you up against the wall, and it will do almost nothing to chase away the bottomless want we both feel."

She gasped. She should leave right now. If Rainer flirted like this with someone else, she would be wrecked with jealousy. He deserved better.

Though maybe that was the true creeping fear that never left her. *Rainer deserves better.*

"My love, you are so wonderfully transparent, and it's one of my favorite things about you. Now tell me that you want that."

Xander's eyes were incendiary. She glanced around the room, trying to distract herself from the dirty words. It didn't work. When she looked at the desk in the corner, she imagined him bending her over it. When she looked at the chair next to the window, she imagined straddling and riding him. When she looked at the bed, she imagined him hooking her calves over his forearms and thrusting into her the way he loved to.

She did not want him, not really. Her restlessness always seemed tipped toward destruction and she wasn't sure how to right it.

She cleared her throat and met his eyes again. "Are you truly satisfied with that? To know you can never truly have me to yourself?"

"I am happy with anything that ends with me inside you." Playful impatience laced his words.

"Be serious."

"Cece, I have made mistakes in the past, but rest assured I will always be happy to have you in whatever way you still choose to give yourself to me. I know what I did. I know what I broke. But I still love you. I will still count on you to see me—however maddening it is when you do. I still want you." His face softened, and he ran his fingers over her hand.

She'd been prepared for sexy Xander, the one who came on to her and flirted with her aggressively even when they were married. What she was woefully unprepared for was sweet Xander. Loving, lost, wounded, wanting-to-connect, looking-right-into-her-heart Xander.

This was what she'd wanted. Proof that she hadn't imagined what was between them. Proof that she could trust herself.

He leaned closer. The plush fabric of her chair groaned as his hands gripped the arms tighter. His breath danced over her lips, sweet, with a hint of whiskey. "Come now, love, you used to be brave."

"And you used to be reckless."

Cecilia felt entirely divided. She wanted satisfaction from her relationship with Xander, and the closer he came to moving on, the more she seemed poised to sabotage what she had. One moment she was clawing her way back from death for Rainer, and the next she was finding new strategies to shove him away. She was as frightened to let him love her as she was of losing him. Since she'd returned from death, she felt a persistent destructiveness inside of her that she could not shake. Every time she thought it had released her, it took on a new form.

Cecilia didn't want to think anymore. She wanted to feel something.

"What are you waiting for? I thought kings took what they wanted."

Xander blew out a breath. "If you want to tear your perfect fairy tale apart with a kiss, I'm not strong enough to stop you. I'd let you ruin me a thousand more times if only to escape one moment of feeling this broken."

The words were like a knife slid skillfully under her ribs. There was no arming herself against this version of Xander. Cecilia thought she wanted answers from him, but now she only wanted oblivion. Perhaps that was exactly the thing he was chasing as well.

23

XANDER

For a year Xander had been poised on the precipice of madness, and Cece was waiting to push him over the edge.

He couldn't tell if she actually wanted to kiss him or if she, like him, had survived death only to throw herself toward every hazard like she was helpless to the call of the void.

He did not want to be the reckless trap she threw herself into, but he'd ached for her so long and he was too weak not to give in.

Xander arched an eyebrow, hunger creeping into his gaze. "Is that what you need? For me to just take you so that you can be blameless?"

Cece licked her lips, dragging her teeth across her lower lip. That shattered his last semblance of control.

Xander kissed her like his entire existence depended on it. The world around them seemed to pause to make space for the suspended moment between them.

It was the same and yet not. Xander was stunned that something he'd done so many times could be equal parts mundane and strange. Their movements were practiced. Memory burned into muscles. His hands as hungry as hers were hesitant.

She put so much godsdamned sugar in her tea. It was disgusting, but it also gave her mouth a sweet lemony flavor. She tasted like goodness itself, if such a thing were possible. At times he thought himself a villain—kissing her like drinking in her sweetness would undo all his wrongs. He wished her lips were laced with absolution—wished it were so simple. She'd always been a blessing he was unworthy of but couldn't stop wanting.

Gods help him—how had he ever stopped kissing her? How could he accept a true goodbye from the person he loved most in the world?

As if one kiss could undo months of hopeless longing. As if he could forget what it was like to fall asleep next to her every night and wake up beside her every morning. As if untangling the roots she'd grown deep in his heart was as simple as untangling his fingers from her hair.

Xander forced himself to focus. To remember the feel of her as she melted against him, soft in all the right places and strong underneath. Her lavender-lemon scent, mixed with his bergamot and cedar, like summer and winter at war with each other. The sound of her whimper as he lifted her and she wrapped her legs around his waist.

He wanted to kiss her all day. He wanted to make love to her until she looked at him and said his name as she always had, like he was the only thing in the world she wanted to see. He wanted to hold her against him all night and listen to her breathing. He was made of nothing but want in every moment with her.

He carried her over to the bed, sitting down on the edge with her in his lap. She hesitated, as if to draw away when he was not ready.

He felt the passion falter. The kiss was a fire burning fast and hot, soon to be struggling for air. The more tentative her movements, the harder he kissed her. He poured all the months of longing into the kiss as if he could breathe desire into her body the way he had so many times before.

His skin tingled at her touch and all his blood rushed south. A year had passed, but his body responded to her as if it had only been hours since they last touched.

His hands tangled in her hair and he tugged gently, tilting her head back to drag his teeth down her neck. He pushed her dress over her shoulders, kissing all the new skin he revealed and slipping his other hand between her legs.

He felt the brokenness in both of them. The familiarity of those shattered pieces trying to find comfort in fitting together. The solace of a bad habit.

Something was off. The desperation—the unmitigated need—in his body met the lack of desire in hers. Reality crashed down on him. The inequity between them suddenly made plain: love versus loved.

She was kissing a memory while he was kissing a wish.

Cece drew back, steadying herself with her hands on Xander's chest, right above the scar of the wound that had nearly killed him.

"I'm sorry. This was a mistake. I never should have come here." He wasn't sure if she meant Argaria or his room. "It was cruel to make you believe—"

Xander ran a hand through his hair, trying to calm the pounding panic in his heart. Her face was flushed, her lips swollen and her eyes glassy with unshed tears because, while he'd felt nothing but relief in kissing her, she'd felt only regret.

Xander sighed. "My love, you are exquisite torture. You grow more lovely every day. It isn't fair."

Cece shook her head, rolling off his lap to put distance between them. She curled in on herself.

Xander wanted to be angry at her, but how could he? He'd always known where he stood with her. He'd just been too much of an optimist and too damn competitive to accept defeat. He'd made her the answer to all of his hurts because it was easier than accepting how he set himself up to lose by repeating the pattern of his entire life— loving someone who put him second. He'd been second in his family and it had insulated him from expectations.

It gave him a risk he could see and take measure of. If he knew where he was vulnerable, he could protect himself. But it had not worked that way with Cece. The more he saw it—the more certain he was that she loved Rainer more—the harder Xander tried to beat the odds.

"It will be okay. He will forgive you."

She shook her head. "It's not the forgiveness I worry about, but the hurt I cause him." She rubbed the bridge of her nose. "The hurt I caused you with my carelessness. Gods, I'm such a fool. Why can I not stop pushing him away?"

Xander took her hand in his. "Name the fear, love."

Cece blew out a shuddering breath. "It's not one fear. It's an army of them. I'm afraid that he will see and know all of me and it won't be good enough. I'm afraid I don't love myself enough to feel worthy of him. I'm afraid I am enough for him now, but someday I won't be. I'm afraid of so many things I cannot even find words for. Grimon warned me—"

Her words trailed off in a gasp. He'd read her words for months, but she'd talked all around what had happened when she'd died. He knew she'd seen Davide and had heard what his brother said to her, but he did not know what she'd been through.

"I see it in my mind and the words get caught on their way out and when I relive it, it's like it's disconnected from me. Like a memory my body does not have and so I'm frozen between there and now— still in suspension, waiting for my life to start." She pressed a trembling hand to her heart, thumb stroking the golden scar through her dress.

Xander swallowed the lump in his throat. "Tell him. Tell him what you have words for."

She stood, trying to smooth her dress back into place. "I'm sorry, Xan. I shouldn't have made you think—"

He winced.

She stopped in her tracks as if realizing her apology was just making everything worse. "I'll go."

She took a rallying breath, turned, and fled his room. He wanted to chase her—to shake the truth out of her. She was not inherently cruel, but she could be so reckless.

The door slammed closed behind her, the sound resonating in his chest like something slammed closed there as well. She'd swept out of the room and taken any remaining possibility with her.

Dread sat like a stone in Xander's stomach. His love hadn't brought her back to life. It had sent her from this world. It nearly sent him, too. Now he was left trying to learn how to live with half a heart.

He thought he'd reached rock bottom, but it seemed there was farther to fall.

24

RAINER

Rainer turned to face his fiancée, eager to see her after a long day. The door clicked shut behind Cecilia and she looked at him, her eyes glassy with unshed tears.

"Rain."

His gaze raked over her puffy lips, the pink skin on her neck, her rumpled dress and hair. She didn't need to speak for him to know what had happened. Her body was a ledger of her guilt.

When he felt the surge of lust and grief a moment before, he'd assumed she was on her way to see him, but now he knew better.

Rainer had left her alone with Xander the first time and she'd returned deflowered, lovesick, and engaged. Why would he not expect the same, or worse, from this trip?

He clenched a fist at his side, trying to summon calm when all he felt was rage, jealousy, and betrayal. Cecilia was chaos, but he wanted her to be his chaos alone.

She'd needed to settle this one question with Xander. Why had Rainer assumed it would be so simple when Xander was the only other man who'd ever been a threat to her heart?

Because she is not my property. Because the more one tries to control Cecilia Reznik, the more she rebels. Because she belongs to herself.

"Rain, I—"

He held up a hand. "No. I don't want to hear it." He snatched his whiskey glass and threw it across the room. It shattered against the far wall.

Cecilia winced, curling into herself, her eyes wide in surprise. "I'm sorry. I don't know what's wrong with me—"

"No," he repeated. "I love you, but I cannot listen to this right now." He scrubbed a hand over his face and looked at her swollen lips and teary eyes. "Did you fuck him?"

"No," she mumbled.

"Did you want to?"

"No. I don't understand why I did it."

"I feel like I'm just sitting here like a fool, waiting for him to steal you away from me." His control was so practiced, but here he was shouting at the woman he loved because he was desperate to keep her when she was constantly slipping away.

Her eyes narrowed, anger overtaking her fear. "He didn't *steal* me away last time. You let me go. I'm not saying that to hurt your feelings, but you told me you didn't want me. I wanted you to fight for me and you wouldn't, and he did. You didn't lose me to him. You didn't want me."

"But I did—" Rainer insisted.

"I didn't know that. I moved on. So you need to let go of this idea that Xander Savero is going to steal me away. I'm yours and—"

"I can't listen to this bullshit right now." His hands were shaking at his sides and he laughed bitterly. "Telling me you're mine while another man's kiss is still on your mouth. I can't stand the sight of you. I need air."

Rainer crossed the room and opened the door.

"Wait! Where are you going?" she called after him.

He ignored the panic in her voice. "Out! Maybe this time you can be the one who sits alone, wondering what the other is up to."

Rainer slammed the door behind him. He stormed down the hallway, making turns with no plan whatsoever, quickly becoming lost.

The castle walls felt stifling. The entire building was a monument to the Saveros.

Rainer was so foolish. How could he have thought he could bring Cecilia back here into the very heart of Xander's power and she wouldn't feel compelled by it?

Raymond had warned him that love could bring down empires, and Rainer had felt so smug when he finally won Cecilia over. But now Rainer was twisted in knots at the thought of losing her.

He was so stupidly eager to see Xander married off—so delighted for a mission to prove his value. All he'd done was make things worse.

Rainer wanted to break something, anything. He wasn't sure he'd ever been so angry.

He had the distinct feeling that his suffering somehow sharpened him into something more deadly and less compassionate. So much of his life had been about control. Rainer had twisted himself into anxious knots trying to bring Cecilia back to herself, and still he felt her holding back, halting mid-sentence, laying awake and staring at the ceiling. He wanted so badly to pull the truth from her layer by layer—to force her to tear down every barrier between them. But he knew that what he wanted was not something he could get by force.

He hated being angry with her. He wanted to be angry at Xander —that was a comfortable place to direct his anger—but Cecilia made her own choices.

Pushing through the door at the end of the hall, Rainer was finally greeted with cool air. His eyes adjusted to the darkness, and he realized he stood on a high castle wall overlooking the lantern lights of the city below. He walked toward the edge, gripping the stone railing tightly, and dropped his chin to his chest, sucking in deep breaths.

"You're not going to jump or anything, are you?"

Rainer startled and spun to find a woman leaning against the stone wall beside the door, sipping a glass of whiskey.

He sighed, running a hand through his hair. "I just needed some air."

"I can understand that. It's stuffy in there and there are about five too many princesses," the woman said, a sly smile on her lips.

At first glance, Rainer thought she was Princess Jessamin of Novum, but then he realized she wore the clothing of the princess's royal guard, a pale purple tunic embroidered with orchids. At one hip, she wore a deadly looking curved blade and at the other a smaller, more ornate dagger. A lavender scarf hung loose around her neck.

"I don't bite," she said, noticing his appraisal. "I'm Isla."

Rainer smiled slightly. "I hope you'll forgive me for saying so, but you look remarkably like Princess Jessamin. I hadn't noticed before."

Isla smiled and held up her scarf. "I suppose you wouldn't, given that I usually wear this over my face."

Rainer stared at her. "You're related."

Isla's eyes went wide in surprise, but she didn't need to confirm it. His guardian training was so ingrained that he took in every face in the room, searching for threats. He'd noticed that one of Jessamin's guards hid her face at all times, but he also knew from stories of Novum that particularly devout women wore such garb to honor the goddess of the stars, so he hadn't thought anything of it. But now he saw it as an excellent way to hide a royal decoy in a foreign court.

"Sisters?" he asked.

"Cousins."

"Do you like protecting the princess?" he asked.

"Do you like protecting a goddess?" Isla countered.

Rainer choked on a surprised laugh. "I like it more now than I used to."

Isla waggled her eyebrows. "I bet you do."

"Sorry, it's none of my business. I can leave you alone if you'd like some peace," Rainer mumbled.

"No, it's a fair question. In Novum, it's an incredible honor to protect what the queen values, and Queen Aisa values her children most. They are the future. Those who protect Princess Jessamin, Princess Karina, and Prince Proco have the most important job in the kingdom."

Rainer nodded.

"Of course, my story is the boring one. I'd love to hear the story of the Lost Goddess from the man whose love brought her back from the dead," Isla said.

Rainer knew that people liked their story. He didn't blame them. If he'd heard it when they were younger, he would have liked it too, but it still filled him with dread, relief, and grief each time he heard a whisper of it.

"We heard about you from Novumi sailors before we ever came here," she continued. "Months ago, they returned with a tale too grand not to be true. A secret goddess who fell in love with her guardian. A duo who share a soul bond that wraps around their hearts. Storytelling is revered in our culture. We all know who you are."

"Cece and I have always wanted to visit Novum. We love myths and legends and fairy tales. We've always wanted to travel there and listen to your campfire stories and learn about the gods you worship and see the summer auroras."

Isla's eyes lit up. "You should absolutely visit. Our people would love to hear your story from your own mouths. The storytelling tradition is strong in Novum and they especially love to hear new stories from foreign lands. You'd be very popular."

"The last year has been hard and Cece could use something to look forward to," Rainer sighed.

"Trouble with your lady?" she asked.

Rainer tried to shrug it off. "She's a complicated person. She's been through a lot, but she drives me out of my mind."

"She loves you very much," Isla said.

It rankled him when people presumed to know him just because they knew part of his story. "How would you know that?"

Isla was unbothered by his sharp tone. "Because I watch. Make sure you don't let your jealousy blind you. Lady Reznik lights up when you're around. She's a warrior, but she lets you stand in her blind spot. If she didn't love and trust you deeply, she'd never allow that. If you paid attention, you'd notice she does it for no other. Not even the king."

It was a strange thing to get an outside view of his love story from a complete stranger, but what Isla said was true. Especially since that day on the beach. It had been especially hard for Cecilia to be open. He hadn't noticed that she still let him stand in her blind spot, still opened her stance, and he certainly had missed that she didn't let Xander do the same things. Rainer took it all for granted because she'd allowed him to do them for so long.

He scrubbed a hand down his face, blowing out a breath that turned into a little white cloud in the cold air.

"Care for a drink? Take the edge off?" Isla asked. Seeing his hesitation, she added, "I stole it from the king's secret stash. I understand the two of you have quite a contentious relationship. I'd love to hear that story."

Rainer laughed. He considered turning her offer down to keep his head clear, but that seemed less important than obliterating his anxious thoughts. He nodded, and she poured him a glass from the fancy set of crystal she'd also swiped.

He downed the entire glass, handing it back to her.

"Take it easy. This is the good stuff," she teased.

"This is taking it easy."

Isla grinned as she leaned back against the wall. "The king is very fond of your lady."

Rainer hummed in agreement.

"It seems she's also quite fond of him—not that I blame her," Isla said. "If a man looked at me the way he does at her, it would be hard to remain unaffected. In a room full of princesses, he has eyes for her alone."

Rainer nodded, surprised by the note of admiration in her tone.

She straightened, as if realizing Rainer's appraisal. "You're not fond of him."

Rainer sighed. "I would be if he wasn't always so...Xander. They're a lot alike. I think I worry that he understands her in a way that I don't. They both have magic and he has access to this wild side of her that I can't understand. No matter how much I read about magic, I can't understand it the way they do."

"You're looking at the one thing you can't have instead of the many things you do, Guardian McKay. You have a direct line to her heart. You read her effortlessly. You're always right beside her. She looks to you when she's worried, not him."

Rainer considered it as he finished off another glass of whiskey. He should slow down, but he didn't want to. He was still so frustrated —with Cecilia, with himself, with the entire situation.

"Perhaps we could talk about something else. Maybe you could share some stories."

Isla smiled, happy to oblige him. Rainer appreciated that she let him brood silently while she spun her tales. She was true to what he expected of someone from Novum—a great storyteller.

After a while and another two glasses of whiskey, he felt thoroughly buzzed.

Isla smiled at him. "You look like you feel better. I'm afraid I must get back to my princess, but feel free to enjoy the spoils of my snooping," she laughed, gesturing at the whiskey.

Rainer watched her silently retreat into the castle. He closed his eyes, leaning back against the wall next to the door, and sighed heavily. He needed to go back in and confront Cecilia, but had no clue what he would say or do. He had his own rooms that he could stay in, but her anxiety buzzed through their connection like a swarm of bees, and he'd not rest until she calmed down.

All those years, all that striving, the desperate desire to be needed. He'd smothered her with his protection because he'd only known how to be valuable when he was doing something for which he could receive accolades. His duty was just a patch placed over the hole at the center of him. A well of hurt so deep he knew he'd never reach the bottom even if he spent his life trying. He'd made Cecilia the solution, the safe way out, because she loved him as much in his weak moments as she did when he was strong.

He owed her the same even if he was angry.

Before he could move to go inside, the parapet door burst open with a bang.

A blur of silk and dark hair ran by, storming to the railing before letting out a frustrated scream.

Rainer froze, unsure if he should try to silently escape or offer to help.

The woman pulled her red silk dressing gown around her more tightly against the cold air.

"My lady?" Rainer said quietly.

The woman jumped and turned to face him. She rubbed furiously at her puffy eyes and the tears glistening on her cheeks in the dim lantern light.

"Oh, I'm sorry, Guardian McKay. I didn't realize anyone was out here. I'm thoroughly mortified. I can go," she mumbled, trying to hide her tears.

He stared at her, trying to remember her name and title. She was one of Xander's marriage prospects, but Rainer could not place her.

"Eloise Spellman," she said. "I see the terrified lack of recognition on your face. It's fine. I'm used to it. The lone lady among princesses is very forgettable. We haven't been formally introduced, but everyone knows who you are." Her cheeks pinked slightly.

"Everyone knows who I am?" Rainer asked.

She giggled nervously, self-consciously patting her face. "Yes, your love story is a legend. You're also very...noticeable."

The old, pre-Gauntlet-finishing Rainer, would have seen an opening to flirt with her. Despite the dim light and her puffy face, she was very beautiful, with black, curly hair in stark contrast to her porcelain skin. Her pale green eyes were ringed in gold and bright with intelligence. The impulse to flirt was still there, but to what end?

"I had no idea I was so memorable."

She looked away. "Oh yes, you're quite the talk among the ladies of the Argarian court."

He took a step closer. "Are you one of those ladies?"

She met his gaze, her hair spilling over her shoulders. "Maybe."

Reality clicked back into place. He was alone with an unmarried woman in a public place and that woman was one of the king's marriage prospects.

Rainer glanced toward the door. "We probably shouldn't be alone. It could hurt your reputation or your chances with the king."

Eloise laughed bitterly. "As if I stand a chance. Even if the king could tear his attention away from Lady Reznik, it wouldn't land on me. I'm just a lady. It doesn't matter if I know Argarian culture and everyone at court, or gods forbid, I'm smart. '*No man wants a woman with a brain. Keep your mouth shut unless it's offering praise,*' my father always says."

Rainer shook his head. "My father used to say a great many foolish things as well, though I must disagree with yours. The king prefers smart, assertive women. If you want to stand out, you should speak up."

Eloise looked out at the twinkling lantern lights in the town far below.

"Do you even *want* to be queen?" Rainer asked.

Eloise looked startled by the question. "I don't know. I don't have my father's taste for power."

Rainer sighed. "I can sympathize with that."

"Truly, I've spent my whole life wanting what he wants and I *should* want to be queen. Argaria is my home and I love it. I like the changes that King Xander's been making. I can tell he's a good man and, gods, he's handsome—but do I want the responsibility? I don't think so. Just this first week alone is enough to put me off of court life. I've spent most of my life at these social gatherings and the women are abhorrent. I think I was just hoping to find partnership. Becoming queen just puts a bigger target on my back when I'd prefer to blend in."

"I highly doubt there's a room where someone so beautiful could blend in." Rainer didn't understand why he said it. It was a reflex from a different time—a different man who used harmless flirtation to shove away his feelings for Cecilia.

Eloise blushed and met his eyes. Her posture shifted, and she placed her palm on his chest, her fingers tracing the embroidery on his tunic. "You think I'm beautiful?"

"You know you are," Rainer said.

"I'm not sure I believe you," she sighed. "Perhaps you could make me feel it."

She leaned closer, tilting her chin up. She was taller than Cecilia, and he'd only need to bend slightly to kiss her. It would be so easy.

He imagined the insane jealousy Cecilia would feel if he kissed Eloise. Would she make a scene? Would she scream at him? Would she try to fuck him until she was sure he was hers?

Then a jarring thought hit him. *Would she cry?* That question brought him right back to earth. He hated when she cried. It was infuriating when he was angry and she started crying, because he couldn't hold on to his frustration when she was so upset.

He couldn't bear to alienate her further. He didn't even want to. Eloise was beautiful and clearly willing, but he only wanted Cecilia.

Rainer sighed. "You're tempting, Lady Eloise, but I'm afraid I'm very much spoken for. I don't think this would make either of us feel better. If you want the king, he likes persistence. Just don't take no for an answer. Insist on time with him."

Eloise sighed, rubbing her puffy eyes. "I knew you would turn me down. You're one of the good ones. Maybe you're right and I should convince the king that marrying me wouldn't be a mistake. It's hard considering what a prick my father is. Frankly, I understand His Majesty's apprehension about getting involved with me." She laughed to herself before trailing her fingers over Rainer's chest. "If you change your mind, the offer stands."

She turned away and slunk back through the balcony door, leaving Rainer alone with his thoughts.

He looked out over the flickering lantern lights until he had a plan.

If Cecilia wanted passion, he would give it to her, and he'd make sure she knew exactly how he felt. He wasn't about to sit helplessly by and let Xander win her back. Tonight, Rainer needed to remind Cecilia what she was to him.

Tomorrow he'd force Xander to confront the same thing, and Rainer would enjoy doing it.

25

CECILIA

Cecilia hated that all she could do was wait for Rainer to cool down and come back. She could find him—their bond meant she could easily figure out where he was—but he'd said he couldn't stand the sight of her. She didn't blame him.

Her bath hadn't been relaxing at all and now her damp hair chilled on the back of her neck. Her mind wouldn't stop spinning as she paced the room with her silk nightgown billowing around her as she walked.

What if this was the last straw? What if he left? What if he tried to kill Xander, and they arrested him? What if he stopped loving her?

She was so stupid. There was nothing like what she felt for Rainer. She would never be able to truly be with Xander again. A year ago she'd learned her lesson the most brutal way possible, and she'd realized whom she couldn't live without. Why had she been so foolish to risk it? Was this just another way she was punishing herself —by sabotaging what she and Rainer had?

In the unbearable silence, she wondered if she was trying to get him to give up on her so that he wouldn't realize later that she couldn't make him happy. Cecilia still didn't trust that he could love who she was now, and here she was ruining her chance at something good so she wouldn't have the rug pulled out from under her later.

The door creaked open and Rainer stepped into the room.

She wanted to go to him, but she was frozen in place.

He ran a hand through his hair. His cheeks were slightly flushed, and his eyes a bit glassy. He'd been drinking. It wasn't a surprise, but it set Cecilia even more on edge.

"I just had a chat with Eloise Spellman."

Cecilia's stomach turned over so violently she stopped breathing.

Rainer barked out a bitter laugh. "Look how your mind is spinning. You go and fool around with the king, but I have a drink with another woman, and you're green with envy."

"Did you—"

"Did I what—touch her? Kiss her? Fuck her?" he taunted. "She's gorgeous, you know. She stood there with those green eyes and perfect lips in just a silk dressing gown. In another life..." He let the words trail off.

Anger burned through Cecilia, but she kept her mouth shut. It was hypocritical to be angry when she'd just been all over Xander.

"She was so...accommodating."

A fierce wave of nausea roiled her stomach. She shifted her feet, unable to tell if he was lying. Her vision clouded with tears. She blinked them away furiously. Her thumb rubbed her inner wrist frenetically as she tried to soothe herself.

Rainer's gaze tracked the movement, and he faltered. He closed the distance between them, taking her chin roughly in his hand, his eyes wild.

"Where did he touch you?"

Cecilia hesitated before bringing her fingers to her lips. Without warning, Rainer kissed her harshly. It was a consuming and unrelenting kiss, like he was trying to recover what she'd given someone else. He squeezed her chin, bordering on too hard, but she didn't pull away. She was too relieved to want anything but him.

Finally, he drew back, meeting her gaze.

"Where else?" He pushed her back against the hard stone wall.

His eyes were lit with fury, and the sight filled her body with feverish heat.

She ran her fingers down her neck and over her shoulders. Rainer pinned her against the wall as he kissed down her jaw and neck, teeth scraping, right on the edge of too much. Her mind spun wildly. She was confused and also incredibly turned on.

"Rain," she rasped.

She arched into him as he nipped her delicate skin and then licked away each hurt. He was incredibly thorough, making sure to cover every inch of her neck and shoulders, reclaiming all the territory Xander had gained until she ached so badly she thought her knees might give out.

He drew back, his gaze simmering between anger and lust. "Where else?"

She hesitated before slipping the thin straps of her nightgown off her shoulders. The silk pooled around her feet in a midnight-blue puddle. Rainer held his breath as she slid her hand over the lacy panties.

His eyes narrowed, and his face dropped into a furious scowl. "Outside or inside?"

"Outside," she whispered.

He lifted her off her feet and carried her to the bed, throwing her down before ripping off his shirt.

She wanted to hold on to her anger, wanted to ask more about what happened with Eloise, but he'd worked her into a frenzy, and now she just wanted him to forgive her.

He grabbed her legs and yanked her hips to the edge of the bed before sliding off her lace underwear.

Rainer towered over her, breathing hard as he pulled her legs up against his chest. "Is this what you need? Do I not want you enough? Am I not passionate enough? Do I not make you feel desired enough?"

She shook her head. "No, Rain, I—"

"I'm going to remind you right now. So just make sure you are paying attention. I'm going to show you how much I want you every day, all day, always."

He turned his head and kissed her inner ankle. He kissed and licked all the way up from her calf to her knee to her thigh before doing the same thing on the other leg.

Cecilia panted and writhed, but he held her firmly. When he finished kissing her other thigh, he kissed up her hip bones, her belly, before teasing her nipples until lust was a full-blown fever burning her from the inside out. Then he kissed his way back down and finally went where she'd been waiting for him to go. He licked her torturously slowly, alternating between his tongue and fingers until she bucked her hips off the bed.

She was so close it almost hurt, but he drew away again. She let out a sound of shock and protest but didn't have time to do more as he flipped her onto her stomach. She waited, expecting him to slide inside her.

Instead, he started kissing up the backs of her legs, continuing his torture the way he had on the front of her body. He kissed up the small of her back, trailing his tongue up her spine all the way to the back of her neck.

"Rain, please," she begged.

"Do you feel it, Cece? It's maddening to want you this way all the time. Do I want you enough?"

It was a challenge, and she should have said yes, but she was too stubborn to give in. "No."

He froze behind her for a moment. The only sound in the room was the faint crackle of the fire and the rustle of him unbuttoning his pants and sliding them off.

Rainer bent over her body, his chest flush with her back, and whispered in her ear. "All right. If you need more, I will show you more. I'll make you really feel it this time."

He thrust into her hard. Her hands balled in the sheets as she tried to adjust to the fullness. She thought he'd just continue, but he waited. He softened his grip, kissing her shoulder.

"Okay?" he whispered.

She brought her hand over his on her hip and prodded him to dig his fingers in slightly harder.

"Don't stop," she rasped. She was furious and terrified he'd leave her, and she wanted everything he could give her.

Rainer gripped her hips firmer and pulled out, thrusting into her again even harder. He hesitated just for a moment, but she pushed back against him, and then he let loose whatever wildness he'd been holding back. He moved hard and fast, lifting her hips so he could go deeper. She moaned, meeting each thrust. She opened up their connection and let him feel how much she loved him.

His pace slowed as the feeling hit him, but he didn't stop. Love careened back down their bond from him in reply, and she blinked away tears of relief.

He bent over her body so his firm chest was pressed against her back. "Is this enough? Do you need more?"

"Yes, more," she whimpered. She was so close to her climax.

"So greedy," he taunted.

He slipped his hand between her and the bed, rubbing her clit as he thrusted. Her whole body went rigid as she finally went over the edge. The intensity left her shaking violently.

Rainer pulled out and flipped her over, dropping to his knees before she was even done shaking. He slid his tongue inside her again. She was so sensitive, but he didn't care. It was precisely what she didn't know she wanted.

He feasted on her, teasing her with the wet slide of his tongue until she let out a strangled cry as another mind-emptying orgasm tore through her. He licked and kissed his way back up her body.

His gaze collided with hers. "Say it, Cece. Say the words I want to hear."

"I'm just for you, Rain." She felt the truth of those words.

He smiled as he pushed back inside her. "That's right. You're mine." With each sentence he punctuated that possession with a thrust of his hips. "So stop giving him pieces of yourself. I don't care if it's selfish. I want every single part of you."

"I'm sorry," she whispered. Tears streamed down her face, and she was overcome by emotion.

"Are you?" he whispered against her lips.

"Yes," she sighed. She pulled him into a feverish kiss full of want and worry.

"I thought of how I'd like you to show me how sorry you are," he murmured, kissing her neck.

He rolled her on top of him so she straddled his lap and sat up so they were eye to eye. She sank onto him slowly. His hands ran up her back, pressing her against his chest as he kissed her. The feeling of being wrapped in his arms and feeling so full was exquisite. She leaned her head against his shoulder, trying to catch her breath.

Cecilia slowly started to move her hips, and he wound a hand into her hair, pulling her into a long, slow kiss. He worked his way down her neck with kisses that grew hungrier and rougher as he went, matching the pace with which she moved her hips.

Finally, he pulled back and met her gaze. His green eyes were blazing with lust and love and hunger. The heady, swimming starlight sensation spread through her. She was so close. Everything about being with him, touching him, feeling him inside her felt so right.

Pleasure buzzed along her skin, warmth spreading through all of her limbs, and she moaned his name like a quiet prayer. Rainer helped her keep the pace. He pulled her down harder, dug his hands into her hips, his fingers a hot brand on her skin.

"Cece, let go. I've got you and I'm going to keep you," he whispered.

He brought his hips up to meet her as he rubbed his thumb over her scar, sending an intense flood of pleasure through her. She threw her head back and screamed as she came apart.

Her body was a flood of sparkling, tingling light, and she opened her eyes to look at Rainer. Love flowed freely through their connection.

She took his face in her hands and kissed him deeply. She whispered "I love you" against his lips over and over as tears streamed down her face.

She didn't know how it could be like this every time she opened up and connected to him—so deep and powerful. It was like looking right into his soul and seeing the truth of how much he loved her. For so long, she'd felt so unworthy of him. His goodness. His joy. His kind, open heart. But when he connected with her, she felt so powerful and lovely.

He kissed her tears away as she started to move faster again, this time for him. He moaned her name and looked into her eyes as she moved. Her hands pressed against his chest and she dragged her fingers across his scar as she pushed down on him, and he groaned and squeezed her tighter as he finished.

Rainer dropped his face into the crook of her neck, kissing her and smiling against her skin. Gradually, her breathing grew less ragged and her heart slowed, but she stayed locked together with him for a few long moments before laying down beside him.

"I didn't do anything with Eloise," Rainer said, breaking the silence.

Relief crashed down on Cecilia.

"I could have, but I didn't. Because I don't want anyone else." He scrubbed a hand over his face. "That's what's so frustrating. I'm so in love with you, and you still love him. I want only you, and you want both of us."

Rainer's words and the look on his face doused her in guilt.

"Rain, I only want you. I got carried away, and I should not have done that because I knew it would hurt you. What I feel for Xander is messy."

"I know."

"It's unfinished, and although I know in my heart it would have always ended this way, it's hard to ignore what we had. But the reality is that's only a symptom," she said.

She ran her thumb over her inner wrist, trying to summon the courage she needed. Tears welled in her eyes, and she wiped them away, frustrated.

Rainer gently took her hand and kissed her wrist, placing her palm over his heart. "What is it?" he whispered as he stroked her cheek.

"I know what you've said about kids—"

"Cece—"

"No, wait—just let me say it because it's really hard," Cecilia started. "I know you've said there are many ways to be a family—that I am worth more to you than just what I can give you. I know that, and I believe that logically. I do. But there is a part of me that can't let it go—that feels like it's selfish to tie you to me when I can't give you something so important. And that same part is afraid that while you are happy now, in a few years, you might not be. You might regret making that choice. I feel selfish for wanting you—selfish for asking you to give up something so important. I can barely reconcile the loss in my own mind. Loving you the way I do, I can't bear the thought of not being able to give you every single thing that you want, because you deserve it, Rain."

Cecilia rubbed her eyes and blew out a slow breath. "I have spent more than a year pulling that final exchange apart because it's not fair and it doesn't agree with the principles of the Gauntlet. Every other exchange required my choice. But the Cave of Longings didn't really give one. Knowing what I know now, maybe if I hadn't agreed, nothing would have happened, but I was in agony and the threat certainly felt real. Even so, an exchange made under duress is counter to the rules of magic. You should only be able to exchange what is freely given. And yet here I am trying to accept a thing that still leaves me breathless."

"Why didn't you say anything?" Rainer asked.

"The same reason you don't say anything to me about it. Because it hurts. Because it's so ugly and it makes me furious and I don't want you to feel that, too." Cecilia swallowed hard, trying to stuff down her feelings so she could get through everything she had to say. "I know that there are parts of me that will always be broken, and I think I was scared that if I was damaged, I didn't deserve you. We have this beautiful, perfect love story, and all of these people were constantly telling me that, or wanting to see my scar, and I just felt like this sad, heart-broken, ungrateful person. I feel unworthy of your love."

Rainer's face fell. He kissed her crescent scar. "You are more worthy than anyone I've ever met."

"I know that now. I know that because I've been thinking about the past year. I've been thinking about how you have taken care of me and have been so incredibly kind and patient with me. Every time you were sweet when I was awful, it just made me feel further from being ready. I know I will never be who I was before becoming a goddess ever again. I won't be the girl you fell in love with ever again. I came out of the dark different and it's not an excuse but I am still healing. I'm deeply flawed. I'm trying, and I'm yours—invisible scars and all."

"Your heart and mine are the same," Rainer started. "Broken in all the same places. I'm still healing too, but I want to be the person you share that with. I know that you'll never be the same, and I won't either, but I don't expect or want you to be. I can't believe for one second that you would feel unworthy of me after sacrificing yourself for me."

"But what if you just feel like you owe me?" she asked.

Rainer sat up, pulling her up to a seat and taking both of her hands in his. "You made me stab you in the heart, Cecilia, and I did it. I—" His voice broke and the ache in her chest stole all the air from the room. "I watched you die. I don't know how I could remain unchanged after that. But I don't want the old you or the old me. I want us as we are now. You astonish me, Cece. All the time. You went through so much so quickly. You came here to try to help Xander and all of our friends. Your courage, kindness, and compassion never cease to amaze me. I fall more in love with you all the time. The only thing that scares me is that you won't need me anymore."

"I don't need you. I *want* you, and that's much better. No one has ever loved me better, and there's no one else I want to spend my life with."

He smiled as he brushed the tears from her cheeks.

"Xander is a distraction. I'm just scared. It's not an excuse, but I'm afraid of letting you down, and rather than do it accidentally, I chose something intentionally, so I won't be surprised by it when you reject me."

Recognition stole over his face. "Is this why you change the subject when I try to set a date?"

Tears streamed down her face as she nodded.

"Cece." His voice was so tender. "Why didn't you just say so?"

"Because it's hard," she sobbed as she tucked her face into his chest.

"I know, but it's me, Cece. I know it will take you a while to believe that someone can love just you when the whole world wants something from you, but look at me. I love you and want you." Rainer shook his head. "I'm sorry I got a little aggressive and punished you for being lost."

She climbed to her knees and took his hands in hers. "First of all, that was hot, and it was hardly punishment, but if that's what you consider punishment, please feel free to punish me anytime. I should have just told you, and I shouldn't have kissed him. I swear I am trying to stop ruining what we have. I'm just terrified that I'm going to be blindsided again."

Rainer cupped her face in his hands. "Cece, I swear to you there is nothing that will make me stop loving you. It makes me blind with fury when I think about him touching you, but I don't love you less."

"I'm trying—I swear I am—but I'm so scared all the time that I'm about to get some terrible news, or something is going to go wrong. I keep waiting for the thing we can't come back from. You are the person I love most in the world, and I don't know what I would do without you. I've already had to think about it more times than I would have liked, and I live in constant fear it will happen again. In some ways, it feels like relying on Xander is safer."

"Because he's still kind of obsessed with you?" Rainer asked.

"No, because it's never been with him the way it is with you."

"How so?"

"Oh gods, it's hard to explain. Everything I feel with you is so powerful. That feeling between us that is *only* between us. I don't feel that with him. Being with you is like coming home. I mean—gods! You try to describe it."

Rainer looked thoughtful for a moment. "When we're together—when I'm inside you, and my arms are wrapped around you, and I'm kissing you—it feels like the only thing I could ever want. Every time, I'm so happy I feel like it will kill me. I feel so much it's a struggle not to cry. It's like it will never be enough. Like, I can't get close enough. Like I can't touch enough of you. It feels like it was worth every bad thing that ever happened to me."

She looked at him with tears in her eyes, and he smiled and kissed the inside of her wrist.

"That was much better than the way I said it, but it's exactly how I feel," she whispered.

She tucked herself into his chest and breathed in his familiar linen, lilac, and sea air smell. He ran his fingers down her back and kissed the top of her head.

"So what did His Majesty have to say?"

"Just that I'm crazy to think you'd ever stop loving me and that if he can't fuck me, he wants to watch you do it," she said with a smirk.

Rainer's eyes went wide. "Wow."

"Yes. I don't expect Xander would enjoy it as much as he thinks."

"I might enjoy it," Rainer mused. "Just once, I'd love to see that smug, self-satisfied smirk wiped off his face. I know it would be if he saw what I see when we're together."

"And what do you see?" she asked.

He smiled and kissed her. "The most beautiful thing in the world —your heart."

Rainer was right. She understood the allure. A part of her felt hot all over thinking about Xander watching her, but she knew he'd be disappointed. It would break Xander's heart because he would know what Rainer and Cecilia had was different.

The kind of love that puts you upright against someone else, heart to heart and soul to soul, and forces you to accept what you deserve, whether you're ready or not.

It was like that every time. There were moments when Cecilia could forget it or temporarily distract herself, but as soon as that connection opened again, it was just the two of them. The castle could crumble around them and they wouldn't notice.

It wasn't what fairy tales were made of. It was vulnerable and raw and terrifying and wonderful. It made them strong in the jagged, broken places, and it belonged to the two of them.

Two best friends who guided each other out of the dark over and over again. Two dreamers who grew up but refused to grow out of their love of a good story. Two souls so entwined with each other they grew stronger together.

26

XANDER

The library was supposed to be Xander's personal haven. He often spent the afternoons there hiding from tedious meetings, and since no one in the castle seemed intent on academic pursuits, it was usually empty. Maybe it was foolish to go alone to meet the man whose fiancée he had just kissed, but Xander had never backed down from a fight before and he wouldn't start now. Not for fucking Rainer McKay.

Xander was already grumpy. A bottle of his favorite whiskey had gone missing from his sitting room and he was now—perhaps fortunately—sober for this meeting. It would be a good thing if Rainer wanted a fight, but a bad thing if Xander was about to get a lecture.

Dust motes swirled in the flickering firelight and the scent of parchment and ink filled the space. He didn't know why Rainer had summoned him to the library of all places, but it irked him that the guardian invited him with a note as if *he* was the king and Xander merely a servant. If anything, he'd expected to be summoned to a fighting ring after kissing Cece—not this forgotten space.

Slumping into a chair by the fireplace, Xander allowed his mind to wander for the first time all day. His morning had been filled by tea with Princess Mayella and a dessert tasting with Princess

Larissa. Then he spent two hours with his council, the members of which all had differing opinions on whom he should marry. The entire time, his mind replayed his kiss with Cece on a torturous loop.

It was one thing to know the loss of her, but another to feel it in her body—her calm in contrast to his starved desperation. In all of his imaginings of kissing her again, not once had he considered she might be unmoved, especially after being so jealous of anyone else holding his attention. The grief of losing her all over again was sobering.

He ran a hand through his hair, wishing for a drink.

A soft whimper cut through the silence. Xander stood and moved toward the sound, following it down a long tunnel of shelves until he reached the back of the room.

Warm firelight from the far wall cast shadows over Cece. She sat on a plush chair hidden in the back corner of the library with a book in her hand and her dress bunched up around her waist. Rainer knelt on the ground in front of her, her legs draped over his shoulders.

"Keep reading, Cece," Rainer whispered as his eyes locked with hers.

She bit her lip, trying to stifle a moan as his mouth moved against her.

Cece blinked wildly, struggling to focus on the book in her hands. "The princess went to the window and—fuck—" The book folded against her chest. "Rainer—"

Rainer's name on her lips would have made Xander feel sick if he wasn't so turned on by the sight of her.

Well played, McKay. He expected retribution for kissing Cece, but he'd anticipated a punch in the face, not a sex show. Shocking that Rainer would do something as bold as invite Xander to watch the two of them. Perhaps the war had put a little darkness into pure and steady Rainer McKay after all.

Then again, Cece was a bit of an exhibitionist. Maybe she didn't mind. But when Xander looked at her, she was lost in what was happening. She didn't seem to realize he was there.

"Shh, better be quiet or someone will hear, sweetheart," Rainer taunted. "Keep reading."

He waited for her to start reading again before he went back to his ministrations. It was the type of game that made Cece so wild. Xander had underestimated Rainer at every turn.

Cece gasped and continued reading. "The brave knight had arrived. He looked up at her and shouted: 'My lady—'" She moaned, and her fingernails dug into the upholstery harder. The sound made Xander rock hard. "I can't keep—oh gods—"

She dropped her head back. Her free hand came to Rainer's head, but he pulled away.

"Keep reading, Cece," he whispered. He stopped moving, and she let out a frustrated whimper. "Keep reading."

She lifted the book and Rainer waited for her to begin again. "The brave knight climbed the ivy on the tower wall until he...reached her window. She threw her arms around him...relieved he was safe and—"

She moaned loudly and dropped the book. It thudded softly on the carpet.

Xander tried to adjust himself to lessen the pressure of his pants and accidentally bumped the shelf. It hardly made a noise, but Cece's gaze shot up and locked on his. There was a flash of surprise in her eyes.

He expected her to say something to stop Rainer. Instead, she kept her eyes on Xander. His body blazed to life as her gaze dropped to his pants and a slight smile played across her lips.

She met his eyes again and maintained their locked gaze as she moaned and rocked her hips to meet Rainer's mouth.

Xander had never been so turned on. Cece liked to be watched, but he expected her to tear into him for even daring to notice what she was up to. Instead, it seemed to make her hotter.

Her moans grew more urgent. Rainer's hand slid between her legs, his fingers working in tandem with his mouth.

"Oh gods, Rain!" She made eye contact with Xander. "Please?"

She was messing with him, knowing how much he loved when she begged.

He shook his head no, and her lower lip kicked out in a pout. He could tell by her flush and the way her nipples peaked against the red silk of her dress that she was painfully close to the edge.

"Please, I need to," she begged, her gaze still locked on Xander.

He shook his head again.

Rainer moved more urgently between her legs, and her eyes squeezed shut as she tried to postpone her climax.

She wasn't letting Xander touch her, but she clearly still got off on him controlling her. He still got off on being in control of her. He stroked his hardness through his pants. She watched the action, licking her lips.

Fuck, she is perfect. Xander missed her. She could slay him with a look. She met his eyes again, a question in her own.

Her hand on the back of Rainer's head pressed down urgently.

"Please?" she begged, her gaze crashing into Xander's.

"Look at me when I make you come," Rainer said. His voice was a gruff command—a reminder to Xander and Cece of who was really in charge.

Cece's gaze snapped to Rainer. "Can I—"

He nodded, and relief flooded her face. She dropped her head back, and as if perfectly reading her body, Rainer's hand shot up and covered her mouth just as she screamed and fell apart. Her legs trembled and her back arched as she rode out the wave of pleasure until she collapsed into the chair again.

"Gods, you are so sexy," Rainer said.

Rainer yanked her to her feet. He bent her over a nearby table with surprising roughness and hiked up her skirts, loosening the ties of her dress to expose the smooth skin of her back. His fingers trailed down her spine, and she shivered. Then he kissed and licked his way back up the line he traced with his fingers. She let out a string of expletives that made Rainer chuckle. He pressed his hand to her back, pushing her chest flat against the wood of the table. He worked himself free of his pants and slowly slid inside her, and they both groaned in unison.

Xander wanted to know what she was thinking, letting him watch her, even if she wouldn't let him have full control.

Rainer thrust into her harder, and she winced. Her cheeks pinked, and she sighed. Her face was awash with a mixture of pain and pleasure. Rainer moved against her, and she pressed herself back into him.

Rainer was utterly lost in her, so much so that he either didn't notice Xander or didn't care if he watched. He held her hips, moving slowly in and out, his gaze locked on where their bodies met.

Cece's eyes blazed with hunger, and Xander could read the word in them from experience. *More.*

"Harder," she panted.

Rainer groaned, following her orders with a vicious thrust, pinning her to the edge of the table.

Xander wished he had ever been clever enough to take her in a library. He'd never thought of anything so hot. He unbuttoned his pants and began to stroke himself.

Cece watched him as she moaned much louder than before. It was a good thing Xander had made the library his personal sanctuary, or they might have been found out.

Suddenly Rainer bent over her body, his thrusts shorter and more urgent as his hand wrapped around her and slid between her legs, rubbing her along with his strokes.

"Do you like it, Cece? Do you like that I can't get enough of you? Do you like when I fuck you in public? Do you wish someone was watching?" Rainer whispered.

"Yes," she groaned, meeting Xander's eyes. She slammed a hand against the table and squeezed her eyes shut.

"I see the way you look at the king. Do you wish he was touching you? Do you wish he was watching?" Rainer asked, a smirk painted on his lips. His hips moved harder and faster. Possessive, claiming.

"Rain," she begged.

"Would you like to feel his eyes on you? Would you like to remind him how gorgeous you are when you fall apart for me and only me? Would you want to make him jealous?"

Her eyes locked on to Xander's, and her back arched, her whole body tensing as she climaxed.

Xander exploded in his hands, his grunt only covered up by Cece's scream. He fumbled in his pocket for a handkerchief to clean up the mess.

Watching Rainer fuck her was as torturous as it was hot. Cece clearly hadn't done this knowing Xander would come in. She got carried away like she so often did. Rainer was the one who invited him, and it was a power play. A reminder that she was his—one that Rainer knew Cece wouldn't mind. If Rainer had told her right then that he'd invited Xander to watch, she would have gotten off even faster.

Rainer flipped her over. Her legs shook, but Rainer knelt and buried his face between her thighs. She cursed, her hand cupping the back of his head. Her legs shook violently, and her whole body seemed to vibrate with need. Her head rolled from side to side and her eyes squeezed shut. She tried to shift, but Rainer's hands cupped her ass, holding her at the perfect height to feast on her. Her heels dug into his shoulders and her toes curled, every muscle in her body tight as a bowstring, ready to snap.

"Rain!" Her fingernails scored the wood tabletop as she came again.

Rainer's hands glided along her skin greedily, pushing her dress higher. He continued to work as she rode out her climax. He kissed her hip bone, her stomach, then the inside of her knee, worshipping her body before climbing back to his feet and grinning at her. She held his gaze. There was pure devotion in his eyes as he pressed into her and her eyes reflected it back.

"You feel amazing," Rainer rasped. "You drive me crazy. The way you say my name, the way you come undone for me. I want to stay inside you all day. I will never get enough of you."

She sat up urgently, and he snaked an arm around her waist. She took his face in her hands and kissed him before drawing back to meet his eyes. He moved against her, and she rolled her hips to meet him. Her hands dug into his shoulders as they moved. Rainer's fingers gripped her hip as he tried to make it last.

It was no longer a show for Xander. Cece was entirely focused on Rainer. Xander couldn't pretend what was between them was just sweetness and lovemaking. He couldn't pretend that Rainer was safe and boring.

"I want to be on top," Cece panted.

Rainer gripped her legs and lifted her off the table, changing places so that he could lie back. Her knees bracketed his hips, and she freed her arms from her dress, shoving it down so her breasts were exposed. Then, she sank down on him with a gasp.

Though most of her movements were hidden by the skirt of her dress, Xander was mesmerized by what he could see. She slid her hands up Rainer's shirt, bracing herself on his chest as she rode him. His hands flexed on her hips, and he groaned. His hooded gaze was locked on hers, and she looked exceptionally pleased with herself. She leaned back, running a hand through her hair as she cupped her breast and sighed in satisfaction.

Xander knew he should walk away, but he couldn't take his eyes off her.

She locked eyes with Rainer, and something silent passed—something unsayable and sacred. Xander felt like he should look away. Still, he couldn't make himself, and he stared on in morbid curiosity at the very thing that would obliterate his heart.

"I'm just for you, Rain," Cece murmured.

Both of their faces were serene. Rainer's hand trailed down over her golden scar. She threw her head back as her spine arched, and she cried out and splintered apart.

Xander had never wanted anything as bad as he wanted her at that moment.

Rainer shuddered below her, his hands gripping her hips tight as he groaned. She leaned forward and kissed him as her fingers threaded through his hair. Xander couldn't make out their whispers, but he could guess what they were saying as Rainer kissed her neck, her face, her eyelids.

Xander stared at them as jealousy rotted his insides. He'd spent days trying to make her jealous, yet she'd only needed to be well fucked by one person to ruin him. Truthfully, he only needed to watch Rainer touch her and see Cece look at him with so much love in her eyes to feel jealous.

Cece was an absolute wonder to Xander. She did the wildest things when she got wound up, and he felt intense envy that she hadn't done that exact thing to him. He wanted to come out of hiding and confront her about it, though perhaps it was his fault for not being creative enough to bring her into the library to begin with. Maybe he'd approached things all wrong, and he should have immediately made himself known. Perhaps that was what Rainer expected him to do. The thought almost made him laugh.

Xander finally ripped his eyes away from them and walked around the corner. He leaned his head back against a bookcase, looking into the shelves in front of him, unseeing. He'd spectacularly screwed things up. As hot as watching Cece was, he was immediately pulled back to kissing her the day before. The way he'd felt her pushing for something she no longer felt. The way he felt his hold on her slip, while she still held him fully in her thrall.

Kissing her at all was foolish, but he'd felt entirely unmoored since the arrival of the princesses in Argaria. The last time he'd felt like he knew who he was was when he was with Cece. Now with his cousin coming for his throne and no courage to ask the question about his true parentage, Xander felt desperate to hold on to her.

He'd wronged her and hadn't had the heart to apologize before he left Olney. Xander wanted forgiveness and also he didn't. He didn't want their business finished. He didn't want to stop owing her something because the debt was a link between them. He'd take anything that still tied him to her.

Like a tree stretching toward the light, he could not stop bending toward her.

People talked about first love like something flimsy, like they'd been drunk or hit their heads too hard. Xander's love for her did feel like a certain type of madness, but it had also given him strength, forced him to stop hiding and playing a role instead of being himself. She'd turned him inside out with her love.

He was momentarily distracted from his swirling thoughts by a shadow above him. Out of the corner of his eye, he saw someone on the upper-level balcony disappear into the stacks. Apparently, he hadn't been the only one enjoying the show.

"Was that a wise decision?"

Xander jumped at the whisper right behind him. He knew it was Evan without turning because he was the only person who could sneak up on him.

"Probably not, but for once, it wasn't my fault." Xander smirked, casting one last glance at the balcony to see if the intruder would show their face, but they were gone.

"It's not your fault that you're in here jerking off on a bunch of dusty old books?" Evan asked.

Xander turned and met his friend's dark eyes. "Rainer summoned me here for that little bit of performance art."

Evan's brows shot up. "Perhaps if you didn't spend so much time flirting with his fiancée, he wouldn't feel a need to remind you what they are to each other."

Xander rolled his eyes. "Yes, and perhaps if I hadn't kissed her last night, he wouldn't feel a need to show me how ardently she loves him. I'm going to pretend I was running late and didn't see it."

It was pointless. Rainer had clearly known he was a spectator. It wasn't like Xander had done much to stay hidden, but he didn't want to give him the satisfaction.

Evan sighed, his jaw clenched, and nodded.

They walked back to the door and closed it loudly before making their way into the center of the room. Cece's giggle bubbled from behind the stacks, and a moment later, she and Rainer appeared. Her long hair was wild as always, but her dress was somehow immaculate. The only sign of her exertion was the flush on her cheeks.

"Sorry I'm late," Xander said. "I hope you weren't waiting too long, McKay... Cece, my love. I wasn't expecting you to come."

Her blush grew brighter, and she looked from Xander to Rainer.

Rainer smirked. Cece watched the exchange warily. Her eyes narrowed on Rainer, but he ignored the accusation in her gaze.

"Xander, I'm so glad you could make it, but I've realized what I thought was a threat was actually nothing at all. You'll forgive me for wasting your time," Rainer said.

Well met, McKay. Xander pursed his lips.

"If you both don't mind, I'm going to sweep Cece away for a romantic dinner. I'm sure you have plenty to do since we only have a few days left until the big announcement," Rainer said.

The reminder sent panic fluttering in Xander's chest. "Of course," he said tightly.

Rainer and Cece breezed out of the library joyfully, hand in hand.

As soon as the door closed behind the pair, Evan smacked Xander's arm.

"What the fuck is wrong with you? Why can't you just leave her alone?"

Xander shrugged, rubbing his arm. "Because she is my greatest weakness."

Evan leaned his head against the bookshelf next to him and crossed his arms. "Are you out of your fucking mind?"

Xander cocked an eyebrow. "I think we both already know that when it comes to her, I am."

"This is too much, even for you."

The words were a gut punch. Evan's eyes went wide, realizing too late what he'd let slip: the words that hurt Xander more than anything else. The words he'd made it a point to never, ever say.

Xander tried to hide his slight flinch, but there was no disguising the skip in his heartbeat—not that it mattered.

Too much. Words Xander had heard his entire childhood. King Damian was always telling him to be less. Less showy, less demanding of time and energy, less than Davide. Xander's instructors thought he was too ambitious. His swordsmanship tutor thought he was too cocky, and everyone thought he was too emotional. His whole life was a parade of people telling him he was too much.

Evan and Teddy had always made it a point to tease or roll their eyes but to never say those dreaded words.

The only other person who'd never once said it to him was Cece, who'd loved his excess. It was part of the reason Xander loved her so much.

"I didn't mean that," Evan said.

Xander shook his head. "Yes, you did."

Evan scrubbed his hands over his face and hair and sighed. "Really, I didn't. I swear. I'm just stressed with everything going on, Xan. We got word from King Marcos that the Olney seer is missing."

Xander's eyes widened. "The Seer who bonded all the Gauntlet duos together?"

"Yes. She bonded Rainer and Cece when they were children."

"What do you think it means?" Xander asked.

"It means that something awful is going to happen," Evan said. "There's no way to know for sure, but if Vincent has the most powerful witches in the kingdom and a slayer, who knows what havoc he could cause with them and any information the slayer stole from Jude Harek?"

Xander turned the possibilities over in his mind. "Jude had limited knowledge—you made sure no one knew everything. So I doubt the slayer got much that would be useful from him. But I'm not sure what Vincent would want with the Seer. She can not only create bonds between witches and guardians, but destroy them. In Olney, if a witch and their bonded guardian had a relationship and were found out, their bond would be severed. It's supposed to be an excruciating process, like having a part of your body cut out. Then one was sent to live in exile while the other remained in shame."

"That's barbaric," Evan huffed.

"But an effective deterrent. It's why Rainer and Cece never got together back then, though it was obvious they were both in love with each other." Xander rubbed the back of his neck. "Does Marcos have any idea what's going on?"

"Marcos said it's possible Vincent just wants her to look into his future, but he also suggested that Cece might have some idea. Has she said anything to you?"

Xander said nothing, but he spun the golden band on his right ring finger reflexively.

"What is that?" Evan asked. "I noticed it the other day."

"It's a gift from Cece." Xander's hand instinctively patted the chain where his wedding ring rested above his heart.

Evan's eyes narrowed with suspicion. "What kind of gift?"

"One to acknowledge what we had and remind me that any ring from her will stay on this hand to make room on the other for a new wedding band," Xander said meaningfully.

Evan frowned. "If you don't tell me what you know, I can't be prepared for how things might go wrong."

Xander brought his hands to Evan's shoulders. "Ev, I get it. I really do, trust me. But even if I told you, it would do nothing to prepare us. The best I can tell is that she's pulling at strings, and it might be nothing because she's been traumatized. I can't tell you more than that, and I need you to trust me when I say it will protect me more if you know nothing. For all you know, this ring is simply a gift from my beloved ex-wife. Do you get it?"

Evan shook his head.

"I'm not telling you to protect both of us. It's a gift from Cece. Let it go. If I have to order you to, I will, but I'd rather not give my second order to you ever."

Evan sighed. Xander made a point not to order him around. It was one of the rules he'd only broken once when he absolutely had to. How else could he expect to maintain a friendship when he was a royal?

"Anything else you want to tell me instead? Other than the fact that you've made sure that one of the people we've brought in to protect you now also wants to murder you," Evan said.

Xander laughed. "He's welcome to try. I might even let him get a free hit in. I deserve it." He drew shapes in the dust on the closest bookshelf. "Before I kissed her last night, Cece mentioned that she caught Princess Clare poking around the royal wing."

Evan stood up straighter. "Did Cece think she's a threat?"

"Cece has hated Clare from the beginning since I showed her so much attention. Hard to say whether she felt Clare was some kind of spy or she'd become naturally suspicious of anyone else who might be sneaking about and trying to fuck me."

Evan rolled his eyes. "You are so pompous."

"You're the one who organized this whole event," Xander laughed. "If you wanted me to have less of an ego, you shouldn't have invited six beautiful women to compete for my heart. I'm a bit embarrassed to say I don't even know what the royal archives contain, so I'm not sure what Clare would even get her hands on. I've never been in there," he admitted.

"They hold the family trees of the Saveros, dating back centuries. There's information on births, marriages, deaths. There are a lot of books on mythology and foreign religions. There are some ancient magic books and lots of maps and history books on Argaria and other kingdoms."

Xander grinned as if he hadn't pored over those very books when he first discovered there were questions about his parentage. "Sounds boring."

"Indeed. I'm glad that these princesses seem interested despite your antics."

"Do you think Clare is an issue?" Xander asked.

"Princess Clare was vetted like everyone else—by two council members or an ambassador. People know her, and her kingdom is right next door. I think it's more likely that she heard rumors around the court and wanted to find out for herself, but that's hardly enough to assume ill intentions. Frankly, if the roles were reversed I wouldn't hesitate to dig through archives. We have a strong enough presence of people in place in Aldrena, many of whom have met her personally and have confirmed her identity and that she's a proper lady."

Xander arched a brow. "So safe to assume she was just looking for me to teach her to be an improper lady?"

Evan laughed. "Indeed. Any chance you're considering taking her up on it?"

Xander shrugged.

"Xan—"

"Despite my antics, I'm honestly trying. Still, I'm not sure I'm ready to have a princess stalking me in the night. I know Clare is the obvious choice."

Evan frowned. "You don't have to pick the obvious choice. I invited these women because they all represent different advantages. We don't need to talk about it now. Just keep your mind open and stop flirting with Cece."

"I'll try."

Evan looked at him skeptically.

"Loving Cece is a hard habit to break."

"No one is asking you to break it. Just to choose a new wife. None of these women are expecting a love match, and if they are, that's on them. But there must be someone that you feel a sense of partnership or connection to."

Xander ran a hand through his hair. Everyone acted like it was so easy to make the decision. Like he should be able to trust himself.

Name the fear and it loses its power. Davide's words from beyond the grave lived in his blood.

Xander shook his head, trying to clear a swirling vortex of fears. *I'm afraid that I cannot trust any of my instincts. I'm afraid I'll get my heart broken. I'm afraid I'll shatter someone else the way I did Cece. I'm afraid no one will ever choose me. I'm afraid to want something I can't control. I'm more afraid to be king than not to.*

Xander endlessly cycled through a litany of fears, giving each a name, and yet, they became no less compelling.

27

RAINER

Rainer woke in a panic. The bed was empty and cool because Cecilia wasn't beside him. She was always still asleep, usually heavily, when he woke up.

Instead, he patted the pillow in the dawn light peeking through the bedroom curtains and found a note on her pillow. *Find me.*

It was a game they hadn't played since they were children, but he was intrigued.

He dressed and gave a tug on his bond with Cecilia and followed the pull to her. He wove through hallway after hallway, trusting his instinct and the magic that connected the two of them to lead him to the right place because he didn't know that part of the castle.

Finally, he came to stand in front of a large, intricately carved wooden door. He paused before pushing it open until he was certain Cecilia was on the other side.

He was immediately greeted with the fresh smell of wisteria and lilacs and the sight of Cecilia's smiling face.

"What's this?" Rainer asked.

He took in the young wisteria trees that formed an arch a few feet away from the roaring fireplace. Beautiful, ever-blooming lilacs in pots next to them filled the room with a sweet, heady scent. The floor was covered in tiny white flower petals, and it looked like a stunning replica of the grove where they trained back in Olney.

Cecilia shifted nervously in front of the arch the trees formed. She wore a dress embroidered with vines and white flowers, the fabric a pale bluish-green—nearly the shade of Olney wedding dresses. The front of her hair was pinned away from her face, but the rest was down. She looked lovely, approachable, and extremely unsure of herself.

"Come in," she said, her voice just above a whisper.

"Did you do all of this?" he asked as he crossed the room to meet her.

"Sylvie helped. I'm fine at growing things, but she's better at getting them to bloom. I wanted it to be beautiful for you. I wanted it to look like—"

"Our grove," Rainer interrupted. "It does."

The same place where he taught her how to fight, where they whispered secrets and stories, where they'd had their first kiss.

"I wanted to surprise you," she said as she took both of his hands in hers.

Her anxiety buzzed through their connection, so he sent her some love to soothe her. Her face relaxed, and she smiled at him.

She swallowed hard. "I have made a lot of mistakes."

"I know, but I forgive you, and we're past that. You didn't have to go to all this trouble." He smiled.

"Just let me get this out," she said. She squeezed his hands and took a shaky breath. "Rainer, I cannot remember a time before loving you. My love for you has grown and changed as I have. I am so very fortunate to be the person who is directly connected to your heart, to know you so personally, because you are the person who inspires me most. We have been through so much together. We have lost so much, but you are the person who lessens each loss with your very presence. You share all my burdens, whether I let you or not. You are my favorite person in the world, and you are my family."

Rainer swallowed thickly. He hadn't realized how badly he wanted to hear that.

"I have not always been good at being taken care of. I am stubborn and willful, and I always think I'm right. I am emotional and wild, and you are steady and kind."

She blinked away tears, and he brushed those that escaped from her cheeks.

"Cece—"

"You are the person I love most in the world, and I don't want to run from this anymore. There will never be a *right time*. I might always carry this darkness in my heart, but it doesn't change what I want. This world we've built could fall apart tomorrow, and if that happened, I would hate myself for making you feel like there was any doubt that I wanted to spend the rest of my life with you. I've said it before, but I'll repeat it—your love is worth saving, even at the end of the world. Rainer Jordan McKay, will you marry me?"

Cecilia knelt in front of him, holding out a simple gold ring.

He stared at her, speechless.

She looked at him expectantly.

"You're proposing," he said dumbly. His brain couldn't catch up with what was happening.

Yes, you idiot, your beautiful fiancée set up this surprise for you because she wanted to propose, and now you're making her sweat it.

"Well, you proposed to me twice, so I figured it's only fair I do it once. Is that a yes?" Cecilia asked.

He pulled her to her feet. "Yes! Of course it's a yes!" He swept her into a tight hug.

She tucked her face into his neck as she relaxed into him. He was so relieved he couldn't form words.

Home was not a place. Home was who he ran to when life got hard, when the sky got dark and his heart was broken and everything in him felt unsettled. In every groundless, quaking moment, he'd found himself pacing in front of her door, hoping she would seek out some trouble so he could have a chance to tag along and be needed.

Cecilia was his home.

"I want to get married this spring—just after your birthday. It's such a pretty time of year. I thought we could just have the ceremony on the beach below the cottage," she whispered.

Rainer swallowed the lump in his throat, his eyes watery as he set her back on her feet. He wasn't even embarrassed because she looked delighted by his overwhelm.

"Rain," Cecilia said, brushing away a tear that trailed down his cheek. "You're so sweet. What did I do to deserve you?"

Rainer could only stare at her—the beautiful woman who wanted to marry him.

Cecilia had obvious strengths, but at that moment, he saw a different strength—a quiet resilience that lived in her. It was the way she could look at all the hard and dark things in the world, could sit with the immense heaviness of a broken heart, and still choose to love. She could look into the face of torture and still reach out with an open heart.

"May I?" she asked, taking his right hand in hers. "I figured I would just let you wear this on your other hand for safekeeping, and I had it engraved like mine."

She held it up to the light so he could see the words *Brave with my heart* written inside the band.

"When did you do all this?" Rainer asked.

Her smile grew wide. "Well, I had the ring made months ago when I had your sword and my dagger made. I just didn't think I'd need it until the wedding. I've been carrying it around for months, and I don't want to carry it anymore. I want you to have it, and I want you to know that I'm ready, or at least as ready as I'll ever be."

He kissed her.

"I want to marry you in front of everyone we love, but I thought today I could make a vow just to you," she whispered.

Rainer's heart raced. He'd lost track of just how many times he'd wished for a moment like this—for the feeling of being chosen and loved exactly as he was with no qualifiers or contingencies.

"I have made a lot of mistakes," Cecilia said. "We both have. But there has never been a single moment when I stopped loving you. I love you, and I want you. I am so grateful for your love and patience with me while I've worked through everything. So I promise you this: I will continue to be brave with my hand and brave with my heart when it comes to you. No more doubts. No more hiding. Every day I choose you."

Rainer could hardly breathe. It was amazing that one moment could make the immensity of the loss and suffering they'd been through seem worth it.

"I can be brave if you can be brave too," he whispered, echoing what he'd said years before when they both sat terrified in the seer's suite. "I promise to continue to be brave with my hand and brave with my heart. I promise to love every part of you. I'll remind you who you are when you forget, because you are undeniable and unforgettable, Cecilia Juliette Reznik."

They may not have been official wedding vows, but they were as official as Rainer needed. She'd finally picked a date, and he thought his heart would burst from happiness. He pulled her into another kiss, crushing her against his body.

He pulled back and arched a brow. "Is this because of what happened in the library yesterday?"

She giggled. "No, I just had time to think and clear my head."

Her fingers wove through his hair, and she sighed in satisfaction. He searched their connection, and there was no apprehension at all, just relief and joy and love. He kissed down her neck as he unbuttoned the back of her dress. Slowly, he worked his way over her chest, dotting kisses along her neckline.

"Wow, apparently that made you very happy," she mumbled between kisses.

He smiled against her lips. "You have no idea. Let me show you."

He brought her down to the floor, intent on showing her exactly how happy she'd made him.

They were in the middle of chaos in a distant kingdom. There were spies at court and people who wanted to hurt their friends. So many things that could go wrong at any moment. There were so many things to worry about, but all Rainer wanted to do was be alone with Cecilia for as long as he could.

PART III:

T⚡ MAKE A KING

28

XANDER

It was too much to hope for one good night of sleep. Xander blinked blearily, roused by frantic knocking on his bedroom door. He cursed, stumbling out of bed naked, grabbing the pants that had been laid out for the next morning and pulling them on.

He yanked the door open. Sylvie stood with her fist raised to knock again, her hair mussed from sleep and her eyes wide with worry. The guard outside his room looked sheepishly from her to Xander to Cal and Evan, who stood behind Sylvie, looking dazed.

"She insisted—"

Sylvie scowled at the guard. "Both Evan and Cal have been spell-bound. I don't know the spell, but I can tell it's ancient magic because I've never seen anything like it—even in my Gauntlet memories. They wandered back from stable poker with the hunter captains in a daze. Maxim Bardenary escorted them and said there's been a report from the borders. Vincent's men have attacked."

"You're sure it's a spell and not—" The thought of his friends having their minds wiped by a slayer robbed him of breath.

"It's not a slayer's work," Sylvie said. "I checked their memories. They're all still there. They're just out of it."

307

Xander ducked into his closet to pull on a shirt. "I'm not supposed to ride out anywhere without Evan, Cal, or—shit."

Sylvie grimaced. "Rainer, I know. What are the odds he'll be willing to help while I try to break this spell?"

Xander sighed heavily. He tucked a bunch of dried chamomile into his pocket and grabbed his armor. Rainer owed him nothing, but he was honorable enough to do it anyway. "Only one way to find out."

Xander walked into the hall and shoved his armor into the guard's arms. "Tell them to ready Biscuit and Rainer McKay's horse, and tell the captains to organize their men. I'll be down in a few minutes."

The man disappeared down the hallway. Xander started toward Cece's room.

Sylvie followed him, dragging Cal and Evan, who mindlessly moved wherever she corralled them. Xander's head spun. It was stupid to go out when it seemed an obvious trap. It was too convenient that Evan and Cal had both been incapacitated when Vincent's men attacked, but it was unlikely they'd be expecting Rainer McKay at Xander's side.

Xander was loath to admit that Rainer was the best swordsman he'd ever seen. As someone who'd been trained to defend his whole life, Rainer was an excellent choice. As someone whose fiancée Xander never stopped trying to seduce, he was not.

Xander summoned all his bravado and knocked on Cece's door.

Rainer answered it, shirtless, hair mussed and eyes heavy with sleep. "What do you want? Cece's asleep," he whispered.

"You should wake her. I need your help," Xander said. "Can I come in?"

Rainer nodded and pushed the door open, letting Xander walk by before Sylvie dragged Cal and Evan in behind her.

Cece sat up in bed in the dim firelight, holding the blankets up to her chest. She grumbled a curse as Rainer tossed her a robe. She carefully wrapped it around herself and stood from the bed.

"Why are you waking me in the middle of the night?" she asked, crossing the room to sit in one of the plush chairs by the fire. Her eyes caught on Evan and Cal. "What's wrong with them?"

"Can you see something?" Xander asked.

"Can't you?" She crossed the room to take a closer look at Cal. "Gods, Xander, I know you weren't trained like the rest of us, but how do you not recognize spellwork when you smell it? You should be able to as well." She shifted to look at Evan. "What did they do to you two?"

Taking Evan's hand, she closed her eyes, and the lemon-lavender scent of her magic filled the room. "I can't see any faces, just a bunch of laughing and drinking. He only had whiskey to drink, but perhaps that was spelled. In the stables, even a hunter with enhanced senses would struggle to pick up the scent of spellwork." She took Cal's hand, then shook her head. "No clues."

"How could this happen to both of them?" Xander asked.

"I don't recognize the magic," Sylvie said. "If I had to guess, it's some type of daze spell, but it's not one I know."

"I agree. It's not one I've ever seen," Cece said. "And the smell of the magic is old—mugwort and blood and moss, like what the Gauntlet caves smelled like. We might be able to find something on it in the library."

Sylvie cocked her head. "Or you could try to summon a spirit that might know. Didn't you say that affinity had been stronger since—" She stopped and clamped her mouth shut.

Xander had put it out of his head, but the memory roared back. The sand grainy on his hands, the pain and exhaustion in his body, the smell of blood and the panic and love in her eyes. He blew out a shuddering breath, trying to rid himself of the perfectly preserved living nightmare of that day on the beach.

Cece crossed her arms and grimaced. "I'd rather not."

Xander hadn't realized she could consult with spirits that way, but it made sense considering her affinity for death and her visit beyond the veil.

He shifted, turning his gaze on Rainer. "That's not all I need. There's been some trouble in one of the cities outside the castle walls, and I need to ride out to help. It's a short ride, but there are reports of

Vincent's men attacking. I'm forbidden from going beyond castle walls during the festival without—"

Rainer frowned and rubbed the back of his neck. "Cal, Evan, or me."

Cece's eyes went wide as she turned her fury on Rainer. "Excuse me? Have you been keeping secrets?"

"I honestly didn't think it would come up since I'd be just as likely to put a knife in his back as his enemies," Rainer said, forcing lightness into his voice.

Cece was not amused. She glared at Xander. "Why do you have to be there?"

"Because the kingdom hangs in a precarious balance. If I don't show up for these skirmishes, it makes me look weak. Since this is very likely a targeted attack, given the state Cal and Evan are in, I need someone with me who I can trust, even if the only thing I can trust him to do is stab me in the back," Xander said.

Cece was quiet for a moment, staring into the fire. "No." She sat back down in the chair.

Rainer knelt in front of her, resting his hands on her knees. "We don't tell each other what we can and can't do, right? That was your rule. I won't ask you not to do something you need to do, and you won't do that to me. Didn't we agree to that?"

"Fine, then I'm coming too."

Rainer sighed heavily. "That's not a good idea. You haven't been shooting, and I know you don't want to. You would be a liability, and we both know it."

Xander hadn't noticed it until now. Rainer used two different voices with her, and the one he was using now was Guardian Rainer voice. It was stern and no-nonsense instead of the softer Fiancé Rainer voice he usually used.

She leaned her forehead against his. "I don't want you to be in danger."

Rainer's face softened. Xander could see her chipping away at his resolve.

"We don't have a lot of time. The guards are already waiting in the stable," Xander said.

Cece gave him a furious look. She stood up and pushed past Rainer. "You know, you might be a royal, but you can't just use us as you like."

Behind her, Rainer ducked into the washroom.

"The answer is no," Cece said to Xander. "Your people won't care if you miss this one time."

"The people who live in that village will." Xander let the truth hit her, but she was unmoved. She was so godsdamned stubborn, and he was running out of time.

She turned as Rainer walked out of the washroom and picked up his sword.

"Rain, no!"

Xander saw the change in her body language, the way her voice grew tight and shrill. He heard her heart racing and her breathing get shallow. She started to argue with Rainer, but Xander didn't have time for that. His people didn't have time for that.

Rainer pulled her into a kiss, trying to calm her down, but she pulled away, rearing back to yell at him again.

Xander pulled a handful of dried chamomile from his pocket and put his other hand on the back of Cece's neck, murmuring the words of his grandmother's soothing spell.

Her eyes went wide with panic as she realized what was happening. "No—"

Rainer caught her as her knees went out and carried her to the bed.

"She's going to be so pissed," Rainer said, covering her with a blanket. He pressed a kiss to her lips before turning to face Sylvie. "You'll stay with her and be here when she wakes up?"

Sylvie nodded, and Rainer followed Xander out of the room.

———

The battle raged as Xander and Rainer rode into Alfasin with a small contingent of guards. The night was so dark that it was hard to tell Vincent's hunters from their own until they were within spitting distance.

The fight was brutal, the night bitterly cold. Fire spread from house to house, urged on by the vicious winds. The storm was unwilling to bend to Xander as easily as it normally would. He felt the press of witches feeding their magic into the storm, trying to make it stronger.

"Rainer, tell the men to take cover," Xander yelled over the roaring wind.

He waited for their men to hustle into the few structures left standing. Then he turned his focus to the storm. The magic grew so loud and discordant, but beneath the cacophony he heard a subtle melody. Xander grabbed ahold of it. He waited, his magic whispering a soothing line of energy into the storm to give it focus. The other storm witches had been feeding it for a while, even before he'd arrived. They had to be close to reaching the end of their magical reserves, but there was no telling how many of them were out there. He let it build for another moment and then he struck.

He forced a huge surge of his magic out at once, drawing as much of it into that one melodic line as he could, then sent it all barreling toward the enemy line. He pelted them with snow, sleet, rain, and wind. He drew down lightning bolts in an unrelenting staccato.

Xander's ears popped with the force of letting it all go at once. He dropped to the ground, cringing in pain as the magic rushed out of him. He pressed a hand to his left ear and it came away bloody.

"Shit." The sound of his own voice was muted. He brought the hand back to his ear and let healing magic flow. When he pulled his palm away a moment later, the screams and groans from the enemy line hit him all at once, but the storm was no more than a light drizzle and a few gusts of wind.

His men emerged from cover and began to engage again. They held the line and, mercifully, the last of the townsfolk were able to flee to safety.

Xander charged into the fray, ignoring Rainer's shout behind him. He sliced and blocked blows. He fought with the same torrent as the storm. As he spun and ducked and dodged blades, he caught Rainer in action, all shining steel and merciless violence. He'd seen him fight before, though never with such fury.

Rainer caught his eye. "Could you please stay behind me?"

"Move faster and I won't have to, old man. It's not my fault your retired ass can't keep up."

Rainer scowled at him, then sliced through a man who charged at him. "I'm not retired."

"But you are out of practice. Too much time sitting at home," Xander taunted, blocking a swipe from an enemy attacker before shoving his dagger into the man's neck.

"Could you have a little more regard for your life?"

Xander understood. If he got himself killed, not only would the kingdom crumble into the hands of his insane cousin, but all that Cece sacrificed would amount to nothing.

Still, Rainer was an asset. He was an incredibly skilled fighter, adept at protecting someone who was occasionally a bit reckless. He anticipated Xander's movements in a way that would have been annoying if it weren't so helpful. Loath as he was to admit it, Rainer McKay was truly gifted.

"Xander, hang back," Rainer called over his shoulder.

Xander tried frantically to use his fire magic to put out a fire before it burned a nearby cottage, but he was still getting the hang of it, and it drained his energy too quickly. He hadn't eaten enough to be prepared for a fight like this.

"These are my people!" he called back.

"And you are their only good option for king!" Rainer yelled.

Xander begrudgingly slowed and fell into step with Rainer.

They fought their way through five more hunters before a horn sounded from the hills above town and Vincent's men began to retreat.

"Should we pursue?" Rainer asked.

Xander looked around at his men as they struggled to their feet.

Some were cheering. Others were helping the wounded. The air was full of smoke and ash from the burning cottages. Blood stained the slushy layer of fresh snow with abstract splotches. The chill in Xander's bones made him long for Olney's more temperate climate.

"We should head back," Xander sighed. "I don't want to pursue without knowing what's out there in the daylight, and we should get back and make sure everything is okay with the princesses and Cal and Evan."

He hated to stand down, but it was the wiser choice. He gave the command to head back to Castle Savero, but he stood proudly facing the hillside where the last of Vincent's hunters were disappearing through the trees.

He and Rainer mounted their horses, and dread sunk like a stone in Xander's stomach. Cece was going to be so furious when they got back. He dreaded seeing her face.

He turned to Rainer. "Is she awake yet?"

Rainer shook his head. "I would know. She's going to be so angry. We shouldn't have left her."

"She'll be okay."

"I'm not worried about her. I'm worried about us. We might have survived this skirmish, but I don't like our chances in that one," Rainer sighed.

Xander half-smiled, picked up his pace, and Rainer followed him into the dark.

———

As soon as they dismounted, footsteps pounded into the stable and Cece launched herself into Rainer's arms like she was shot from a catapult. Her legs wrapped around his waist, her arms around his neck, and despite the crowd of guards in the stables, she kissed him in a mad frenzy.

They both seemed utterly unconcerned with their passionate public display of affection. Some of the guards shifted, averting their eyes, but Xander couldn't tear his gaze away.

Cece wound her fingers through Rainer's hair. His hand slid up the back of her tunic. For a moment, Xander thought he might fuck her right there, in front of everyone—obviously he wasn't afraid of a little public sex—but finally, the guardian pulled away.

Cece gripped Rainer's face in her hands. "Don't ever let him do that to me again, Rainer McKay." Her voice wavered, and Xander couldn't tell if it was fear or fury making her shake.

"I won't. I'm sorry. I won't," Rainer said, cradling her head against his shoulder.

She closed her eyes and took a shaky breath before pulling back and letting him set her on her feet, then she turned and stalked toward Xander. His guards stiffened, but he held up a hand, stopping them. He held his arms out to Cece as if he expected her to do the same thing to him as she'd done to Rainer. He hoped the humor would dispel her anger, but instead of kissing him, she punched him in the face.

He stumbled back, surprised by the force of the blow.

"Don't you ever do that to me again! I don't care what you're king of! If you ever use that magic on me again, if you ever put my love at risk, I will end you!"

A guard took a step forward, but Xander waved him off. "I'm fine. You're dismissed. I had that coming." It was less his face than his heart that was bruised.

His men looked skeptical, but they listened to his command, shuffling out of the stable quietly.

Cece pressed a hand to her chest. "Do either of you have any idea what it was like waking up and realizing that Rainer was gone? I couldn't breathe. I have already been robbed of so many choices. You can't take my choice away like that!" Her breath came in short pants, and suddenly she collapsed to her knees with a ragged sob.

Xander didn't move. He just stared as Rainer knelt next to her and placed a hand on her back.

"You can't do that. You should both have known what that would feel like to me. How could either of you?! You can't leave me like that.

I can't lose anymore. I can't—" She broke off, dissolving into sobs as Rainer pulled her into his lap.

The heavy silence was punctuated by Cece's sniffles.

"Sweetheart, shhh...it's okay. I'm right here. I promise I won't ever do it again." Rainer whispered soothing words, but Cece couldn't stop shaking.

She fell apart right there on the stable floor. She broke, and something inside of Xander broke too.

He'd only ever seen her strong, even in the moments she'd been terrified and felt lost and sad. But at that moment, she seemed completely shattered. Even when she made Rainer stab her in the heart, she didn't look scared. Xander had never seen her unable to hold it together until she was in private.

It made sense that she would be triggered by having her choice taken away, but Xander hadn't considered it at the time. He should have thought about how it would feel to her to wake up and know Rainer was gone and feel helpless. The guilt froze him in place.

For the first time, Xander could feel the invisible scars that Cato had left behind on the woman he loved. He'd been so wrapped up in the joy of seeing her, he'd all but ignored the fact that she might still be hurting. Even when he got Cece's heartbreaking letters, he had so much confidence that she would bounce back. It felt impossible for her spirit to be broken. He didn't realize how much had permanently changed for her. It was easy to look at how strong she'd been through so much and think that wouldn't ever change.

Rainer whispered comforting words in her ear and kissed her softly on the forehead and temple as she curled into him. Her sobbing subsided, but she still clung to him.

"Cece, I'm sorry—" Xander started, but she held up a hand.

She climbed to her feet. Though Xander stood a foot taller than Cece, the look she gave him made him feel small.

"I don't want your apology. I hate that after all this time you still haven't learned not to take my choices from me. That is unforgivable." She turned on her heel and stomped away.

He'd gone too far. Xander was too much to be trusted with a kingdom. Too much for his court. And finally, he was too much for the person who'd always loved his excess.

To his surprise, Rainer hesitated, falling behind as she stormed off. He turned to Xander, his face full of pity. "She'll cool down and be herself again. She has a hard time with some things. I should have known that would set her off."

"You did know. I just didn't realize she was so...scared. I've never seen her like that. It's one thing to hear about it or read about it. It's another to witness it. I really am sorry. I would never hurt her like that on purpose," Xander said quietly.

Rainer was good enough not to mention that Xander's intentions didn't matter or that he'd very much hurt Cece on purpose before. He turned and followed his fiancée.

Xander stayed in the stable for a long time, waiting for his guilt to abate.

29

RAINER

Rainer felt terrible. Cecilia was still shaking when they got back to their room. He sat on the bed and pulled her into his lap, rubbing his hands on her arms even though he knew she wasn't shaking from the cold.

Fighting was something he was good at, especially without worrying about Cecilia being hurt. He'd been prepared for her anger, but not this terror. His body was relaxed with the satisfied soreness of battle, but hers was rattled by waking in a panic.

She alternated between hyperventilating, crying, and saying a bunch of words he could barely make out.

"I don't know why this is happening," she said shakily. "I can't breathe. It doesn't make sense. I know you're safe now."

Rainer brought her hand to his heart and held it there for a moment. "It doesn't need to make sense. Just breathe with me. All is well. I won't let Xander do that again. I won't leave while you're sleeping like that. I promise. I'm sorry. I should have realized how you would feel. Just breathe."

Her blue eyes were wide, but she finally focused on his face and took a deep, shaky breath.

"I'm right here. Just keep breathing with me. I'm not going anywhere."

She took a few more deep breaths. As she calmed, he pulled her tight to his chest. She rested her head on his shoulder and tucked her face into the crook of his neck, and she breathed along with him, pressed together, heart to heart. She seemed incredibly small in his arms—too fragile and breakable. He hated seeing her that way.

Her weight settled into him more heavily as she calmed.

"Tell me the story about the village where it rains stars. It always calms you down."

She ran her fingers through the hair on the back of his head. He needed a haircut—it was starting to curl around his ears, but she loved it like that, so he let it grow.

"Go ahead, tell me," he said, kissing her temple.

"Once upon a time there was a village where for one night every year it rained stars." She took another deep breath.

"Go on," he whispered.

"The villagers ran outside with empty jars to collect them, because each star was worth one wish. One of the villagers, a man named Jack, was very in love with one of his fellow villagers, a woman named June. Every year he'd use his wishes for very practical things: good crops for the village, safety for their people, and health for his parents. But he always saved one star for a special occasion. June, on the other hand, was fast and often caught the most stars. She was also generous, blowing through her wishes within the first week of getting them. She wished for things to take care of everyone else in the community because she wanted everyone to love her. So, most of the year June would be without any wishes and every week she would ask Jack what he was saving his last wish for. But he never answered."

Rainer grinned as her story halted.

"What is Jack saving the wish for? I always fall asleep before you get to the end and it doesn't say in your book of fairy tales," she whispered.

"You're telling the story. What do you think he's saving it for?"

She smiled against his neck. "I think he's saving it to wish for her dream house."

"Why do you think it's the house he wants to wish for?" Rainer said.

"Because June wants a home."

Rainer smiled and kissed the top of her head.

Cecilia shifted, running her fingers over the scar on his neck. "Am I right? Is that what he wishes for?"

"Do you think there's a right answer?"

She let out a frustrated huff. "I think there's an answer you had when you told the story initially."

"I left it open-ended."

She pulled back and met his gaze. "What did you wish for the night of the Summer Firestorm meteor shower?"

"I can't tell you unless it comes true."

"What else could you possibly want when I'm right here?"

Rainer laughed. "Maybe a more modest fiancée?"

She pushed her lip out into an exaggerated pout. "You are no fun."

Rainer grinned and flipped her onto her back, settling between her legs. "Let me assure you that I am plenty of fun."

Cecilia let him prove it.

———

After all the stress of the morning, Rainer was eager for the control he felt in the kitchen. Woodworking helped focus his mind, but he still wasn't skilled enough to control outcomes the way he could in the kitchen, and Cecilia had no interest in learning to carve. She did, however, love to eat.

The scent of freshly baked bread hit him as he rounded the corner to the castle kitchen.

"I don't know why you are dragging me to the kitchen. Are you trying to prepare me for you to win our bet? It's not nice to gloat,

Rainer," Cecilia said as Rainer pulled her into the loud, cavernous room.

"I'm not taunting. I was going to teach you to make pasta like Aunt Clara taught me and would have taught you if you weren't so impatient. This is a win-win, Cece. You get to spend time with me, and you get to eat something delicious when you're done."

"Fine."

The kitchen staff looked mildly disturbed by the two of them being there, especially the former princess, but the head chef had laid out everything that Rainer requested. He got to work tying an apron around Cecilia's waist. She regarded his seriousness with amusement. The kitchen staff watched them with curiosity.

Cecilia nodded to the crowd. "I think you have some additional willing students."

Rainer grinned at the group. "I'm happy to teach you all as well, if you like. Lady Reznik has historically not been the most willing or attentive student, and she would benefit from some healthy competition," he said, placing a kiss on the top of her head.

"That was rude," she said.

"Or just true," Rainer teased.

The servants hesitated.

"If you're worried about the king, he will not give you a hard time," Cecilia said as if reading their doubt.

That was enough to win them over.

Before long, six kitchen workers were lined up across from Rainer, learning how to make pasta from scratch. Cecilia did a terrible job of paying attention and cutting her pasta into even shapes.

Halfway through, Evan appeared in the doorway and caught Rainer's attention.

Cecilia eyed him warily. "It's good to see you looking like yourself again."

"I understand I have you and Sylvie to thank for that," Evan said.

Cecilia shrugged. "Sylvie did the heavy lifting of the spell. I just found the right one."

"I'm grateful all the same." Evan nodded at Rainer. "To both of you."

Cecilia crossed her arms, still eyeing Evan with caution. "We'll take your thanks, but if the king needs something from me, you can tell him exactly where to stick his request."

Evan smirked at her misshapen pasta. "Domestic affairs suit you, Cece."

Cecilia glared at him. "For a spy, you sure are a bad liar." She brushed her hair out of her face with her fingers, leaving a trail of flour in their wake.

"Actually, I was hoping to speak to Rainer," Evan said.

Rainer nodded and met him outside the kitchen doorway. He didn't want to be put between them, but Evan was smart enough to know that if Rainer was made to choose between staying and supporting their friends or leaving because Cecilia wanted to, he'd choose the latter in a second.

Evan leaned back against the stone wall. "Xander wanted me to check on her and you to see if you're leaving. As her friend, I'd understand, but as his, I'm willing to beg you both to stay. I feel like we are right on the edge of figuring all of this out."

Rainer brushed his hands on his apron. "She's not going anywhere."

"You're sure? I saw Xander's eye." Evan smirked.

"She likes to pretend she would walk away, but she's in this for the long haul. She wants to figure out what's going on as much as the rest of us, whether she admits it or not. I know she wants him to find someone," Rainer said. "I'll talk to Xander."

Evan's eyes went wide. "Should I be there to supervise?"

"I've always been nice to him. He's had a problem with me since the beginning. At the moment, I think I'm the safer bet," he said, nodding his head toward Cecilia.

She sat on the counter covered in a film of flour, eating a peach tart that she'd swindled from one of the kitchen servants. Her eyes were closed as she took a big bite, as if tasting it required her full concentration. Her whole face lit up with a smile as she turned to the waiting baker, clearly trying to express her approval.

Gods, she was cute.

Rainer turned back to Evan. "I'll find him a little later tonight."

Evan nodded and left them to continue their cooking lesson.

————

Rainer ran a hand through his hair and paused outside the king's rooms. Strange that he'd felt envious of Xander and now he felt nothing but pity. The man had been his nemesis for so long, but now all he could see were the ways their lives mirrored each other—the way he understood how awful it must be for Xander to put his duty above his happiness. He'd thought Xander's life was charmed, and in some ways it was, but now Rainer understood that for all his wealth, he had no family, no respect from the people for whom he was clearly working hard, no safety from those who wanted him dead, and no choice but to marry someone for his duty.

The guard outside Xander's door eyed Rainer expectantly.

"I'm here to see Xan—the king."

The guard nodded to the door, and Rainer knocked. A moment later, Xander answered, his eye mottled with color where Cecilia had punched him.

Xander raised his brows. "You are just about the last person I was expecting."

"That's quite a shiner, Your Majesty," Rainer said with a smirk.

"Who taught her that right hook?" Xander asked.

Rainer couldn't help but feel proud.

"I thought you said she hadn't been training," Xander said, gesturing for Rainer to enter the room. "I wasn't expecting her to hit quite so hard."

"I said she hadn't been shooting. She still does hunter workouts every day," Rainer said.

"That explains it. For a moment, I thought maybe she maintained some of her goddess strength," Xander said, leading him to two chairs by the fireplace. "What can I do for you?"

"I came to check on you."

"Strange. We're not exactly friends," Xander said quietly.

Rainer stood there awkwardly, trying to decide if it was better to stay or go. "Maybe it's time that changed. I know we haven't ever seen eye to eye, and I still want to punch you every time you give Cece that look, but I also know that out of all of us, you've probably lost the most." He took in the surprise on Xander's face with amusement. "Look, you messed up with Cece. Big time. We both did, but after the stable I thought maybe you might want to talk to someone."

Xander nodded, pouring them each a drink from a decanter on the table beside him. Rainer surveyed the room around them as he sipped from the crystal glass. The bedroom was sparse, save for a few personal items. A wooden box overflowing with letters sat on his nightstand and Cece's dried bridal bouquet hung by the closet door. Several wood carvings of small animals stood on the mantel. He was about to ask if Xander had done them when he spotted one of Lady Rosalee Reznik's paintings above the fireplace.

In fact, he knew well it was Cecilia's favorite because it was one of the few that portrayed her.

Xander caught him staring at it. "A parting gift."

"Why?" Rainer couldn't stop himself from asking.

"Because I recognized her the first time I ever looked at it. I still recognize her in it. The next best thing to looking at her lovely face, I suppose."

"But she loves that painting." Jealousy twisted in Rainer's stomach. He'd wondered where it had gone.

"She does. I thought about sending it back a hundred times, but I couldn't bear to part with it." He swallowed hard as he broke their eye contact and looked into the fire. "How is she?"

"I know she'll be okay, but those moments when she's not are the scariest thing that I've ever seen," Rainer admitted. "Scarier than the gods, than the caves, than fighting off hordes of hunters...maybe even scarier than watching her die. It's like she's trapped inside herself, stuck under the surface, and I can't get to her."

Xander nodded.

Rainer hadn't realized how much he'd missed having someone to talk to about Cecilia. He talked to her about all of the big things in his life, but he'd missed the chance to share his worries about her.

He rubbed a hand over the back of his neck and met Xander's eye. "Every day she decides if she can let me love her. It's hard for her. I guess that's the immeasurable cost of all we've been through. Some days she wants to fight it and I have to make my love smaller—crush it down into something she can accept. Other days she can't get enough, like it's the glue holding her together. Those are the good days—when I can let my love exist in its true form—something large enough to swallow both of us."

Xander looked contemplative as he nodded. It seemed he understood what Rainer meant. Perhaps he'd blamed himself for Cecilia's wounding, but Rainer didn't. Xander had made one mistake that he'd more than paid for, and he wasn't responsible for the things that hurt Cecilia most.

Xander was quiet for a moment. "And what about you? You talk a lot about Cece, and I know that worrying about her is more than one of your jobs, but how are you handling everything?"

"I'm probably going to need another drink if I'm going to talk to my fiancée's ex-husband about my feelings," Rainer said with a smirk.

Xander laughed and poured them each another glass of whiskey.

Rainer drained half the glass before speaking, the pleasant burn warming his chest. "I thought I was okay for a while, but now I am afraid all the time. I am afraid of the echo of every old hurt I cannot love away. I am afraid of the haunted look in her eyes. I wake Cece up a couple times a night to make sure she's still breathing. I have nightmares of the knife going into my heart and then me stabbing Cece, but in the dreams she doesn't wake up. Sometimes I wake up screaming. Sometimes it's enough just to feel her breathing beside me. But sometimes I have to shake her awake and see her eyes to know for sure that she's all right. How selfish is that? I will still not let her have a good night's sleep after a year."

Xander shrugged. "I couldn't let her have a good night's sleep the entire time we were together, but for a way worse reason. I'm sure she doesn't mind."

Rainer gave him a scathing look. "She doesn't, and that's almost worse. It feels like nothing will be normal again."

"What is normal anymore?" Xander asked with a sad smile.

"That's a fair question, I guess. I just would like to feel that Cato didn't break all of us. Like there are some parts of all of us that aren't ruined by this whole ordeal. I know she's not the same, and I don't expect her to be. All I want is to marry her, to spend my life with her —not some perfect idealized version of her, but this version of her," Rainer said, taking a long gulp of his drink.

"She's getting there," Xander said, refilling Rainer's glass without prompting.

Rainer ran a hand through his hair. "You know, I tell her all the time I can't remember the exact moment I fell in love with her. That's almost true. It definitely happened in little ways over time, but there was a moment I knew for sure. It was when my mom was dying."

The fire flickered, and Rainer took a long drink of whiskey. He could still see the whole vision in his mind's eye, as burned into his brain as the day she'd given him the ribbon.

"I was eighteen, and Cece was sixteen. She lost her mom when she was really young, but she was so distraught because she was really close to my mom, but also so steady in the face of loss. Anyway, there was one night toward the end when I was afraid to sleep because I didn't want to miss her passing. We were camped out on the couch in my mother's room, and I told her I was too worried to sleep. Cece just wrapped herself around me, and she said, 'Rain, you go to sleep. I'll wake you up when you need to worry.' She stayed up so that I wouldn't miss anything."

Swirling the whiskey in his glass, Rainer struggled for the words. "That would have been enough, but I woke up a while later, and she was sitting on the edge of my mom's bed. My mom said how tired she was, and Cece just looked at her and said, 'Mama, I'll take care of Rain. You can go. I'll make sure he's okay. You don't have to worry. I'll love him enough for both of us.'"

Love had never felt like a certainty until Cecilia promised to love him. It always felt like something that could be taken away if he wasn't good enough, especially with his mother dying. But the moment Cecilia said those words, the moment he felt the truth of them in his chest, Rainer knew what real love was.

"Then Cece laid down next to my mother and told her to share any memories that she wanted to make sure I had. The whole night she stayed up and let my mom send through all of these memories of me as a kid. Cece woke me up in the morning when she could hear the death whispers and stayed with me the whole time and after for days." Rainer's eyes burned and he blinked away tears.

Xander didn't say anything. He just nodded.

"I never told her I heard that."

"Why?" Xander asked.

"I don't know. I think before this, admitting it would have been admitting how much I loved her, and I couldn't stand to look too closely at that."

Rainer remembered the way he'd been broken by grief; the way Cecilia had crawled into his bed. He'd buried his face in her neck and cried, and she'd whispered his favorite stories into his hair. She knew what he'd needed, and she'd given it to him without hesitation or tending to her own grief.

When he met Xander's eye, he expected teasing, but there was only understanding.

They both sat there, drinking in silence, both knowing what it was to be saved from drowning in grief by the same woman's love.

A warmth and lightness spread through Rainer's limbs and he was beginning to think he'd had too much to drink. He hadn't been drunk in years. Not since before they left on their last Gauntlet run, and even then, the occasions were few and far between. Still, he poured himself another glass.

Rainer cleared his throat, trying to sound more sober. "But I'm not here to talk about me, Xander. We need to talk about you. What are we all doing here? Are you actually trying to find a wife or will you continue to try to win back my fiancée?"

"It all feels impossible," Xander said, leaning back in his chair. "I agreed to this because some part of me hoped maybe I would meet one of these women and feel something, but after this morning's needlepoint exhibit, I feel like I don't relate to any of them. I finally understand why Cece hates it so much. It's remarkably boring and I felt like an idiot trying to compliment them." He scrubbed a hand down his face. "I never wanted to be king. I never expected to be, and I feel like I can barely hold myself together, let alone a whole kingdom. I'm terrified of letting everyone down."

"So, what will you do?"

"What would you have done? If I hadn't fucked up. If she'd stayed with me. Would you have moved on?" Xander asked. It clearly wasn't meant to be a challenge or a test. His face was full of honest curiosity.

Rainer refilled his glass. Somehow he'd gulped down several drinks without feeling it, but now he felt a heady lightness in his mind. His thoughts floated away like leaves in the breeze. "I don't think I ever could have really moved on. I don't think I could have been alone forever, but I don't think I ever could have truly been with anyone, either."

Xander frowned. "I'm not sure if you know, but my mother had a consort for many years. My father was not particularly sentimental, but he was vindictive and possessive. He liked to win. He didn't so much resent the affection my mother showered on her consort because he wanted it, it was simply that he saw my mother give someone else what she couldn't give him and he never forgave her for it. Even if I could marry a queen who didn't expect my full affection, I couldn't subject children to seeing that. I doubt my feelings about Cece are a mystery to anyone in this kingdom, and certainly not to those princesses."

"Do you think they care?" Rainer asked.

"I think they can convince themselves now that they don't the same way all women convince themselves they can change a man.

But over time, when they see up close and personal the way I pine for her, I doubt it will be so easy not to care. I'm not exactly discreet."

Rainer's gut churned at that. "You know you can't have her, right? I'm not letting her go again."

"I think the whole of my king's guard knows that," Xander said, smirking. "But yes, the day she died is as imprinted on me as it is on you. I remember whose love she came back for and whose killed her." He looked back into the fire. "I know I can't have her in the same way ever again. It changes so little in my mind. You should know well that love is beyond reason. I'll love her the same whether I can or can't have her."

Suddenly, the door swung open and Cecilia burst into the room. She stood in the doorway with her hands on her hips.

It was a testament to how drunk Rainer was that he hadn't felt her before she appeared.

Rainer stared at her, a vision in a scarlet off-the-shoulder dress. The entire neckline was covered in large rosettes, and buttons trailed all the way down the front. Rainer wanted to undo those buttons immediately. He wanted to run his fingers through her neatly pinned-up hair and wreck it. He wanted to kiss her until she was breathless—until she begged him to do more. She was so much fun to rile up, and he was the one who got to spend his life riling her.

"You've got to be kidding me. We are all down there working our asses off planning a talent show for the princesses tomorrow, and the two of you are up here getting drunk?" She sulked as she stepped into Xander's room.

Rainer glanced guiltily at the nearly empty decanter of whiskey.

"A talent show?" Xander asked.

Cecilia grimaced. "Yes, Xander. A talent show for them to show you their considerable poise and talent or whatever else princesses do."

Rainer frowned. "That sounds horrible."

Xander burst out laughing. "It does."

"What? You two are friends now?" she asked. "I can't tell if this is a dream or a nightmare."

"I think we both know it's more of a fantasy," Xander said with a wink.

Cecilia blushed a deep crimson.

"Has your fierce temper cooled, my love?" Xander asked.

She didn't respond as she crossed the room to stand in front of Rainer.

"Cece, we were just talking," Rainer said, his words slightly slower than he meant them to be. "I thought you wanted us to be friends."

"You are an adorable drunk," she said. She ran a hand through his messy hair. He leaned into her touch and then pulled her down into his lap, nuzzling into her neck.

"Wow, you are drunk," she said. "If I didn't know any better, I would think you two had been enchanted by some foreign magic."

"Ugh, could you be slightly less in love? You're making me nauseous," Xander groaned.

"He's just jealous because he saw you in the library," Rainer whispered loudly.

"He's not wrong," Xander laughed. "It's pretty much all I've thought about since."

Rainer glared at him, but Xander just shrugged.

"Just being honest. Would you want to be with anyone else after being with her?" Xander asked.

Rainer tilted his head, considering. "There's no one else like her," he sighed, kissing her cheek.

"All right, let's get you to bed," Cecilia laughed. "I bet you're going to be feeling great tomorrow."

She barely acknowledged Xander as she dragged Rainer out of the room and back to their chambers. When they got there, Rainer tried to undo all the buttons on her dress but got frustrated halfway through and let her take over. He wanted to kiss her for hours, but the whiskey and warmth of the room and Cecilia whispering a bedtime story had him drifting off before he could even kiss her good night.

30

EVAN

E van was happy for the crisp morning air as he and Xander rode through the old hunter training grounds toward the edge of the castle grounds. The past few days had been frustrating. He still didn't know how he and Cal had been spellbound, and no matter how he searched his memories, he could not find the answer.

Beyond that, the festival was flying by. Just over a week remained before Xander needed to choose a wife. Evan wasn't good at planning dates or getting a read on the princesses. He needed to focus on the things he had some semblance of control over, and keeping Xander focused on his prospects was at the top of that list.

He hoped visiting one of their old haunts would help bring both him and Xander some clarity.

"Remember when we used to hide notes out here when you were in training and I wasn't supposed to see you?" Xander said.

Evan grinned, remembering how morose Xander had been, cut off and alone in the castle while Evan, a year older, did the most intense part of his hunter training. "I wonder if there are any notes still hidden out there."

Xander laughed, looking more like himself than he had in weeks.

"Doubtful. You made it your mission to find even my best-hidden notes."

Evan pulled back on the reins and his horse came to a stop. Xander pulled up beside him, reaching for his canteen of coffee. He uncorked it and steam rose from the opening.

"Are you ready to have a serious conversation about your prospects?" Evan asked.

Xander met his eye, took a hard swallow of his coffee, and nodded.

"Let's talk about Eloise Spellman."

Xander barely reacted. "She's very beautiful and, mercifully, seems to be nothing like her father. I'm sure she would be a powerful ally within the kingdom, and I can tell by looking at her that she has a certain edge. I overheard her taking down another lady who'd been rude to a servant once, and you know how I feel about a woman with a sharp tongue."

"I'd think you'd be wary about getting involved with another woman that appears to have an eye for Rainer McKay," Evan said.

Xander choked on his coffee. "What? How do you manage to know everything about everything?"

Not everything. Not the most important thing. Not what Vincent looks like or how to stop him.

Evan shrugged. "I caught the end of a conversation between them the other night on the balcony at the end of the east hallway. It must have been after your antics with Cece, because Rainer was flirting with her. She spoke right to his hero complex."

Evan studied the king carefully.

Xander's eyes narrowed. "Why would he do something so incredibly foolish?"

"Why do you?" Evan challenged.

Xander sighed, leaning back in his chair. "To make Cece jealous."

"Regardless, while Rainer's flirtation with her appeared to be harmless, hers seemed born of genuine interest."

"Of course. Who doesn't love perfect Rainer McKay?" Xander huffed, sulking into his coffee.

Evan almost laughed. He'd never seen Xander jealous of anyone. Normally Xander's confidence was his biggest liability, but Rainer's hold over Cecilia made him the only person in the world Xander was genuinely envious of.

"Well, I won't make that mistake twice. I've already lost one love to Rainer. Do you see Eloise as a real prospect?" Xander asked.

"Honestly, no. In that same conversation with Rainer, she admitted that she didn't have a desire to be queen. She seems burned out on court life, and while I don't think she'd try to wrestle power from you, I'm not sure she'd be happy. Beyond that, she would be a help in securing your standing among the Argarian aristocracy, and the family is fabulously wealthy. Still, I think she's probably not the best option." Evan paused to sip his coffee. He wanted to look casual because he wanted Xander to seriously consider the next candidate. "What about Jessamin of Novum? She seems intelligent, beautiful, fierce."

Xander eyed him suspiciously. "She is. You think she's the best option?"

"I think that all of those women want something and pretend not to. She seems the only one willing to be up-front about it."

Xander's eyebrows shot up as he considered.

"I think she has the most to gain through this alliance, the most buy-in to make it work," Evan said.

Xander frowned.

"You don't find her attractive?" Evan asked.

Xander laughed. "I'd have to be blind not to. Princess Jessamin's beauty is only surpassed by my Cece."

Evan rolled his eyes. "You really need to stop calling her that."

Xander shrugged. "I like Jessamin. She's a very adventurous dresser. She's clearly intelligent. She has a warrior's instincts. I understand she can hunt and fight, which I find both terrifying and comforting. The stories about Novum's female warriors are fascinating, though I do worry about having someone who could easily snuff out my life and take the throne for herself sleeping in my bed every night."

"Didn't bother you before."

Xander chuckled. "Yes, but Cece loved me. These women have no such liability."

Jessamin was the most obviously dangerous of the prospects, but her kingdom also had the most to gain from an alliance and, therefore, the most incentive to make it work. Evan knew from his spies that the queen of Novum was extremely anxious to strike an alliance and that Xander was an obvious choice because of Argaria's recent alliance with Olney. It was a two-for-one alliance deal for her and would likely open up trade in a whole new way, stimulating both kingdoms' economies.

Beyond that, Jessamin seemed temperate and smart. Evan thought that they'd be well-matched—at the very least as friends, if not eventually more.

"I understand your concerns, but Jessamin has likely been here long enough to understand how your own kingdom views you as an outsider, and that's been a challenge to your reign," Evan said. "Even if she killed you, she must see that they wouldn't accept her as queen. She's still here, which indicates a commitment to see this through. My spies tell me that Jessamin is extremely pragmatic. You could use someone more steady in your corner."

"You mean someone other than you," Xander taunted.

Evan cleared his throat, trying to think of the right entry into the conversation. "Xander, I will always be your friend and advisor, but I need someone to share the weight with me. I have other responsibilities I'd like to take on, and I can't do that if you don't get married."

A smirk stole over Xander's face. "Would those responsibilities have to do with Lady Brett?"

Evan glared at him. "You know they would."

"She wants you to give me up?"

"She wants me to give up babysitting you because you're a grown man," Evan said curtly.

Xander smirked. "I thought that was what you sent those murderous whores to do."

Evan winced. He still felt terrible about the fire witch who nearly killed his friend.

Xander smoothed his shirt and tugged at his sleeves, not meeting Evan's eye. "You're serious about Sylvie."

"You know I am." Evan had no idea what to expect from his friend.

A host of emotions washed over the king's face. "I'm happy for you. Sylvie is—well, she hates me, but she's a lovely and talented woman, and I know we'd be lost without her."

"We would." Evan was relieved. He didn't need Xander's approval, but he was the closest thing Evan had to family and it meant a lot that he liked Sylvie.

The horses stirred as if uncomfortable in the silence.

"What are the drawbacks of Jessamin?" Xander asked finally.

"There aren't any, although it wouldn't be a bad idea to secure the border where Vincent is causing such chaos. He'd be less likely to continue his attacks if he knew Aldrena was on the other side of him, ready to help us defend ourselves."

Xander nodded. "Princess Clare, then?"

"Thoughts?"

Xander ran a hand through his hair. "She's beautiful, but she seems torn between pretending to be what she thinks I will like and actually being herself."

Evan could feel his friend faltering. He needed some kind of win, even if it was just a small one. "Maybe she's nervous. We could arrange a date for you so that you could actually talk to her."

He held his breath, waiting for a rejection that didn't come.

"Fine," Xander said.

Evan kept his face placid even as he rejoiced in his head. "I will take care of everything."

"You always do," Xander sighed.

Evan wanted to offer encouragement and approval, but he knew by the far-off look in Xander's eyes not to bother.

———

Sylvie barreled into Evan's room like a lovely storm of color. Her blue dress was covered in golden lace accents, the colors giving a supernatural sparkle to her eyes in the firelight.

"Please tell me he's decided on a queen," Sylvie said.

Evan promised her that he'd have the hard conversation with Xander. He'd simply hoped that Xander would have agreed to more than just a date.

He held up a hand, and her face fell.

"He has another week. Before you get angry—"

"If you're going to tell me anything other than he'd chosen a wife, consider me already furious," she quipped. "I spent the whole morning at the Temple of Aurelia with the priestesses and the women from that village he and Rainer defended the other night."

Evan held up his hands. "Sylvie—"

"No, I don't want to hear it! This has to end."

Evan frowned. He knew there was something she wasn't saying, but he was terrified of what it might be. "He has eliminated several options, and he agreed to a private date with Clare, who I think you will agree is a very promising option."

Sylvie backed away from him. "This is just another excuse to delay."

"It isn't."

"It's hard for me to take him seriously, and I'm not trying to marry him, Evan," she huffed. She slumped into a chair. "I am so tired."

"I know, but we're almost there," Evan said softly.

She shook her head and looked up at him. "No. I'm tired of waiting for you to want to start something with me. I'm tired of your commitment to me coming after your commitment to this kingdom. I have planned and schemed and lied for you, but I am so tired of waiting."

Evan frowned. He understood she was empathetic; every time she came back from the temple, she was more tightly wound. It was like she'd absorbed all of their pain and needed a place to let it out in anger. But pushing Xander now would be a mistake.

"Just let me explain—"

She held up a hand, squeezing her eyes closed. "No. I've had enough, Evan. You swore this would be different. You know that I am tired of being put after him, and he shows no real progress."

"He does!"

"He doesn't. He's playing you like he always does, and it's beyond frustrating that you can't see it," she said.

Evan was so exasperated. Xander really was finally trying and now she was ready to give up. "He isn't. He's serious this time."

"Forgive me if I don't hang my hopes on the whims of a desperate, sad king. You know what?" Sylvie paused as if unable to get through the rest of her words. "For over a year, I have sat back and been patient as you've named thing after thing that would solve our problems. The number of times you've told me that things will change 'as soon as' whatever mystical thing happens. The truth is that nothing will change the dynamic between you two. As long as you are there, Xander will act like an ass because you'll pick up the pieces. I want —" Her voice cut off, strained by emotion, and he was startled to see tears in her eyes.

"Syl—" he said, reaching for her hand.

She stepped out of his grasp. "I want more. I've done everything I can to make this alliance successful. I have waited and waited for you to see me—to really see me."

"I do, I swear I do."

"No, you don't," she said bitterly. "Or maybe you do, and you're just not who I thought you were. If you were, you'd see me and you wouldn't let anything keep you from me because I am one of a kind. There is no one like me, and if you were really paying attention, you'd stop putting me after everything else. Either you don't see me, or you just can't want me how I need to be wanted, but either way, this isn't enough anymore. I don't want to be a secret, and I don't want to wait until you have time to make me a priority because if I do, I'll be waiting forever."

"Sylvie, where is this coming from? Just let me explain—" Evan tried.

She paused, looking at him as if seeing him for the first time.

337

"Have you ever watched Cece and Rainer? Really watched them? Have you seen the way he can't take his eyes off of her? The way he kisses her in front of people, even though he shouldn't, because he truly can't help himself."

"Yes, I've watched, but—"

"Two days ago, I helped her propose to him."

Evan frowned. "But they're already engaged."

"I know. But he asked her, and she wanted to ask him too. So I helped her grow plants to look like the grove where they trained for years. I spent hours with her because it was important for her to dazzle him. She was so nervous and afraid to be so vulnerable, but it was so important that she let him know how much she loved him— how unafraid she was for other people to know."

Sylvie looked away, her eyes glassy. "I know that I can't have exactly what they have, but I don't want to be a thing that's hidden and put after everything else. I can't pretend it's okay because I felt the ache in my chest the whole time I helped her. I felt it because I wanted someone to risk that for me, even in private. I wanted someone that I love that much to put me first. What I realized is that you never will, and I just cannot listen to one more excuse. I don't have any grace left to extend you. Because I'm spectacular, and I deserve to be treated as such."

Evan could say nothing. Some deeply buried part of him was afraid of this. He'd had so little love in his life that all the words for how he felt were forever trapped in his chest. Xander was the closest thing he had to family, and this kingdom was his home. He was the son of a warrior, forced to fight his way to power and lie to keep it, and yet he was unsure how to fight for the woman he loved.

Sylvie was so far above him in station and wealth. She deserved more than he could give her. He couldn't promise her anything, even if he wanted to. He would never be someone like Xander who could make grand romantic gestures. He could barely admit to himself how he felt about her. She deserved someone who sang it from the parapets.

She wrung her hands and met his gaze. "I am done waiting for you, Evan. Whatever is between us is over."

He reached for her again involuntarily. This time she finally used the technique he'd taught her to break his grip, but his pride in her using it was drowned out by his grief that she was done with him.

She left the room without looking back, and that was the moment he knew that it was more than just a strategy. She wasn't working him. She was truly done waiting.

The castle felt suddenly claustrophobic, the walls of his life closing in. He stood with a start and tore through candlelit halls until he broke into the cold air of the gardens. He paced through the maze of flowers, drawing in deep breaths, and he tried to calm the panic that rose in his chest.

"Rough evening?"

Evan turned and found William Arvato sitting on a stone bench in the garden with a glass of whiskey in his hand.

As much as Evan was disturbed by the apparent friendship between William and Sylvie, he appreciated that William had been such a firm advocate for Xander at their council meeting the previous day. He had shared his confidence in the king when Lord Spellman started to drone on about the urgency of the king's decision, which, of course, focused on the many benefits of marrying his daughter, Eloise. William said that a few more days for the king to make his decision wouldn't make a difference. He'd also offered to send some of his own men to the borders to ensure peace for the next week and through Xander's marriage ceremony.

It wasn't a huge sacrifice since it was in William's best interest not to give another council member more power. Plus, his lands and men were mostly located in the east, where Vincent's men were attacking. Still, Evan appreciated it.

"Yes. It seems I've upset Lady Brett," Evan sighed.

"Ah, Lady Brett is a formidable woman."

Evan smiled. "That is one word for her."

William eyed him with a sympathetic smile. "I find that it always seems to be the things we love most about a person that are also the most frustrating."

"I didn't think you were married, William," Evan said.

He chuckled darkly. "I'm not, and that's the exact reason why."

Evan fought off a grin.

"My advice—give her time to cool down and then make a grand gesture," William said with a smile.

"I'm not sure there's a gesture that gets me out of this one." Evan didn't understand why he was talking so openly about his feelings, but the anxiety of losing Sylvie was worse than any he'd felt in the past year of trying to hold the kingdom together. "I'm afraid she's done with me."

William chuckled. "Women rarely mean that when they say it, in my experience."

"Lady Brett is a woman of her word," Evan said.

William shrugged and placed a hand on his shoulder. "You never know. The next few days will change so much for all of us. She might feel differently when dazzled by a royal wedding."

Evan shrugged.

"In my experience, paying reduces the drama," William chuckled as he rose and gestured to a blonde woman walking toward them.

Evan's gaze fell on Mika, the only whore Xander had spent any time with—one of his only friends and confidants in Argaria. She also happened to be one of Evan's spies. He couldn't pretend he didn't know who she was, but he also couldn't be too familiar.

"Lady Notte," Evan said with a slight bow. "Thank you for your advice, William."

Evan watched the two disappear into the dark and hoped William was right. Still, there was a certain finality in Sylvie's tone and demeanor that he couldn't shake.

Footsteps echoed down the trail, and a moment later, Cal appeared holding a flask.

"You look a sorry sight," Cal said, half-joking.

"I'm sure I feel worse," Evan said.

Cal sat down on the bench beside him and handed him a flask.

Evan knew this guardian technique well. He'd learned a lot from watching Cal and Sylvie over the past year.

"It's not that I don't want her. I just don't know how to be who she deserves," Evan said.

"I know," Cal sighed.

"I want to. I want to tell her so many things. She's the only woman —" Evan couldn't finish the sentence. She was the only woman he'd ever loved. "I am very serious about her. I really wanted to make things—"

"Gods, you're terrible at talking about how you feel. No wonder she's so frustrated," Cal teased.

Evan shrugged, taking another pull from the flask.

"I know you love her. You don't have to say it. I know she loves you too, but Sylvie is stubborn. She's proud. She can rule a room of men with far more power than her, but what she wants to know is that she has you, because the only person she really *wants* to know she has dominion over is you."

"But she does."

"Does she?" Cal asked.

"I swear I am trying to get through this, and I have a plan. I have everything. I just needed a little more time. The more that happens here, the more certain I am that someone inside the castle is working against us. I just need her to wait until this chaos is over."

"I think you need to ask yourself—knowing what we all know about how quickly things can change—are you willing to risk being too late?" Cal questioned.

"I don't have a choice, Cal. Two kingdoms rely on Xander making this choice and solidifying this alliance. If I push Xander now—"

"He'll have to stand on his own?" Cal asked.

Evan sighed and ran a hand through his hair. "What happened between you two years ago? I'm not jealous. I'm just curious."

Evan's life was full of secrets—he collected them, tucked them away for safekeeping—but he could not stand the few secrets that he didn't possess. He knew Cal and Sylvie had been in love when they were younger, and while it was clear that was in the past, Evan desperately wanted to know how someone as kind and thoughtful as Cal had failed with her. Whenever he asked Sylvie, she just said they were young and it didn't work out. It was the same way she always deflected that set something off in his mind.

"That's Sylvie's story to tell. You know you don't have anything to worry about from me in that regard. I will always love and care for her, but she and I could never get back what once was," Cal said.

There was a hint of sadness in his voice, but he said nothing else, leaving Evan to stew in regret.

31

XANDER

Xander genuinely tried to pay attention to the beautiful woman sitting across from him.

Clare Pyke was smart and charming. Not in the way Cece was, but few people were. Still, she knew how to carry conversation and flirt. He should have loved her company.

"Your Grace, you look far away," Clare said, interrupting his thoughts.

He shook his head. "Please, just call me Xander when we're alone. I apologize. You're wonderful company. There's just so much happening all the time. My mind wanders with worries for my people."

What an idiotic lie.

Clare's brow creased with concern. "Of course. A king's work is never done." She bit her lip and looked down demurely before taking his hand in hers. "I'd like to help you share the weight. I think we'd make a good team." She smiled earnestly, and he saw her in a new light.

She was beautiful, with shiny blonde hair that hung in perfect ringlets and eyes of a faint gray-green that seemed to change in shade with whatever she was wearing. Her proper upbringing was apparent in how she held a teacup and sat straight in her chair with her ankles crossed. Her every movement and laugh were regal and elegant to the point where Xander found it distracting. Everything about her was pleasant and accommodating.

He should have liked it—should have seen the merit in it, at least, since he needed a queen—but he couldn't stop comparing her to Cece.

Cece, who had good manners and held her teacup properly but still appeared to somehow resent doing so. He'd loved watching the way she railed against decorum.

Was he truly obsessed with his former wife, or was it normal to compare every other woman he met to his first love? He hadn't the faintest idea. Men didn't talk about such things, and Evan would probably laugh if he asked. He was certain Evan had never pined over anyone. Perhaps he could ask Cal.

"I'm sorry. I know I am lousy company these days. I look forward to having someone to share these burdens with. Now tell me again what you were saying about the vocal performance and symphony," Xander said. He had to practically grit out those last words. Of all the things to force interest in. If Cece could see him in the midst of this conversation, she'd laugh her head off.

Clare droned on about the latest musical performance she'd attended.

Xander wanted to scoop his eyeballs out with his teaspoon. Perhaps he was approaching this the wrong way. Maybe he simply needed to approach Clare the same way he had Cece.

"Clare—" he interrupted. "I hope you'll forgive me for being so bold, but is this what you actually want to talk about?"

Her eyes went wide in surprised panic. "I—"

"It's not that it isn't interesting. I simply have very little time to find a wife, and I'd like to get to know the real you, not the version of you that you've been coached to be."

Clare's lips parted with a small puff of air. She leaned back in the chair, her posture relaxing slightly. She studied him as if trying to decide if he was messing with her. "Do you have something stronger than this?" she asked, gesturing to the teacup. "Whiskey, maybe?"

Xander couldn't hide his shock.

"Don't look so surprised. If we're going to have a heart-to-heart, I'm going to need something with more bite," she said.

For the first time, Xander had the impression he was looking at Clare Pyke instead of the princess of Aldrena. He stood abruptly and crossed the room, retrieving a decanter of whiskey and pouring two substantial glasses.

Clare took a long gulp, closing her eyes as if enjoying the burn in her chest before meeting his gaze again.

"You want to talk in truths? I want to know about Lady Reznik," she said.

Xander cringed. He did not want to talk to this woman about Cece, but honesty was an exchange of sorts and you couldn't get it without also giving some. "What about her?"

"She was truly a goddess?" Clare asked.

"Yes."

"And she still retains her powers?"

Xander hesitated. It wasn't the question he was expecting. If she was coming from a place of jealousy, he'd expect her to ask how frequent and involved Cece's presence would be, not about her powers. "Some of them. This is a strange line of questioning."

"Is it? Your ex-wife is a former goddess who may be able to smite me with a look. I'd prefer to know of what I'm dealing with," she said pointedly.

Xander sat back. Clare's demeanor softened.

"What do you want to know?" she asked.

"Do you actually want to marry me?"

She laughed.

"That's funny?" Xander asked, smiling genuinely for the first time.

"Yes, it is. It's funny how ignorant you are to your privilege," she said, taking another long pull of her whiskey. "Xander, you're a young, incredibly handsome king who just managed to help bring down one of the last living gods and forged an alliance with Olney after centuries of war. You are the greatest catch in the world right now—if not ever. You have your pick of women."

Xander sat back in his chair, unable to contain his surprise. It was interesting to see an objective outside opinion.

Clare shifted uncomfortably in his silence. In hunter training and more recently in council meetings, he'd learned the importance of using silence to get others to share more than they wanted.

"I have other prospects, yes, but all pale in comparison," Clare started. "We live in a world that does not consider my wants, but yes, I want someone young and handsome to start a family with. I don't want to be saddled with some old man. Moreover, I want actual responsibility. Rumor has it that you were very demonstrative with Lady Reznik when you were married. I appreciate a man who is decisive and unafraid to show his feelings, but more than that, I think this world needs leaders who have compassion and humanity. The era of perfect kings and queens is over. I want to be human."

Clare took another long gulp of whiskey, and still, he didn't speak. He waited to see if she would rise to the occasion or unravel completely. Maybe it was cruel, but Xander needed a queen who wouldn't crack under pressure.

"I think you and I could make a huge difference in our two kingdoms, probably even in Olney. An alliance between our homelands, but it would also be between us. I want to share my life with someone. I want to share responsibilities, and hardships, and victories. The world, my parents—everyone wants me to be a prop. What I want to be is a partner." She sat back and took another long swig of her drink. "What do you think?"

Xander sipped his whiskey, letting a tense moment stretch out between them. "That's very compelling. Much more compelling than when you were playing the fool earlier."

"Well then," she said, finishing her drink and setting the glass down on the table. "Perhaps you'll find this even more compelling."

She stood abruptly and straddled his lap.

Xander leaned back in genuine shock. He was not expecting the swiftness with which she came out of her shell.

She ran her fingers through his hair and leaned in close. Her breath smelled of sweet tea and whiskey as she brushed her lips over his, and it broke him out of his trance.

Xander kissed Clare with the wild frustration that had been building in him for months, trying to push Cece from his mind. He was so angry that she invaded everything. There was a beautiful woman straddling his lap who wanted him, who would likely let him do anything he wanted, a woman who wanted to be his partner.

Why couldn't he stop thinking about how her kiss felt wrong? Why couldn't he stop wishing she was Cece? Why couldn't he want someone—*anyone*—else? Why, out of all the women in the world, did his heart so stubbornly long for the one person who didn't want him? It was maddening.

He pulled away abruptly.

Clare looked dazed and worried.

Xander refused to give up so easily. He drew her back in again, crushing her body against his. He tugged on her hair, gently pulling her head back, drawing a line of kisses down her neck to her collarbone and back up the other side. She moaned and ground her hips against him. She brought his hand to her breast, encouraging him to touch her more.

He played with her peaked nipple through the silky fabric, and she arched into his hand. He nipped at her earlobe, and she whimpered. She ground her hips against his hardening cock, pulling him into a deeper kiss. He was almost relieved that someone else could stir up desire in him after months of nothing. Clare didn't mind his roughness. In fact, she seemed to enjoy the passion.

She worked the laces at the collar of his tunic and slid her hands under the hem, feeling along his skin. Her hands felt lightly callused but soft, and they reminded him of Cece's. He groaned. Hiking her dress up to her thighs, she guided his hand between her legs.

Clare whimpered his name, and everything heated in his body iced over.

He hated the sound of it on her lips. It was so sexy, but also wrong. His body instantly rebelled at the fact that she was not Cece.

She pulled back and looked at his face. "Did I do something wrong?"

Xander struggled for words as he shook his head. "No, you're perfect. Beautiful, sexy, smart. I just feel like maybe we're moving a bit too quickly."

She pulled at the chain on his neck, lifting his wedding band from beneath his shirt. She dropped it like it burned her and shrunk away from his lap. She sank into her own chair, instantly sliding her prim and proper mask back into place as she adjusted her dress and fixed her ruffled hair.

"Clare," he said softly, but she wouldn't meet his eyes.

"I can help you get over her, you know," she whispered.

"She's unforgettable."

"Because she was a goddess?"

"*Is* a goddess," he corrected.

"What makes half of her better than all of me?" Clare challenged.

He was going to answer, but Clare's eyes had shifted from anger to interest. Xander sealed his mouth, realizing that she'd moved from fury to assessment and information-gathering. He didn't like the feeling of sharing parts of Cece with someone who saw her as competition. For years he'd watched women of the court tear each other down over men, and he didn't want any of them to have an easy way to wound Cece.

At his abrupt silence, Clare's face clouded with frustration and humiliation.

She stood abruptly. "Very well. Even if you can't forget, I could help you move on. If you decide you want that, let me know."

She turned and breezed out the door. There was a finality to the way it slammed behind her.

Xander slumped into his chair. He was frustrated with himself, frustrated that one woman had rendered him so irreparably broken that he could no longer access the carefree hunter he'd been before they met. For years, he'd been practical about romantic pursuits, but now he felt wholly dismantled and unable to find that practicality again. He felt panicked at the thought of failure.

A light tap on the door startled him.

"Come in," he said.

Xander was divided. Part of him wanted it to be Clare, and the other part of him prayed desperately it wasn't. He didn't know what to say to her when he was barely holding himself together. He had no clue what he needed.

His breath came in rapid, shallow breaths. He was losing it.

The door creaked open, and Princess Jessamin entered the sitting room. "Your Grace," she said as she dipped into a curtsey.

"Yes, hello," he said, realizing too late he was supposed to get up and bow.

He brought a hand to his chest, trying to slow his racing heart. *What is wrong with you?* He chugged his glass of whiskey.

Jessamin looked stunning in a burgundy and gold gown that showed off her figure while also highlighting the strength in her arms. She studied him quietly, her warm brown eyes going soft. "Is something wrong, Your Majesty? Are you well?"

"I'm—I'm not sure," he admitted. A cold sweat broke out on his back.

"I saw Princess Clare retreating, and I thought perhaps you might want company, but I can come back."

"Please!" He jumped to his feet. "Please don't leave."

He tried to calm his breathing, but it was so rapid and shallow. His vision narrowed.

Jessamin hesitated where she was as if trying to decide if it was best to leave him with whatever shred of dignity he had left or stay and try to help.

She chose to stay.

"Sit down," Jessamin said forcefully. He sat back in his chair, and she dragged the other chair right next to him. "Put your head between your knees and try to take a deep breath."

He followed her orders without question simply because she sounded like she knew what she was talking about. Her cool hand alit on the back of his neck.

"It's going to be okay, Your Grace," she soothed.

"Call me Xander," he rasped.

"It's going to be okay, Xander," she said, rubbing slow circles on his back.

His breathing was still too rapid, and he worried he might faint and then eventually die of humiliation when he woke up, but before any of that could happen, Jessamin started to sing.

Her voice was clear and beautiful, and the song was lovely and haunting. He wished he spoke Novumi because he wanted to understand the words.

Her song had its desired effect; he was so distracted by it, his breathing began to even out. His heart rate slowed. Eventually, he sat up and looked at Jessamin. Her eyes were squeezed closed as if she was too nervous to look at him, but her body swayed with her words as if she contained too much emotion to express. It was beautiful.

"What is the song about?" he asked when she'd finished.

"It's about a woman whose husband loses pieces of himself every time he kisses her. But he loves her so much he simply can't stop. So he goes on kissing her until there's nothing left of him and he disappears. She's grieving him even while he's still in her arms because she can see the end of their time together each time, with each kiss."

"That's heavy," he sighed.

"It is. My mother used to sing it to me as a child when I couldn't sleep."

Xander cocked an eyebrow. "Seems a strange song to sing to a child."

Jessamin shrugged. "Not to her. She was trying to warn me of the dangers of loving. You can't love someone without losing parts of yourself."

"But don't you also gain things? New things? New parts of yourself that are excavated and waiting to be discovered?"

Jessamin's face broke into a wide, beautiful grin that crinkled the skin around her eyes. "That's what I said. I've always felt that way."

"So you've been in love before?" Xander asked.

"Just once."

"How did you get over it?" He meant it earnestly.

She placed her hand on his and squeezed. "I wish I could give you the magical cure, but I'm afraid I'm still learning."

He smiled at her knowingly. At least there was one other person in this dreaded castle who could understand his plight.

"You can talk about it if you want. Or I can just sit with you. Or I can leave you alone with your thoughts," she said. She poured herself a cup of tea and took a sip.

Xander hesitated slightly. He wasn't sure he understood himself, but beyond that, she was from a neighboring kingdom that could use the information against him.

"Everyone is relying on me picking a new wife at the end of this. My people, my kingdom's alliance with Olney. All of it falls apart if I don't find a partner to build a life and future. I have less than a week left."

Jessamin nodded. "That's a tremendous amount of pressure."

"It is, but the pressure I'm used to, and certainly not anything you aren't dealing with, too. The problem is that I am pretty obviously in love with my ex-wife, who is madly in love with her fiancé and who deserves much better than me. I have talked myself out of it. I have tried to push it away with logic and reason, but there is no reasoning with this side of me. I can't stop feeling what I feel, even if she doesn't feel the same."

He drank the rest of his whiskey in one gulp.

"How can I have a clear enough head to make such a big decision when she consumes me? I swear I'm trying, and it's not for lack of lovely, charming women around me. I just cannot seem to let go."

"Then why did you invite her?" Jessamin asked.

He wanted to admit that he hadn't. That he'd needed her to come protect him yet again. But he didn't need to share any more secrets with someone he didn't know if he could trust. "Because I value her opinion, and she knows me better than anyone in the world."

He expected Jessamin's gaze to be judgmental. Instead, he was met with warm brown eyes full of compassion.

"Then maybe what you need to do is take her advice. Hear her out. Maybe you need to count on her to love you enough to see clearly when you can't. If you truly trust her the most and you can't pick on your own, let her pick, or at least weigh her opinion heavily along with your own."

He considered it. Cece would be happy to share her thoughts, and she'd spent enough time with the women to have a feel for them. Even better, she had a sense of people and could read their emotions.

"Maybe you don't need to let go so much as to make more room." Jessamin shook her head. "What do I really know about this? I suspect I'm as clueless as you. I hope you'll forgive me for speaking so freely."

"I encourage you to always speak so freely with me. I find court speak exhausting and wasteful."

A light tap on the door interrupted them. Xander beckoned the person in. A redheaded woman stepped into the room, bowing to both of them. She was dressed in the lilac Novum princess guard uniform.

"Your Highness, I'm sorry to interrupt, but you'll be late for cocktails if we don't get you back to your room soon."

"Thank you, Maren. I'll be right out," Jessamin said. She watched her guard go before turning back to Xander. "If you don't trust yourself now, trust who you were when you loved her. Trust you would only love someone who had your best interests at heart."

He nodded as Jessamin stood to leave.

"For what it's worth, I think you deserve more love than you'll let yourself receive. Look for someone who gives it to you in a way that you can take it," Jessamin said.

He nodded as the words settled into his mind. More love, different love. Not completely letting go, but making space. That felt doable.

"I'll leave you to your thoughts. I hope you find some peace."

He wanted to argue with Jessamin, but his head was a mess. He stared at her for a moment, truly seeing her for the first time. He wrote her off as too beautiful when he'd first seen her. Most beautiful women didn't bother to have substance because the world wasn't interested in it. But now that he looked closely, he saw how her eyes could be both warm and cunning, joyful and serious; how she could read a situation with a hunter's mind and respond with a queen's grace. If he hadn't been such an idiot, he might have seen her as a choice before he let her ruin it by comforting him in a moment of impending dread.

"Jessamin," he started. She paused at the doorway but didn't turn. "Thank you."

"You're welcome," she whispered before slipping out, leaving him with nothing but her lime-and-ginger scent on the air and a harsh sense of regret.

How could a warrior princess ever respect a king who'd fallen apart in front of her like a child? His plight to find a wife seemed more impossible than ever. He was humiliated that Jessamin witnessed his distress. She'd obviously been kind out of pity and obligation, which spoke to her character. But he didn't know how he could face her again after making such a fool of himself.

32

XANDER

Xander tossed and turned, trying to make a decision. He had two days until the ceremony where he was supposed to choose a bride.

Jessamin's words bounced around his head. Every time he closed his eyes, he tried to envision himself with one of the ladies available to him, and every time his mind floated back to Cece.

When he wasn't thinking about the decision awaiting him, his mind meandered to the magic to which Cal and Evan had fallen victim. Worries chased his chance for sleep until he thought he'd go mad with exhaustion.

He was right on the edge of dreaming when the creak of the passage door startled him. He blinked his eyes open, his whole body coming to life. He knew her by scent, by the patter of her footsteps crossing the floor.

Before he could react, Cece pounced on him. Her silk nightdress hiked up as she straddled him.

"Xander, I need you," she moaned, grinding over his quickly hardening cock.

Cece was still barely speaking to him. It had to be a dream.

He sat up, pulling her close, kissing her neck.

He slid his hands under the hem of her nightdress. He was overwhelmed by the softness of her skin, her smell mixed with an herbal scent he didn't recognize, and the intoxicating feeling of her body against his, the familiar muscle memory clicking into place. She was frantic, her fingers tugging at his hair, pulling him closer. She rolled her hips against his hardness.

"Touch me," she whispered.

He was desperate to have her, worried he would climax just from her grinding.

"Please, Xander," she whined.

She could probably make him come just from begging like that, but he needed more. All he had to do was shift the sheet covering his lap, and he could be inside her. He was desperate to feel her warm and wet and tight around him. He started to shift the sheet down when he heard the passage door again. He cracked an eye open and saw Rainer standing there.

"What the—Cece?" Rainer said. Cece pulled back and turned to look at Rainer. "What the fuck are you doing?"

Xander was thrown off by the strange turn the dream had taken, but Cece dug her fingernails into his shoulder, and he drew back as he realized he was very much awake.

Cece turned back to look at him. Xander glimpsed her eyes in the dim firelight. There was a strange haze in them, as if clouds floated over her irises.

Xander cursed. Suddenly, the strange smell around her made sense. It was the same wet, earthy smell of the magic that had affected Cal and Evan.

"She's bewitched," Xander said. "I'm sorry—"

Cece interrupted Xander by trying to kiss him. He held her away.

"I thought I was dreaming."

Rainer looked at him skeptically, but he tilted Cece's chin up and saw the cloudiness in her eyes.

"Well, it could be fun to have both of you at once," she said, looking from Rainer to Xander.

Xander choked on a laugh. "How do you want us, Cece?"

Rainer gave him a dirty look. "You shouldn't take advantage of her altered state of mind to ask her something like that. She's going to be mortified."

"You're not the least bit curious?" Xander just wanted to hear her say it.

Rainer looked torn between worry and laughter as Cece drew him closer. Xander had definitely not given the man enough credit. Rainer was much more honorable, but he was clearly very curious.

"Cece, what happened to you?" Rainer asked.

She practically climbed his body, wrapping herself around him, kissing his neck.

Rainer frowned. "Tea. She made some tea before bed. The servants have left it there for us each night. I didn't have any tonight. I just don't know why she sought you out when I was asleep next to her."

Xander tensed. Footsteps echoed down the hall—coming quickly. "Someone's coming. I think they're hoping to catch us in the act. Hide in the passageway."

"What if it's someone trying to kill you?" Rainer asked.

"Then I'll be ready," Xander said, pulling on his robe and grabbing the sword tucked next to his bed. He went to stand next to the bedroom door.

Rainer hesitated for a moment before ducking into the passageway, dragging Cece with him.

The bedroom door opened, and a disheveled Evan appeared with Princess Brytta's guards. Xander recognized them by their gold uniforms embroidered with mountain emblems.

They looked surprised to see Xander with a sword in hand.

"What is the meaning of this interruption in the middle of the night?" Xander asked.

The guards looked at each other and then back at Xander.

One of them spoke. "Your Majesty, we beg your pardon, but we heard reports that you had one of the princesses here with you this evening, and we needed to be certain that wasn't true to protect the dignity and reputation of Princess Brytta."

"Where did you hear this report?" Evan asked from the doorway.

"I'm afraid I'm not at liberty to disclose the source," one of the guards said.

Evan crossed his arms, leveling the two guards with a stoic glare. "Then you better get at liberty fast, or your princess will be out of contention."

They said nothing, both looking at their feet.

"It's a shame. She was going to be my choice at the announcement tomorrow," Xander said.

The guards' eyes went wide, and they looked at each other before one spoke. "It was a guard from the Jeset court—one of Princess Mayella's."

Xander nodded. "Very well. You're dismissed."

The guards mumbled apologies. Evan shepherded them out and closed the door behind them.

When they were gone, Rainer pushed back through the passageway. His hair was mussed and his lips were swollen. He was still actively restraining Cece.

"What is going on?" Evan asked.

"We have to figure out how to break this spell," he huffed. "I don't really feel comfortable taking advantage and she is shockingly strong."

"Always so gallant," Xander teased.

"Another spell? I'll get Sylvie," Evan said.

He left and reappeared with a very sleepy Sylvie a few moments later. She crossed the room to look at her friend, but Rainer could barely hold her still.

"Oh honey, what did they give you?" Sylvie asked, resting a hand on Cece's cheek. She turned back to Xander and Evan. "I don't know what it is. Just like what happened with Cal and Evan. It's old magic and not something I know how to break."

"I could put her to sleep," Xander offered.

"No, I promised her I wouldn't let you do that again. I couldn't do that," Rainer said firmly.

Xander nodded, guilt settling like a stone in his stomach.

"You know who could fix it?" Sylvie said. "Grimon would probably know, and if he didn't, Samson would."

Rainer cocked his head, considering. "It's not a bad idea. Cece—what do you think? Want to summon Grimon?"

"You want me to fuck Grim?" Cece asked, her eyes going wide. "While you watch?"

Xander laughed because Rainer looked stunned by the question. Sylvie looked equally amused, and Evan had no idea what to make of the whole thing. As usual, he was trying to stay all business in an insane situation.

"No, I just want you to summon him to break the spell," Rainer said tightly.

"You're no fun at all," Cece sighed, but she kissed the mark on her wrist to summon Grimon.

A moment later, the god of death appeared in a rush of smoke and ash.

"Lady Cece, this is a pleasant surprise, though I must admit that I'm surprised at the late hour," Grimon said, smiling at her.

"Grim!" she squealed, breaking out of Rainer's grip and launching herself into the arms of a very surprised Grimon. She whispered something in his ear, and he pulled back and looked at her.

"She's bewitched," he said. "A lust spell, and a very old one."

Cece rolled her hips against him, and Grimon's jaw clenched. He held her firmly so she couldn't move. Xander admired his self-control.

"Can you break it?" Rainer asked, watching where the god's hands rested on his fiancée's thighs.

"I can't, but my brother should be able to. I suspect you won't like his methods, though," Grimon said. "He feeds off these kinds of things."

"Just summon him. We don't have any other options, and we don't have a lot of time," Xander said.

Grimon shook his head. "Very well, don't say I didn't warn you. He's going to have way too much fun with this."

A moment later, the temperature in the room spiked, and Samson stepped out of the flames in the fireplace.

"Little Goddess!" Samson purred, looking at Cece in his brother's arms. "Who got to you?" He laughed as he sauntered over to her.

"Finally, someone who will let me have fun," Cece sighed, exasperated.

Samson put a hand on Cece's cheek. "Let me see those pretty blue eyes, Cece."

"I'll let you see a lot more than that," she said smoothly.

Evan let out a choked cough. Samson turned to look at him.

"Well, if it isn't my favorite hunter. You just keep getting better-looking. I've missed you. I do love a man who knows how to keep a secret. It's always the quiet ones that are the most fun," Samson said, winking at Evan.

Sylvie giggled, but Evan looked like he didn't know whether to stay or run.

"We were just leaving," he finally said, taking hold of Sylvie's wrist, which she promptly yanked away as she followed him out of the room.

It seemed Xander's friend was no closer to healing his relationship. The thought left him feeling guilty.

Samson turned his attention back to Cece. He closed his eyes, resting his hand on her cheek. After a moment, his eyes fluttered open.

"I can fix it, but you're not going to like it. I haven't seen this kind of magic in centuries. I didn't even know anyone was still practicing it. The reality is, it doesn't have a timeline. If you don't do something, she will stay this way, which I find incredibly appealing, but I imagine you will find inappropriate for court."

"How do you fix it?" Rainer asked.

"It's essentially like she's overdosing on lust. I can draw it out of her, but she's going to have to—" He let his words trail off, but Rainer and Xander both understood the implication. "It's going to get really intense, and I'd be lying if I said that I wasn't going to thoroughly enjoy it. Think you can control your jealousy, guardian?"

Rainer scrubbed a hand over his face and sighed in frustration. "It's not something I can do?"

"No, it's actually a good thing neither of you fucked her, or you would catch it, too. This type of lust spell is made to spread and cause a frenzy."

Xander cursed. "So it's likely that someone did this so we would all be sex-crazed and distracted?"

"Is that different from your baseline mood?" Samson asked, his eyes bright with amusement. "I can pull it down for a moment to get her consent, but she'll be in excruciating pain when I do that." The god shifted his hungry eyes back to Cece in Grimon's arms. He brought his hand to her cheek. "Cece, I know you're in there. I need to do something to break the spell, but I won't do it without your permission."

For a moment, her eyes cleared, and she took a deep breath. "Do it. Please make it stop. You have my permission." Her voice sounded weak, and she looked like she was in agony.

"With all of them here?" Samson asked.

"I don't care," she mumbled.

Samson took her out of Grimon's arms with a smile.

"Could you look a little less delighted?" Rainer grumbled.

"Relax, it will be over soon. She's in agony now, desperate for release. This is quick and easy, and everyone enjoys themselves," Samson said plainly. "Plus, as I understand it, she enjoys spectators."

Samson pinned Cece against the wall and she wrapped her legs around his waist. Her cheeks were flushed, her eyes fiery even through the fog that hung over them.

He turned to Grimon. "It wouldn't be a bad idea to create a little sound damper because I'm going to make her scream the walls down."

Grimon rolled his eyes and went to work. Xander didn't need to see the god of death's magic to feel it. A heaviness spread through the room, and the usual noisy din from outside the hallway quieted as the air filled with the cinnamon and ash smell of Grimon's magic. The only sound was Cece's breathing.

Samson met her eyes. "Little Goddess, I want you to give me everything."

She nodded. Samson slid a hand between her legs. She gasped at the same time he cursed and started to move his fingers. Cece tensed, digging her fingernails into his shoulders as she shuddered. Samson leaned in, whispering something Xander couldn't hear in Cece's ear. Apparently, the god of lust knew how much she liked dirty talk.

Cece had said that all the gods could see the truth in different ways. Reading desires must have been one of Samson's lesser-known powers.

As her breathing picked up and her moaning grew louder and more urgent, Xander tore his gaze away to find Rainer and Grimon looking just as enraptured by the scene. He looked back at Cece, and he could tell that she was already close.

Xander wanted to touch her so badly. It was torture to see it now when he was trying so hard to move on. Perhaps that had been the point of this spell—maximum emotional destruction for Xander. If so, it was clearly created by someone who knew him well.

Cece leaned her head back against the wall, rolling it from side to side as Samson's fingers pumped into her.

"Don't fight it, Cece. Let me take it. Give it all to me. You'll feel so much better. Come for me, Little Goddess," Samson grunted, his hand moving faster as she rolled her hips to meet his pace.

Every muscle in her body tensed.

She screamed, her hips still rolling to meet thrust after thrust of Samson's fingers. The release crested. It rolled on and on, seemingly unending, as Cece screamed and moaned and came apart in a frenzy. It was one of the hottest things Xander had ever seen. She had no shame at all. She surrendered, wave after wave crashing over her as she thrashed against Samson.

As if it was possible to die from jealousy, Xander keeled over immediately.

Finally, after a few long minutes, the tension in Cece's body eased, and she leaned her head back against the wall with a soft whimper.

Samson withdrew his fingers and fixed her nightdress back into place.

"Fuck," Samson murmured, looking over his shoulder at Grimon. "If I had access to a pussy like that, I'd be eating it morning, noon, and night."

Cece blushed and curled into Samson, going limp in his arms.

"How do you feel, Cece?" Grimon asked.

She cracked an eye open and looked at him.

"Normal and exhausted. Rain?" She reached for her fiancé.

Samson carefully handed her over to Rainer, who held her close against his chest, kissing her hair.

"I'm sorry," she mumbled.

Rainer cradled her in his arms, kissing her temple. "You don't have to be sorry. I'm glad you're all right."

"She's out of the spell, although I expect she will have some extra steam to burn off for the next few days if you know what I mean. Good news is that it won't be contagious anymore," Samson said, winking at Rainer. "You are a very lucky man."

Cece looked at the two gods. "Thank you for coming to help." Her head lolled against Rainer's chest.

"Happy to *come* and help anytime. That's the most fun I've had in quite a while, you fiery little goddess," Samson said honestly.

Grimon gave him a dirty look. "All right, brother, you've had your fun. We should be off. Plenty to do."

Cece studied Grimon carefully.

"He's skittish," she mumbled sleepily. "Avoiding me."

Xander studied the god of death. She was right. Grimon had been strangely absent, skipping opportunities to toss underhanded insults at Xander and flirt with Cece. With so much happening, Xander hadn't noticed.

"Why, Cece?" Xander asked, but she was already asleep against Rainer's chest.

Grimon met Xander's eye and then glanced at the bedside table where the mirror was hidden. He arched a brow. "There are many reasons why one might avoid things."

Xander wanted to know for sure that was the reason Grimon had been so cagey. "Wait—"

It was too late. The two gods disappeared in a puff of smoke and mist, leaving behind a faint tinge of tobacco, vanilla, cinnamon, and ash.

"I'll ask her about it tomorrow," Rainer said. He turned to leave.

"Rainer," Xander called after him.

Rainer paused at the passageway door.

"I swear I really didn't know. Not until I saw her eyes. I just thought I was dreaming, and then when I realized I wasn't—she's very hard to say no to."

Rainer sighed. "I believe you."

He said nothing else as he disappeared into the dark passageway.

Sleep would be impossible now. Xander glanced at the stack of parchment Evan had organized on each of the princesses. He could read through it again to see if there was something that made one of them stand out, or he could face the truth he'd been avoiding for months.

"Name the fear," he whispered into the dark.

I'm afraid I'm Damian's son, but I'm more afraid I'm not.

Xander scrubbed a hand over his face. How could he decide what princess was right for him if he didn't even know who he really was? He couldn't in good conscience burden one of these women with a dangerous secret.

He slid the drawer of the nightstand open and the hum grew deafening—as if the mirror could tell that he was tempted after months of ignoring it to finally look into it and see his truth.

For months he'd sworn that as soon as he was ready to know for certain, he would look. But time flew by and he still didn't know how he'd react either way.

He knew for certain that the mirror would reveal his true father because there was no truth that was more fundamental to who he was.

If he was Damian's son, that meant he might possess the same mean streak, the same selfish desperation for power that meant waging a twenty-year war for the sake of his own ego.

If he was the son of his mother's consort, Arthur Randal, it meant he was a bastard with no claim to the throne and further solidified that he had no business trying to rule a kingdom.

Both options were bad, but one would burden a new wife with a terrible truth that could put her in danger as well.

Xander lifted the mirror from the drawer and pulled it free from the velvet wrapping with a trembling hand. It glinted in the firelight. He tilted it from side to side and the humming grew so loud his ears rang.

"Gods, all right already, I'll look, just give me a moment of peace," he grumbled.

The sound cut off so suddenly that Xander nearly dropped the mirror from sheer shock.

"If I am who I've been raised to believe I am, then nothing has changed."

He didn't know why he said it aloud. Perhaps it made it feel more official—more like he was deciding something instead of possibly having his world shattered.

"If I'm Arthur Randal's son, I'll—" The breath rushed out of him. "I'll not burden one of these women with my lack of love and my lack of security. I'll call the whole thing off."

He tried to take a deep breath, but his chest was too tight, the fear and panic sending his heart into a thunderous frenzy.

He lifted the mirror and looked at his reflection. In the silver glass his face was pinched with worry, a deep line between his brows, a downward tilt to his mouth.

"I'm ready to see the truth."

He waited for his face to morph into someone else's, but it remained the same. Instead, a shocking pain lanced his hand, shooting up his arm, through his neck, and into his head.

He squeezed his eyes closed and his mind lit with a memory.

———

Xander was staring at his mother's worried face. She looked younger than the last time he'd seen her, with fewer lines around her eyes.

They stood in the sitting room next to his bedroom and there was a half-packed leather saddlebag open on his bed.

"Alexander, I need you to listen to me right now. I know Damian supports this wild plan you have of going to Olney and finding the Lost God yourself, but there are things you don't know. Very important things, and I cannot let you go until you know them."

Xander sighed. "I told you. I've made up my mind. You won't dissuade me. My father—"

"Your father is Arthur Randal."

Xander froze, a sick feeling twisting in his stomach. "You're lying. You'll say anything to get me to stay."

But that was not how his mother operated. She'd never been manipulative. In fact, she was always painfully honest with him, trying to balance out the attention that Davide received by showering Xander with her praise and attention.

"But you weren't with him when I was born."

She shook her head, looking down at the ground. "Not officially, no. I'm not proud of my actions, but this is the truth. Damian and I were in a rough patch, so we weren't sleeping together. He had his whores and I had Arthur."

She wrung her hands. "It was not supposed to be a relationship. It was just meant to be a comfort for me when I needed affection. But Arthur was kind and a good listener and over time we fell in love. If you won't listen to me...listen to him."

She walked to the door and opened it, and Arthur Randal entered the room.

Looking at the man then, Xander could see himself in some of his mannerisms—in his hazel eyes and the tilt of his smile.

"Alexander, it's nice to meet in truth for the first time," Arthur said.

"Are you here to try to convince me not to go?" Xander asked. He sounded so childish in his own ears.

"If I can, yes. Unlike your mother, I am certain that you will be well. You've excelled in your training here and I have no doubt you will do the

same wherever you train. Still, you must know the additional danger this secret poses, not just to you but to the doubts it could stir up about the line of succession."

"So my father—" Xander cleared his throat. "The king knows?"

Juliana nodded. "He does."

"Your storm magic comes from my family line. Though I don't possess the ability, my mother did, and my sister does as well," Arthur said. "We're also talented artists, so that's probably where you got your talent for drawing."

Arthur gestured to the open sketch pad on Xander's desk. Xander felt furious and exposed by his lack of knowledge; by being known by someone he didn't know.

"Does Davide know?" Xander asked. It broke his heart that the brother he loved so much, who had always taken care of him, was only half-related.

His mother shook her head. "No."

"Is it possible that he—"

"No," Juliana said. "That was before I met Arthur. Davide is Damian's son."

Xander wanted any reason not to believe her, but it was as if he'd been looking at his life through foggy glass and someone had finally wiped it clean. The way Damian never seemed satisfied with him. The way Arthur Randal had taken so much extra time teaching Xander when he started hunter training. The way Damian hated his storm magic instead of encouraging him to use it.

Now it made sense why the king had so quickly agreed to this plan. Why Damian had always resented his magic—magic that did not come from the Savero family line.

His mother took his hand in hers and looked at him pleadingly. "Davide was born of duty, but you were born of love. I regret that my actions hurt Damian and that they hurt you, but I will never regret you, my beautiful, talented boy. I am not above begging to keep you safe. I am sorry that I kept this from you for so long, but I wanted you to have as normal of a childhood as possible and you already felt so inferior to Davide."

Xander was furious—not just at her, but at Damian for not being *honest with him. So many of the king's actions would have felt less personal if Xander had known this one thing.*

"I won't stay where I'm not wanted," Xander snapped.

"Alexander, please."

The agony in his mother's voice was almost enough to stop him in his tracks, but he pushed through and went back to the closet to gather more of his clothes.

If the king was sending Xander away thinking that he'd fail, he had another thing coming. Xander would go to Olney, become the best hunter he could possibly be, and return to Argaria with the Lost God in hand if it was the last thing he did.

———

The memory winked out and Xander blinked his eyes open.

That was his memory. The mirror had helped recover his own stolen memory.

Fury burst to life in Xander's chest. How dare his mother rob him of something so fundamental? How dare she take so long to tell him to begin with?

He felt a sinking sense of betrayal mixed with love for his mother.

He shook his head; it wasn't as if it was some great loss. Up until that point he'd assumed he was Damian's son despite the speculation. Without this memory, his life and opinion of himself would have remained the same. That's what she'd always wanted—for him to feel as important and deserving as Davide. But now Xander felt robbed of the chance to know himself.

Finding out now, when he was trying to become the king that everyone else needed him to be, was terrible timing and he didn't want to doom a wife to keep the secret with him, and certainly not about something this catastrophic.

Xander pressed his hand to the shimmering line of Grimon's favor on his wrist. A moment later, the god of death appeared in a cloud of ash and smoke. His gaze instantly narrowed on the mirror.

"You knew," Xander said.

Grimon nodded. "The mirror was your mother's—a wedding gift she received from one of the Argarian court families. It doesn't show truths, but it hums when a truth needs to come out. She thought it would serve her well as queen and let her know who was trustworthy and who wasn't, and it did for many years. But when you were so determined to leave, she needed a backup plan if you couldn't be convinced. Rare magical objects like this can act as a conduit for memory, but this one was unique as only you would be able to retrieve the memory because it belonged to you and it was tied to the deepest truth about you. So when she confessed to you and you still weren't swayed, she had Magdalena take the memory from you so that you wouldn't be a risk to yourself."

Magdalena had stolen his memories. Xander hadn't even known she was adept at memory magic. He'd always assumed she was just a healer.

Xander shook his head. The sense of betrayal made him feel sick with grief and gratitude for his mother. He never would have willingly told anyone, but a memory witch could have stolen the secret from him if his cover was blown and that would have put not only his safety at risk, but Davide's as well. It would have thrown the whole line of succession into question.

Grimon frowned, a hint of sympathy passing over his usually stoic face. "I'm sorry you found out this way."

"How did you find out?" Xander asked.

"When she passed and I greeted her, she asked me to go retrieve the mirror from her room to give to you. I admit I waited until things had settled some before I handed it over."

Xander swallowed thickly. "Get out."

"What will you do with what you know?" Grimon asked.

Xander shook his head. "I said *get out*."

Grimon dissipated into smoke and Xander shoved the now-silent mirror back into the bedside drawer and collapsed against the mattress, wrung out from grief and betrayal.

33

CECILIA

Cecilia walked through the small family cemetery on the perimeter of the Castle Savero grounds. She tried to settle the restless anxiousness that had buzzed through her all morning. She'd woken from yet another dream where she'd felt like she was being watched, and now she felt it again, the hairs on the back of her neck rising as she moved through the rows of carefully tended graves.

If anything, coming to Argaria seemed to make it worse. So much had happened since she'd arrived that she busied herself focusing on everything else. Now it felt impossible to ignore, and the same sense of foreboding settled into her.

She wasn't sure if it was her imagination, but since she'd died and been reborn, her sight for spirits had seemed sharper. They still appeared fainter and less corporeal than the living, but her sense of them was as present when she closed her eyes as it was when they were open. Maybe that was why she always felt watched.

Grimon appeared, startling her from her daze. He held out an Olney lemon. "Here you are. As requested."

Cecilia took it and turned it over in her hands. "Walk with me?"

He shook his head. "I'm afraid I have too much happening today."

"You're avoiding me." She didn't know what it was. Perhaps he could not look at her without seeing her in death. She felt a bit of the same when she saw him, but she hoped it wouldn't always feel like this: like she was looking at her own friend and he was looking at her ghost.

He winked. "I wasn't the other night."

"Pervert."

Grimon began to waver and ripple.

"Don't run off yet."

"I'm afraid I must—"

Then he was gone, and Cecilia was left alone. She followed the pathway to two impressive-looking headstones, pausing in front of a white marble marker.

Cecilia stared down at the name on the headstone: *Juliana Marie Savero – Beloved Wife, Mother, and Queen.* She placed a rose on the stone and bowed her head.

She'd always felt gravestones were silly because spirits were free to roam, not contained to a cemetery, but now she understood the markers were more for the living than the dead.

"I promised I would take care of him and I swear I'm here trying," she whispered. Cecilia worried her presence wasn't enough; that she was somehow letting the late queen down.

Looking up at the stone castle walls, she sighed. She'd been a little embarrassed by the way she'd behaved the night before. She knew it wasn't her fault—it was simply the result of magic. Still, she had a sinking feeling that she'd thoroughly embarrassed herself in front of Xander and Rainer. Rainer had a look of pure amusement on his face when he woke her that morning, asking what sort of fantasies she'd been keeping from him, but she knew he was just trying to make her feel better.

Cecilia shook the thoughts from her head as she continued down the row of late kings and queens, and the next row of great warriors and heroes of Argaria. She came to a stop in front of a newer stone, the marble edges sharp and clean. She'd been avoiding this sight since she returned to Argaria. She couldn't bring herself to look directly at it, even if that was her entire reason for visiting the cemetery.

She laid the Olney lemon atop the headstone, swallowed hard, and finally read the inscription: *Theodore Andrew Reynolds – Friend, Protector, Hero*. The dates turned her stomach. He'd only had twenty-five years, but he'd left such a void that she missed him after having known him a mere few weeks.

The lemons were more for her, to honor a promise she'd made to Teddy. Grimon had been nice enough to act as her courier, bringing her several fresh lemons so she could honor the man who'd saved her life. The whole world knew about how Rainer had saved her, but only their tight group knew about how Teddy had befriended her when she was behind enemy lines and saved her in the wild.

She said a silent prayer that she wouldn't have to bury any more friends. She couldn't bear it.

Footsteps behind her startled her. She turned and her breath left her in a rush. She'd heard that Reese Reynolds looked like Teddy, but the resemblance was astonishing. Only their eyes were truly different.

"Apologies, Lady Reznik. I didn't mean to startle you," Reese said.

She smiled. "It's quite all right, it's just a bit like seeing a ghost... and I say that as someone who sees them all the time."

Reese smiled. It was Teddy's smile. "Lemons?" he asked, gesturing to the fruit.

Cecilia nodded. "He wouldn't stop talking about them. Lemons the size of your head. I was going to take him to the groves as soon as we got to Olney." She was surprised by the tears welling in her eyes. "I'm very sorry that I never had the chance to."

Reese nodded, and the two of them stood in silence for a few moments.

"I was hoping I'd have a chance to speak with you." Reese's throat bobbed. "I wanted to thank you for what you did. Evan and Xander told me what had happened. You found a way to bring him peace, and if I couldn't be there, it's a comfort to know that someone was. Evan said he whispered something to you right before he died. If you don't mind, I thought maybe you could share it."

Cecilia brushed tears from her cheeks, remembering the words.

"He said—" She took a deep breath to steady herself, and Reese took her hand, giving a light squeeze for encouragement. She looked into the eyes of the man who wanted any last piece of his brother he could get.

"He said, 'I wanted to tell you that you're really brave. You're brave how you fight, but you're braver how you love—with your whole heart. I understand why they both fell in love with you. Don't lose that. Even if it hurts. Don't let them lose it, either.'"

Reese smiled. His eyes were glassy.

"I'm not sure I've done the best job of that," she sighed.

Reese shrugged. "I've seen you and your fiancé. I'd say you're doing all right."

"I meant more with Evan and Xander. Xander refuses to consider any option that isn't me, and Evan is just so stubborn when it comes to Sylvie. I don't know how to convince them to do something I can barely do myself," Cecilia sighed.

Her mind drifted to the last conversation she'd had with a very distraught Sylvie. Sylvie had broken off her courtship with Evan, and while Cecilia understood where her friend was coming from, she saw the way she sulked and stared at Evan whenever they were in a room together. Sylvie might have wanted to be over the hunter, but it didn't seem like she was yet.

Cecilia couldn't decide if she should put her money on Sylvie making Evan jealous enough to get over his hangups or on Evan doing something blatant enough to lure her back in. She hoped for both of their sakes that they'd make their way back to each other.

"Walk with me?" Reese offered her his arm, and she took it. He led her toward the rose garden. "I see the way you interact with the king and with Evan. I think you're good for them. You do a lot of the same things Teddy did. It's no wonder he liked you so much. You had the same ability to lovingly force them to confront the things they're too stubborn to confront on their own. Obviously, you both have your own styles of doing it. Where Teddy had the ability to play dumb and act as if he didn't know he was challenging, you are a bit less subtle, but I think you have the same effect."

"That's high praise coming from you," Cecilia said.

"It's simply the truth."

Cecilia and Reese walked through the garden for another hour, laughing and crying as they shared stories about his late brother. Each tale lightened the grief she felt as if simply speaking the words released the weight she'd carried for more than a year.

34

XANDER

Xander heard Evan's hushed arguing through the door. It didn't matter how frustrated his friends were—he was not going to doom one of these women to his shitty fate.

As far as Xander was concerned, the issues were twofold. He was a bastard—only half-royal and with no right to the throne. If he married one of these women and tied her to him, he'd be dooming her, too.

People would assume she was complicit in the lie and even if they didn't, her virtue would be gone and she'd have no viable marriage prospects. He would not ruin someone else to save himself.

The other problem was that he could not even guarantee to love the person who would be sacrificing her entire future for him.

How could he possibly agree to a marriage that he didn't want—where he'd never be able to give someone the kind of love they deserved? Especially with the risk they'd be taking on.

Xander tried to stop, but loving Cece bled into everything. Even when she wasn't there, she was. Her absence was as much a reminder as her presence—confronting him with that which he could not give—his heart. It felt wrong to enter into a commitment without the very vitality the commitment required.

Evan's voice crept under the door. "He's being difficult. We're supposed to make the announcement tomorrow, and he's insisting that he's sending them all home."

Xander huffed a frustrated breath. Why couldn't anyone understand him? He wasn't trying to be difficult, but he wished just once they would choose to investigate his behavior before judging it.

"Seriously? After all of this?" Cal asked, his annoyance clear even through the door.

"So, what do you want us to do? Go in there and tie him up until he decides?" Rainer asked.

Sylvie's voice slid under the door. "Maybe we can use some sort of decision-making spell."

"You're sure he won't decide?" Cece's smooth voice cut through the others.

"Yes," Evan said.

"I don't know what else to do. I've done everything to try to convince him," Cece said. "Rain and I are getting married in a few months. Short of marrying Rainer today, I don't know how else I can convince Xander that I'm not an option."

"We could arrange that," Rainer said softly.

Xander bristled.

"I am not letting some spoiled king dictate anything about our wedding," Cece said loudly. "I will try to talk to him one more time."

Evan sighed in a familiar and belabored way. "Should I search you for weapons, Cece?"

"Have you seen His Majesty's shiner? I don't need any weapons," she said. "You all stay here in case I need backup."

"How will we know?" Evan asked.

"If it gets too loud—or too quiet," she said solemnly.

The door creaked open, and Cece walked into the room like she owned it.

"My love, were you lonely? Is Rainer not doing a good enough job satisfying you that you needed to call on me this evening? I'm not complaining," Xander said, looking up from his chair with a smirk.

"I think you know why I'm here. It's time to decide."

"I'm sending them all home," Xander said emphatically. "I'm not choosing someone. Even you won't change my mind."

Part of him wanted to tell her. She would understand if he did. Of that, he was certain. But the secret felt too large, too overwhelming to explain when he didn't even know how he felt about it.

She stared at him, and he felt the pulse of a storm inside her. She was furious. "Are you fucking kidding me?"

He should have calmed her down, but he enjoyed stoking her fire. "I thought that was what you wanted—for me to choose you. It's no contest. I could search the whole world, and I wouldn't find your equal. What's the point of pretending?"

"What's the point? I think the point is to grow the fuck up, Xander. The point is that you're in charge of a kingdom. The peace in our two kingdoms relies on you being established and having good allies. That's the point."

He didn't like the way her words stung, but he liked their angry bite. He liked that he could still get a rise out of her. "I don't want the weight of that."

"Well, too bad. You have it!" Cece huffed. "Do you think I wanted the weight of being the Lost Goddess? No! But I took it because there was no other choice. I had no choice but to make it work and figure it out."

He held up a hand. "I dream about the simplest things."

She stood preternaturally still as Xander continued.

"Picking out your clothes in the morning and then seeing you wearing them, or how you'd wake up in the middle of the night and not want to wake me, so you'd just lay there staring at me for a long time."

A lovely blush warmed her cheeks. "You knew about that?"

"I can hear your heartbeat, love. I know when you're asleep or not."

"Why didn't you say something?" she asked. She poured herself some whiskey and took a long gulp.

"I was curious what you would do, and if you just wanted to look at my handsome face, who was I to stop you?" He smirked.

She rolled her eyes. "You had my heart. I trusted you. I was so open and so vulnerable, and you did nothing but lie. You had the opportunity to start fresh, and you still didn't tell me. You broke me, Xan. I trusted you so completely. I let you see all of me. I was open and vulnerable, and scared. I left myself out there for you, and you crushed me. It's still hard to reckon with it."

"I was out of my mind."

"You had every chance before that to be honest with me. But instead, you broke my fucking heart," she screamed.

He deserved to see the hurt on her face, the tremor in her voice. He deserved all of it. "I know. I'm so sorry. I've never been more sorry about anything. I just wish I could undo it."

"I gave you so many chances. I put my whole self out there for you. I fucking trusted you so completely. I opened up to you like I never opened up to anyone else, and you *crushed* me. You called me barren." She seemed surprised by her own anger.

He ran a hand through his hair. "I know what I did. I feel the echo of it in every moment of every day since. I'm sorry that I broke such a beautiful, precious part of you. You deserve much better."

This was a losing fight. He needed her out of his room. While he could work around everyone else, Cece was the one person he could not ignore.

"Xander, I know you don't want to. I know it's not ideal, but you have to choose a wife," she whispered.

"I already did."

"You have to choose." Her eyes were wide and panicked.

"Why are you so adamant?" Xander asked.

"Because here you are wanting to fight for me when it's too late—when you should be fighting for yourself." She swallowed thickly. "I have fought for myself in every long dark night, through every doubt, through every raw wound that feels like it will never truly heal. Because I know that I cannot put my salvation on someone else. Just like I know you cannot fight for your kingdom if you won't first fight for yourself."

The words hit him like a body blow, knocking the air from his lungs.

"I gave up a lot for this peace," she whispered, blinking tears from her eyes. "I gave up my father, my humanity, my innocence, and my life. Some days I wonder if I gave up my sanity. I can't touch my bow without feeling crushed by grief for my father. I'm nervous if I'm separated from Rainer for more than a few hours. You saw me fall apart on the stable floor. Is that the girl you fell in love with?"

He swallowed around the lump in his throat. "This girl is better. I can't be with someone who doesn't understand what it is to lose. I lost one of my best friends, both of my parents, my brother, and the woman I love more than once. I also lost my mind. Do you think any one of those princesses has experienced even a whisper of the kind of suffering I've been through? I don't—" His voice broke. "I don't even know if I can love someone again."

There it was—the name of the fear. Speaking it aloud did not banish the specter of it from his mind.

"You don't have to love her to marry her. It's a business transaction to honor the memory of all those people we've lost. Love could come later," she said.

"Or resentment could, when she realizes I cannot give her a fairy tale."

He felt as if he was tearing apart at the seams. The more he shared, the less solid he felt. His hands trembled, his chest growing tight. He could not panic again. Not in front of her.

"I don't want to be my father," Xander said.

He didn't want to be Damian, the father who raised him, who was cruel and careless. But he also didn't want to be Arthur, who lied to him his whole life and died before Xander had a chance to know him. He felt robbed of the opportunity, and his mother and Arthur had both sanctioned the theft of that memory.

"You're not. Don't be so morose," she said.

"Would you prefer I be playful?" he asked, pulling back.

This was what he needed. A distraction.

She read him well. She took a step back, but he caught her around the waist and pinned her against the wall. His hands slid down to grip her thighs and he laughed when he felt her dagger pressed into his neck.

"Gods, I missed this." He leaned in, truly not caring if the blade cut him.

Cece flinched back in panic, smacking her head on the wall. Warm blood trickled down his neck.

"Drop the dagger, Cece."

"No. We aren't doing this again," she said firmly.

He couldn't stop staring at her lips.

She pressed the dagger in. "How can you go from being so sweet to so infuriating so quickly?"

"Talent and practice."

"Put me down."

"Make me, Goddess," he said, pressing into the blade more as she gasped.

"Did I get too close, Xander? What are you trying to distract me from?" she asked.

Suddenly, he didn't feel playful anymore. He felt something desperate clawing at him. Grief choked him, and a sob ripped from his chest.

Cece went still, looking at the wound on his neck. But it wasn't physical; it was the pain of losing her. It was the loneliness that dogged him. Everything that had been tucked carefully away behind bravado, flirtation, drinking, and fighting came tumbling out.

She was so vital and angry. So furiously alive that he couldn't believe he'd once watched her die. He'd watched too many people he loved die. First Teddy. Then Davide. But when Cece's string snapped, it changed him, brought something cold and frozen right into the center of him and he still hadn't thawed.

Now he was stuck in his life, a man stitched together with secrets. One wrong move and what was left of his life would unravel. He was terrified.

"Xan?" Her face was a blur, but her voice was concerned.

"Everyone is gone," he whispered. "I'm really alone."

He blinked away the tears in frustration. He couldn't pull back on the grief. It flooded to the surface like a mighty river.

Rainer and Evan burst through the doors and stared at Cece, pinned against the wall in Xander's arms. Evan's eyes went wide with alarm.

"Talk to me about what's really going on. Rain and Evan kept me in the dark," she whispered. "What happened while I was gone, Xan?"

He blinked away tears, meeting her worried blue eyes. She held a hand up to Rainer and Evan to shoo them away, but they stood frozen, as Xander tucked his face into Cece's neck and two years of grief hit him all at once.

She wrapped an arm around him, her hand stroking his hair in the way she knew he loved, and he fell apart. He held her so tightly, but she didn't complain. He felt so lost, floating out to sea with nothing to anchor him but her.

"Xander," she whispered. "I'm right here."

Rainer and Evan shifted by the door.

Xander turned and walked to the bed, sitting on the edge with Cece in his lap. He kept his face tucked into her neck, too embarrassed to let anyone but her witness his grief.

"Rainer and Evan didn't tell me anything specific. They just said it was bad. They said it was yours to tell. Talk to me, love," she said, bringing her hand to his cheek.

Part of him was embarrassed. He didn't want her to know. Another part longed to unload all of it and just sit with her. His eyes darted to Evan and Rainer. Cece turned and shooed them away again. Evan reluctantly left her alone with the king, but Rainer hesitated.

"It's not like before, Rain. I crescent promise," she said. He nodded, taking in Xander's mortified, teary face, and left them alone.

When Xander was sure they were gone, he finally spoke.

"Evan found me up on the castle wall one night." He planned to say more but fell silent at the look on her face—devastation that he experienced that kind of pain, and fury that she couldn't undo it.

"Tell me about it," she said softly, running her fingers through his hair.

He took a deep, shaky breath. It was a comfort he didn't deserve or realize he needed. He slid a hand up her shirt, and she tensed for a moment until she realized he just wanted to touch her skin. His fingers idly brushed along her waist as he tried to summon the courage to speak.

"I didn't know how to lose you. I deserved to, and you deserved to be happy. But letting you go was the hardest thing I ever did. And then I came back here, and everyone was gone. Everything familiar in my life is gone. My parents, my brother, Teddy, you. I grew up in Olney, and I was back here with none of the people I knew and with advisors and people who didn't know or like me. My heart wasn't in it. It never was. As you know, I wanted to be a prince, not a king. It was so much pressure. I was hanging by a thread, and then I found a note you'd tucked in an old jacket of mine."

He swallowed hard. "It said: *Xander – Don't let King Hector intimidate you. You are wonderful and charming, and I love you. You will be great today. Love, Cece. PS. Come back to bed and make love to me immediately.*"

She smiled sadly.

"It just wrecked me, love. I missed how unbelievably grumpy you are in the mornings, and the way you'd let me lay out your dress, but you'd wait until I left to get into it so I wouldn't immediately take it off. I missed the little songs you used to hum when you were roaming around the cottage, doing the most mundane things. It all sent me into a spiral. I don't know what I was planning to do. I just didn't know how to keep going."

"Let's make a deal right now that if you ever feel that way again, you will come to talk to me first, please," she said, kissing the top of his head.

He nodded.

"I love you very much, Xan, and losing you like that—losing you

381

at all would break my heart. You must know I wouldn't be here if you weren't very important to me. I know I can't be what you want me to be anymore, but I will always love you. You're still one of my best friends—or you were before you ignored me for a year."

"I'm sorry."

"Don't be sorry," she sighed. "Just promise that you will reach out when you need me."

"I promise."

"And stop trying to antagonize Rainer."

"I won't promise that," Xander said. "I deserve to have my fun. He gets to have you. I should at least get to drive him crazy if I want to. It's only fair that I return the favor." He lay there as she wound her fingers through his hair. "I forgot how nice it is to be touched like this."

"You could have this in a queen, love. Why must you resist it?" she asked.

He wanted to tell her the truth of who he was, but the secret was too large—the weight of it meant for someone who wanted to share the burden. He'd already given Cece so much of himself. If he didn't stop, he'd have nothing left for someone else. The possibility felt distant and impossible, but still there was a nagging ember lit in his heart that wanted to hope.

"You know why I resist love," he said quietly.

"Queens don't expect love. They expect respect and partnership."

"But how could I settle for that after what we had?" Xander asked.

She frowned. "You mean what *you* had, Xan. You had someone who loved you like crazy, and was open and honest, and trusted you with her whole heart. I did not have the same."

He knew the words were true, but they were still hard to hear.

"I'm not saying it to hurt you."

He held her tighter. "I know."

"You have to move on."

"I'm not ready and my choice will tie someone to me. If I go down, she'll go down with me. Things are precarious. I don't want to ruin someone else, especially if I can't at least give them love." It was as close as he could get to admitting the truth.

Cece sighed. "You don't think I felt the same responsibility to you? We all have our lots in life, and the only thing we can control is our reaction to the challenges that appear before us. You can fight against it, or you can accept it."

"And did you just accept it, Goddess?"

She was quiet for a moment. "More than just your happiness relies on this."

"You think I don't know that? It's the only reason I'm entertaining this idea."

She frowned at him, her fingers brushing his neck. "I should heal this—"

"Leave the scar," he whispered.

"Why?"

He swallowed hard. "Better to have a visible scar than one I can't see that still hurts."

Xander unbuttoned two more buttons of his tunic and placed her hand over his scar. "I'm grateful for this one every day."

She lifted the chain that held his wedding ring.

He'd become so accustomed to the feel of it he'd forgotten it was there. Now he felt exposed with her holding it in her palm.

"You still wear it."

Xander swallowed the knot of emotion in his throat. "Close to my heart."

"Why?" Her voice was breathless, her gaze watery.

He lifted the ring from her hand and tucked it back under his shirt. "This ring and this scar are bookends on our love. The start and the end, both beautiful and ugly. I like to keep the truth of that close at heart."

Someday he'd stop wearing it, but not yet.

Cece went quiet, tilting her face toward the fire. A storm passed over her features. She was always like that, a tempest brewing just under the surface of her skin. He wondered if that was one of the reasons he'd taken to her so quickly. The Storm Prince and his stormy princess.

The firelight gave her face an ethereal glow. In the past he'd try to sketch that fierce radiance. But since she'd arrived, he'd finally laid down his charcoal and stopped drawing her. Finally, he saw her as she truly was—someone he could never capture.

35

XANDER

Xander expected to feel humiliated after falling apart, but Cece had been so gentle with him last night.

Still, he dreaded saying goodbye to her more than choosing his future wife.

He stood on his balcony looking down on Ardenis. The city was bustling with activity, the people preparing for the his announcement and wedding to follow. He wondered if that town crier was still out there spreading the truth about him.

He shook off the thought, making his way back to the table where he had information on each of his potential brides spread out in a mess. Every single one had benefits and drawbacks, but each time he thought of their eager faces, he felt nothing but guilt for tying his fate to theirs and for not being able to care for them the way they deserved.

If he'd never fallen for Cece, it might have seemed the most natural thing in the world to marry someone he didn't love. Now he knew what it was to marry someone he'd hopelessly fallen for. He remembered the night they were married. He remembered the stunning joy of it, and anything else felt like he'd be cheating himself and his bride.

Name the fear and it loses its power over you. *I'm afraid I will never love again. I'm afraid my wife will resent that I cannot give her that part of myself. I'm afraid I have no birthright to be the king.*

He waited for the fears to abate. Even if they all came true, he'd feel no worse than he already did. He sighed. He'd already survived it. That thought alone eased some of the tension in his chest.

He forced himself to be logical. Clare Pyke of Aldrena made the most sense. She was beautiful and edgier than he'd expected. She also seemed somewhat frustrated by his love for Cece, but not completely put off by it. Maybe she'd learn to live with it?

The only other viable option was Jessamin Orum of Novum, but he'd made an absolute fool of himself in front of her. His ego was substantial, though perhaps not enough to get over that. She had a regal quality, but she knew what it was to love, which meant she'd recognize the lack of it, and he hated the idea of letting her down that way.

He sighed in frustration and shoved the papers off the table. They flew through the air, landing in a scattered mess on the floor.

Maybe Jessamin was right that he should ask Cece for her opinion, but he couldn't do that now. Not when she was coming to give him closure. He didn't want to think about anyone else when he was trying to make peace with his past.

There was a light tap on the door, and Cece pushed into the room. She took in the disheveled papers before her blue eyes settled on him.

"Seems like it's going well," she teased.

Xander stared at her. She was striking in a simple red silk dress with her hair loose around her shoulders.

"As well as can be expected."

"Well, I'm here for your closure, love," she said.

Crossing the room, she pulled him into a hug. He held her against his chest, tight enough that she wheezed.

"Xander, you are a good man and you'll be a great husband because you learn from your mistakes. You deserve companionship and happiness. I love you very much, but I can never be to you again what I once was. It makes our time together mean no less. It makes me feel no less affection toward you. It's simply true."

He relaxed into her, burying his face in her hair and kissing the top of her head. After a few moments like that, she pulled back and looked at him.

"It's not easy to let go," Cece whispered. "Sometimes you think you want something, but what you need is to let go. I was lost to you before you ever had me."

He stared at her. That statement was true in more than one way. Her love had already belonged to Rainer when they met. Also, he'd made the deal that ruined them before he fully understood her. She had been his, and she had not. The story he conjured in his head for all those months may as well have been a fairy tale.

He'd fallen in love with a beautiful girl the whole world overlooked. He'd watched her when she thought no one was looking and fell in love with her quiet kindness. She was a woman who had no reason to be so kind or to try to correct injustices that she had no part in. Yet she never stopped doing so. Cece wasn't the damsel in distress. She was the knight in shining armor.

He'd created the circumstances where she needed him, or at least been complicit in them. Then he'd made the mistake of believing the story himself. Believing he was doing something good. Believing he was liberating someone who needed his help. The truth was, he couldn't free someone who was never imprisoned to begin with. He'd been the only one who ended up believing the fairy tale he created. A prince who saved and fell in love with a beautiful goddess. The truth hurt, but it removed the shackles of his past.

"The feelings I had were real, but the circumstances that created them were not. I could never pull the two apart," she admitted. "I think if things had been different—if I'd met you in any other circumstances—even if you were still you and I were still me, and you were undercover in my kingdom. I think even if I knew that, I still would have fallen in love with you. But you never gave me the chance to figure it out. Because of that, I could never be certain. That's why you never really had a chance."

"If I could go back to that first night by the river and tell myself what I know now—how it all turned out—I'd love you anyway. Even if I'd known you would wreck me, I wouldn't surrender any time with you," Xander said.

"I don't regret it," she whispered. "It hurt me deeply. Worse than anything else has. But I'll never regret you. You did what you thought was right for your family and your people. I learned so much from you. I loved you, and I always will."

"There's room in a heart for all that and Rainer?" Xander asked.

"There's room in mine."

And he knew it was true. Cece had the biggest heart he'd ever seen, and he was lucky to have a piece of it, even if it broke his own every day.

"You know, Argarians marry for life," Xander whispered. "We don't have divorce or dissolution of marriage. Those vows are forever. What I promised you, I will always promise you. What I promised you can't be promised to another. But I will try to find new things in myself to promise."

It was all he could offer with his heart so broken, and he knew from the look in her eyes hers was too.

"I love you, Cecilia Reznik, and I always will. And because I love you, I will let you go."

Love was different things to different people, but to Xander and Cece, it was the same. Love was being seen and understood. And that was the love they could both keep.

"I am releasing you so that I can hold on to a part of you I couldn't otherwise have. You gave me something I desperately needed. You saw me when no one else did, and for that, I will always be grateful. I thought maybe we could make some new vows—an exchange, if you will," she said.

"Vows?" he asked.

She placed his hand over her heart and hers over his and looked into his eyes.

"What is yours is no one else's. What is mine is mine alone."

He swallowed hard and repeated the words back to her.

"I release you in love, and I wish you every happiness."

Xander forced himself to say the words and mean them. They stared at each other as if waiting to feel a physical severing that never came. He pulled her into a tight hug.

He couldn't fight the tears that clouded his vision.

For so long, their love had seemed eternal. Staring down the true end of it was excruciating.

"Xan, don't cry," she whispered, her own eyes glassy.

"I hate endings. They're always sad," he mumbled.

She cupped his cheek and smiled. "This isn't the ending. It's the start of a new story. Trust me. I'm an expert at storytelling."

He laughed through the tears. In the past, he would have been embarrassed to let her see them, but she wiped them away with such tenderness he didn't feel anything but loved.

"What's the new story?" Xander asked.

"The story of my new best friend," Cece replied.

"I thought Rainer was your best friend."

"Rainer is my fiancé, and he's wonderful, but I've found it's difficult for him to be all things. He's the love of my life, but he can't be both things. How will I talk to him about him when he annoys me?" she asked, arching an eyebrow.

Xander laughed. "And does that ever happen?"

"Have you met the man?" Cece asked sarcastically. "Have you ever met anyone so self-righteous?"

Xander barked out a laugh. "You are a menace."

"I know."

Silence swelled between them, stretching out as he imagined a hundred different lifetimes where they didn't say goodbye, where they easily fit together, where they fell in love and stayed that way.

Cece held Xander's face in her hands and kissed his forehead.

"You are a good man, and you will do so much good in this world. I'll never doubt that," she said.

"Never say never, love. Never is a challenge."

Her eyebrows shot up. "Did you just quote Cato to me?"

"Maybe."

She scrunched her nose. "I hate it."

Xander chuckled. "If we can't laugh at it, it's just sad."

She smiled and her eyes lit up. "I'm so proud of you. I think your mother would be too. This is your chance to be the person she and I always knew you could be. The person Teddy always thought you were. The person my father trained and admired so much. Don't let us down, Xan. But most of all, do this for you. Do this because you deserve to be taken care of."

She always said the right thing. It was maddening how wonderful she could be. He pulled her into a tight hug before placing her back on her feet.

One last time, he stared into her eyes with all the love in his heart, and she stared right back. Because she could meet his vulnerability with her own. Finally, she drew back to leave.

"I'll leave you to your decision. See you at the announcement."

She retreated and left him alone in his room.

As soon as she was gone, he felt like the walls would close in. He could not stand to be there. He fled his room and charged toward the training rooms, his guards keeping a respectful distance behind him.

He was tired of their hovering, but now maybe they could truly make themselves useful and spar with him to burn off his restless energy. Perhaps a fight would be clarifying.

When he entered his private training room, there was already someone on the mat. A blur of lilac moved around the room, tossing knives at targets placed around the periphery. Xander paused in the doorway, afraid to enter and break her concentration. His guards reached for their swords, as if concerned for his safety.

But Xander recognized the lilac blur. It was one of the Novumi princess guards. She'd propped open the doors to outside, setting up an elaborate training course for herself. She moved from target to target with grace, swiping blades from her vest and tossing them with precision. She flung a final blade behind her back and it sank into the center of the target on the far side of the room. Then she somersaulted to her left, scooped up a bow, and shot off three arrows, all of which hit the targets placed in the yard outside the training room doors.

He sensed the danger before she even turned to look at him. It wasn't the kind of danger that accompanied an immediate threat, more an ominous sense of foreboding. Because Xander was turned on.

He clapped.

She didn't turn to look at him. "Your Grace."

"How did you know?" Xander asked.

The woman finally turned toward him. Most of her face was covered by a lilac scarf. Evan had explained that it was a practice for many devout followers of a certain Novumi goddess to wear such garb. The tease of only being able to see her eyes stoked Xander's curiosity.

"Hunter's senses. You have a distinct scent."

Xander cocked his head to the side. "Not a bad one, I hope."

She shook her head and set the bow on a rack on the other side of the room. "It's not unpleasant."

"You're very good with those knives and with a bow," Xander said, nodding to the targets. "Care to spar, Lady—"

She crossed her arms. "Not a lady. Just a guard."

"And what shall I call you?"

She said nothing, but her gaze flicked to the guards behind him. "You needn't call me anything. You're a king and I'm a princess guard. Don't you have people for that?"

Xander grinned. "For learning names? No, I'm afraid I don't have people for that and I would very much like to know yours."

"Why?"

"Because I have a thing for exceptional women."

She crossed her arms and tilted her head to the side. "Then why haven't you sent these fluffed-up princesses home?"

Xander stripped off his jacket so he was in just his undershirt. "You'll try to sell me on yours?"

She huffed a breath that ruffled her scarf. "No. If you need

391

convincing that Princess Jessamin is your best option, it's because you're a man of poor judgment and quality."

Xander tipped his head back and laughed. "I'll give you poor judgment, but I consider myself to be of exceptional quality in both looks and swordsmanship, and possibly also good intentions."

She took a step toward him. "Intentions do not save realms and your swordsmanship seems only marginally better than most."

"Ah, but I note you'll grant me my good looks."

The corners of her eyes crinkled. There was something compelling about a woman who could smile with her eyes like that.

"Is this how you normally meet women?" she asked.

"In my private training room? No. But historically, I prefer to meet women while they're bathing. If you give me a time, I'll be happy to drop in on you." He winked and her heartbeat spiked.

It had been so long since he'd had such interesting banter with someone. It felt for a moment like he was returning not to his old self, but to an evolution of who he'd been. After having his entire world shattered, it felt good.

"That won't be necessary," she said, taking a step away from him.

"Very well," he said, gesturing to the mats. "Why don't we spar and I can try to earn your name?"

Her eyes crinkled again. "If you're determined to embarrass yourself, I'm not kind enough to stop you."

They moved into position across from each other.

"You don't understand my apprehension to marry, considering how things went last time?" Xander asked, sticking out his foot and tripping her.

She recovered quickly, darting left and then right and catching him in the ribs with a surprisingly vicious punch. Xander could have tried harder, but he liked studying her fighting style, so he let her lead.

"I think such apprehension is the luxury of men who get to use one hurt as an excuse to never take a risk again. Men fear humiliation so much they'd prefer to be alone."

No one spoke to Xander that way.

"Why do you fear settling down? What makes you so restless with this decision?" the woman asked. She feinted left like she was going to punch his face and instead hit him in the gut.

Xander gasped and stumbled back, fighting off a laugh.

Gods, he loved to fight.

"I don't fear settling down. I fear being unable to give someone young and eager that which I no longer have. I fear burdening them inequitably."

He blocked three quick blows. Catching her around the waist, he took her to the mat. She quickly rolled him beneath her so that her hips straddled his.

"Successful marriages have been built on practicality," she said breathlessly. "Love is not necessary."

"What do you know of what makes a successful marriage? I don't see a ring on your finger," Xander said, nodding at her hand.

Her eyes lit up again. "I'm afraid I've not met my match. Most men are too weak, too proud, or too busy looking up from their backs at me."

Xander grinned, an old fire stirring to life in his stomach. "Truthfully, I enjoy this view."

He gripped her thighs and flexed his hips, lifting her off the ground.

Her whiskey-colored eyes, the only facial feature not hidden by her veil, went wide. Her hands came to his chest and for a moment, Xander was very much not thinking about fighting. He was entirely focused on the woman straddling him.

She was tall, nearly as tall as him, with thick, firm thighs and an hourglass figure that hid surprising strength. Perhaps it was just the position, but he wondered what else her body could do.

A gusty breeze from the open doors stirred her scarf and all at once, Xander felt the hum of a storm slicing its way through the mountains around Ardenis.

"What is it?" she asked, rolling off of him to gaze out the door into the darkness.

Xander sat up and listened closely. The pulse of the wind, the clashing of fronts vibrated in his chest, his magic surging to reach out and play with it. "It sounds like a blizzard."

"Sounds like?"

"Storms have a sort of melody. There are the spring thunderstorms that are loud and clashing and sound like a discordant symphony, but a blizzard starts low and crescendos."

She turned and looked at him, her head cocked to the side like she couldn't tell if he was messing with her.

"I was nine the first time I heard it—or I suppose, the first time I realized what I was hearing."

"Like the Storm Prince story," she said, more to herself than him.

"Yes, like the story. Would you like me to hum it?"

Her shoulders relaxed as she sat up straighter. "Yes."

He leaned closer so she would hear it clearly but his guards would not. He felt suddenly self-conscious sharing it. It was a sentiment he hadn't even expressed to Cece, though he wasn't sure why. She probably would have been one of the few people he knew who understood the vibrational pulse of a storm.

He took the woman's hand in his, placed it over his heart, and began to hum.

When he was finished, he blinked his eyes open and met her assessing gaze. The room was silent, nothing but the whistling wind tearing through the space and the sound of her rapid heartbeat.

Finally, she spoke. "Can I offer you a piece of advice, Your Grace?"

"I suspect I'd like anything you offer me," he said.

She leaned in closer so her veiled mouth was right next to his ear.

"No matter how romantic or clever you think you're being, don't flirt with someone while you smell like another woman. Lady Reznik's scent is all over you." She launched to her feet and darted across the room, pausing in the doorway. "It was a gallant effort and you have excellent taste in whiskey."

So that was who had stolen a bottle of his finest whiskey. He'd begun to worry the hunters had figured out his hiding place.

The smiling glimmer returned to her eyes as he laughed.

She turned to leave, pausing with her hand on the doorframe. "My name is Isla."

Xander watched her go from where he lay on the mat laughing. He felt no closer to deciding, but at least for the first time in a very long time, he felt like himself.

36

RAINER

A cold breeze whipped across the training grounds, but Rainer barely even registered the chill.

Turn. Swipe. Advance. Step out. Half turn.

The routine was practiced and second nature, his legs and arms moving in perfect unison. Rainer tried to bring a beginner's mind to it each day to see where he could still improve, even after more than twenty years.

The weeks away hadn't left time for the routines he found so grounding, and being outside in fresh cold air as he worked through his usual warm-up was a welcome change from the stale air in the castle.

As he moved through the third sequence, he thought about home. Olney was probably getting chilly. By the time he and Cecilia returned home, the sea would be too cold for his morning swims and he'd have to switch to running for the winter months. Still, he'd be happy to be home and back in his normal rhythm, start his apprenticeship, and once the weather warmed again, he and Cecilia would finally get married.

He lowered his sword as a stiff wind swept across the field and chilled the sweat on his skin. He pulled his latest star flower carving out of his pocket and turned it over in the sunlight. It was more detailed than any he'd done before, but something about the sizing was off. It frustrated Rainer that he couldn't figure out what exactly it was.

"That's not a bad star flower."

Rainer spun, blade ready. It was an instinct trained by years in the field, but he stopped short of the man's chest.

The man held up his hands. "I should know better than to startle a man with a weapon in his hands."

Rainer recognized him from Xander's council but could not summon his name.

The man smiled at what was surely a panicked look on Rainer's face. "William Arvato. Don't feel bad. If you weren't the fairy tale all the ladies of court have been gossiping about for the past year, I wouldn't have remembered your name either. A lot of unfamiliar faces at court these few weeks."

Rainer wasn't sure how to respond. He used to want to be a fairy tale but now it felt like people looked at the beauty of the ending without seeing the pain underneath.

"You're a carver?" William asked.

"I dabble. It's just a hobby." Rainer cringed internally.

He wasn't sure why he couldn't claim the new career for himself. He didn't even need his father's judgment to feel ashamed of it.

William picked up the wooden flower. "It's pretty good."

"It's more the focus it provides."

William grinned. "I'm not one to judge the plight of a retired warrior. I get quite restless at court myself. While I've always felt at home with a sword in my hand, I've long felt like an imposter at a table talking politics. In many ways, the two are the same, and in others they very much are not."

Rainer nodded. He knew that feeling well. "I'd rather come up with the defense plan for a castle than try to steer a future path with no boundaries."

"Was your father one for court or the battlefield?"

Rainer hesitated, torn between claiming his birth father or the man who'd raised him. It was hard to admit that he'd likely fall short for both, though less so for Raymond McKay.

"He was one for whichever could gain him the most political advantage."

William laughed. "Sounds like we could be brothers."

Rainer grinned. "It's a comfort not to be the only one. Does yours also disapprove of your every choice?"

"He'd have to do it from beyond the grave."

Rainer blanched. "Apologies, I didn't realize—"

William held up a hand. "No apology necessary. I wouldn't be here now if he hadn't, and he was far too idealistic to make real change."

"You think idealism doesn't belong in the council chambers?" Rainer asked.

William sighed and turned in a slow circle, moving around the training grounds. It was a footwork sequence, Rainer realized after a moment.

"My father had a good heart, but he did not understand how to choose his moments. Imagine, if you will, an opponent on the battle-field who runs straight at you." He took three quick steps toward Rainer and paused. "Sure, that's technically the fastest path forward, but is it the best?"

He turned away and went through the sequence again, moving around Rainer in a series of dips and slides. "I understand that progress must be incremental. Often the best plans involve meticu-lous patience and studying your enemy. I imagine that's how your lady became the fighter she is."

Rainer grinned. "It is."

"Those who have a natural disadvantage need to be studied and ready to anticipate any weakness in their opponent." William glanced up at the clouding sky. "What I mean to say is that real, lasting change requires patience and planning so that when the right moment arises, you're ready to act. I give His Majesty a hard time in council meetings occasionally, just to pressure test his plans, but he has the right idea. Things are tense now but they won't be forever."

Rainer considered the truth in his words. When they first arrived in Argaria, he'd expected less unrest, but Xander was changing things that had been the same for centuries. Progress was slow. Rainer learned that from Evan's letters, but also from life in Olney City. People so accustomed to war were more restless in peace, looking for a fight and keeping the hunters of the Olney City watch busy with their antics.

"So what will you do now that you've laid down your blade?" William asked.

A rush of irrational embarrassment rose in Rainer. It was impossible to tell if he was ashamed of his new apprenticeship plan or if he was adopting his father's feelings about it like he had so many times before.

Cecilia was so supportive, but she was so enthusiastic about everything he pursued it was hard to tell if she actually liked his work or just wanted him to feel free to experiment. She'd immediately taken to displaying his terrible carvings all over their cottage like they were great works of art instead of blobs. Each night she rubbed his aching hands with oil as she admired whatever he'd worked on that day.

"When we return home, I'm continuing with a carpentry apprenticeship."

William's eyebrows shot up.

Rainer felt immediately humiliated. Why had he admitted that to a lord in a foreign court, one he didn't even know?

Rainer cleared his throat. "I know it's unconventional, but I appreciate the physicality of it and it's a practical career."

"Don't mistake my surprise for judgment. I was merely thinking of your age."

Rainer burst out laughing. He hadn't thought much about it himself, but most apprentices started at eighteen. Rainer was ten years older and starting over like he'd just finished schooling.

"I suppose I hadn't thought of it that way."

William grinned. "You're never too old to learn something new."

"You're not going to say what a waste it is?" Rainer asked.

William shrugged a shoulder. "The point of life is to live, right? Not to endlessly chase down death. Why shouldn't you try something new?"

They fell into a comfortable silence as William adjusted his sheath to prepare for training.

The loud clang of steel meeting steel stole their attention. On the far side of the training grounds, two men were locked in a battle.

"Do you know them?" William asked.

Rainer squinted at the men. "I know Reese—or rather I've met him. I knew his younger brother. I'm afraid I've not formally met the other man, but I know he's from Xander's council."

William nodded. "Chris Lamotis. A curious thing, two wealthy land-owning men jousting, don't you think? Most wealthy men don't bother learning how to fight other than for the sake of having a hobby, but they're clearly well-trained and they're out here almost every day."

Rainer narrowed his gaze at William. There was suspicion in his tone, but Rainer was not sure what he was implying. Evan was convinced there was a spy in their midst, but Rainer found it hard to be skeptical of Teddy's older brother.

"You know them well?" Rainer asked.

"I haven't been on the council long, but they always seem to be in the know about their lands and everyone else's," William said. "One wonders what they're training for and how they're so well-informed."

Rainer watched the two men run through another drill. Chris landed on his back. Reese laughed, saying something too quiet for Rainer to hear before helping his friend to his feet and clapping a hand on his back.

"I suppose you're not the only restless former warrior in need of exercise," Rainer said.

William shrugged. "I suppose not." He nodded at Rainer's sword. "That's a beautiful weapon. May I see it?"

Rainer held the hilt toward him, and William took the blade. He stepped back and made a few swift strikes through the air. His movements were compact, precise—a clear sign he was not just a trained warrior, but one who had seen enough battle to abandon the grand moves that looked good in motion but were impractical when an enemy was coming at you.

"Very well balanced," William said, holding the flat side to his palm to read the inscription on the blade. "*Brave with my hand.* Lovely notion. I like the crescent moon on the hilt."

Rainer was suddenly uncomfortable with a stranger holding such a personal gift. He took back the blade and sheathed it. "Thank you. It was a gift from my fiancée."

"Yes, the lovely and spirited Lady Reznik," William said, looking toward the castle.

"Speaking of her, she is no doubt wondering where I am. I have to go wash up before the selection this evening," Rainer said.

William rubbed the back of his neck. "Apologies for taking so much of your time. It's nice to see a new face around here, especially one so skilled and with no agenda."

Rainer laughed. "I hope you find many more. Let me know if you need a sparring partner. We're here until after the wedding."

William stood a little straighter. "I've heard stories of your skills, and I will certainly take you up on it. What man doesn't want a crack at the famous Rainer McKay? I have age and experience on my side. I'd prefer having you fighting beside me but I bet I could take you down," he said, his tone teasing.

Rainer grinned as he walked toward the castle. William could certainly try, but Rainer would be damned if he was brought down by a puffed-up Argarian lord.

37

XANDER

Xander could not remember a time he'd been so nervous. He tugged at the collar of his tunic. It felt like it had shrunk since he left his room, squeezing his neck as he descended to the ground floor of the castle. He'd always been impulsively decisive.

Now his palms were sweaty, his heart pounding as he lingered at the end of the hallway that led to the ballroom. He'd spent hours going over everything he'd learned about the princesses. While he'd eliminated two of them in his mind, the rest had as many benefits as drawbacks.

If he didn't decide now, he'd be letting everyone down. He rested his forehead against the cold stone wall. His guards shifted behind him.

"You're dismissed. I will be in the ballroom in a moment. I just need to collect my thoughts."

The guards looked at each other, torn between obeying their king and whatever threat Evan had leveled at them. Finally, they turned and left him in the dim hallway. He ducked into an alcove under the stairwell and tried to calm his pounding heart. This hideout was temporary, and if the same panic was coming on that he'd felt the other day, he needed a more substantial hiding place.

He stumbled down the hallway, counting the doors. If he sought shelter in the wrong room, someone important would see his weakness.

It was happening again—the same thing that had happened the other day with Princess Jessamin. So far all the assassins had failed, but his body seemed determined to finish the job for them. He drew in gasping breaths, his limbs tingling, vision narrowing as he finally reached the sanctuary on which he was counting. He shoved the door open and stepped into the closet, forcing the door closed behind him.

It wasn't until he leaned back against the door that he realized he wasn't alone. He'd expected the room to be dark, but a candle sat on a shelf stacked with tea sets. Its flickering light illuminated Princess Jessamin, frozen in fear with her hand up her pretty redheaded guard's tunic.

A hysterical laugh bubbled out of Xander's chest, the shock of having caught one of his marriage prospects in the midst of her own romantic tryst so absurd that it startled the panic from his body.

He muffled the sound as the two women stepped away from each other.

"Your Majesty, I can explain," Jessamin said, her hands lifted to brace against his anger.

But Xander wasn't angry. He was stunned. All of the pieces clicked into place in his mind. When they'd been alone in his room, she'd had a unique understanding of his predicament, one she admitted she was trying to navigate herself. He'd noticed the way she'd lit up when the redheaded guard—Maren, if he remembered correctly—popped her head into the room to summon her. But he'd assumed Jessamin simply preferred the company of her familiar guards.

The candlelight guttered and set the glittering gems on Jessamin's dress sparkling.

"I feel foolish for not noticing sooner," Xander said. "You prefer women?"

"I prefer Maren," she said.

Maren straightened her shirt. "Your Grace, I'm sorry for any embarrassment we might have caused, but please do not punish Jess. This is entirely my fault, and I will accept the punishment."

"Please don't tell anyone. If my parents find out—" Jessamin started. "Our kingdom may be progressive in some ways, but not in this one. They would not be understanding."

Xander shook his head. "I'm not angry and I have no desire to ruin either of you for the absurdity of our world, which only accepts love that looks one way." He met Jessamin's gaze. "I wish you'd told me the truth because it would have saved me some trouble. Why are you here?"

Jessamin wrung her hands. "I need to make a good match. The only reason I came was that I hoped a king who was already in love with someone else wouldn't mind if he didn't have my heart. I have every intention of doing my duty as a wife and queen. I want to be a mother and I want a partner to rule with. But I've known Maren my whole life, and I love her. Even in Novum it's considered deviant behavior, but—"

"It is no such thing, and don't you ever let someone tell you otherwise," Xander said sternly. "Love grows where it will. I would never judge you for feeling what you feel. As if any of us can help who we love."

He placed his hand on the princess's shoulder. A brand-new idea was forming in his mind. He'd been humiliated by his emotional display in front of her the day before, worried that a warrior of her stature would be eager to exploit any weakness. But she'd looked at him with kindness and, as far as he could tell, she'd told no one.

If he married her, it would take all the pressure off of him. She did not expect romantic love from him because she already had it. They could be partners—friends—and perhaps in time he could find a consort to share his heart with.

"Do you want to marry me? I recognize this is not the most romantic proposal, but I want to know if you think you could honestly be happy here. You're far from home and I know how that can offer both freedom and grief."

Jessamin stared at him, her face awash with disbelief.

"Do not look so stunned. I have been worried about sentencing one of these dreamy-eyed women to a loveless marriage—worried that I'd be an echo of my parents, who were forever unhappy and sentenced to stay together." He ran a hand through his hair and forced a smile. "I am relieved that you need partnership and friend-ship—two things I can easily offer. I have lost so much of myself over the past two years. It's a relief that you can make use of what's left of me."

Jessamin's face softened. "It seems what is left of you is of higher quality than most of the men I've met."

Xander smirked. "That's kind of you to say, but the bar isn't exactly set high."

Both women laughed, dispelling the tension in the small closet.

"Rest assured, I will accept it if you want to be open about your love, or if you wish to keep it to yourselves," Xander said. "I cannot control everyone in the kingdom, but I will not abide bigotry in my court. I will not expect you to hide what you have. My mother had a consort."

Jessamin smiled sheepishly. "We know. We have heard the rumors."

Xander froze, looking from her to the guard. He'd hoped the rumors wouldn't make their way to the ears of the women he was courting, but he shouldn't have been surprised that they had. If he were in their position, he would make it his mission to know as much as possible about his prospects. It was to be expected in matters of love and war.

"We don't listen to idle chatter because it's so often untrue, but if by chance it was, it would make no difference to me." Jessamin's response was clever and kind in that it did not require he deny the truth. "I've seen nothing but the quality of your character since we've arrived."

"The quality of my character." Xander laughed. "Is that what you call being lovesick?"

"It speaks to your loyalty that you carry your commitments in your heart even after the obligation has ended."

Xander had not thought of it that way, but he supposed she was right. He had many flaws, but being changeable was not one of them. He leaned his head back against the door as relief swept over him. If Jessamin didn't look equally relieved he would have been concerned it was all too good to be true. She may not have known the full truth of him, but she knew enough that he didn't feel guilty.

He was almost through this horrible ordeal, and he couldn't wait for things to go back to normal.

"I appreciate your offer of secrecy, but I'm wise enough to know that you need to share our arrangement with your friends," Jessamin said. "What they don't know could hurt them and a wise king keeps his trusted advisors informed."

Xander nodded. "I suppose we should go face our future. We can't stay in this closet forever." He bowed to the two women. "Don't forget to look surprised."

With that, he left Jessamin and Maren in the closet amongst the tea sets and antique candelabras and marched toward the ballroom with newfound determination.

He bore the weight of every eye in the room as he stepped into the bustling space. He'd forgone being formally announced in hopes of slipping in unnoticed, but that was too much to ask.

Evan waited for him on the dais. "Are you ready?"

Xander nodded, looking over the crowd before meeting his friend's eye.

"Xan—" Evan rubbed the back of his neck like he did when he was trying to figure out how to express something.

They both struggled with these more emotional moments, the two of them stumbling through, trying to figure out what Teddy would say if he were there.

"I'm good with it. I promise."

Evan's relief was instant. Xander hadn't realized until he saw the tension melt from Evan's shoulders how much the pressure had weighed on his friend.

"Are we just about ready?" Cece asked as she made her way toward him.

Xander nodded. "Thank you."

The rest of their small group huddled close for assignments, Cal with Sylvie on his arm and her narrowed eyes on Xander, Rainer with his stern appraisal of threats in the room, and Cece in her spectacular shimmering dress and bright smile.

Evan cleared his throat. "All the princesses are here and ready. Sylvie, you'll be with the princesses. Cece and I will be with Xander. Rainer, you and Cal will be midway through the room for cover. I'm not expecting anything crazy, but we can never be too careful."

Sylvie darted over to the princesses, who were lining up with their guards behind them.

Rainer and Cal stationed themselves on the periphery, taking a glance over the room.

This was it. Xander was going to do this last thing to secure the throne he didn't really want for the good of his people. He'd expected it to feel more terrifying, but he just felt relieved that the decision was made and the emotional fallout would be limited to a few disappointed princesses.

Across the ballroom, a lilac blur caught his eye. She darted through the crowd, finally coming to rest behind Jessamin. *Isla.* She still had the scarf wrapped around her face but Xander swore he could feel her intense gaze fixed on him. He wondered what she would say about his choice. After seeing her train so fiercely, he was happy she was on the winning side of his selection.

"Good evening, everyone!" Evan called out, waiting for the room to quiet. "We are so delighted that you've all been able to join us over these past few weeks. It's been such an honor to the kingdom of Argaria to have so many wonderful, talented princesses here for this. His Majesty, Alexander Savero, is very happy to announce that he's chosen the new queen of Argaria."

A hush went over the crowd, and Xander took in the nervous faces of the princesses as he took center stage.

"I'm so grateful to all of you for coming here and allowing me to get to know you," Xander said. "As you can imagine, this was a very difficult choice with so many exceptional women here. I would be lucky to have any of you as a wife. I am so grateful that you all took the time to travel here and get to know me."

Each princess smiled back as if she was certain she would be chosen.

Xander cleared his throat. "After much careful deliberation, I have decided to extend my hand to Princess Jessamin of Novum."

Just like that, he conquered his fear in front of his court. Perhaps he could be a good king after all.

Jessamin looked genuinely surprised. She took a step forward, ready to join Xander on the raised dais.

Then pandemonium broke out.

38

EVAN

Evan was so relieved that Xander had consented to pick a queen that he hadn't worried sufficiently about how the other princesses might react. Though he had expected some level of angst with the announcement, he was unprepared for the complete chaos that broke out.

Immediately, he wished he'd stationed more guards closer to the dais. He watched in horror as Princess Clare charged at Xander. Cecilia cut her off, blocking the strike of her dagger with her bare arm.

The blade tore through Cecilia's skin, and she let out a yelp. She looked at Evan with surprise on her face, and he knew instantly something was wrong. Rainer and Cal charged toward them, and it suddenly occurred to Evan that this was more than an angry princess. It was an ambush. All of Clare's guards were charging toward them.

Cecilia fought Clare off as best she could with only a dagger. They dueled as Clare's guards in their bright blue Aldrenian garb advanced on Xander's guards.

Xander tried to reach for Cecilia, but Evan forced him back. Cecilia swept Clare's legs out from under her, bringing the princess to the ground, then hopped up and let Xander tie a strip of his under-shirt around her bloody forearm.

"What's going on, love?" Xander asked.

"I can't use my goddess magic," Cecilia said breathlessly.

"At all?" Evan asked.

She shrugged, turning her attention back to Clare. "Godsbane, maybe?" she said. "I had a glass of bubble wine earlier."

Evan grimaced. Someone could have spiked all the wine with Godsbane. He wasn't even certain what it tasted like, and he hadn't thought to check for it.

Evan put himself between Xander and the melee, as his instinct demanded, despite Xander's protest. It wasn't that Evan doubted his skill, but Xander had no weapon on him, and while it was easy to see the enemy on the battlefield, it was much harder in a room of should-be friends.

Cal and Rainer were both engaged with Clare's guards. Someone swung a blade at Cal. He jumped aside and it narrowly missed him. He unsheathed his sword, prepared for the next blow. He fought with the guard for a few moments before burying his blade in his gut. Cal turned to check on Sylvie.

One of Clare's guards had broken through the line of king's guards and charged toward Xander. Evan drew his sword and blocked the blow. They parried until Evan landed a killing blow, only to be immediately engaged with another Aldrenian guard. He wanted to keep at least one of them alive for questioning, but it was too dangerous when he didn't know who in the room was friend and who was foe.

Evan searched wildly for Sylvie, spotting her next to Jessamin, whose guards had surrounded the future queen and were engaged with several Aldrenian guards. Her eyes met his, and she threw out earth magic to grow roots around the feet of one of the guards who fought with Cal.

She shot Evan a smile. He smiled back, but he'd been distracted, and yet another guard charged him, sinking a sword into his side. He was surprised by his sloppiness. All he could do was stumble back.

Sylvie screamed Evan's name as he fell to the ground. He looked up at the advancing guard, who lifted his sword. He was about to sweep it down when William Arvato shoved a dagger into the guard's side and twisted, pulling it out viciously.

"William," Evan choked.

William gave him a half-smile and salute and jumped back into the melee. Evan knew that William had served in the hunter army for a while, but he'd expected the lord to cower as soon as the fighting broke out. He watched William disappear into the fight, working alongside Reese and Chris.

Evan sat up and looked around, the wound in his side protesting. It was serious, but not mortal.

Cecilia's fatigue was obvious. She stumbled to the side as she continued to spar with Clare. The princess was an exceptional fighter.

Clare knocked Cecilia aside and advanced on Xander, who appeared frozen in place as she swung her dagger down at his chest. Time stilled, and Evan couldn't breathe as he helplessly watched someone try to kill his best friend. At the last second, Cecilia brought her own dagger to Clare's neck, and the princess drew up short.

"Drop it," Cecilia said.

Clare dropped the blade.

Evan's gaze darted back to Sylvie. She was charging fearlessly toward him. He loved her so much he wanted to ask her to marry him right there.

Another blur of color and flashing blades tore across the room—another princess and her guards. Cal intercepted one guard and Rainer intercepted the other, but Princess Brytta kept charging at a defenseless Cecilia.

Who were these women? How had they managed to pass Evan's background checks? Unless, of course, this was truly an enemy kingdom trying to start a war, which would have been much worse.

Evan reached for his dagger, ready to throw, but Princess Jessamin beat him to it, impaling Brytta in the back, and nodded at Cecilia.

The distraction had been all Clare needed. She ducked away from Cecilia and grabbed her dagger from the floor, tossing it at Xander.

Evan jumped to his feet. Cecilia dove toward Xander. It wasn't until Evan stumbled that he realized that the blade didn't hit Xander. It didn't hit Cecilia or Evan either.

When the movement settled, Evan was shocked to see the blade buried in Sylvie's chest.

"No!" Cecilia and Evan yelled at the same time.

Cecilia grabbed Sylvie as she tumbled to the floor, and Evan knelt next to them.

A scream tore through the room. Cal grabbed his chest and turned toward them, eyes wide as he felt Sylvie's pain through their bond. His eyes lit with fury and he bolted toward them.

Time slowed, weighed down by Evan's horror. His mind could not catch up to the wild fear in his heart. Sylvie could not be hurt. She was capable of handling herself. She wasn't a damsel in distress, but a mastermind moving pieces around her chess board.

But now she was bleeding on the dais with a dagger in her chest.

"Cal!" Cecilia screamed. As if knowing what she was asking, he ran toward her and brought his blade down to kill Clare.

"Don't kill her!" Cecilia shouted. "Just protect me. We'll need to ask her questions."

Evan's heart was in his throat as he crawled closer. Xander knelt beside them and Evan took one of Sylvie's hands. It was ice-cold.

"Syl, look at me," he said insistently.

She smiled at him, her eyelids fluttering. "I was coming to save you, you stubborn ass."

Evan choked on a startled laugh. "I know. You were so beautiful tonight, it distracted me."

Sylvie winced in pain as Cecilia prodded her wound.

"Okay, Xander, pull out the blade. I'm going to have to work fast, and I might need you as backup, okay?" she said. "Sylvie, you're going to stay with me. I've done this before. I can do it again, but I need you to stay awake."

Sylvie tried to nod. Her lips moved, but her whisper was too faint for them to make out.

"What's that?" Cecilia asked.

"No scar," Sylvie rasped.

Cecilia laughed through her tears. "Oh my gods, you're so vain. Live to scold me if I don't do a perfect job."

Evan leaned down and whispered to Sylvie. Everything that had felt too trite to express how he felt about her came out all at once.

"Sylvie, I love you. I should have said it so much sooner. It's always been true. I'm sorry I couldn't say it until now. I couldn't say something I have felt for so long. You are so brilliant. I have never met anyone with a better mind for strategy and I have spent every moment since we met trying to earn your love with gifts and surprises when I should have just told you that I am so ridiculously, inconveniently in love with you."

He'd bought her dresses and made sure she knew the moment new fabrics were arriving at her favorite seamstress so she could debut the most stylish items for every social event. But what did that really amount to but research? He hadn't made her *feel* loved. He'd made her feel like a secret, like something shameful he hid from the world, all because he was afraid of having a weakness that could be exploited.

He watched in horror as Xander pulled out the blade and Cecilia placed her hands over the wound as blood rushed from it.

Evan kept whispering soothing things to Sylvie and kissing her hand. Finally, Cal rejoined them, but he was facing out toward the room, making sure the threat had passed.

"Cece?" Cal said, his voice tight with fear that mimicked Evan's.

"I have to concentrate, Cal. I'm doing my best."

Rainer stood next to his friend, narrating what Cecilia was doing. Evan had seen enough injuries to know that it would be a mortal wound without the help of magic. But Cecilia was a goddess who'd come back from death. She'd saved Xander from a similar wound. If anyone could do it, she could.

There was blood everywhere, and Cecilia strained to staunch the flow as she healed.

Sylvie had been running past Xander to help heal Evan. It was his fault she was hurt.

"I'm such a fool. I cannot lose you," Evan murmured as Sylvie slipped from consciousness.

Evan didn't realize he was shaking until he felt Xander's hand steady on his shoulder. He could not lose someone else he loved. Someone who loved him. He couldn't imagine a life where he wouldn't hear her say those words again.

She said them with such a casualness, as if loving him was easy and not a chore. As if she was certain he was just a day, an hour, a moment from prioritizing her above the kingdom. Sylvie had faith in him and this is what it had gotten her—a blade in the chest two kingdoms away from her home, all for a man who couldn't say how he felt about her.

Finally, after a few long, painful moments, the wound was healed. Sylvie was still breathing. Her heart was still beating, but the wary look on Cecilia's face said something was wrong.

"What is it?" Evan asked.

"Death whispers," she said, squeezing Sylvie's other hand. "I think...I think I need to..."

Before they could react, Cecilia stood and left the room. Nervous murmurs spread through the crowd.

"Where did she go?" Evan asked.

"I think she went to talk to Grimon," Xander said.

"But I thought he didn't decide who lived or died," Evan said.

He fought hard for composure, but his voice was shaking. Panic tightened his chest. He could hardly breathe.

"Yes, but if she's in between, he can help. We just have to pray that's the case," Xander said, placing a hand on Evan's shoulder. "You should let me heal you. You'll need your strength."

The Castle Savero healer, Magdalena, managed to make her way through the crowd and knelt beside Evan. She took Sylvie's pulse and then turned to him.

"I can take care of that. You'll be good as new." She lifted the hem of his shirt without waiting for him to answer and placed her hands over the wound, pressing the tingling healing magic into his skin.

Cal met Evan's gaze, looking more lost than he'd ever seen the guardian. Cal whispered to Sylvie, soft, pleading words. He and Evan took turns until Cecilia walked back into the room and knelt next to Cal.

"Keep talking to her. Grim is doing what he can, but ultimately it's up to her if she comes back. We can't make her. It has to be her choice," she said solemnly.

Evan wanted to scream. How could he sit by helplessly and do nothing but talk? It was the thing he was worst at. His words were clumsy and stupid. The only woman he'd ever loved was hanging to life by a thread, and all he could do was hold her hand and beg her to come back. He'd been such an idiot not to propose sooner. He'd been a fool to not keep her away from the chaos of court life. He'd made so many mistakes he might never get a chance to make up for.

Princess Jessamin tentatively approached.

"Thank you, Your Highness. You saved my life. I owe you," Cecilia said to Jessamin.

"You owe me nothing, Lady Reznik. Friends take care of each other," Jessamin said with a nod.

Although he recognized the need for alliances, especially in the midst of this chaos, the love of Evan's life was a steep price to pay for a new friend in their fold.

———

Cal stood vigil over Sylvie with a stoic stillness that Evan couldn't fathom. He couldn't stop moving, constantly walking between their friends in the meeting room next door and Sylvie, who lay so still on the sitting room couch.

Evan checked her pulse incessantly. She should have been awake by now. He wished he could bring her back through sheer force of will. Cal wandered toward the window to give Evan some space.

Evan couldn't imagine what the guardian was going through. He'd seen how frantic Cecilia had been when Rainer almost died. He knew the bond between guardians and their witches being severed was like having a part of your body cut out. But if Evan was honest, that was exactly how he felt.

He knelt beside her and leaned his forehead against her hand.

"Gods, Syl, please come back. I know I've been an absolute shit, but I love you. I've never had a way with words. I've always prioritized the wrong things and realized too late, but I swear I will fix this if you come back to me. I have a ring. I won't make you wait anymore. Just come back, and you'll always be first. No more telling you to wait. There's nothing else I want to wait for. I'd marry you tomorrow. I love you. Please don't leave me."

The words were pathetic and way too late, but he couldn't stop them from coming out. He could have sworn her pulse kicked up slightly, but when he looked at her face, there was no sign of her waking.

"I have a ring and everything. You just wake up, and I'll go get it and ask you right now. I'm on my knees already. Just please come back and marry me," he whispered, smoothing her hair back from her face. Even unconscious and bloody, he thought she was the most beautiful woman he'd ever laid eyes on. He kissed her hand and crossed the room to Cal.

Cal stared out the window into the courtyard, where Evan's guards were sorting through the guests for questioning.

"I don't know what I'll do if—" Cal started.

Evan clapped a hand on his shoulder. "I know."

Early in their relationship, in a moment of jealousy, Evan had asked Sylvie how their guardian bond differed from Rainer and Cecilia's soul bond, and she'd explained that Cal didn't get quite the same level of detail on her feelings. Every bond was as unique as the corresponding duo, but she and Cal didn't have a soul bond—just a protection bond. Fear and pain came through, but the rest was veiled and dull. Still, she'd told him that losing Cal would be like losing a part of herself.

"It's my job to protect her. I just couldn't get to her in time. I didn't know where she was going, and I realized she was moving too late," Cal said. He swallowed hard.

"Cal, I know. I feel the same, but you know how she is. She's a force of nature. To think either of us can predict exactly what she will do, it's just not fair. I feel the same way, but she's going to be okay," Evan said. He wished he felt more confident.

They stood together in silence, watching the hunters outside the window. It was a complete mess. If things were different, Evan would have been in the middle of the interrogation, sorting things out right along with them.

He was furious and terrified. Someone had come into his castle and hurt the woman he loved. He wanted to go outside and deliver as many beatings as it took to get to the bottom of it.

Instead, he was inside where he could do nothing but reevaluate every moment he had made Sylvie wait for him. All the nights he stayed up late answering letters from his network of spies. All the days he spent trying to lobby for Xander with council members. Even the time he spent paying town criers to sing Xander's praises. It all meant nothing without Sylvie.

It was the worst time to realize it. He was ashamed to be the kind of man who didn't know what he had until he was at risk of losing it. It made him no better than every other suitor she'd ever had.

If he had another chance, he would tell her exactly how he felt and he wouldn't make her wait. Sylvie would come first and perhaps letting Xander clean up his own messes would inspire him to truly lead instead of letting Evan be his crutch.

Evan wasn't one for praying, but he believed in commitment, and if he had another chance he would commit himself to being worthy of her—to learning how to tell her what he felt.

A soft groan startled him from his thoughts. Evan turned, afraid he'd dreamed it, but Sylvie's eyelids fluttered open and she forced a pained smile.

"Are you just going to stand there sulking, or do you want my answer?" Sylvie asked.

Evan was across the room in a heartbeat. "Answer?" he asked, barely breathing as he took her hand in his.

"Yes."

"Yes?" Evan asked.

"Yes, I'll marry you. Now don't make me almost get killed so that you'll set a date. Let's do it right now." She grinned weakly.

The relief brought him to his knees. For a moment, he could not even look at her. He pressed his forehead to her stomach and tried to stop trembling from the unbelievable comfort of her teasing.

He kissed her. He poured all of the madness he'd staved off the past few hours into that kiss. When he pulled back, she was laughing, and Cal was clapping somewhere behind him.

"Gods, take it easy, Evan. I just came back from Grim's doorstep," she teased. "I'm never going to let you live down this or the fact that you didn't tell me you loved me until I was dying."

He didn't mind the ribbing. He'd take whatever she dished out for the rest of his life.

"So when do I get to see this ring?" she asked.

Evan and Cal laughed, happy to have her back and in good spirits, even if everything else was falling apart.

39

CECILIA

After the havoc of Xander's announcement settled, Cecilia gathered the group in a meeting room. The pervasive uneasiness she felt seemed to have settled now that Sylvie was awake. The whole group looked exhausted and overwhelmed. She didn't blame them. It was hard to tell where to start, and it was demoralizing that all of their well-laid plans had been ripped apart by several well-positioned assassins.

Evan's hunters were still figuring out exactly what had happened. All they'd uncovered so far was that the delegations allegedly from Aldrena and Krysk were responsible for the attacks. The assassins might have succeeded if not for their friends and several of Xander's council members.

"This is the last one," Evan said.

Two hunters dragged a man into the room and forced him to sit in the chair in front of Cecilia. They tied him to the chair, but his mouth was bloody and he had bandages wrapped around his chest. He didn't seem in a state to make a run for it.

"He's the last guard left. He must know something," Evan said.

Cecilia brought her hands to the man's cheeks. "It hurts less if you don't fight it."

He grimaced at her and stuck out his chin in defiance. She pressed her magic into him, rooting through his recent memories. She saw the ballroom and the memory of coming to the kingdom, but when she tried to focus in on any of the commanding male figures in his memories, there was a strange blurriness to the face, a distortion to the voice. Every single scene in every attacker's memory had the same haziness.

Cecilia blinked her eyes open and studied the man before her. Her friends were counting on her to figure out this puzzle. Someone was responsible. If Vincent was behind it, there had to be more to his plan—a hint of what was to come or a glimpse of one of his top advisors.

She closed her eyes and dug deeper, following the strings between memories, searching for a common thread. But the more she pressed, the more she ran into muddled faces and different voices. In all her years, Cecilia had never seen someone cloak memories so effectively. Vincent either had a fantastically talented memory witch working for him or—

She wouldn't even think it. It was just the fear trying to feed itself on the remnants of dread in her mind. Cato was dead and his brand of manipulation was finally gone from the world. Perhaps it was the work of the slayer who'd gone missing from Ardenis.

She drew away from the prisoner and shook her head.

Evan scowled, nodding to the door. She followed him into the hall and down the corridor to where the rest of their friends were gathered.

"I've never seen anything like it," Cecilia said. "It must be some sort of cloaking spell, though not one I've ever seen. I can go through the archives again—"

"It's been the same with every prisoner." Evan rubbed the bridge of his nose. "I've sent messengers to Aldrena and Krysk to figure out if they were duped as we were or if their parties were set upon on their way. This is turning into a complete inter-kingdom nightmare. Not to mention the fact that we questioned the other princesses. It borders on a diplomatic disaster."

Cecilia and Evan entered Xander's sitting room. Their friends all relaxed at the sight of them.

"No luck?" Xander asked.

Cecilia shook her head. She felt terrible for letting him down when he sounded so hopeful.

Evan ran a hand through his hair. "I'm baffled by how Vincent would have the funds to pull something like this off. How has he managed to infiltrate our court with such ease? How would he even know all the kingdoms we'd sent invites to? If I could just figure out where the money is coming from, we could get to the bottom of this."

"Honestly, it feels like every time I take a step in the right direction, things fall apart even more. Do you think I'm cursed?" Xander asked.

"The drama," Cecilia teased, forcing lightness into her voice.

She knew Xander, and at that moment, he needed levity. "Look, we are almost there, and it seems like we rooted out the issues in court. Obviously, it's not ideal, but you have your alliance. We can assume we know the cause of all this is old magic. We will question those we've captured and get to the bottom of it."

Her gaze fell on Jessamin's wide, worried eyes. "What's wrong?" Cecilia asked.

"Did I just start a war? I killed the princess of Aldrena," Jessamin said.

"I believe it was an act of war when she tried to kill your husband-to-be, so we should be okay," Cecilia reassured her. "Evan is looking into the actual whereabouts of the foreign princesses, and we are questioning the rest to figure out exactly what happened. But so much happened so fast. It might help if I pulled the memory from each of you, and we can see if we can rebuild the entire scene to figure out how things fell apart."

She sat with each of them, drawing their memories of the attack so that she could see the room from different angles. It took a few minutes to pull them all, but they were patient while she worked.

"What I can't figure out is how someone managed to sneak you Godsbane without you noticing," Rainer said.

She sighed. She'd been wondering the same thing herself. She recalled the memory. She was standing to Xander's right. Beside her were Reese Reynolds and Chris Lamotis from Xander's council. On the other side of Xander was Evan, next to William Arvato and Edward Spellman and the rest of the council members that she didn't know as well.

She replayed the memory over and over, but she couldn't quite zero in on when she'd lost touch with her goddess magic. She hadn't realized until she'd been engaged with Clare. She blinked her eyes open and shook her head.

"Either way, it's safe to say that whoever planned it chose the perfect moment, and it was well-orchestrated," Xander said. "It was almost impossible to tell who was coming at us, and it was the one event where I didn't have a weapon. They also chose the moment when I'd have the least number of guards around me."

Cecilia read the subtext of what he was saying, and it sent a chill through her. Only someone with intimate knowledge of the inner workings of their court ceremonies would have known all those details. If someone in his council was leaking information, it could be catastrophic. But there was no way to prove it wasn't a well-placed servant who overheard their conversations.

There was a knock on the door, and it cracked open, revealing one of Xander's council members. Cecilia searched her memory for his name—William Arvato. Amidst the fighting, she had missed that he was very handsome with dark hair and a muscular build, exactly as Sylvie had described him. She grinned at the way Evan glowered at the man.

"William, did you need something?" Xander asked.

William smiled as he leaned into the room. "I just wanted to say that I heard the good news that Lady Brett has woken. I was hoping that I could visit, or at least send my good wishes."

Cecilia smirked. Sylvie had told her how she'd used her friendship with the handsome William Arvato to stoke Evan's jealousy, and it was clear the nobleman was smitten. She couldn't blame him. Sylvie's gift for manipulating men was supernatural.

Xander smiled. "I'll be happy to pass along your wishes, but I'm afraid she's not up for visitors just yet. She'll be pleased to hear you were checking on her," he said. "Thank you again for your help today."

"I'll have her favorite tea sent up tomorrow to help her build back her energy," William said.

Cecilia tried not to laugh at the scathing look on Evan's face.

"I'm quite capable of helping my fiancée heal without any assistance," Evan said through a tight smile.

William's eyebrows shot up, but he nodded and took his dismissal, closing the door behind him.

"So now what?" Rainer said, sitting down at the table.

Cecilia thought that Sylvie waking up would relieve the uneasiness she'd been feeling. What could be worse than another of her friends nearly dying? But the feeling hadn't abated. She squeezed her eyes shut and considered sharing her suspicion with the rest of her friends. She'd insulated them from the fear until that moment, certain it was a figment of her imagination.

She looked around the room at Xander, who was teasing Evan, and Rainer, who was leaning against the wall and laughing with Cal. She could grant them this one victory—this one day of feeling triumph. Once they made it through the wedding, she would share the quiet fear that grew louder with every memory she sorted through.

For now, she would take the win.

40

XANDER

Xander fidgeted next to Evan as they watched Jessamin's maids walk down the aisle toward the temple altar. Light poured in the stained-glass windows, casting a rainbow of color over the white walls. An obscene amount of red roses lined the aisle, and the altar was covered in tall cream-colored candles.

This was it. Nearly three weeks of chaos and the wedding had finally arrived. Xander was finally solidifying an alliance that would hopefully end this long, miserable fight with Vincent.

Xander could sense Cece trying to catch his eye, but he couldn't bear to look at her. He might not go through with what he needed to do if he did. As relieved as he felt to have the pressure alleviated, marrying someone else still felt impossible. It helped that he and Jessamin had talked for hours and come to an understanding of what their marriage would be—more friendship and partnership than romantic love. It meant that he left that space open for himself whenever he was ready. If he was *ever* ready.

Though he was sure that he never would be, his bride-to-be was certain. He appreciated Jessamin's confidence and direct communication style. She insisted he would find a new love, eventually.

Still, Xander was sure if he looked at Cece at the very moment he was supposed to let her go, he might lose his nerve.

Trumpets blared as the doors at the back of the temple were drawn open, and Jessamin appeared gilded in sunlight. Hushed whispers filled the temple as she walked down the aisle, and Xander forced a smile. Evan elbowed him, and he met his friend's eye.

"I'm proud of you," Evan whispered, low enough that only Xander would hear.

The recognition knotted in Xander's chest. Evan was the person who'd known him the longest. Though he wasn't a brother by blood, he was the closest thing that Xander had left, and his approval meant more to Xander than he could say.

In a moment of weakness, he looked at Cece. She was in the front row in a midnight-blue dress, a serene smile on her face. Her lips moved, and he strained to hear what she said.

Underneath the din of other whispers, her steady voice was still easy to pick out. "What is yours is no one else's. What is mine is mine alone. I release you in love, and I wish you every happiness."

Xander swallowed hard. It was like an incantation. As if she said it to break a spell between them. Cece was still trying to take care of him. It shocked him that she always seemed to understand what he needed to hear.

He smiled as he looked away from his past and toward the woman who would be his future. He was momentarily distracted by a slash of lilac by the back doors of the temple. *Isla.* He looked forward to hearing what she had to say about his choice, and perhaps now she stay for a while.

He forced himself to focus on Jessamin and smile. He had to admit his bride looked stunning in a bright scarlet dress and golden veil.

Xander held out a hand to her, helping her up the steps to the altar, and they turned to face each other in front of the high priestess of the Temple of Aurelia. Jessamin gave his hands an encouraging squeeze as the high priestess led them through their vows. The impersonal nature of the ceremony made it easier. It was in such stark contrast to the moonlit midnight ceremony he'd had with Cece. It was easier to simply repeat the traditional vows.

He slid the large ruby ring onto Jessamin's finger. She grinned at it and him.

He'd let Jessamin pick from a collection of Savero family heirlooms. He'd expected it to be a challenging experience, but Jessamin made it a delight. Since she was known as a warrior, he hadn't expected her to be so dazzled by jewels, but she was ecstatic over the options. He was only beginning to understand his new wife, but he was amused at how she effortlessly walked the line between warrior and courtly lady.

She also had understood the importance of following the somewhat strict and archaic Argarian traditions that he planned to do away with for further generations, including the long, boring ceremony, reception, formal brunch the next day, and the consummation witness.

He'd thought for sure she would have protested having someone witness their wedding night, but it worked out since the witness was meant to be someone from the queen's court, and Maren was already her lover. Though Xander worried how Maren would react and if jealousy might become an issue.

While Jessamin seemed happy and willing to fulfill her duties as wife and queen, he wasn't sure what to expect from her pretty redheaded lover, Maren, and he wasn't so sure he wanted a Novumi princess guard on his bad side. Also, it was one thing to know something was happening and quite another to witness it, as he had learned recently when watching Rainer and Cece.

Jessamin squeezed his hands again, bringing his attention back to the priestess, who was waiting for Xander to respond. Waiting for him to consent to taking Jessamin as his wife and queen.

"I do," he said.

He was relieved that this wedding bore no resemblance to the intimate ceremony he'd designed for his first marriage, though he missed his mother's presence deeply. He wondered what she would think about all of this.

Cece had insisted on giving his mother's ring back, no matter how he'd argued with her. He knew she'd done it with the intention of him giving it to Jessamin, but that would've felt wrong—like he was exchanging one wife for another, instead of ending one story and starting a new one. When he looked at that ring, he thought of Cece, and he couldn't stand the constant reminder. He'd taken it with the intention of someday giving it to his son or daughter to give the same approval his mother had once given him.

Jessamin listened intently to the high priestess, repeating after her to accept her new role not just as Xander's wife, but also to coronate her as Queen of Argaria. Xander smiled at her as she finished her vow of allegiance to the kingdom.

"By the power given me by the Argarian monarchy, I now pronounce you married. You may kiss your queen," the high priestess said.

Xander leaned in and gave his new wife a chaste, temple-appropriate kiss. The crowd erupted into cheers. Chants of "Long live the king" and "Long live the queen" broke out as they walked down the aisle together.

He was relieved the ceremony went off without a hitch. It had been impossible to relax the entire time when he was worried Vincent would show up in the middle of the ceremony.

As they exited the temple, Xander was congratulated by his council, who all seemed pleased with his choice of bride. Reese and Chris gave him and Jessamin hugs, while William Arvato settled for a handshake. The rest of the group was more subdued, offering simple nods of approval.

Even Edward Spellman congratulated Xander. He didn't miss the opportunity to express his disappointment that his daughter Eloise wasn't chosen, but was appeased when Xander promised to make her a good match.

As quickly as he could manage, Evan corralled Jessamin and Xander to their carriage so that they could get back to the safety of Castle Savero for the reception.

When they were finally alone in their carriage, Jessamin sighed and leaned her head back against the carriage wall.

"Doing okay?" she asked.

"I should be asking you that, darling," he teased.

"Of course you should, but I got everything I wanted today, and you made a sacrifice for the good of your people," she said thoughtfully.

Xander smiled weakly. "I'm a very lucky man. I could do much worse than a beautiful new bride."

She laughed and turned her attention to the gathering crowd, waving at them as they rode through Ardenis to the castle gates. Just a few more hours, and Xander would be free from the fear that had chased him for months.

PART IV:
DEATH OF A
MEMORY

41

RAINER

Rainer stood next to Xander and Jessamin. The new queen had changed from her scarlet ceremony gown into a form-fitting red dress for the reception portion of the evening.

The party was well underway with musicians playing, people dancing, and drinks flowing. Rainer was restless, wondering what was keeping Cecilia.

The king and his new queen had already made their grand entrance and had their first dance. It was tradition for the ladies of the court to change into new dresses, but Cecilia had been gone a while now.

He looked to the ballroom doorway and spotted Sylvie arriving in a beautiful purple dress. She walked toward them, curtseying to Xander and Jessamin.

"Don't look so worried, Rain. She's right behind me. I just didn't want to be upstaged at my entrance," Sylvie said with a smirk.

Evan appeared out of nowhere, and Sylvie threaded her arm through his. Rainer didn't miss the beautiful diamond on her ring finger that shimmered in the candlelight. He was relieved to see that not only had Sylvie survived her wounds, but she'd also agreed to

Evan's proposal. It was good to see Evan, ordinarily stoic, looking so happy.

"That's one way to make an entrance," Xander said.

Jessamin grinned as she looked from her new husband to the ballroom door.

Rainer turned and spotted Cecilia walking in. His focus narrowed on her as she strode across the floor toward them. She was a vision in a sleek, long-sleeved teal velvet dress that clung to her body, showing off her curves before flaring out at the thigh and showing a glimpse of her left leg through a slit. The front of the gown plunged, a draping crisscrossed neckline accentuating her waist and leaving her golden scar on display.

Rainer wondered how on earth it was staying in place. All he could do was stare at her like a fool.

Cecilia curtseyed to Xander and Jessamin. "Your Majesties, I'm sorry I was late. My seamstress just finished."

"It seems like it was worth the wait. I told you it would be spectacular." Jessamin smiled, kissing Cecilia on the cheek.

"You were right, Your Grace," Cecilia laughed.

"Nonsense, call me Jess."

"This is your doing?" Xander asked his new wife.

She nodded. "In Novum, this style is all the rage, and I just knew it would suit Cece. A larger gown would swallow her up, but this puts her assets on display. No need for so much embellishment when you have a body like that."

Rainer was inclined to agree.

"It seems your new queen has quite an eye for design," Cecilia said, smiling at Jessamin.

Rainer was happy to see they'd become such fast friends. Anyone married to Xander would need the support.

"Give it a spin," Jessamin suggested.

Cecilia stepped back and spun slowly, showing off the draped open back and the way the fabric clung to the curve of her ass.

Rainer fought the urge to immediately toss her over his shoulder and carry her back to their room. She grinned like she was reading his mind.

"Lady Reznik, what sort of magic is keeping such a flimsy dress in place?" Xander asked.

"Just a bit of sugar paste and a lot of luck."

Rainer stepped forward. He brought a hand to her hip, bending low so that his lips were right next to her ear. "I'm going to lick this dress off of you later," he whispered.

"I'm counting on it," she countered.

He kissed her cheek and pulled back. "You take my breath away in that dress. Would you like to dance?"

She nodded, and Rainer led her onto the dance floor. It felt as though every eye in the room followed them. He pulled her close, resting a hand on her lower back, his thumb skimming her skin right above the draped back of the gown. Rainer fought the urge to kiss her. He might have already done so in a room full of their friends and a few princesses, but doing so in front of half the kingdom might have been a step too far. No matter how ridiculous the rules of proper courtship were, he could follow them for a few more months.

"Were you trying to catch someone's attention this evening?" he asked.

"Just yours." She smiled.

"Well, it seems you've caught everyone's." Rainer spun Cecilia away, and it was then that she noticed all the eyes on them. He turned her back, and she leaned into him.

"I wasn't really expecting anyone to notice other than you," she said nervously. "I suggested a lace panel for the front, but Jess insisted it would look better open and that I should show off my scar. She said that their people need fairy tales now more than ever. I suspect she didn't enjoy being the center of attention and wanted a distraction."

"Well, you are an excellent distraction," Rainer laughed. "How long do we have to stay down here?"

She grinned at him, a glint of trouble in her eyes. Although Rainer had always been cautious, he lived for the spark he saw in Cecilia, unsure from one moment to the next if she would burn the world down or shine much-needed light into dark places. She had always been worth the risk of finding out.

"I just got here, and this is what we've all worked so hard for. We deserve to enjoy it. Plus, I want to get some use out of my pretty dress," Cecilia said.

"Honestly, I think you should only wear that dress from now on, although it makes it very difficult to behave appropriately."

"I was hoping it would inspire some very inappropriate behavior," she said, pressing her hips against him. She was shredding his self-control, and she knew it. The song ended, and he bowed to his fiancée.

Xander appeared next to them. "Lady Reznik, I was hoping you would do me the honor of a dance."

Rainer didn't like the look in his eye, but she couldn't exactly say no to the king on his wedding day.

"I would be honored, Your Majesty." Cecilia took Xander's hand, and he pulled her close.

Xander rested his hand the slightest bit too low, just above the curve of Cecilia's bottom. She gave him an exasperated smile and he pulled her closer until their bodies pressed together. They moved with each other like they were made to, two bodies so attuned to each other that it seemed effortless. Rainer knew their history, but it still bothered him. He didn't blame the king for wanting her, but it irritated him that Xander was so obvious about it.

"Do you still get jealous?"

Rainer turned to find Jessamin next to him, a knowing smile on her face. She handed him a whiskey.

"I suppose I do," he said.

"Understandable. Your fiancée is lovely and also very easy to like."

"That she is. I just wish he wasn't so—"

"Intense?" Jessamin suggested. They both laughed, and he nodded. "I see nothing wrong with a king who shows his love so freely. Why shouldn't he still have love and respect for a woman he made vows to?"

"I'm happy for you two." Rainer was surprised at the truth in his words. Despite Xander's incessant flirting with Cecilia, he'd lost so much and he deserved a happy ending too. "Do you get jealous?" Rainer asked.

Jessamin smiled. "Of a man honoring his commitment? Who is steadfast in his love? No. I don't get jealous." She grabbed a glass of bubble wine from a passing servant and took a sip. "I hope you two will stay awhile and visit often. I could certainly use Cece's wisdom and counsel. The king brightens up when she's around."

"I expect we'll visit a few times a year. Despite the king's best efforts to sour me, I have actually grown used to him. He is a good influence on Cece. I just want her to be happy."

"She does have a haunted look in her eye at times," Jessamin said quietly. "To be expected with all you've been through."

"I wish I could save her from it," Rainer said. He hadn't meant to say it out loud.

Jessamin's face softened. "You do, in small ways all the time. You must see that. The way she lights up whenever she sees you." Her face shifted as if a shadow passed over it. "We all have our demons we must dance with. Clearly, she's a strong woman. This world doesn't reward weakness, so trust that if you're the person she shows the broken parts of her heart to, then she must really love you. She must trust you. And if the stories are true, trust must be difficult for her."

Rainer nodded. He hadn't been prepared for Jessamin to be so wise, or for her words to make him feel so much. He swallowed around the lump in his throat and looked back at Cecilia.

Finally, the song ended, and Xander bowed to Cecilia, kissed her hand, and pulled Jessamin onto the dance floor. Rainer pulled Cecilia out next to them.

The song was slower this time, so he drew her close and swayed gently with her to the music. She rested her head against his chest, and he pressed his lips to the top of her hair. Warmth and joy spread through his whole body. It took him a moment to realize she was using her goddess power on him. He closed his eyes and relaxed into it. He could have stayed there all night with her.

"I love when you do that," he whispered.

SHEILA MASTERSON

"I wish we could get married now," she sighed.

"I will marry you tomorrow if you want," he said.

"That would be nice, but I am already attached to getting married at home. I can see it in my head and Aunt Clara will kill me if I get married without her a second time," she said with a dreamy smile.

"Well, you don't need a ceremony to have my heart, Cece. That's just a formality. I'm yours," he said, brushing his thumb along the inside of her wrist. She closed her eyes and smiled.

"I'm just for you, Rain," she said.

He felt like his heart might burst at the words no matter how many times she said them. They finally felt true. Xander was married. Finally, they were going to have their happily ever after, and it had been a long time coming. It felt like the future he'd always hoped for was in his grasp.

"I can feel you trying to find the next thing to worry about. Just enjoy this," she said, leaning her head against his chest.

"I wish we didn't need to be responsible for anything else," he sighed. "How do you manage to be so calm?"

"I don't know," Cecilia said. "In some ways, it will always be our responsibility to save this peace we've built. Maybe it shouldn't just rely on us, but I wouldn't trust anyone else with it. I'm less calm than resigned. Maybe happily ever after is just all of us trying to pick up the pieces and move on, however messy, emotional, and imperfect that may be. Maybe we get to be in love, but we still have the burden of keeping the dark at bay. Maybe Evan loses a friend but gains the love of his life. Maybe Xander moves on in the way he can. Maybe I'll always have moments of fear and panic, but you'll always be there to sit in the dark beside me. Maybe you'll always worry too much, but I'll be there to make you forget in whatever creative way I can. I think I expected we could somehow come out of this at peace with the whole thing. Maybe finding peace is like marriage, and you wake up every day and have to recommit to it and work for it. Maybe that's the real struggle."

Rainer stared at her.

"What?" she asked, alarmed.

"I just love you so much." He smiled and slid his hand slightly lower, cupping her bottom.

"Rainer!" she scolded.

He laughed and slid his palm to her lower back. "Sorry, it's just very tempting in this dress. I think if you'd worn a dress like this back in Olney, I would have dragged you back to the cottage and ruined you. Rules be damned."

"I wish I'd known that then," she said. "It's funny. The night I met Xander in the woods, I was thinking about just stripping off my bathing gown and letting you come back and find me naked."

"You were?" Rainer couldn't hide his surprise.

"Yes. It occurred to me that you were fighting it so much, and you'd already almost given in. Maybe if I just gave you a little push, you would go for it."

"I wish I hadn't been captured."

She giggled.

"I couldn't have done that, though," Rainer sighed. "I wouldn't have wanted your first time to be out in the woods. I got carried away that one morning because I wanted you so badly, and I'd been fighting it for so long, and you kept moaning, but I think I would have stopped things."

"I wouldn't have. I would have let you have me right there. I wanted it."

"I know," he said. "I could tell. Honestly, the way you were moving against me—"

"I wish we hadn't been interrupted," Cecilia said. The look in her eyes made him want to sweep her back to their room immediately.

"Me too."

Rainer went rigid as his eyes locked on the man standing behind Cecilia. Fear rendered him speechless. For a moment, he was certain he was dreaming. He had either conjured a ghost or he was truly staring at Cato. Rainer's chest ached as if he felt the god's blade sinking into his heart all over again.

The apparition smirked, cocking his head to the side, dark hair falling over his forehead. His gray eyes flashed with menace as he set his sights on Cecilia.

Rainer gripped the dagger at his waist. He wanted to throw Cecilia over his shoulder and run. He wanted to rip Cato limb from limb for even looking at her. He wanted so badly to protect her from turning around and reliving the worst day of his life.

"What?" Cecilia asked, turning to come face to face with the god.

Rainer waited for her to scream, to grab the dagger he hoped was strapped to her thigh.

But she looked almost relieved.

"I knew it," she said, shaking her head, dread spiking through their connection. "I knew you weren't really gone."

Rainer felt betrayed that she hadn't shared her suspicion.

Cato winked at her. "Happy to see you too, Little Dove. May I have this dance?"

It went against every instinct for Rainer to hand her over to the trickster god, but Cecilia nodded, offering Rainer one last reassuring look before she placed her hand in Cato's.

Cato pulled her against his body, and the two former gods started to dance.

42

CECILIA

Relief and worry warred in Cecilia, her whole body gone cold as Cato spun her on the dance floor. As they turned around the room, his face moved in and out of shadow so swiftly she found it hard to read a single emotion.

Most people had stopped dancing, warily loitering around the edges of the dance floor, their eyes fixed on the trickster god. Their fear and unease swelled and rushed through the room like an oppressive fog. Cecilia tried to ignore it but her own icy panic made her palm clammy against his.

"I knew it was too good to be true. I knew you weren't really gone," she said.

She'd worried she'd made it up—that her worry was just another symptom of the fear that lived in her body, or perhaps a slow madness creeping up on her in the wake of her death. It was almost a comfort to know she hadn't imagined it all these months.

Cato smirked. "How did you know?"

"How did you survive?"

Cato lowered her into a dip. "I called in the last of my favors when I crossed the veil between life and death after you so viciously

439

stabbed me." He faked a pout. "Samson met up with me and guided me back to the living world."

Fury rose like bile in Cecilia's throat. Samson had plenty of time to prepare them. "Is there no one who doesn't owe you a favor? How have you stacked up so many?"

Cato spun her. "I find it's best to figure out what people value, so you can be there the moment they need it. Lucky for me, Samson can be impulsive, and a few years ago, when he needed a reviving potion for a favored lover, I provided it with the caveat that he owe me a favor and hold on to a second revival potion just in case."

"It's a spell?" Cecilia asked.

He nodded. "Made by your birth mother, in fact. She had a little-known gift for death summoning that piqued her interest in such things. Samson's closeness with his brother means he was intimately acquainted with the afterlife realms. I also called in a favor with Aurelia. I'd been holding on to that one for years, but it finally came in handy. She distracted Grimon for me so he couldn't stop me from leaving. And because time moves differently there, I was back in my body before it had even begun to cool. Far from ideal, but Samson, being the honorable god he is, made sure I had the potion and was back on my feet before he left me in this wretched mortal body."

Cecilia stumbled a step. "You're mortal."

She should have known the moment he appeared. He no longer felt like a looming magical presence. There was a hint of a magical buzz around him, but it was more akin to what she felt from Xander or any other powerful witch than that of a living god.

"So are you," Cato said. "Why do you think you agreed to the dance so quickly?"

"To get you away from Rainer." She had been certain of it at the time, though now she wasn't.

Cato's grin grew wolfish. "It's best to enhance a desire that's already there."

Cecilia fought the urge to run from him. The second his attention was off of her, it could switch to any of her friends. "If your power works on me, then mine will work on you."

"Which is why I'm behaving myself." His gaze dipped to the cut of her dress and the scar on her chest. "You know, I think you're in less clothing every time I see you. If I come back again, will you simply be waiting for me naked?" he teased as he pulled Cecilia against him.

She frowned. "What inspired this bold reentry into court?"

"I felt pretty certain that you couldn't manage a weapon under this scandalous dress."

"I thought you would be done underestimating me by now," she taunted.

"Perhaps I should be," he said, looking her over again like he might have missed a hiding place. "Though I'm not sure how. Tell me, are your more scandalous dress choices Rainer's influence, or is this who you always would have been if you didn't have to care about appearances?"

She wished desperately that she hadn't forgone her dagger.

"I think I'm more myself now," she said. "Why are you here interrupting the king's wedding reception?"

Cato ignored the question. A new song started and he led her through the beginning of the next dance. Everyone else in the room had stopped dancing, but Cecilia refused to take her eyes from Cato's for fear it would draw his attention to someone she wanted to protect. Rainer tugged at their bond and she sent a glimmer of calm back to him. She wanted him far away from Cato. Just the thought of Rainer being this close to the god who had almost killed him made her heart thump harder.

"Tell me, how have you been feeling since coming back from the dead?" Cato asked. "Was it all happily ever after, or did the grief finally catch up with you? Did your loves finally get to see what I saw —how bitter and broken you were by the time I was done with you?"

He was trying to bait her, but Cecilia had no idea why. "We're all broken in our own ways, Cato. What do you want?"

He hesitated, his face awash with confusion. If he was expecting the old her, he was going to be disappointed.

"Can I assume that the old spells we've encountered and the ancient witches who've gone missing are your doing?" Cecilia asked.

Cato spun her and pulled her back against his body. "Safe assumption. I thought they might know a thing or two about how to transfer your power to me."

Cecilia burst out laughing as she spun back to look at him. "Have you learned nothing? Those witches know how to bind magic like the Gauntlet but never without an exchange, and the only equally valuable thing you have is your magic."

He rolled his eyes. "Yes. Yes. You witches are all the same—so concerned with balance. It's ridiculous because you never even wanted the power."

Cecilia stomped on his toes. "Well, it's mine now, and I've finally found a good use for it."

"Your little healing clinic?" Cato rolled his eyes.

"I know you don't understand now, but maybe you will in a few years. Now that you have a mortal lifespan," Cecilia said.

"I'm unwilling to wait and see. I'd hoped I could regain some power, but it seems I'm stuck with what I have."

Cecilia bit back a laugh. She should have felt terrified of him, but she only felt smug now. "The witches escaped, didn't they?"

Cato dipped her and yanked her back up. "They claim they only go where they wish to and that they were captured by my men so they could deliver the message themselves that I would not be able to weather the exchange." He tipped his head back with a huff. "Fucking witches."

"So why not just enjoy your short mortal life now?"

"Why don't you?" Cato countered, arching a brow.

"I'm trying," she huffed. "But someone keeps causing chaos and, I suspect, working with yet another Savero. Have you learned nothing?"

His hand drifted lower on her back, his thumb brushing her bare skin. It sent a shiver up her spine.

"So, why are you here? Why now?" Cecilia asked.

Cato pulled her closer so her body was flush with his. She braced herself for him to open a fold in space and drag her through. Instead, he leaned in so his lips brushed her ear.

"Besides the fact that I like to make an entrance?" Cato said, his tone playful. "I noticed something peculiar when I was in Olney. It seems I cannot break into the impenetrable mind of King Marcos and his guard and advisor, Anders Everett. Any idea why that might be?"

Cecilia bit her lip to keep from sighing in relief. The warded rings worked. It was a contingency plan, but it worked. If she made it back to Olney, she was going to have Rainer bake an entire batch of lemon cakes for Devlin to thank him.

"I haven't the faintest idea," she said. "Perhaps you're just not as strong as you once were and you're unwilling to accept your limitation. That's been an issue for you historically."

He sighed heavily. "Have it your way, Little Dove." He pulled away from her so quickly she stumbled. "I warned you that love would make you weak. People who love are so easily manipulated."

"Only you would see love as a weakness, even after witnessing what you've seen from me."

Cato set his sights on Xander and for the first time Cecilia noticed a sort of weariness in the trickster's eyes. Perhaps court intrigue did not suit him the way it used to. Perhaps a mortal lifespan had made his games lose their luster.

Cecilia let herself look at Xander for the first time since she'd started dancing. Evan and Rainer bracketed him. Jessamin was gone. It would only be a moment before Cato figured out that he couldn't manipulate Xander and he'd switch to Rainer, who stood poised with a dagger in his hand.

She needed to do something, but Cato would be ready for techniques she'd used before. If she just tried to take control of the mind Cato already held, they'd go around and around until one or both of them spent all their magic. Cecilia needed to get ahead of him.

Her memory witch magic would only work if she touched Cato, but the remnants of her goddess magic—though not as strong or permanent—would still work over a distance.

She could not anticipate who he'd go to next, but she could use her magic to take something from him. She dove into his mind with a precise strike. He was already using his magic, or at least trying to, so it was easy to locate the memory of how to influence and manipulate people. She gathered all the threads of memory of that part of his magic and yanked hard.

When she blinked her eyes open, Cato was wincing and rubbing his temple. He looked at Rainer with murder in his eyes and Cecilia waited for him to realize what memory she'd stolen from him.

Cato cocked his head to the side and turned slowly to look at Cecilia. He chuckled and shook his head. "That was very clever, though I have to assume if your power is like mine, it's a temporary solution. It will wear off."

Cecilia shrugged a shoulder, feigning a casualness she didn't feel. "Can you just let it go now?" she asked. "Even I can tell your heart isn't really in this. Your jokes were better when it was."

"You know nothing, Little Dove. You're still so young." He brushed his dark hair back from his forehead, the candlelight dancing over the scar above his eye. "I can't let it go. Last chance, Cece. Tell me why I can't influence the kings."

"You know I won't," she said.

Cato dipped her again and she dug her fingernails into the back of his neck.

"Haven't you done enough? Why do you continue to mess with all of us?"

The song ended. Cato set her back on her feet, bowed, and kissed her hand. Then he opened a swirling portal.

She drew back so he wouldn't drag her in. He met her gaze right before it snapped closed and said, "Because I can. I'll see you soon."

43

EVAN

Nothing fun ever happened in a library. Of that, Evan was certain.

It was almost midnight, the silver light of the moon cascading through the windows of the dusty library. Evan's eyes burned in the dim light, their candles having melted down to nubs.

Across from him, Xander lit a new candle with a flicker of fire magic. He rubbed his eyes and leaned back in the chair. He should have been enjoying his wedding night, not here doing research.

Their group had been gathered in the library for hours, searching for anything on Cato and preventing godly influence.

Evan slammed a heavy book shut, kicking up a cloud of dust.

Sylvie startled where she lounged, dozing on the plush chair beside the fireplace.

"Sorry," he said.

She waved her hand, then caught a glimpse of the diamond on it and grinned before flashing it to him. Evan couldn't help but smile back. Despite all the chaos around them, and even with purple splotches under her eyes, Sylvie looked lit from within. That was the only magic he'd ever wanted: to make the woman he loved light up.

Cecilia shifted in the chair beside Sylvie's, holding a book up to the fire before dropping it on the floor with a thud. Evan scowled at her.

"Stop giving me that look, Evan." She rubbed a hand over her face. "The damage is done. Cato tried for Xander first, and he'd already tried for Marcos. He will know that it's not just me working against him, and what we need is for the rest of us to be protected."

Evan was ordinarily able to control his temper, but the events of the day had burned through all his patience and left him running on pure frustration.

Cato and Vincent working together explained the coordinated timing of spellwork and the fact that the magic used was so old. Cato had taken the ancient witches from both kingdoms in the hope of transferring Cecilia's remaining powers to him.

But Evan was furious at Cecilia for letting him be blindsided and angry at himself for being bested by the trickster god once again.

He had the ominous feeling of history repeating itself, except this time he had a best friend, a kingdom, and a fiancée to lose.

Cal walked out of the stacks and dropped a new book on the table in the empty spot across from Evan.

"How long have you known he was alive?" Evan asked, tapping each of his fingers to his thumb in an attempt to calm himself down.

"I didn't know," Cecilia insisted. "I had a feeling. Between the dreams, and then a conversation I had with Grimon. I just suspected, and I didn't want to tell you because I thought I was just being paranoid."

"But I could have prepared us better!" Evan almost shouted.

Rainer peeked his head out of the stacks, but Cecilia held up a hand to him and pinned Evan with a look.

"How? How exactly would you have prepared us for Cato's return, oh wise strategist?"

Evan rubbed the back of his neck. Cecilia was right. He had no idea. It was a variable he wouldn't know how to deal with at all. Cato was far too unpredictable for plans, and he'd already learned that the hard way. His gaze strayed to Sylvie, who was stronger but still deathly pale and weak.

"I thought I was imagining things. I did my best to protect what I could and buy us time to come up with a solution," Cecilia said.

Evan nodded and relented. He wasn't mad at her; he was angry at himself for not even dreaming up this possibility when it had clearly been in her head from day one.

"I can only assume he won't give up on claiming my powers so easily, but I'm not going to let him," Cecilia said. "I'm helping people back home. I've been able to help those with failing memories and tremors and those who are depressed. And it goes without saying that I'm certain that Cato wielding both of our powers would be a truly terrible idea."

"I think we all agree on that," Xander said.

"What about Marcos and Anders?" Evan asked.

"They're both okay. I just had Grim check, but also I just know," Cecilia said. Her eyes met Xander's briefly, then they both looked away.

Evan crossed his arms. "How?"

She cocked her head like she was patronizing a child. "Evan, I just know, and I can't tell you why. You are the one who believes in compartmentalizing information."

Evan sighed in frustration. He hated being in the dark, though he supposed that was how everyone else felt around him the rest of the time. He could see in Cecilia's eyes that he needed to trust her.

"For now, Marcos, Anders, and Xander are all safe, but the rest of us are not," she said. "I can protect people I'm with, and if Cato's power is like mine, he'll be depleted faster and unable to do as much. I had him forget to use his power temporarily, but we can't count on that working long-term. Plus, if he's smart, he'll just try to control me."

Rainer sucked in a breath and leaned against the arm of her chair. "Didn't you just take away his memory of how to use his magic? Won't that be enough?"

Cecilia shrugged. "I used my goddess magic because it's more precise and it works at a distance, but it's not as strong or permanent as it once was. Some patients at the clinic require regular maintenance and not just a one-time treatment. Of the people I've worked with at the clinic, a desire to remember a joyful memory or forget a painful one affects their outcome. But Cato has strong motivation to remember."

"Why would someone want to forget?" Cal asked.

Her face softened. "For some older people, it's easier not to remember those who have passed on. Regardless, we can't build our plan around hoping Cato doesn't remember."

"We could try wards?" Sylvie suggested weakly.

Evan hated that Sylvie was even participating in the conversation. She should have been resting after nearly dying. Even as she recovered she'd insisted on coordinating everything for the wedding and reception. She'd barely slept, but Evan refused to leave her alone. If nothing else, he wanted Cecilia near her to protect her.

"Would that work?" Evan asked.

"I was thinking about it because of all the spells that Vincent's people have used. Wards are old magic like those spells," Sylvie said. "There's probably information about them in the archives. I have to think with so many gods walking among men years ago that the witches would have guarded their minds to keep out godly powers. The witches who created the Gauntlet must have had some way that they protected their intentions to take what Cato desired most and all the Gauntlet caves had wards to keep out anyone without magic."

"You're right! Gods, I didn't even consider it because I'd never thought about painting them directly on a person. How else could they have pulled one over on him?" Cecilia said, clapping her hands together.

That was Sylvie. Brilliant all the time, even when she was still healing and exhausted. Evan briefly considered crossing the room to kiss her, but decided against it. No need to get carried away. He could wait until they were alone.

"I can ask the spirits if they can point me in the right direction," Cecilia continued, turning to smile at Xander. "I think we're good for one night. Xan, go make this marriage official or all this trouble will have been for nothing."

Xander held her gaze for a moment, then nodded. Evan waited with bated breath for a snarky comeback. He'd expected an argument from Xander, or that he'd use this emergency as an excuse, but it seemed he and Cecilia had finally made peace.

Relief washed over Evan, and the weight of his exhaustion crashed down on him at once.

"You should all go to bed," Cecilia said. "Rain and I can take it from here, but I'll be around in the morning to paint everyone's wards, so be bathed and ready bright and early."

Evan rose and helped Sylvie from her seat. She cocked a brow and nodded at Cecilia. She wanted him to apologize.

He sighed and turned toward her. "I'm sorry I got frustrated that you were withholding vital speculation about our enemy."

"Oh, Ev, if you don't stop being so nice to me, I'll start to think you've warmed to me." Cecilia winked and disappeared into the stacks.

44

XANDER

Xander stood in Jessamin's chambers, feeling nervous and unsettled. It wasn't the excitement of the evening that had him uneasy. It had been far too long since he'd been with a woman, and he was afraid it would be a disaster.

The sight of Cato after all this time had left him in a panicked cold sweat. He spun the warded ring around his finger. It could protect him from the god's influence, but not from Cato plunging a dagger into his chest.

He toyed with the sash on his robe. "I'd hoped this night would be different and not haunted by the specter of my past."

"I won't let him hurt you," Jessamin said. Her tone was fierce and protective.

Xander appreciated the sentiment, but all he really wanted was to feel like he could protect himself this time.

"Either way, he's not here tonight and I'd prefer to put it out of my mind," Xander said.

Jessamin stood on the other side of the intricately carved four-poster bed in a lilac silk robe.

He cleared his throat. "I know you'll find it hard to believe, but I haven't been with a woman since Cece."

He was embarrassed to admit it. For most of his life he'd relished being a more experienced partner, teaching a lover how to find pleasure with him or on her own. He liked sharing that power. But now he felt self-conscious—afraid he would fall short of his new wife's expectations.

Jessamin's face softened. "Your commitment to her is admirable."

"We don't have to do this. So much has happened and I never want you to feel pressured or uncomfortable," Xander said.

Jessamin held up a hand to stop him. "Let's make an agreement right now that if you do anything that makes me uncomfortable, I will tell you, and vice versa. I don't want secrets between us. We are a team now. Your problems are my problems and your triumphs are my triumphs."

Relief flooded Xander. Partnership was something he could do—something he craved.

"As a partner, I expect honesty, and I will give you the same respect. In light of that commitment, I am very comfortable doing this, as is Maren. As I've already said. This agreement between us is more than I could have hoped for, and it wouldn't be the first time we've brought another to bed with us."

Xander's eyebrows shot up as he looked at Maren, who leaned against the wall by the fireplace, her green robe slipping open to reveal the pale curve of her breasts. She didn't look jealous so much as curious.

"Furthermore, I happen to know that I'm at the right moment to conceive, and being a mother and carrying on both of our family lines is very important to me," Jessamin said. "I'd like a big family. I've made an offering to the goddess of the stars—who grants fervent wishes—and the goddess of the moon—who blesses fertility."

Xander had never been particularly devout, but he supposed it didn't hurt. He had only thought of having children in the abstract. He'd put the desire to do so to bed when he found out that Cece couldn't conceive. He'd told himself he didn't want it and that it didn't matter to him, but Jessamin's words unlocked a longing that he'd shoved down for so long.

He'd always wanted to be a father. Maybe it was arrogant to think he could do a better job than Damian—who'd focused so much on making him hard and competitive that he'd never had a chance to know the man—but Xander wanted the chance to try. He'd always wanted to have the chance to raise children who were as kind as they were strategic and as brave as they were compassionate. If they had magic, he wanted them to embrace it, not hide it away.

"Xander?" Jessamin's voice interrupted his thoughts.

"I would love to do that," he said. "Are you sure you feel ready?"

Jessamin nodded as she slipped off her robe and stood before him in a silk nightgown. She sat down on the edge of the bed and gestured for Maren, who sat down beside her.

For just a moment, Xander felt like the man he'd been before he'd fallen in love. He knew he would never be the same person he was before Cato ripped his life apart, and after seeing the god tonight, that reminder was fresh. But it was a relief to know that part of him still stirred to life after being buried for so long.

Xander could do much worse than going to bed with two beautiful women.

———

Xander rounded the corner, feeling more relaxed and at peace than he had in a long time. The sun was shining. The castle was already alive with servants preparing the post-wedding brunch, and his friends were temporarily warded against godly influence. All they needed to do was get through this brunch, and then they could figure out how to solve the problem of Cato.

Seeing Cato the night before left him with a creeping dread in his bones, but at least for now his friends were safe.

He walked down the grand staircase to the lower level. Earth witches tended to enormous garlands of red roses wrapped around the banisters and down the ceiling of the main hall. Fire witches walked through the halls, lighting a ludicrous number of candles.

Fiddlers tuned up in the foyers. Xander had to admit that the aesthetics added a certain romance to the castle.

The extravagance was a bit much for brunch, but it had been years since a royal wedding. His and Cece's ceremony had been a romantic secret. Evan felt that the aristocracy and the common folk both needed to believe in the fairy tale of it all.

That was why Jessamin had taken a carriage through the streets the day before on her way to their temple ceremony. The people had gathered in the streets, throwing flowers and welcoming their new queen. Evan was a nervous wreck about the whole thing, but it had gone off without a hitch.

Xander was relieved to be one event away from being done with all the visitors in the castle. He was looking forward to getting back to the day-to-day ruling of the kingdom, something only Cato's chaos could make him wish for.

He looked forward to getting to know his new wife and sending a strong, unified message to Vincent that an attack on Argaria was also an attack on Novum. Hopefully, that would be enough to discourage his cousin once and for all.

All things considered, his wedding night was a success, though perhaps not as memorable as his first. Especially since he'd made his way back to his own room to sleep. Waking up alone wasn't as strange as realizing that he had a new wife in the room next door. Still, he found himself looking forward to talking with Jessamin and watching her interact with his council since he'd announced his desire to add a seat for his new wife.

He rounded another corner and nearly ran into Mika and Magdalena. Mika's eyes darted from Xander to the healer nervously before she slid her flawless mask of calm back into place.

"Your Majesty," they said, dipping into curtseys.

"It's good to see you both. I didn't realize you knew each other," Xander said, eyeing Mika suspiciously. She was more private than he'd realized, though he supposed privacy was an asset to someone in her line of work. Still, he was surprised to see that she and Magdalena were so close.

"As you can imagine, with my profession, it's important that I regularly see Magdalena," Mika said, as if sensing his suspicion.

"Of course," Xander said. He made a mental note to mention this interaction to Evan. There was something off in her tone.

"You look good, Your Grace. Marriage agrees with you. Your new queen is lovely, and I look forward to getting to know her," Magdalena said.

Magdalena had served Xander's family for years. She'd helped his mother deliver Xander. She'd healed Cece when she was poisoned, and she had helped Sylvie recover from her near-death experience.

"Will I see you both at brunch?" Xander asked.

"We wouldn't miss it," Magdalena said with a sincere smile.

Xander excused himself and found his way down to the dining room, where his council and several prominent members of the Argarian aristocracy would be meeting for brunch. He scanned the guards in the room, his own guards in Argarian red mixed in with Edward Spellman's men in navy and red and William Arvato's in black and gold. It was still startling to see them comingled with his trusted guards. As much as Xander appreciated the extra support, he was looking forward to going back to business as usual. It was beyond time for things to calm down in his life and in the lives of his people.

He scanned the rest of the room, his eyes connecting with Reese and Chris, who were discussing something in hushed tones off in the corner. He made his way over to them.

"Everything okay, Reese?" Xander asked.

"Other than the return of a dead god? Of course," Reese said, but the look on his face suggested the exact opposite, as did the jump in his heartbeat.

"How worried are the people?" Xander asked.

Chris smiled sheepishly, his eyes crinkling. "You know how it is— bad news spreads like wildfire."

Xander blew out a harassed sigh. "Of course. We will stay vigilant until we know more."

"We were just discussing some logistics for the morning. We were hoping to catch up with Evan. Have you seen him?" Reese asked.

Xander shook his head. "I haven't seen him yet, but he's been hovering over his lovely fiancée quite a bit since the incident at the announcement ceremony."

"Understandably so," Chris said.

Reese and Chris locked eyes before looking around the room again.

"I suppose I'll leave you to it unless you think there's something I can help with," Xander said.

"Oh no," Reese said. "Don't worry yourself. We'll discuss it with Evan, and we'll all enjoy brunch."

Xander wanted to ask more questions, but was interrupted by applause at Jessamin's arrival.

He'd grown accustomed to compartmentalizing. If he didn't panic, his council wouldn't panic, and he needed them to fall in line for the next day. Just until the princesses departed and everything calmed down.

Xander smiled and introduced people to his new wife. He drank to toasts and hardly had a moment to catch his breath.

Despite all the chaos, it was good to see his friends laughing and interacting with the court. Sylvie and Evan spoke with Cal and Lady Tanya McGraph. Rainer spoke with Reese and Chris, and Cece chatted animatedly with William Arvato. In the far corner of the room, Mika and Magdalena whispered and smiled as they nibbled breakfast pastries.

Jessamin hung on Xander's arm like a doting queen, chatting easily with some of the stuffier members of his council, who seemed to be won over by her beauty and charm.

Xander had been certain at the opening ball he wouldn't get here, but somehow it had all worked out. He felt nothing but love and gratitude that he'd made so many mistakes in his life, but still managed to have such a wonderful, capable group of friends to weather the coming storm alongside him.

45

EVAN

Evan should have been able to breathe easier. The visiting dignitaries would be out of the castle within hours, along with the extra security from Spellman and Arvato. They'd made it through the engagement, wedding, and brunch successfully.

Instead, he was met with more bad news.

Reese and Chris had pulled him aside before brunch and mentioned that neither of them had heard from their network of spies throughout the kingdom after their last two rounds of messages.

Evan was having the same issue. He could have written it off as an isolated incident if it was just him. Spying was dangerous, and there were a whole host of reasons he might not have heard back from his contacts. But the fact that well-connected Reese and Chris were having the same issue simultaneously was a sign of a much larger problem.

He'd hoped that Xander's marriage would have squashed Vincent's hold on Argaria, but it appeared Vincent was desperate and making a last-ditch effort at usurping.

Every step forward seemed to lead two steps back. The marriage was a huge win, but now they were staring down yet another problem. It was beyond frustrating.

Xander handed him a glass of bubble wine. "For the love of the gods, will you finally relax? This is your victory, Evan. We'll solve the rest tomorrow when all these strangers are out of here. Now will you wipe that grimace off your face and take the win?"

Evan sighed, accepting a glass and clinking it against the king's before taking a sip. "Congratulations on finally rising to the occasion."

Xander arched a brow, a teasing gleam in his eye that was familiar but had long been absent. "I assure you, I rose to the occasion several times. I've not enjoyed my official duties so much in quite a while."

Evan barked out a laugh. "It is startling how you can be so very different and yet parts of you remain unchanged."

"Some might say the best parts. Shall I ask my bride if she can attest?" Xander asked.

Evan shook his head and downed the rest of the wine.

Xander placed a hand on his shoulder. "Seriously, Ev. Thank you. I know I didn't make it easy. I know how much you've done for me the past year and I know what it almost cost you. I'm ready for the next steps and I know you're ready for yours too."

Evan swallowed thickly and nodded. "It was about time you stop forcing me to choose between you and Sylvie. I'm proud of you."

Xander nodded, his throat bobbing as he looked around the room at their friends laughing happily together.

"It's not over yet," Evan said, soft enough that only Xander could hear.

He turned to meet his eye. "That may be so, but we still deserve to celebrate how far we've come and I'll not let you skip it."

Evan followed Xander over to their friends. He wished he could ask Rainer and Cecilia to stay forever. Although things between Xander and Cecilia seemed to have settled, he was sure she and Rainer were eager to start preparing for their own wedding. He made a mental note to ask how much longer they were willing to stay when they'd only been planning for the festival.

"Sylvie, you weren't kidding about Lord Arvato. He's very charming," Cecilia laughed, fanning herself. "He was chatting with me at brunch. He has the most unusual eyes. I've never seen any like that. So dark they're nearly black, with flecks of gold."

Evan's stomach plummeted. "What did you just say?"

Cecilia frowned, clearly picking up on his fear. "William Arvato was talking to me at brunch, and he was very flirtatious. I see why Sylvie enjoys talking—"

"No, what did you say about his eyes?" Evan demanded.

"That they were nearly black with flecks of gold."

The one defining characteristic they knew Vincent possessed.

Xander set his glass on the table with a loud clang, his face reflecting the horror Evan was feeling.

"Fuck!"

William Arvato *was* Vincent Savero. Their nemesis had been right in front of their faces the entire time, and they hadn't noticed. It explained everything. He knew how to anticipate their every move because he was helping make them in the council meetings.

"What?" Cecilia asked.

"William Arvato *is* Vincent Savero. It's the only thing that makes sense. I cannot believe we didn't notice." Evan ran a hand over his face in disbelief.

How had he never noticed the eyes? He wracked his brain.

Cato, that was how. Cato could disguise appearances as he'd done the day Endros showed up appearing as Davide years before. It would have been simple magic. He only needed to change William's eye color, something that should have been manageable to Cato, even in his current mortal state.

"Evan, you aren't making any sense," Sylvie said.

"Think about it," Evan said, trying to breathe through the tightness in his chest. "When William arrived to take over for his father, almost no one had met him before he showed up. The only reason we let him on the council—"

"Was because I insisted that fresh blood would be a good thing," Xander said, rubbing a hand over his face.

Evan shook his head. "No, three of the other council members vouched for him and they could have lied. But I pushed for it too because Spellman was putting so much pressure on us and the rumors had become so pervasive, I thought he'd be an ally."

Panic twisted in Evan's chest as he continued. "We don't know what Vincent looks like, and his only distinguishing feature is his eyes, so he had Cato disguise them. But as we've learned from Cecilia, in her current state, her powers don't always last as long as before."

Cecilia went pale. "The same is true for Cato and if I took away his ability to use his power last night—"

"It makes sense that the disguise wouldn't last through the day today," Evan finished. His stomach plummeted. "We knew someone on the council had to at least have been leaking information. Otherwise, they wouldn't have known the exact moment to attack during the announcement ceremony, and they wouldn't have been a step ahead of us for months. The last place we'd ever look for Vincent is in our fucking council. I can't believe it!"

And Evan personally had written off his suspicion as jealousy that the man was always flirting with Sylvie.

Xander's eyes went wide. "And we just gave him the literal keys to the kingdom after the incident at the announcement ceremony that he probably helped orchestrate. He acted like a hero, so we'd give him trust. I let him bring in more guards."

"We need Spellman's men to get out there and stop this. They can give us the numbers against Will—Vincent," Evan corrected.

Rainer tucked Cecilia against his side and whispered something in her ear. Evan was surprised to see the fear on Cecilia's face. In the past, she'd shared a similar lack of self-preservation instinct and inconvenient bravery as Xander. Evan remembered how many times he had to talk her out of running down to confront Davide on the beach the day she'd accepted her goddess powers. He hadn't let himself sleep that night because he was certain she'd sneak away and be a hero. Still, it was clear that crossing through the veil and back had left its mark on her.

"I have a really bad feeling about all of this. I think we should get Jessamin and Sylvie out," Cecilia said.

"I think we should all get out," Sylvie argued.

"I can't leave my people behind. I have to at least get the staff out of the castle," Xander said.

Sylvie laughed morosely. "What a time to start acting like a king."

Evan looked frantically from Xander to Sylvie.

How could he be faced with the same choice that he'd been struggling with over and over? He needed to choose Sylvie first, without question, but he couldn't leave Xander behind.

"Evan," Cecilia interrupted his thoughts. "Take Jessamin, her guards, and Sylvie and whoever else you can to safety. Rain and I will stay with Xander and try to get all the staff out of the castle."

"I am not going to leave my husband," Jessamin said firmly.

Maren took her hand. "Please, Your Majesty, you can't be the queen of anything if you're dead. Tell her," she said, turning to Xander.

"Darling, I will never command you," Xander said gently. "I respect your ability as a fighter, but it's not just you that you're fighting for. A good warrior knows when to stand and fight and when to retreat and regroup and live to fight another day."

Jessamin huffed out a breath, realizing the logic in what he was saying. He'd already learned how to speak to her in a way she understood and didn't make her feel powerless.

"I'm going with Sylvie—" Evan cleared his throat. "And the queen, of course." When he met Sylvie's gaze, he saw relief that he chose her. He knew it was the right choice, but it went against every instinct to leave Xander behind.

"We don't have time to argue," Cecilia said. "I promise the three of us will stay together, but you all have to go. I am going to ask the spirits to guide you out. Follow the passages that open for you and don't try to get through those that don't."

"I can stay," Cal said.

"No, Cal, I appreciate it, but the fewer minds I have to keep tabs on, the better," she said. "Those wards have held so far, but if any of them get smudged or stop working, it will be a disaster. I know Evan could use the help."

"Evan, get them out," Xander said. "Go to the new Temple of Aurelia on the south side of Ardenis. Once everyone is there safe, you can come back—carefully—but we will probably be out by then."

Evan sighed but nodded.

Xander pulled Jessamin into a tight hug and kissed her cheek. "Be careful, darling. I'm sorry that our honeymoon is so chaotic."

Jessamin laughed. "At least it's not boring."

"You're armed?" Xander asked.

She slid her hand down her dress. "There are ten blades hidden in my bodice alone. I'll be fine."

Sylvie hugged Cecilia. "Don't be a hero again, or I will come back and kill you myself."

Cecilia laughed. "I have done that enough. I'm just corralling His Majesty, as is my gift."

She stood quietly for a moment with her eyes closed, then pointed to the passageway at the far side of the room. The door creaked open on its own, and all of them turned and looked at her.

"What? I told you they would help," she said with a grin. "They don't like strangers invading their home."

Evan ushered everyone into the passageway and turned back to look at his friends, who had crossed the room to the other passage on the far wall. Xander gave him a nod. Then, the three of them disappeared into the dark, heading down to the kitchens.

Evan couldn't get over the feeling he was saying goodbye, as if there was permanence to it. He had the nagging sense that he was forgetting something important, but he shoved the fear away.

He closed the passageway door and led the rest of his friends into the dark.

46

XANDER

Xander could barely breathe around his shock and outrage as he rounded the corner into the kitchen.

The head chef looked up with wide, panicked eyes. "Your Grace, we weren't expecting—"

"My cousin's men are in the castle. I need everyone to evacuate immediately," he said.

He expected chaos but the staff just brushed their hands and glanced at each other for a long moment. The head chef whispered with one woman who held a tray full of freshly baked rolls. She nodded and ushered some of the younger women toward the rear exit. The rest of the men stayed where they were.

"If it's all right with you, Your Majesty, I think the rest of us would prefer to stay and fight," the head chef said.

A lump formed in Xander's throat. Maybe it had nothing to do with loyalty to him, and these people just wanted to protect their home, but their commitment to the cause was a relief. No one wanted to feel like they were alone in a fight.

"Very well. We are going to clear the floor. Can you defend the way out for anyone we send your way?" Xander asked.

The chef bowed. "We'd be honored to, Your Grace."

Xander nodded in thanks and darted out of the kitchen with Cece and Rainer on his heels.

They rounded the corner and continued down the corridor that led to the training rooms, taking turns clearing each room as they went and sending any remaining castle staff to the kitchens to escape.

They reached the end of the hall and turned back to clear the next wing, but at the junction a group of guards in black and gold regalia were waiting for them. William's men—or, rather, Vincent's.

Xander and Rainer drew their swords, with Cece poised between, a flame sizzling above her palm.

She tossed fireballs at the first line of men before they could draw their blades. They screeched, frantically patting their clothes before crumpling to the ground, screaming. The smell of charred flesh made Xander's stomach heave, but he focused on the rest of the group. There looked to be about thirty men.

Rainer peeled off to cover Cece's right flank and Xander turned to face the left. Fighting alongside them was easy, a relief, as if it was always meant to be the three of them working side by side to save the kingdom.

It felt good to fight—to take all the fear and rage that had stirred to life in him since Cato popped up at his wedding reception and channel it into something he could act on. Xander was a lousy politician but an excellent fighter, and he'd be damned if he let his own house fall to his cousin.

Cece bumped against his back and Xander stole a glance at her. Her hem was marred with blood and she held a sword that was too large for her. Still, she fended off the guard she was fighting.

She froze one guard in his tracks, grabbed his blade, and sliced it across his throat. He fell to the ground in a bloody heap and she jumped over his body, but missed another charging at her. The man grabbed her by the throat and slammed her into the wall. Xander gasped.

The dull thud of her body hitting stone sent Rainer into a frenzy. He ripped the man away from Cece and shoved his sword through the guard's chest. He pressed a foot to the dead man's back and shoved him off his blade. A wet sucking sound filled the air as the sword slid free and the guard's body slumped to the ground.

Rainer spun and slit two more guards' throats before they had a chance to get more than a swipe at him. Two more men came at him. Rainer fended them off with frenzied violence born of the pleasure of hurting those who had tried to steal what wasn't theirs.

A man grabbed Cece and she deflected him, throwing an elbow into his gut and a fist into his jaw. She jabbed her dagger into his side and twisted before pulling it out.

The guard stumbled away from her, but another came up behind her, grabbing her hair, yanking her head back, and squeezing her throat. Cece gasped and stabbed her dagger into the man's thigh, but he hung on.

Xander shoved his blade through the gut of his opponent and dashed toward Cece. Before he could reach her, Rainer yanked her assailant off of her by his collar, plunged his dagger into the man's chest, and twisted slowly.

The guard dropped to the ground, gurgling, blood pouring from his mouth and chest.

Rainer smiled at the remaining guards. "Touch her and I'll make sure you die drowning in your own blood."

The five guards charged Rainer all at once.

Xander was stunned at the graceful violence. Rainer fought with rage that Xander had never seen in him. His violence was arresting— a marker of how much they had all been through. It was the vicious, single-minded fight of a man who'd seen the woman he loved broken and would not stand to see it again.

Rainer laid waste to twenty of Vincent Savero's men and, one by one, Xander and Cece watched them fall. When the last man went down, Rainer finally lifted his eyes to look at Cece. He looked feral. He panted, his damp hair falling over his blood-splattered forehead.

He sheathed his blade and crossed the hall in a blur to kiss her. Drawing back, he leaned his forehead against hers. "Are you well?"

"Yes," she said breathlessly. "Are *you*?"

He grinned. "Better than I've been in a while. Now let's go clear this floor."

"Let me know if you need a hand next time, McKay," Xander teased.

"Shut up. You're the king. You're supposed to stay back," Rainer said, shoving the sweaty hair back from his forehead. "Let's finish this."

Xander led them down the next wing, where they found Edward Spellman gesturing animatedly down the hall and barking commands at his guards.

Edward looked up and his shoulders slumped in relief. "Your Grace, I just heard what happened. We were worried you'd been captured."

"Were you really? I thought you'd be happy to be rid of me," Xander joked.

Edward looked mildly offended. "I'll not have our kingdom in the hands of a madman. Better a young, untested king than a mad dog."

The honesty was a relief. Perhaps Edward Spellman was just one of those men who wanted something to complain about.

"Will you help me clear the staff from this floor?" Xander asked. "I want to make sure the castle staff are safely evacuated before we take the fight to him."

Edward nodded to the south wing behind them. "We've cleared the south. We were about to head to the north wing."

"We'll go with you," Xander said.

He charged down the hall, bracketed by Rainer and Cece. The rooms in the north corridor were empty, doors blown open, furniture tipped.

"Look alert," Xander said, peeking into the dining room.

The feast had been cleared away but the remnants of brunch remained in empty place settings and glasses tinged with dregs of red wine. Something nagged at the back of Xander's mind—like he'd forgotten something important.

He rolled his shoulders to shake the feeling off, the vigilance and fear of a distant struggle becoming present.

Spellman's guards were close on their heels as they reached the sitting room. Xander shoved the doors open and stepped into the bright sunlit room.

Vincent Savero stood smiling, a group of his men gathered behind him as if they'd been waiting for Xander.

"Cousin," he said with a smile. "It's good to finally meet again, true face to true face, true name to true name."

"You're outnumbered," Xander said. "Surrender now and I'll give you a swift death."

"Do I not deserve mercy?" Vincent asked.

Xander laughed bitterly. "You come into my house in an attempt to overthrow my rule and expect mercy?"

Vincent looked too relaxed, too utterly certain of himself. "I am the rightful king."

Xander nearly choked on his anger. "There's a difference between claiming a thing and it being true." He held his blade at the ready. "You've invaded the house of power in this kingdom with no evidence of your claims. You've harmed my people for your own gain. You have no right to my throne or my mercy."

Vincent cocked his head to the side, his gaze darting past Xander. "Where's Evan? Has your minion abandoned you?"

"He's around, but he's not your problem right now. You're still outnumbered," Xander said, but he frowned. Something was wrong. Vincent's men weren't moving into position to defend him. They didn't even have blades drawn.

Cece spun her quiet curse, making Xander's blood run cold. "Spellman is in on it," she hissed.

Rainer turned so the three of them were back-to-back, but there were nearly fifty men surrounding them and, even with his and Cece's magic, that would be a challenge.

Xander didn't want to believe he'd had not one but two traitors on his council, but it all hit him at once. Evan had never been able to figure out how Vincent funded his army, but Spellman was the wealthiest man in Argaria.

Before he could lift his sword, an arrow struck Cece in the arm.

466

She yelped, yanking it out and tossing it on the floor. She covered the wound with her hand to heal it and Xander's heart leapt into his throat as he looked for the next hunter to fire.

But no one did. All the men looked calm, poised to fight if they needed to but somehow certain they wouldn't.

Cece turned her angry gaze on the first line of men, but nothing happened. "Godsbane," she mumbled. "The arrow had Godsbane."

Xander pressed his back against hers. They were sitting ducks here. On the far side of the room, beside the fireplace, there was a passageway, but they'd have to fight off a lot of men to get there.

Before he could suggest they try to head that way, Spellman's men attacked. Xander fought as hard as he could. Cece was cut off from her goddess powers but she stabbed and ducked and threw fireballs as much as she dared without setting the whole castle on fire. Rainer picked up the slack with his fierce fighting.

"The fireplace," Xander grunted as he ducked out of the way of a sword swipe.

Rainer nodded subtly as he tucked Cece behind him. A huge hunter came at him hard, his large broadsword whistling through the air. Rainer tried to block, but the blow was brutal; he ducked to the side and his sword was knocked from his hand. The man grabbed for him and Rainer caught him in the jaw with a right hook before another burly guard came up behind him and pressed a blade to his throat.

Cece stopped moving immediately and dropped her blade.

"Smart girl," Vincent said.

Xander turned wildly, summoning his storm magic. It was hard to use this deep in the castle. He could blow out the windows in the room, but trying to funnel a storm through a small opening was not very effective. He wanted to stand and fight, but doing so now would get his closest friends killed. It would probably get him killed as well.

"No shame in admitting when you're outmatched, cousin."

Xander felt crushed under impotent fury, but he dropped his blade and held his hands up. Guards charged him and Cece, snapping Unsummoner bracelets on their wrists.

He narrowed his eyes at Vincent, trying to remember the young cousin he'd grown up with. He looked nothing like his old self. The years had carved away any kindness and left him with sharp features and the dark eyes for which he was known. Xander was sure they hadn't always looked like that. He would have noticed.

The moment Xander's magic severed, he wanted to slump in defeat. He forced himself to hold his head high.

"Those are spelled," Vincent said. "You won't be able to get them off without magic. Ancient magic. You may have sneaked those witches away, but not before they did me a few favors. Not your basic everyday Unsummoner bracelet. You're quick, taking so many of my men out before they could subdue you. Honestly, you all nearly foiled my well-laid plans when you had the wedding so soon. I almost couldn't get my men here in time."

Vincent grinned as he looked at the three of them. "I thought a couple of fake princesses would add enough chaos to the mix, but I must admit, you weathered it much better than I expected. There were so many moving pieces and I nearly missed my timing." He brushed his hands down his fine tunic. "I see the gears turning. You're wondering about the eyes. Unfortunately, Cato's power is not what it once was. It wore off sooner than expected this time, since the lovely Lady Reznik temporarily stole his memory of how to use it. So she noticed when I was mesmerizing her with my charm at brunch."

Both Xander and Rainer bristled at that, but Cece laughed.

Oh, gods. Please, Cece, don't be yourself right now. Don't be brave. Be sweet and timid. Just this once, Xander silently begged.

"That's funny?" Vincent asked, a slight grin on his face.

"Yes. It's just that all of you Saveros think you're so different, but you equally overestimate your ability to charm women."

Vincent tipped his head back and laughed. "You are certainly spirited. I'll give you that. I love a feisty woman." He walked toward her, and Cece paled. "I understand you're still available," Vincent taunted, looking from Rainer to Cece.

"I'm engaged," Cece said.

"Until the deal is sealed, I consider you still available. It's McKay's fault for not securing you when he had the chance." Vincent reached out a hand and stroked her cheek.

To Cece's credit, she didn't shrink away.

Beside Xander, Rainer thrashed against the guards. Xander met his eye and shook his head as if to say, "*Don't give him the satisfaction.*"

Vincent looked at Rainer as he let his fingers trail down Cece's neck, over her exposed shoulder, and then along the neckline of her dress, letting his finger skim right under the edge of the lace. Cece's heart raced loud enough for Xander to hear from where he stood, but she didn't move.

"So soft," Vincent whispered.

Rainer stilled, his brow creased with helpless worry as he watched.

Cece met Xander's eyes over Vincent's shoulder and gave the slightest shake of her head.

"I'll make this simple. Why is it that the trickster hasn't been able to get into any of your heads? Or the king of Olney's?"

Xander shook his head. "I don't know."

"If you're a good king, that's a lie. But if you're a good friend and ex-husband, it isn't. As I understand, you spent quite a bit of time protecting Guardian McKay for your dear ex-wife. Is that true?"

Xander wasn't sure how to answer. He felt like he was struggling in an undertow, and every wrong answer was going to sweep him into deeper water. He'd been strategically outmaneuvered for months. He wouldn't suddenly be able to come out on top, but he was the king. He had to do something.

Just holding Vincent's attention might be enough. The longer they distracted Vincent and his men, the more time the staff had to escape. He crossed his fingers that they were smart enough to flee and had somewhere to go. Hopefully, Evan was intercepting people. He prayed their friends made it to safety.

Vincent nodded, and two guards dragged Rainer forward. They stripped him of his fine tunic and undershirt so that he stood shirtless before they bent him over the mahogany table. They bound his wrists to either side, immobilizing him.

Cece faltered, taking a step toward him. His gaze was locked on hers, and he shook his head. Tears welled in her eyes, but she smiled halfheartedly as he sent something through their connection. "*I love you,*" he mouthed.

Cece gritted her teeth and dug her nails into her palms to keep herself from crying. The frustration on her face mirrored Xander's own. He hated feeling helpless.

Vincent pulled off his fancy tunic and rolled up the sleeves of his undershirt, revealing scarred forearms. "Here's what's going to happen. You can tell me why the trickster can't get into your heads." He picked up a switch. "For every minute it takes you to tell me, I'm going to give Rainer a lash. If you tell me now, he won't get any. Look at that perfect skin, Lady Reznik. You've done such a good job keeping him in one piece all these years. Are you willing to throw that all away now? As I understand, lashings are very hard to heal, even for talented healers, because of the way the skin splits. They almost always leave scars."

Reality set in. They'd faced cruelty before, but never such sharp violence. Cato's psychological warfare had been brutal but always with a goal in mind, and he hadn't relished physical pain in conjunction with it. His violence was a means to an end. Vincent seemed to bask in their fear, his eyes lit with excitement at the prospect of inflicting pain.

"We'll start in one minute. If you tell me before, then I won't whip him at all."

Cece glanced helplessly from Rainer to Xander. Rainer met Xander's gaze and gave the slightest shake of his head. He wanted the king to know he could take it.

Beside Xander, Cece was standing tall, but he could tell by the look in her eye and the way her heart pounded that she was crumbling.

"Let Lady Reznik go. She doesn't know anything. She only recently recovered from her ordeal," Xander said.

Rainer looked relieved by the plea. Xander didn't understand why he was doing it. Cece wouldn't leave, but he just wanted her out of the center of Vincent's attention. She did not deserve to be the object of any more cruelty.

Vincent just laughed. He smiled at Cece as he brought the switch down on Rainer's back. The sound reverberated through the room like a crack of thunder.

Rainer gritted his teeth against the pain, immediately meeting Cece's gaze. She closed her eyes and tears streamed down her face. Rainer's face went calm and serene with her. Xander was struck by the juxtaposition of the horror of the violence combined with their beautiful way of silently communicating.

Xander didn't know how much Cece could take. She already looked like she was about to crack.

"Lady Reznik, perhaps I'm asking the wrong people. Perhaps you know. Why can't the trickster get into your friends' minds?" Vincent said.

"I don't know," Cece gritted out.

Vincent slammed the cane down again. Xander and Cece flinched.

The same game went on for far too long as Vincent taunted and tortured them. The more frustrated he got with their defiance, the more brutally and faster he hit Rainer. No matter how many times they said they didn't know, he didn't believe them.

Vincent whipped Rainer three times in quick succession and Cece yanked herself free of the guard who'd been holding her back, running to Rainer. He squeezed her hand, and she kissed his knuckles. Her cheeks were flushed and damp with sweat.

Xander couldn't imagine the agony of both watching and feeling the pain of the person she loved most. If it had been her on the table, Xander would have cracked instantly.

Rainer's back was a sliced-up, bloody mess. The pain must have been staggering. The air smelled like copper. The table, the floor, and Vincent's clothes were speckled with blood and sweat.

Cece met Xander's eyes. He saw her waver. Her hand was poised over her heart as tears poured down her cheeks. It wasn't Vincent's torture that had her sobbing. It was that Rainer was hurting but still sending reassurance through their bond. Xander knew what it was to protect Cece at his own expense. He'd done it for months while Cato tortured him. He saw it now in the way she cried harder a moment after the strikes, her palm pressed to her heart. Xander had never respected Rainer more.

"I can do this all night—until he's fucking dead. One of you is going to crack," Vincent snarled, preparing to strike again.

Cece curled over Rainer's body protectively, and Vincent drew up at the last second.

"No," she snapped. "We don't know. I made Cato forget how to use his magic. Maybe it has to do with that, but none of us know why he can't do it."

Vincent laughed. "You are very tricky, Lady Reznik. The problem is that I'm a liar, and I know a liar when I see one. This is the last piece of information I need to fulfill my deal with the trickster. I'll have it now, and I'll enter this era with myself as a king with no debts left to pay."

"He is barely conscious," Cece said.

"Are you offering to take his place?" Vincent challenged.

Rainer looked up at her sharply, but Cece said nothing.

"I am," Xander said.

Vincent blew out a breath. "Oh, cousin, come on! We've seen this little drama play out before. Plus, I need you able to move around freely and charm these people. You are part of my succession plan. I need the goodwill you've harnessed with the common folk and aristocracy. I also need you to smooth things over with your new in-laws, so we'll eventually need your new wife as well. You're lucky, you know. You have a longer-term purpose than your two friends. Unfortunately for them, they were caught with you. Once I have what I need, and I've closed off my deal with Cato, they have no purpose. I do hate waste," Vincent threatened.

He turned back to Cece. The feral look on his face made Xander's stomach plummet.

"Very well. If none of you want to talk, perhaps I haven't tried the right strategy yet," he said.

Vincent grabbed Cece, pulling her back flush to his front. He held her securely around the waist. He didn't need to say anything for Xander to recognize the look in his eye.

"*There are much worse things than death,*" Cato had told Xander years before.

Once again, Cato was right.

Ever since Cato had reappeared like a living nightmare the day before, dread had prickled Xander's skin. The hairs on the back of his neck stood on end, reminding him that a reckoning was coming. Now that Vincent held Cece against his body, Xander knew what it was.

Two guards untied Rainer from the table and dragged him to a chair. He winced as his back hit the wood, slumping over, unconscious. He quickly regained consciousness as they tied his wrists to the chair—as if he needed restraints. The man looked half-dead.

"If the two of you won't talk, there's only one of you left to hurt," Vincent said. "Now, while I assume she's the one pulling the strings in all of this, I know that the two of you must also know why it is that Cato can't influence Marcos."

Xander looked warily at Cece, but she looked resigned.

Somehow, that was no comfort. Xander knew she could take the pain, but he wasn't sure he could.

"No takers? Good! I was getting bored with this. I have something else in mind for the lovely Lady Reznik."

Vincent put a hand around her throat, caressing her bodice with the other.

Xander's stomach dropped. He went rigid. The guards tightened their grip on his arms. Rainer rolled in and out of consciousness beside him, in too much pain to connect the dots. If Cato was the brilliant psychological strategist, Vincent was the ruthless, brutal tyrant. He had Cato's flair for manipulation and, thanks to his time undercover in their court, a deep understanding of the dynamics that played out between the three of them.

Cece was doing a good job of hiding her fear, but her heartbeat raced, and if Xander could hear it from ten feet away, Vincent could most certainly feel it at the pulse point in her neck.

He didn't seem satisfied with their reaction. His hand tightened on her throat.

"In fact, I think I'll do it right here. Let you both watch. How many men can say they've fucked a goddess?" Vincent taunted. "And I'll have proof. Maybe I'll let my men each take a turn after me."

Vincent's guards grinned at each other and chuckled as if he'd told a hilarious joke. Every story Xander had been told about the trail of violence Vincent left in villages along Argaria's borders rushed into his head at once.

"Maybe if she's as good as you all seem to think, I'll keep her," Vincent chuckled. "Would you enjoy that, Goddess—having my men and your men watch me take the spoils of this war?"

She refused to cower. "The only thing I will enjoy is watching you bleed out from my blade."

Vincent stepped back and backhanded her.

Xander tried to stand, but two guards forced him into a chair.

Cece quickly stood up straight and lifted her chin in defiance as Vincent admired the blotchy red mark rising on her cheek. He brushed his fingers tenderly over it.

Xander was desperate for a way out. He looked at the dagger on the hip of the guard to his left. He could probably get it and take the man down, but Cece would be on her own and there were six other guards in the room. Two beside Rainer, two beside Vincent. There were probably men outside the sitting room doors as well.

No matter how badly Xander wanted to help her, if he acted rashly now, they'd all suffer for it. He'd get one chance, and he'd have to make it count. "Stop this. You should keep her for yourself—as a queen," Xander said. "She's a goddess. No one would cross you. If you shame her in front of your guards, she can never be that."

Vincent laughed. "She was never going to be my queen, cousin. I saw the game you three played in your library. She doesn't fuck like a queen. She fucks like a whore, and that's what she'll be to me. She will be treated to every deviant, twisted thing I can't do to a wife. What a lucky girl you are, Lady Reznik. I have so many creative ideas for you. So many dark, destructive things for you to try."

Cece paled, her panicked gaze shifting from Rainer to Xander.

"You smell so sweet." Vincent's nose grazed up the column of her neck, and she shuddered as his tongue darted out to lick up the same line.

Rainer mumbled something between breathless grunts of pain.

"Trying to give me pointers, McKay?" Vincent chuckled. "I think I know what she likes after that day in the library."

Her knees buckled, but Vincent held her firm. He sank his teeth into the place where her neck and shoulder met, and she flinched. The guards holding Xander in his seat tightened their grip on him. All he could do was watch as Cece tried to squirm from the pain.

"The only way out is through," Vincent whispered. "My patience is wearing thin. If you tell me now, I won't hurt you, Cecilia."

A hysterical giggle bubbled from her lips.

Vincent went rigid. "Why the fuck is she laughing?"

"Because you already hurt her. She feels what Rainer feels," Xander said.

Vincent was quiet, considering this. Then, with deadly precision, he cut through the strap of her gown and the front folded down to her waist, revealing her lacy mauve bustier.

Vincent clicked his tongue. "Would you look at that? It's like she was expecting me."

Several guards laughed.

Cece tried to squirm away, but Vincent pressed his blade to her throat again. "Move again, and I'll have my men break the bones in your fiancé's fingers one by one. Hold still."

His hand brushed over the lace.

Xander watched as Cece's eyes glazed, like she was trying to send herself somewhere far away. She tipped her head back and stared at the ceiling.

"Please stop," she whispered.

"I'll stop when you tell me what I want to know," Vincent said, his gaze meeting Xander's once again.

There was no winning now. Xander knew enough about interrogations to know the pain would not end if she told Vincent what he wanted to know. Interrogations ended in death or escape, and Xander had no escape route for them. If Cece gave up what she knew, she'd no longer be valuable.

"I don't know," she whispered. "None of us do. Only Marcos knows for sure. We compartmentalized knowledge for this very reason. I would have told you when you were brutalizing Rainer if I knew."

Vincent clicked his tongue. "Perhaps you all truly don't know. Only one way to know for sure." He stood straighter. "Enough games, Xander. Be a king for once in your pathetic life. Be a leader and make the right choice. Tell me now, or I'm going to take her to the other room and find out what all the fuss is about. I'll fuck the information right out of her, and if that doesn't work, I'll let my men take turns until the truth comes out. There won't be anything left of her."

Rainer shook his head violently. He mumbled her name, but he was barely conscious.

Two kingdoms balanced on the edge of a knife.

Xander clenched his jaw so tightly he worried his teeth might shatter.

It was Cece or his kingdom.

Xander hated being king. It was a thankless job that he could never do right because it was impossible to know what was right for so many people when he was just one man.

But he loved his home, and he knew that Vincent would destroy it.

Cece met his gaze, a faint, resigned smile on her lips, like she knew before he did what he would do. But he did not want this. He did not want to have to choose between seeing a person he loved hurt and the safety of his kingdom. There was no real greater good.

There was only the man he was now who had learned that being king was about surrendering selfish desires for the safety of his people. It felt wrong to choose anyone other than Cece, but he forced himself to stay still.

It should have felt like a triumph. Like he was finally evolving from Storm Prince to Storm King, but the victory felt hollow.

Cece nodded at Xander. It was barely perceptible. "Don't," she said, her voice low enough that only he would hear. "Don't take this on. You're doing the right thing."

"Very well," Vincent huffed. "Get her ready for me, Grant."

He shoved Cece into the arms of his guard, who dragged her kicking and screaming into the connecting dining room.

"Last chance to save her," Vincent said, his dark eyes roaming from Xander to Rainer.

Rainer surged in his chair and it tipped to its side, landing him in a heap on the floor.

Vincent laughed and sauntered into the dining room, leaving the door open a crack—so they could hear, Xander realized.

A new terror gripped him as a scuffle echoed from the adjoining room. Then, all went silent. And then the screaming started.

47

CECILIA

Cecilia's heart was in her throat as she struggled against the two guards dragging her toward the dining room table. Her knees shook so violently she could barely stay upright.

Name the fear and it loses its power. She'd brought those words back from death and though she knew how to name this, it brought her no comfort at all.

I'm afraid that this is the thing I cannot come back from.

Vincent's threat was the kind that never lost its potency. The familiarity of that violence was so ingrained in women from the time they were young that the first thing she'd come to fear was the mind of a deviant man.

Rainer and Xander had done a terrible job masking their fear, but she supposed they hadn't had years of practice. They might have worried for her, but they didn't understand the dread of that particular violence was as much a part of her as the knowledge of how to do her hair in the morning, how to act at a courtly function, or how to shoot a bow. It was reflected in every interaction with men: *How many people are in this room? Am I wearing something too revealing? Am I being too flirtatious?*

A lifetime of the burden of curbing men's urges had ensured that doing so was so ordinary Cecilia couldn't imagine her life without it.

But now the fear was uncaged, its talons hollowing out her chest.

Her hips hit the table with a thud and the man on her right shoved her chest onto the surface. She glared at him. Grant. She'd heard Vincent call him that.

He seemed too comfortable with this—too used to pinning a woman down—for her to believe he hadn't done it many times before. Her mind spun, remembering what Sylvie had told her about Vincent and his men hurting women in the border villages.

"Why do you play along?" she asked. "Can you only get that which you take? Are you so satisfied with leftovers?"

Grant smirked. "How do you know I don't prefer it that way? Maybe I enjoy watching you struggle."

Cecilia's rage momentarily anchored her. She was going to kill Grant the first chance she got.

Footsteps marched along the stone floor behind her and she stopped squirming.

"The three of you are a perfect ecosystem," Vincent said. "You pull Xander's strings. Rainer pulls yours. I know exactly where to apply pressure to shatter each of you. Those men would do *anything* for you. So this is the last test to see if they really don't know."

She wished she could feel relieved that only she and Xander knew the answer to why Cato wouldn't get into Marcos and Xander's minds.

Rainer knew nothing. He'd been tortured brutally for nothing. If she hadn't given it up for him, she certainly wouldn't give it up for herself.

Vincent's fingers trailed down her back.

Only you can decide who fear will make you, the seer had once said to her. Cecilia knew how to deplete the advantage of an opponent larger and more powerful than herself, but she was tired of running toward the blade. She wanted to flee and hide. She wanted to take Rainer and Xander and all their friends far away from the madness and just let the world fall apart.

Fear made her a trembling victim. Her body rebelled. Her mind rebelled. Her very soul rebelled. She hated it, but she would endure it.

Cecilia thrashed in the guards' hands, nearly slipping away, but it was too late. Vincent's hand shoved her firmly against the table. He hiked her skirts up, and she tried to kick him, but the guards quickly subdued her legs. He hacked at her skirts with his blade until they were less cumbersome. Red silk fell to the floor around her in shredded bits, landing in jagged pieces like claw marks on the stone floor.

She struggled until she felt Vincent's hand on her bottom.

"Look at that ass. It looks exquisite in these lacy little panties," Vincent taunted.

His fingers dug into her skin as he palmed her. Her stomach heaved. She hated how he touched her. She wanted Rainer's hands on her to wipe away the memory of that feeling.

"One last chance," Vincent shouted to the men in the next room.

Please say nothing, Xan, she begged in her mind. Another voice screamed for him to blurt it out and save her. She didn't realize until then that she truly thought he would. She could always count on the intensity with which he loved her. Until then.

She knew it wasn't about that. Like convincing Rainer to plunge the dagger into her heart months before, it was bigger than her. It was about not just saving two kingdoms of people, but protecting the legacy of their friends who had already died for peace. Beyond that, there was no guarantee that Vincent wouldn't enact the same violence once he got the information he wanted. It was the wise decision not to tell.

Tears streamed down her face.

"Don't cry, love." Vincent ground his hardness against her. "I have a feeling you'll enjoy it."

"Fuck you." She jerked her head back, connecting with his cheek, and he stumbled, cursing.

"Hold her still. You're going to pay for that, Cecilia," he said as the guards held her more firmly against the table. Their hands were like iron bands on her arms.

Vincent brought the butt of his blade down on her left hand. A bone snapped and she yelped involuntarily.

"That's right. Let me hear those sweet little screams. Let your men enjoy your agony."

She bit her lip as he brought the butt of his blade down again, refusing to give him the satisfaction.

"Yes, please defy me. It will make it so much more satisfying when I break you," he whispered before shattering another bone. "Scream," he commanded. She kept her mouth shut. "Scream, or I'll give you a reason to really scream."

Fear sliced Cecilia in half. Rainer tugged hard on the other side of their connection, but everything in her was ice-cold fear. She'd hoped he would be unconscious, but there he was trying to fight his way back to her, if only through their bond.

Vincent dropped to his knees, and she felt a blade slice into her left inner thigh. She screamed in surprise and pain.

She bucked wildly, and his hand slapped her ass hard again.

"Stop it, Cecilia." Vincent's angry whisper cut through her. "Stop moving! I'm not doing what you think. I'm marking your inner thigh with my initials so that every man who ever gets between these legs will know I was here. So that you'll never forget. Now scream your fucking head off, or I really will fuck you."

She couldn't understand what was happening. Confusion clouded her mind until she felt another slice of the blade, and she screamed.

"More," he threatened.

She screamed louder. She begged him to stop.

Rainer's love surged through their bond, mixing with his fear and her pain.

You're not alone, it seemed to say. That broke her. She sobbed because she didn't want to be alone, but she didn't want him to feel her fear and pain either.

It was so cruel. Vincent wanted Rainer and Xander to think he was hurting her, and he was, but not in the way any of them had expected. Her relief was short-lived when she realized that in not doing it now, he could keep the threat of it fresh for whatever lay ahead.

Time slowed, marked by the fiery slash of his blade on her thigh and the hysterical sobs that ripped out of her. She waited for the fear to leave her, but she couldn't stop shaking.

By the time Vincent was done with his carving and yanked her shredded skirt back into place, Cecilia's throat was ragged from screaming, but he hadn't done what she was afraid he would.

She told herself that she'd been through worse, but it was cold comfort. She felt dazed and unable to concentrate. The first glimmer of her goddess power flickered to life in her chest, but she couldn't focus her mind. The pain was too bright and her fear too biting. Her skin flashed hot, then cold.

Vincent dragged her back into the other room, tossing her on the floor in front of Rainer and Xander. Her dress was shredded, slicked with sweat, and stuck to her skin. Her legs were tacky with blood that had dripped from her inner thigh down to her ankles.

Rainer's eyes dragged over her, looking for injuries. When they locked on her blood, he lost it. He screamed her name and bucked in his chair.

Tears streamed down his face and Cecilia couldn't find the words to reassure him.

Vincent leaned a hip against the table. "I guess you all really didn't know, huh?"

Rainer's eyes held the murderous promise of a slow death.

Cecilia wanted to tell him that it wasn't what he thought it was, but she felt no less terrorized and humiliated. She couldn't stop shaking, her mind trying desperately to send her far from this room and the scent of blood and sweat and fear in the air.

Vincent hadn't taken what they were afraid he had, but she felt no relief. Instead, it felt like an executioner's blade hanging over her, poised to drop at any moment. There was no guarantee that he wouldn't resort to that violence the next time he didn't get what he wanted. Vincent understood the power of a threat, and he knew that he had very few punches left to pull.

Rainer's love surged through their connection. It reminded her of the way he'd followed her through the wild, the way he'd promised that he'd follow her into any darkness.

You were never alone, it seemed to whisper.

She knew it was true, but her mind no longer felt like it was her own. Cecilia closed her eyes and surrendered to the nightmare.

48

RAINER

Rainer had never felt like more of a failure.

Vincent hurt her—his beautiful Cecilia, who was just coming back to herself, who had just asked Rainer to marry her. Vincent hurt her in a way that Rainer had no idea how to guide her back from.

Rainer could barely look at her. She looked so small and vulnerable sitting on the floor. She winced as she tried to hold her dress together with her broken hand.

Gods, he wanted to hold her, but she had a startled, far-off look in her eye and she'd wrapped her arms around herself like they were the only thing holding her together. The damage was done.

Was anything worth this? Was anything worth seeing someone he loved so much hurt like this?

Her eyes met his, and she shook her head. He didn't understand what she was trying to communicate. Fear and rage consumed him.

Rainer wanted to cut Vincent apart piece by piece and have a healer put him back together so he could do it again, even slower and more painfully. He wanted to kill him a thousand times over. Rainer had never felt so helpless and consumed by fury.

As if summoned by the profound misery, Cato sauntered into the sitting room.

The trickster god took in the scene with apprehension. His eyes passed from Cecilia to Rainer to Xander and finally landed on Vincent.

"You've made quite a mess, Your Majesty," Cato said.

Vincent sighed. "They won't tell me why you can't control Xander or Marcos. I follow through on my deals."

Rainer could have sworn he saw concern on Cato's face when his eyes took in the blood on Cecilia's legs. She met Cato's gaze with indifference.

"You're off the hook on that. I don't need to know now," Cato said blandly. "I don't want Reznik's magic anymore."

"Why not?" Vincent asked.

"I can't pay the price," Cato said dismissively. "Fucking witches and their transactional magic. It's exhausting. I couldn't find an exchange I could live with."

Rainer felt the slightest bit of satisfaction. His back was screaming against the chair. He swore it hurt worse to look at Cecilia. He was terrified to know what Vincent had done and more afraid that it would finally push her beyond Rainer's reach. She'd fought so hard to get back to where she was.

"In that case, I'm going to kill McKay. I enjoy Cecilia's company, so I'll hang on to her for a bit," Vincent said menacingly.

Cecilia's eyes widened. Her panic surged in Rainer's chest as Vincent moved toward him with his dagger in hand.

"Wait!" Cato said. "He's the best swordsman in all of Olney. Hails from a very impressive family. Could you not use such a man on your guard?"

Rainer froze. Of course Cato knew his lineage. He only hoped the god didn't share it with the whole room. He could not bear the weight of it on a day he'd failed so miserably.

Vincent turned on him. "You think I could control him?"

Cato smirked. "I think he could become controllable."

"Until the moment he uses that well-trained sword hand to bury a blade in my back," Vincent snapped. "What kind of fool do you take me for?"

Cato narrowed his eyes. "The kind with access to the goddess of mind and memory and the god of manipulation and influence."

Rainer thought it was impossible to hate Cato more than he had that day on the beach a year ago, but he did now. His mind was sluggish with exhaustion and pain, but he saw the spark of interest in Vincent's eyes and knew it couldn't be good.

"What do you have in mind?" Vincent asked.

"Make Cecilia make him forget her instead," Cato said, buffing his fingernails on his tunic. "That would be much more potent torture than the mercy of a swift death. Then I can manipulate what memories he has left to make him the kind of soldier every king needs—a blindly loyal one. Rainer McKay does so love his self-righteousness. If he believes you're the rightful king, he will stop at nothing to make sure you hold on to your throne."

Cecilia's burning hot rage shot through Rainer's chest. He would have felt the same if he didn't catch how Cato seemed eager for Vincent to agree. Why would Cato want him alive? Rainer tried to think clearly, but it was hard to think around anything but the pain in his back and his fear for Cecilia.

Vincent gazed curiously at the trickster god. "Why would I do that when I can so easily dispatch him?"

Cato grinned. "It will keep all of your tools in place until you need them. She won't run if he's here, and Xander won't run without her." He leaned in close and whispered in Vincent's ear.

Vincent's eyes lit up, and a half-grin tugged at his lips. He was interested. Rainer watched as the self-proclaimed king calculated things in his mind. "He *is* an excellent swordsman."

"The best," Xander said. "Better than me, even."

Xander was clearly seeing something that Rainer couldn't.

He hated the idea of being used as a tool or a way of controlling Cecilia, but it was better than death. Rainer also couldn't imagine forgetting her. She was woven into every part of him. She had been the biggest fixture in his life since he was eight years old.

"I'll need you to add some of your own power to make this a reasonable option. I need him pliant and motivated," Vincent said.

"If we do this instead of killing him, I'll consider us even," Cato said meaningfully.

Vincent's face lit up. He had what he wanted. "I could just have a slayer do it," he mused.

"No!" Cecilia shook her head. "Slayers are butchers. You need someone who can surgically extricate bits and pieces. I can do it."

It was clear from her face that she didn't want to, but she was resigned to it all the same. It was their only chance.

Vincent sighed heavily, as if he was making a great sacrifice. "All right. If this clears the ledger between us."

Cato shook his hand and looked at Cecilia with a shrug.

"All right, here's the bargain I can offer," Cato started. "Cecilia will pull all of his memories of herself. No one can remind him when he wakes. You can't interfere or have someone else interfere for you. If he gets his memories back, he has to do so independently. That's to make things fair." He winked at Cecilia. "I can't have you make him forget only for you and Xander to instantly help him remember. I will walk through the castle once a day to enforce that manipulation on everyone in residence here. You won't be able to tell him anything that has happened here today via any method of communication, spoken or written word or memory, unless he remembers on his own. No one in the castle will be able to speak of what has happened here aloud. It will simply be as if he has amnesia, and it's best that he remembers on his own. We will say it's the healer's orders."

Cecilia and Xander both nodded, and dread rose in Rainer's stomach.

"You both have to say it," Cato said.

Cecilia gritted her teeth, her face a mix of fear and anger. "I agree."

"I agree," Xander said, turning to look at Cecilia. "Can you do it now with the Godsbane in your system?"

She nodded. "It's almost worn off."

"Have at it, Little Dove." Cato gestured toward Rainer.

She knelt in front of Rainer and cupped his cheek with a trembling hand. Rainer had never wished for magic as much as he did at that moment. She was hurt and terrified and all he wanted was to go back in time and never have brought her here to begin with.

Her eyes were glassy as she kissed him. All the emotions she'd been holding back flooded their connection at once. She was a wreck of fear and grief and rage.

"Sweetheart, it's going to be okay," Rainer promised. The words meant nothing. Everything was already so wrong.

Still, he clasped her face in his hands and kissed her to calm her. He covered her face in kisses, tasting the salt of her tears.

"What if I take too much?" Cecilia sobbed.

"Cece, I could never forget you. You have my whole heart." Rainer tried to sound reassuring.

"I don't know, I'm really talented, Rain," she mumbled through her tears.

Rainer laughed. Only she would joke at a time like this. "And so modest. I crescent promise I will come back to you. Just trust me like I trusted you last time."

"But I was lying." She crumpled over under great, heaving sobs.

Rainer briefly met Xander's eyes over her shoulder. Xander swallowed hard and gave him a firm nod. They didn't need to speak the words for Rainer to know that Xander would protect her as best he could for as long as he could. It was the only comfort Rainer could hope for, though it wasn't as potent as it would have been even a day earlier.

But Xander had let Cecilia be hurt. He'd finally become a king and chosen his kingdom over his love for her. Rainer truly never thought it would happen, even if it was the exact thing they were all hoping for.

Still, he knew from the pain in Xander's eyes that it was an impossible choice, and the guilt of it had taken something from him he couldn't get back. Rainer put his faith in his long-time rival, his love, and their friends who had escaped. Most of all, he put his faith in himself that he'd be able to remember the person he loved most in the world.

Rainer knew exactly what she'd be taking. There was hardly anything he could remember before Cecilia. There was so little that existed without her. Even when she wasn't around, he'd be worried about her, thinking of her, or feeling her emotions. He couldn't let her know how scared he was of what he might become without the memories of the person who'd brightened all his days.

So he took her hand and forced a smile like he had so many times before when he wanted to protect her.

49

CECILIA

Cecilia's broken hand throbbed, but the terror of taking Rainer's memories sharpened her mind. Of course, him losing his memory was better than losing his life, but she couldn't bear to rob him of the history that was so fundamental to everything that had made him the man she loved.

"I am less worried about you not remembering me and more worried you won't remember *you*," Cecilia whispered. "Memory is so complex. I'm in all of your developmental memories. You might have a completely different personality."

She didn't want to oversell herself, but a life without her meant a life without most of the memories of her father and Aunt Clara and many memories with Rainer's own mother. If he was left with only memories of Raymond McKay, he was sure to be colder, rougher, more competitive. She could not imagine who Rainer would be if his father had his way.

"You've told me memory is more than just the mind," Rainer said. "It lives in the body, the emotions. I won't forget me because I won't forget you. I crescent promise," he said, kissing the scar on her palm. She winced in pain as his lips brushed the skin that was already beginning to bruise.

"Do you really think my heart could forget you when you've been wrapped around it for more than half my life?" Rainer whispered. "Do you think I wouldn't feel you the moment you're close to me? I could never forget you. You and I are *infinite*."

She shook her head, her panic like an icy fist squeezing around her heart. "Please don't ask me to do this."

Cecilia wasn't even sure if she was talking to him or Vincent. Through every awful thing that had happened to her since that last Gauntlet run, Rainer had been there to anchor her. Now she would have to be strong for both of them. Fear clawed at her chest and she could not make herself move.

Rainer brought a hand to her chin, wincing as he tilted her chin up. "I would know you even if battle blinded me. I would know by the way you quiet the rest of the world to a hum, by the breath you take before you speak and the way you hold it when you're trying not to cry. I would know the scent of you on the wind and the way it's stitched to every memory of love in my life. And I would even know the absence of you if we'd never met, like a dark night sky aching for the shine of stars. I will always know you, Cecilia."

She choked on a sob. "And you say you're not good with words."

Rainer smiled and kissed her forehead. "If you need to borrow my certainty, you can, because you are unforgettable. I'm going to remember you, and then I'm going to spend the rest of our lives making new memories—writing new stories."

He looked at her. Waiting for her to say it. Waiting for her permission.

"Brave with my hand," Rainer whispered.

She leaned in and kissed him long and slow and sweet—until the knot in her chest began to unwind and she was breathless.

"Brave with my heart," Cecilia rasped, her chin quivering.

Rainer nodded. She pressed her hand up to his sleeve, discreetly wiping away one of the wards from his skin and ensuring that her goddess magic would work on him.

"How long will it take?" Vincent asked. "I'll take the bracelet off while you're working, but if I get even a hint of trouble, the guard will kill Rainer."

A guard stepped behind Rainer, pressing a dagger to his throat. She tried not to wince when Vincent removed her Unsummoner bracelet.

Her magic rushed back to her like a burst of energy. It was tempting to try to use it, but she wasn't thinking clearly, and she didn't trust herself to take all of them out before they could hurt Rainer or Xander. Especially since several of Vincent's guards had magic. One false move and he'd have a slayer rip away Rainer's memories and they wouldn't care at all about preserving the man she loved.

"Truly, I don't know how long," Cecilia admitted. "I've never taken so much from someone. There are limits to my power. I can only do so much at a time. It might take days or hours."

"Very well. Do it already," Vincent said. There was no compassion on his face. No understanding of what it was to love someone and wipe every bit of shared history from their mind.

"The deal has been made, and she must follow through," Cato said. "You may as well busy yourself with your next bit of chaos. Your men and I can oversee this. I'll report back to you when it's done, and we can discuss what else you'd like me to do."

Vincent nodded and left the room with several of his guards.

Cecilia brushed against Rainer's mind, and he let her in. She paused right on the precipice of beginning. Her goddess powers weren't as permanent anymore, evidenced by how many of her memory loss patients needed to return to the clinic for treatment. Perhaps she could use that power to place a sort of mental wall between Rainer and the most precious memories in the hope that it would eventually crumble and he'd remember her.

She went back over Cato's words. According to her agreement, she wasn't allowed to help Rainer remember anything, but this was technically just a different way to make him forget. She'd need to be careful, meticulous, and incredibly intentional with what she erased forever with her memory witch magic, and what she preserved behind a wall of goddess magic.

"Bring to mind a memory of a time when you were very in love with me," she said.

Immediately, his mind came to life with a vision of her on her knees, proposing to him just days earlier.

Cecilia fought off tears as she tugged on the emotional signature of the memory. It connected to so many others in a web, some with thick, corded lines, other with finer gossamer threads. This was her. This was the entirety of her presence in Rainer's life. Seeing it all at once stole her breath. Her magic wavered, the lit pathways in his mind flickering.

Her blood started to burn as she tried to fight the deal she'd made with Cato. This is what happened if you tried to go back on a godly bargain; your body boiled until you obeyed.

She was such a bright presence in his mind, woven into so many areas of his consciousness. She didn't want to take it. But she forced herself to pull on the thickest cords.

There was the moment she'd died on the beach; the first time they'd slept together; the night under the Summer Firestorm meteor shower when he refused to tell her what he'd wished for; all the way back to the day they met when she'd handed him her green ribbon.

Collecting them like golden thread on a tapestry, she cut the cords between them and the rest of the bunch. Seeing his most precious memories of her, all connected and bright with love, was enough to make her feel like she was going to implode.

"Please." It came out in a breathless sob—a prayer to herself. *Please be good enough. Please don't ruin this person I love more than life itself. Please let him still love me.*

Of all the things that broke her heart, nothing had ever cut so deep, left her feeling so raw and helpless as being forced to rob Rainer of his joy and rob herself of his love.

She tugged on the thickest corded threads until they were all wrapped together in the bundle of memories. Carefully, she used her goddess magic to build a box around them. As a last touch, she tucked in the memory of her being dragged away by Vincent, of feeling her fear through their bond and Rainer's desperation to get to her. The memory of his failure. That alone would ensure that he was wary of even trying to recover these. It was a risk, but it also tied remembering her to remembering what had left him with no memory to begin with. If he was brave enough to recover it, he might recover her, too.

Maybe it was the hope in her, the magic that she'd used to save the two kingdoms, that made her believe it could work. Or maybe she could not survive if she took the rest without trying to preserve some of it.

Now it was time for the hard part. Her eyes burned, and she blinked away tears as she laced her way between the rest of the thinly braided memories. One by one, she began to tug them into her own mind. She vented as much old memory as she could risk losing so that she could keep as many of his memories as possible.

Rainer held on. It was a reflex—she knew that from years of practice—but his desperation to keep her sent her into a fit of sobs.

"I'm sorry, Rain. I'm trying to be gentle, but don't fight, or it will hurt more," Cecilia whispered.

He leaned his forehead against hers and relented to her magic. Rainer let her rip herself from his mind bit by bit. At first, it was okay, but as she went on, fear and anxiety spun through their bond.

"It's okay," she soothed.

She used her hope magic to calm him. He relaxed as her hand pressed to the skin at the back of his neck.

She was relieved and terrified when he stopped struggling and let her take them.

The more she stole, the more fear took root in her. She didn't want to see his eyes open and look at her with no recognition.

Cecilia had been saved by Rainer's love. Losing that felt like dying all over again.

50

XANDER

Xander watched as Cece removed herself from the mind of the man she loved. Slowly, painfully, meticulously, with exhaustive attention to detail. It was clearly draining magic. She worked through the night and into the next day, her body hunched over Rainer's, her hands trembling.

Last time, Xander had been able to insulate her, but this time he could do nothing but watch her suffer through it.

It was clear from Rainer's wincing that it was painful for him, psychological torment to go along with the physical torment of the severe wounds covering his back. For Cece, it was only emotionally destructive.

Xander stood watch, occasionally forcing her to take a break when he saw her faltering.

"Cece, rest for a little," he pleaded. "Eat something. We need Magdalena to look at his back, anyway."

"She didn't get out?" Cece asked, finally lifting her weary gaze to look at him. Her eyes were bloodshot and puffy from crying, and her posture was so crumpled a stiff breeze could blow her over.

Xander shook his head. He peered into the hall and asked one of

Vincent's guards to summon the healer, and Magdalena appeared a moment later.

"You were supposed to leave," Xander said.

Magdalena had brought him into the world. He was the first baby she'd ever delivered. She'd been like an aunt to him through the years, tending to the cuts and scrapes born of reckless youth. He wished she'd made her way to safety with the others, but he was glad she was there to help Rainer.

"Actually, I chose to stay. I've served this family my entire life, and I refuse to leave the king in a lurch. Especially with the two of you cut off from your powers," Magdalena said, gesturing to the Unsummoner bracelets.

"I can do it," Cece insisted. "I can keep going."

She sipped some water and flicked dry blood away from her inner ankle. Xander's heart sank at the sight of it. He'd promised he would always protect her, and he hadn't.

Twice in two days, he'd chosen his kingdom over Cece—once in his heart and once in a much more literal way. He was sure he'd made the right choice in not speaking up, but knowing it was right made him no less heartbroken and sick to his stomach.

Magdalena crossed the room to where Rainer lay on his stomach on a bench. She shook her head and tutted at the grotesque lash wounds on his back. She was practiced and incredibly talented, but Xander couldn't imagine that she'd be able to fix the gruesome mess of blood and broken skin.

Magdalena and Cece worked side by side, Cece destroying Rainer's mind as Magdalena healed his body.

In the end, it only took a little under two days for Cece to rip herself from a lifetime of Rainer's memories.

Cece was dead on her feet. Magdalena had stayed up with her all night, healing the lashing wounds. It took hours, even with her years of skill and experience, and considering what it had looked like to begin with, she'd worked a small miracle. Rainer's skin was as good as it would get given the lashing he'd taken. His back was covered in long, shiny scars, a shade or two lighter than his skin.

Magdalena took Rainer's pulse, her gaze locked on the writing on his inner wrist.

"Wards," the healer said. "I haven't seen this kind in years."

"So that's how you kept me out."

Xander startled. Cato leaned against the doorframe. He'd left a half-hour before to get breakfast, and Xander hadn't heard him return.

"It makes sense," Cato laughed. "I should have realized sooner. I knew that stone wall sensation. I just haven't felt it in many years. Other than when I talked to those damned ancient witches."

"I hope you're enjoying this," Xander said morosely. He expected to be more afraid of Cato after all the god had done to him, but now he just felt weary in a bone-deep way.

"On the contrary. I'm not enjoying it at all, but I assumed when faced with the death of the love of her life and the death of his memory, Cece would choose the latter," Cato sighed.

"Why would you care?" Xander asked. "You wanted to kill her before."

Cato glanced warily at Cece. "I never wanted to kill her. I didn't even want to kill you. You were all just a means to an end. There is a great deal of violence I am comfortable with and some that I am not."

Cece refused to look at him. Her gaze was still glued to Rainer's sleeping face.

"You got tired of the games, but you got tired too late," she rasped.

Cato frowned and swallowed hard, his gaze wandering to the blood on her legs. "I did, and I'm sorry that Vincent—"

Cece's laugh was brittle and disbelieving. "Oh, is this the line, Cato? This the violence you can't speak of? All that lying and manipulating, but you cannot bear to even speak of the fallout? Blood on my chest is fine, but blood on my thighs is not?"

Cato flinched. He'd been heartless for so long, but Xander wondered if his newfound humanity and the frailty of mortality had put him in touch with emotions he'd ignored for years.

"Go away," she said. "I can't stand the sight of you, and I'm not done with him yet."

"You haven't worked on him in fifteen minutes now. You're done. I need to work on him. I have instructions from the king and a bargain I'm compelled to honor. I know you don't see it this way, but this was the best option. If I hadn't stepped in, Rainer would be dead," Cato said.

Cece still refused to look at him.

"I have to manipulate what memories he has left to believe that Vincent is king or else he will wake up and be even more confused and likely violent. I made a deal. I cannot go back on it now. I have to make him into something that Vincent finds useful or else he might just kill him," Cato said. His voice was almost soothing.

Cece's head was bowed in resignation. She scooted away, resting her head against Rainer's thigh, her eyelids fluttering as the weight of her exhaustion pressed down on her.

Xander sat down beside her, between her and Cato.

The trickster god knelt beside Rainer's unconscious body and worked for another hour as Cece dozed. Xander watched her, his mouth crammed with questions he didn't dare speak. She had to still be in pain. She needed to be examined, but he was too afraid to startle her from whatever survival mode had kicked in.

Finally, Cato stood and gestured for the guards to carry Rainer up to his new room. Xander, Magdalena, and Cece followed.

Magdalena tried to get Cece to take a bath and change, but she only agreed to let the healer fix her broken hand before she climbed into bed next to Rainer and fell asleep beside him.

Xander and Magdalena sat vigil, waiting for Rainer to wake up, but he slept through the next day and through that evening too.

Xander watched Cece desperately whispering to Rainer, trying to wake him up.

"I might have taken too much," she said, running her fingers through Rainer's hair.

"You didn't," Xander assured her.

"You don't know that. I was in so much of his life. I just don't know. Maybe he can't make his way back to the surface. And who knows what Cato did," she said, brushing away a few tears.

"It's going to be all right," Xander insisted, but he knew the words were hollow. What was it worth to try to save her now when he'd just let her down so badly?

Xander's timing had always been terrible. It figured that he'd managed to become the king everyone wanted him to be just days before his crown was taken by his cousin. He supposed he deserved it. He'd spent a year doing nothing but resenting the responsibility.

Xander gave up Cece and she gave up parts of herself that she'd never get back. The guilt made him sick and hot with impotent rage.

He sent up a silent prayer that Evan, Jessamin, and the rest of his friends had made it out safely. He made a mental note to sneak out and drop a message in several of their contingency locations. Evan's contingencies had seemed over the top. Now Xander was grateful his friend made him memorize so many fallback plans in case of an invasion. He was comforted by the fact that Vincent would have flaunted it if he'd captured their friends.

If Xander really wanted to prove once and for all that he was the leader Argaria deserved, he needed to stand and fight now, however he could. While Vincent still needed him, Xander needed to do exactly what his cousin had done and sweep his power right out from under him. He'd play along. He'd keep Rainer and Cece out of trouble, and when the moment was right, he'd return the favor and knock his cousin off the throne.

51

EVAN

Evan paced the center aisle of the Temple of Aurelia. He'd succeeded in getting Jessamin, her guards, Cal and Sylvie, and much of the Castle Savero staff out before Vincent's men closed in. It felt like a hollow victory. He'd protected the woman he loved and his new queen, but he'd let Xander down. He had missed a piece of the puzzle, and it had cost his friends dearly.

He'd forgotten the money. It was the same piece that had nagged at him for months.

Three full days had passed, but the shock was still fresh. Candle-light flickered through the stained glass of the temple, casting eerie reflections on the ceiling.

Evan tapped his thumb against each of his fingers, trying to settle and focus his mind, and turned his attention back to Jessamin.

"We need to go back! We cannot leave my husband to that animal," Jessamin insisted.

Maren laid a comforting hand on her shoulder, and another of her guards, the one who wore a veil, whispered softly in her ear.

Evan knew how Jessamin felt. After they realized Spellman had betrayed them, they were trapped in the passageway, listening to Rainer be tortured. It was excruciating listening to their friends suffer when they could do nothing to help. Then, a passageway door to their right had opened. Evan and Sylvie were several rooms away when the screaming started. He had to practically drag Jessamin and Sylvie out.

"I promised Xander to get you to safety. You can help much more from here than you could inside. We need your people," Evan said, bringing his attention back to Jessamin.

Jessamin's eyes went wide as reality settled in. Her face fell. "My mother is complicated. I'm not sure she will send battalions, and even so, it will take some time."

Evan leaned his head back against the wall and sighed. It was precisely what he feared from Novum. They expected an alliance that meant support of goods and trade, not a military force. He would need to tread carefully and speak to the warrior in Jessamin. His new queen was very temperate—careful but also proud. She wouldn't want Vincent to think he could march into her kingdom and take over her new house.

"Your Grace, we will figure this out," Sylvie said, placing a hand on her shoulder. "The three of them are a good team. If anyone can get out of this, they will find a way. Cece has been trapped in that castle once before, and Xander grew up there. They will be able to find a way out. Rainer is strong. He will be okay. They will figure out a way to sort this out. The best thing we can do is be ready when they need our help."

Her voice was soothing, and her words seemed to settle Jessamin, but when her eyes met Evan's, he saw his doubt reflected.

Screaming. The last thing they had heard was Cecilia screaming her head off. It went against everything in him to leave them, but Xander and Cecilia had both made him promise to get Jessamin and Sylvie out.

What truly disturbed him was imagining what could have made her scream so violently. He'd seen Cecilia barely flinch when five bones were broken in her hand. He couldn't imagine what would have made her wail like that. He kept his concern to himself, though he assumed that Sylvie was thinking the same thing.

He was grateful that he and Xander had long ago put contingency plans in place for this type of situation. They had three separate methods of communicating, assuming Xander wasn't simply thrown into a dungeon.

From what Evan knew of Vincent, which was clearly not enough, he wouldn't get rid of Xander until he ceased being useful. For now, he'd need the former king to establish credibility with any of the nobility he didn't already own. They were split pretty evenly down the middle. It would be foolish of Vincent not to manipulate Xander into cooperating. It was likely that the imposter king knew Xander well enough to realize that Cecilia was all the leverage he needed to keep Xander well in hand.

It was entirely possible that was the whole reason Cecilia was being tortured. Evan shuddered at the realization. She would provide leverage against some of Xander's impulses. He wouldn't leave her there, and it was likely that Xander was more useful under Vincent's thumb than out in the wild, at least for the time being.

Vincent would also likely use Rainer as a way to get Cecilia to do his bidding. That was a bigger concern.

Evan wondered who was still on the inside. Perhaps Chris and Reese had escaped, or perhaps they could help. Only time would tell.

He was startled from his thoughts by Sylvie's arm sliding around his waist.

"I can't get the sound of her screaming out of my head. We shouldn't have left," she whispered. She leaned her head on his shoulder and burrowed into his arms.

He loved having her there, solid, warm, steady, grounding him from the rush of his thoughts.

"We don't know what it was," Evan said. "She's bounced back from worse."

"There's only one thing that would have made her scream like that," Sylvie said, her voice tight with grief. She shook her head. "You don't know what it's like to feel helpless like that when someone is holding you down—to feel like it's somehow your fault and you can't fight back. To feel like no one will believe you because you're pretty and you flirt and so you must have been asking for it."

Terrible recognition stole through Evan—the last piece of a puzzle clicking into place. Sylvie was speaking from personal experience. This was why she'd taken the violence against the refugees sheltered at the Temple of Aurelia so personally. That was why she spent hours volunteering to help the women there. Some man— some dead man, if Evan had his way—had hurt her and he could do nothing to make it better. Rage climbed up from his stomach like vines that threatened to choke him.

"When that happens—" She cleared her throat. "If that happens, the wounds are more than just physical. It can take years to come back. Evan, the damage—"

"When?" he asked. "Who did that to you?"

Sylvie shook her head and swallowed hard. "It's not important. It was a long time ago, and Cal took care of it. It wasn't what it could have been, but it still affected me for years. It's part of the reason why Cal and I—"

She didn't finish, but suddenly something Evan never understood clicked into place. Someone had hurt her and it affected her so profoundly that she'd ended her relationship with Cal. Evan had only ever seen from the outside the way that assault affected relationships. He'd watched peers struggle to understand and support friends and lovers who had been through it.

Now it felt impossibly personal. Evan wanted to burn down the two kingdoms just to be certain he'd wiped whatever fucker hurt Sylvie from the map. Instead, he shoved the anger away and struggled for some clarity.

He refused to admit that it could be a possibility because the thought of that happening to Cecilia now was unbearable. It was yet another failure that he couldn't accept as fact until he had to.

Evan tried to sound reassuring. "She'll be okay. Xander wouldn't let her be hurt like that, and neither would Rainer. We have to have some faith in them...even if it's hard. I wanted to charge in there as much as you did. But we are of much more use to them on the outside with Jess's army than we are captured along with them. We have to keep our heads."

She looked up at him with tears in her pale blue eyes.

"I know," he whispered. "I feel the same way, but we have to keep it together so Jess stays calm. We can figure this out. I have ways of communicating with Xander. We'll know soon what's going on in there, but I need to sneak away and check our drop-off spots, okay? Can you and Cal distract the girls while I'm gone?"

She nodded. "You'll be careful?"

"Of course." He pulled her into a quick kiss, and she tried to hide her surprise. He made a point of only showing affection in private, but he could tell she needed it. She smiled faintly as she waved to him, and he sneaked out the door.

As he made his way into the frozen night, his breath pushing out in front of him, he prayed to any god that would listen that things inside the castle weren't as bad as he feared. He hoped there would be a note waiting at one of their checkpoints.

Evan crept through the quiet city of Ardenis, ducking into shadows whenever guard patrols marched through the streets. A hush had fallen over the town as if they, too, were trapped under a blanket of grief and loss. The lack of bustling even around popular pubs was unnerving.

He checked the first drop point on the old hunter training grounds, poking at loose stones in the wall. He found nothing. Anxiety pounded through him, his heart racing as he moved on to the second drop point. As he rounded the corner to the royal stables and ducked into the pen at the far end, he saw it.

Tucked into an old worn-down saddlebag was a tiny bird-shaped note. He let out a quiet sigh of relief.

Hope was a fragile thing, but Evan clung to it.

52

CECILIA

Cecilia lay in a bed in the healer's suite. She hadn't moved since Vincent's guards dragged her out of Rainer's arms and tossed her there.

He wasn't waking up. It was her worst fear. Worse even than Rainer forgetting her was Rainer never waking up because he didn't have enough of his mind left to resurface.

Cecilia was wrecked. She'd ruined the love of her life. Even trying to lead him out of the dark by telling familiar fairy tales hadn't roused him.

Now Xander and the healer were hovering around her, waiting for her to let them help, but she didn't want to talk or be touched or comforted.

"Cece, I'm sorry," Xander said.

He reached for her hand, but she shrunk away.

She couldn't stand to be touched, nor could she stand the pity on his face. If she thought about what might have happened—what still could happen—she would break. She shuddered at the thought of it. Her stomach heaved.

Magdalena cleared her throat, crossing the room to sit next to the bed.

"Dear, you have to let me examine you," she said softly. "You have to let me heal you. The king has insisted."

"The king is not the king," Cecilia mumbled.

Magdalena smiled sadly. "That may be true, but we are still at his mercy."

Days had passed but Cecilia still couldn't stop shaking.

"Your Grace, please leave so I can speak with her alone," Magdalena said.

Xander hesitated but nodded and left them. Even with his presence gone from the room, Cecilia knew he was just pacing outside, likely hearing everything she said and feeling guilty for something that was in no way his fault.

Mika appeared in the doorway. "Lady Reznik, may I come in?"

Cecilia nodded. "Please make Xander leave. I'll find him later. I just can't have him there. I can't have him hear everything. Please?"

Mika nodded and disappeared, returning a few moments later. "He's very devoted to you. He didn't want to leave. He feels terribly guilty."

Cecilia shook her head. "He thinks I blame him, but he made the right choice."

Mika nodded. "He'll be fine."

"And Rainer?" Cecilia asked.

Magdalena and Mika locked eyes.

"He's still sleeping," Magdalena said. "I promise we will tell you as soon as we know more."

Cecilia swallowed hard. "I don't know what that much memory loss will do to a person. It could change his entire personality. What if—"

Mika held up a hand. "Let's not go there. That's not a burden you need to carry yet. Right now, you need to worry about yourself."

Cecilia wanted to lash out at the woman for her pity, but when she met the healer's eyes, she saw stark recognition.

"What would Rainer do if he were here?" Mika asked.

Cecilia wanted to hoard the memory from these strangers as much as she wanted to speak it to comfort herself. "He'd lay in bed beside me, hold my hand, and ask how heavy it is. Then he'd let me pass my feelings across to him. It's like our own language. If I send grief, he'd take it and send love back. If I sent anxiety, he'd send calm. It's like what he feels makes room for what I feel, and vice versa. We've always done that when one of us is struggling."

Mika and Magdalena stared at her.

"What?" Cecilia asked.

"That just sounds so wonderful," Mika said softly.

Grief was a boulder in her chest. "It is. It's second nature at this point. I can just feel what he needs and make room for whatever is weighing on him. I take it for granted. I miss it."

"Is the connection gone?" Magdalena asked.

Cecilia felt into her heart space. The anxious baseline of Rainer still buzzed there, warm and familiar, like a soft blanket around her heart. "No, it's still there, but he's going to be confused enough as it is with none of his memories."

She would try to close it off to keep from confusing him, but she had no doubt that the more stress she was under, the less she'd be able to control it. The bond was meant to protect her, and if she was in peril, which she would be daily now, Rainer would feel it.

She tried to imagine feeling the bond with no understanding of what it was. It would be like getting hit with a flood of emotions with no context or reason.

The women fell into a heavy silence.

"Do you want to talk about what exactly happened? Mags says you haven't said anything about what Vincent did," Mika said, sitting on the edge of the bed.

Cecilia looked down at her hands in her lap and said nothing.

"Xander said you were bleeding. You must be in pain. Will you let Mags heal you?" Mika's voice was soothing, gentle, inviting.

"I'm okay," Cecilia said, finally meeting her eyes.

Mika's face softened. "You don't have to be."

"I don't even know you." Tears sprung to Cecilia's eyes, but she blinked them back. She wasn't sure she'd be able to stop if she started, so she refused to cry. "Nothing happened. He didn't—it's a cut on my leg. It's not what it looked like."

Mika's face went steely. "It's not *nothing*. Any time a man puts his hands on you unwelcome is not *nothing*. Any time a man makes you feel afraid of what might happen and you would be powerless to stop him is not *nothing*."

Cecilia met her eyes and knew that Mika was speaking from personal experience. She reached out her hand and Mika took it.

"It's not nothing," Mika repeated. "I'm sorry that happened to you."

She and Magdalena exchanged a look.

"It's a club that no one wants to be a part of, and no one talks about membership to, but far too many have been subjected to that violence," Mika continued. "I'm here to tell you that you will handle it however you want to. You might have a reputation for being brave, but you don't need to be in this room. In here, it's just the three of us."

Magdalena finally spoke. "And all three of us are part of that club or have lost someone to it."

Cecilia squeezed Mika's hand.

Finally, the tears came. She sobbed. She let herself fully feel the terror she'd felt when Vincent bent her over that table. When the guards held her pinned there when he sliced his dagger into her inner thigh. Her body shook with the sobs.

"Can we hug you?" Mika asked.

Cecilia nodded, and the two women—two strangers who were bonded to her by horror alone—wrapped her in a cocoon of their arms.

When she finally settled, she let Magdalena lift her dress and look at Vincent's initials sliced into her thigh. Magdalena and Mika looked ill at the sight of it.

"Is it bad?" Cecilia asked.

Mika swallowed hard. "No, but it needs to be cleaned. And unfortunately it's familiar. We've worked with many of the women sheltered at the Temple of Aurelia, but we also recognize it for a more personal reason."

Sadness swelled in the air around Mika and Magdalena.

"I've been instructed to leave his 'brand,' as he calls it, but I'm not going to do that," Magdalena said.

While it made Cecilia feel sick to think about Vincent leaving a permanent mark on her body tied to the memory of that horrifying day, she worried if it was healed, he'd simply do it again.

"I'm afraid it will get both of us in trouble if you do that," Cecilia said. "I have a better idea. Can you heal it, and then maybe we can cast a glamour of it being there? Do you know someone...someone you trust enough to do it?"

Magdalena winced. "The only person I know who could is—"

The realization struck Cecilia like an arrow. "Cato."

Magdalena nodded. "He's still here. I will summon him."

She hurried from the room before Cecilia could stop her. She didn't want to see Cato again and she definitely didn't want Cato glamouring her inner thigh, but she also didn't want to get Magdalena in trouble, especially after she'd done such a meticulous job healing Rainer.

A few moments later, Magdalena returned with Cato.

Mercifully, he said nothing, perhaps because Cecilia wouldn't even look at him, or perhaps because he had run out of ways to taunt her.

Magdalena sat on the edge of the bed. She wiped the wound clean with alcohol before placing her palm over it. Tingling warmth spread down Cecilia's thigh and the relief was instant. The healer drew away and Cato took her place.

Cecilia held his gaze as his warm hand brushed her thigh, but she refused to flinch and give him another victory.

"Little Dove, I—"

"Are you finished?" Cecilia snapped.

Cato nodded.

"Then get out."

Cato didn't argue. He stood and left the room without another word.

She expected Magdalena and Mika to leave as well, but they hovered.

"You both don't need to babysit. It's not a big deal. Vincent didn't do anything more than touch me and cut me," Cecilia said.

"That's enough," Mika said. The hard line of her jaw silenced any argument from Cecilia.

"Why are you both helping me? It could get you killed," Cecilia said.

A look passed between the two women. Magdalena nodded at Mika.

"Vincent Savero took something from me," Mika said.

Cecilia swallowed hard. Her anger was swift and vicious. "This same something?"

"No. The love of my life, Ivy. He hurt her. He left the same wounds as well as some I couldn't see," Mika whispered.

Cecilia's stomach dropped. "I am so sorry."

"So am I, but that's why I'm here," Mika said. "It's why I've been working with Evan and why I've been waiting four years for this. Four years to get my revenge. We both have."

"Mika loved my daughter," Magdalena said. "My Ivy was going to serve as healer to Davide when he became king. She was helping tend to a village on the outskirts that was dealing with winter fever when Vincent's men attacked. When she returned, she was not the same and we could not bring her back to herself and because of his violence—" Magdalena's voice broke. "We lost her."

"I am so sorry for your loss," Cecilia said.

"Thank you. I'm sorry for yours."

"It cannot compare," Cecilia said, shaking her head.

"Nor should it be compared," Magdalena corrected her. "Take it from a healer. Comparing wounds is pointless. Our attention needs to be focused on those who afflicted that damage."

"I have trained and fought and fucked for this," Mika said, her voice full of venom. "I will kill Vincent Savero. I promise you that. We just wanted you to know that what happened to you—what happened to our Ivy won't happen to anyone else ever again. We are going to end this."

Magdalena nodded. "What we want to know is—will you help us?"

Cecilia smiled faintly. An army of women, young and old, taking down a tyrannical usurper. She thought nothing would drag her from that bed, but the two of them might have found the one thing that could.

"What can I do?" Cecilia asked.

Magdalena and Mika nodded their approval and sat down with her to scheme.

Revenge wasn't the best motivator, but Cecilia would help them take down Vincent Savero, and then she was going to get *her* Rainer back, no matter how long it took. She'd promised him the rest of her days by his side, and that was a promise she intended to keep.

AFTER

RAINER

R ainer felt like he was swimming through dark water. Each time he thought he'd rise to the surface, he was sucked back under.

He was aware of so little. He drifted in and out of memory or dream. It was impossible to tell.

Other times he stirred restlessly, becoming more aware of the sheets tucked tightly around him.

Grief, loss, and fury swelled in his chest until he thought he might explode. Each time he felt on the verge of combustion, a small, warm hand slid into his and a soft voice whispered in his ear. He couldn't make out the words, but he always found it comforting. When the whisper stopped, he was desperate to hear it again—to open his impossibly heavy eyelids and gaze upon the only thing that felt real.

At times, it was a comfort. Other times he became even more agitated, and the whispering began again in earnest. On rare occasions when panic, rage, and fury burned through him like a fever, he'd be grounded immediately by the feeling of a warm body pressed into his side, a soft hand resting on his bare chest. Those times, a tingling warmth spread through him like sunlight on a bright spring day. The whisper would become louder, pleading, lovely. Still, he couldn't make sense of it, but he was grateful for the anchor when he felt completely unmoored in his own mind.

He was most aware of his body when the whisper—no, not a whisper—a woman was pressed against him. When she was there, he tried to pull her closer. He could sometimes tip his head and smell the sweetness of her skin. She smelled like summer in Olney. She smelled like the holes punched in his swirling memories.

Something was desperately wrong, and if he could just wake up, if he could finally kick hard enough to break the surface of his own mind, he knew he'd figure out what to do.

But he was so incredibly tired. So incredibly lost. So unbearably empty.

"Rain—"

A moment passed. He wanted desperately to respond.

"Rainer, I need you to try to wake up. Please, I—"

The whisper was clearer than ever, and there was sadness in the woman's voice that echoed through the hollowness inside him.

"I need you."

He swore a jolt went through him. A cord in his chest was attached to the voice and he experienced a deep need to comfort her. He *needed* to wake up and make sure she was okay. She was hurt. He could tell. He needed to fix it.

There was another whisper from the other side of the room that he couldn't make out.

"I'm going to tell you a story. Follow the fairy tale. You'll remember it. It will lead you back. I know you're tired and confused, but you can do it. Follow my voice back."

She was quiet for a moment, and he felt fingers in his hair.

"There once was a village where it rained stars. Once a year, on a very special night, the residents of the town would gather to collect them. They put out all candles and lanterns. They wandered into the dark, trusting that it would happen as it always did. The light of falling stars would brighten their way. Do you remember what happens next?"

Something happened in Rainer's mind. A hint of a memory. He

was talking. He was telling this story. He couldn't quite pull the memory into focus, but his mother's voice rushed through his mind. *Someday you will be old enough to need those fairy tales again.*

Yes. That was what he needed now—a story to hold on to. He waited, listening closely to the woman's words.

It snapped into place, and he flinched at the deep ache in his head. Maybe that was why he didn't want to wake up. It felt as though someone had taken a chisel to the inside of his skull.

"Did you see that? He flinched!"

There was another whisper Rainer couldn't make out. He wanted the girl to keep talking. Her fingers moved to stroke his jaw, and he tilted his cheek slightly into her hand.

"I think you remember, but I'm going to keep going. Just follow my voice. Come back to me," she said softly.

Rainer listened, all the while pulling on the cord that connected his heart to her voice. Waking felt impossible, but the urgency to do so was relentless, so he pressed on.

———

When Rainer blinked his eyes open, he was met by the face of the king of Argaria. Vincent Savero sat next to his bed, his brow furrowed.

Rainer was expecting the woman whose whispers led him out of the dark. He was expecting to be looking into bright blue eyes. He wasn't sure why, but he swore he could remember them. Instead, he was met with eyes that were dark, nearly black, with flecks of gold.

"Thank the gods! He's waking. Rainer, can you hear me?" Vincent asked.

Rainer tried to speak, but his mouth was so dry it came out in a croak. "Yes."

Relief was apparent on Vincent's face.

"Fetch Magdalena," the king said to a servant girl by the door.

The girl disappeared to find the healer as Vincent handed Rainer a glass of water.

Rainer turned his head and caught sight of Xander Savero standing by the door. He looked warily from Rainer to the king. Xander made him uneasy, though he didn't know why he was so concerned about the Storm Prince.

Something was missing. He just couldn't remember what.

"What's wrong?" Vincent asked.

Rainer shook his head. "I'm not sure. Something doesn't feel right. What happened to me?"

Vincent sat back in his chair, his brow creased with concern.

"We were afraid this might happen," he said. "There was a coup attempt. Some rogue supporters of Xander went behind his back and mine and tried to install him on the throne. Unfortunately, you were caught in the crossfire as my king's guard. I'm sorry to say that you were captured and tortured. You survived an attack by a slayer. The rebels used that slayer to try to get information out of you. We were worried your memory wouldn't be intact. We were hoping that wasn't the case, but Magdalena warned us it would be a strong possibility. What do you remember?"

Rainer leaned his head back on the pillow and squeezed his eyes shut. There was something painful he wasn't remembering. Was it just the torture? He focused hard, but nothing came to mind.

"I remember being whipped, falling on the floor, so much blood..." It came to him like a bolt of lightning. "There was a girl!" He couldn't see her face in his mind, just an outline of her. Rainer blinked his eyes open, and Xander was staring at him. He looked even more concerned.

"What do you remember about her?" Vincent asked.

Rainer shook his head and met the king's eyes. "I don't even remember her face. Just that she was crying, and they pulled her away. Is she okay? Who is she?"

It suddenly felt like the most important question in the world to him. He desperately needed to know that the girl he couldn't remember was okay.

Vincent cleared his throat. "You saved her. She's well. I'm incredibly grateful to you, Rainer."

Rainer sighed in relief, but when he looked to Xander again, the prince's hands fisted at his sides and his jaw clenched. Rainer didn't understand his fury. Maybe just that someone was hurt in an attempt to restore him to the throne that he didn't want.

"What else do you remember?" Vincent asked.

"I remember Xander taking the throne temporarily when Davide died but handing it over to you because you were more equipped to rule, and he never wanted to. I came here to help with the alliance and the transition of power. I'm a guardian." That much was clear as day in his mind—the urge to protect. "Where is my witch?"

Vincent's face fell. "The healers said it's best to let you recall on your own so you aren't overwhelmed. It'll come back eventually, and we'll help you rebuild. We'll let you rest for now. I have no doubt that you'll be back on your feet in no time. I won't soon forget what you've done to protect what's mine."

For some reason, that last sentence made Rainer irrationally angry, though he couldn't place why.

The king patted him on the shoulder and then brushed past Xander to leave the room.

Xander lingered in the doorway.

"What am I forgetting?" Rainer asked.

Xander paused and turned to look at him. "I wish I could tell you, but we've been told to let you remember on your own, and any help we give you could be damaging. Let's just say that I hope you're as good at recovering your memories as you are at being self-righteous."

With that, the prince slunk out the door, leaving Rainer with nothing but the half-formed memories buzzing through his head.

Cryptic fucking Storm Prince.

But the prince's taunt left Rainer with a pervasive sense of dread. There was no denying he was forgetting something important.

The Adventure Continues June 3, 2024 in...

THE GODLESS KINGDOM

A king ripped from his throne. An imposter wearing the crown. A court balanced on a knife's edge.

In the wake of a violent rebellion, Cecilia and Xander are trapped behind enemy lines under the thumb of a cruel tyrant. It's impossible to know who to trust with the culture of fear Vincent has instilled in the Argarian court. Clawing back the power he stole requires slow and careful progress. The vicious king needs them both alive for now, but one wrong move will land them in tower jails or worse.

Outside the castle walls, Evan enlists his network of spies to help his friends escape. But moving through town freely and accessing the castle grounds requires accepting help from an unexpected ally.

In the heart of Vincent's court, Rainer is rendered from an aching past he can't remember and is desperate for the glorious future he's been chasing his whole life. Torn between his duty, his honor, and his heart, Rainer must decide what he wants most and what price he's willing to pay for it.

They all walk a perilous line and one misstep will cost them their lives and the chance at the happily ever after they've fought so hard for.

Order the exciting final installment in The Lost God Series now:
https://www.amazon.com/dp/B0CV85H95F

Scan the code to order:

Thank you for reading

THE ST⚡RM KING

Did you like it? Love it?
Read it because you started the series and now you feel compelled to finish it?

✦ ✦ ✦ ✦ ✦ ✦ ✦ ✦ ✦ ✦ ✦ ✦ ✦ ✦

However you feel about it, I would be so grateful if you would **REVIEW** it on Amazon.

Reviews help indie authors like myself reach new readers and they help readers determine if this book is for them.

Please take a moment to write a short review.
THANK YOU!

Scan the code to review

✦ ✦ ✦ ✦ ✦ ✦ ✦ ✦ ✦ ✦ ✦ ✦ ✦ ✦

You can also get a BONUS CHAPTER featuring a villain POV by following this link:

https://starsagespirit.ck.page/tskbonus

or scanning this code

ACKNOWLEDGMENTS

The first thanks go to Mike for saying "sounds good" when I suggested putting a book out on our anniversary. Thank you for reading this book (twice) in two months. Thank you for believing in me enough to invest your time and energy in my dreams. I love you.

To Tanya - If you had not listened to me talk through my plans for this book and said, "Maybe the series four books," I might still be here trying to cram two books into one and making myself crazy. Thank you for your wisdom, your cheerleading, and your keen eye for detail.

To Liz - The job of a writing wife is not for the faint of heart. Thank you for letting me whine my way through two incredibly challenging developmental edits of this book. This was the big one—the book that tried to kill me. You were the life support keeping me and my terrible metaphors going. Seriously, thank you for being a sounding board as I turned this story over and over until I finally got it right.

To Erin - Thank you for your eagle editorial eyes, for understanding these characters so well, and for double-checking my spy work, since I am sadly, not a spy. Once again, your encouragement came at the exact right moment.

To my beta readers - Michelle, Christa, Fil, and Lauren you are the absolute dream team. I'm so grateful to you for coming along for the series so far and for your brilliant suggestions.

To my sensitivity readers - Thank you for taking the time to explore challenging topics with empathy and grace.

To Andrea - You have outdone yourself yet again with this cover and I'm still amazed that you can capture the vision from my chaotic art briefs. Thank you for being a true partner and putting so much intention into every detail.

To my writer found family - Em, Helen, Kara, Les, Nicole, Penn, Tay, and Vanessa. I am lucky to have you all in me corner. Thank you for sharing your collective knowledge and your spotlight. It's good to be here sprinting alongside people who are eager to lift me up when I'm struggling.

To my business witches - Four years you've been sharing your magic with me and I'm so grateful for your support and for "friend podcast". Whenever I need a pick me up, or an astroweather forecast, you are there, sharing your brilliance.

To my family - I really hope you listened to me and didn't read those chapters I suggested skipping. If you didn't that's on you.

To my friends - thank you for the love and encouragement, for recommending my books to your local bookstores, and for sharing them with your book clubs.

To all the fellow indie authors who have included me in give-aways and shared advice and resources - I love being part of your community.

To my amazing ARC team - Thank you for your enthusiasm, creativity, and art, and for making me cry on an embarrassingly frequent basis. I am so grateful for the way you have championed this series.

To every reader who has read my books, posted about them, recommended them to a friend, bought them as a gift for someone they love, sent me unhinged reactions in my Instagram DMs - THANK YOU! Your enthusiasm and support carried me through the series so far and I know it will continue to lift me through the end.

ABOUT THE AUTHOR

THE STORM KING is Sheila Masterson's third novel. When she's not writing fantasy romance novels, you can find Sheila practicing yoga, or curled up reading tarot or a book. She lives outside of Philadelphia with her fiancé and way too many houseplants.

instagram.com/sheilareadsandwrites

ALSO BY SHEILA MASTERSON

The Lost God

The Memory Curse

Made in United States
Orlando, FL
13 March 2024

44742703R00321